Cosmonaut
Keep

Also by Ken MacLeod

The Cassini Division

The Star Fraction

The Sky Road

The Stone Canal

Cosmonaut Keep

KEN MACLEOD

TOR®

A TOM DOHERTY ASSOCIATES BOOK
NEW YORK

COSMONAUT KEEP

Edited by Patrick Nielsen Hayden

A Tor Book
Published by Tom Doherty Associates, LLC
175 Fifth Avenue
New York, NY 10010

www.tor.com

Tor® is a registered trademark of Tom Doherty Associates, LLC.

Library of Congress Cataloging-in-Publication Data

MacLeod, Ken.
    Cosmonaut keep / Ken MacLeod—1st ed.
       p. cm.
    "A Tom Doherty Associates book."
    ISBN 0-765-30032-X (alk. paper)
    1. Life on other planets—Fiction.   2. Human-alien encoun-
ters—Fiction.   3. Computer programmers—Fiction.   I, Title.

PR6063.A2515 C67 2001
823'.914—dc21

                                                    2001017086

First Edition: May 2001

Printed in the United States of America

0   9   8   7   6   5   4   3   2   1

For Iain

Some of the ideas in this book were inspired by those on the website of the late Chris Boyce, http://www.et-presence.ndirect.co.uk.

An earlier version of Chapter Two was published as a short story in *IT@2000,* a special supplement to *Computer Weekly,* 25 November 1999.

Thanks to Carol, Sharon and Michael, for everything; to Tim Holman, for editorial patience and plot logic debugging; to Tim Adye, for some speculative physics; to Farah Mendlesohn, for reading and commenting on the draft; to Ellis Sharp, from whom I stole a ship's name; and to the Marine Biology Station on the Isle of Cumbrae, for a happy and busy week long ago.

and one of the chiefe trees or posts at the right side of the entrance had the barke taken off, and 5 foote from the ground in fayre Capitall letters was graven CROATOAN without any crosse or signe of distresse

Contents

Cosmonaut
Keep

0

Prologue

Y OU'RE NOT HERE. Try to remember this.
Try not to remember where you really are.

You are in a twisty maze of dark corridors, all alike. You slide down the last of them as smoothly as a piston in a syringe, and are then ejected into the suddenly overwhelming open space of the interior. Minutes ago, you saw outer space, the universe, and the whole shebang itself didn't look bigger than this. Outer space is, fundamentally, familiar. It's only the night sky, without the earth beneath your feet.

This place is fundamentally unfamiliar. It's twenty miles long and five high and it's bigger than anything you've ever seen. It's a room with a world inside it.

To them, it's a bright world. To us it's a dark, cold cavern. To them, our most delicate probes would be like some gigantic space-ship hovering on rocket jets over one of our cities, playing search-lights of intolerable brightness across everything. That's why we're seeing it through their eyes, with their instruments, in their colors. The translation of the colors has more to do with emotional tone than the electromagnetic spectrum; a lot of thought, ours and theirs, has gone into this interpretation.

So what you see is a warm, rich green background, speckled with countless tiny, lively shapes in far more colors than you have names for. You think of jewels and hummingbirds and tropical fish. In fact the comparison with rainforest or coral reef is close to the mark. This is an ecosytem more complex than that of the whole Earth. As the viewpoint drifts closer to the surface you recall pictures of cities from the air, or the patterns of silicon circuitry. This, too, is apt: here, the distinction between natural and artificial is meaningless.

The viewpoint zooms in and out: from fractal snowflakes, rainbow-hued, in kaleidoscopic motion, to the vast violet-hazed distances and perspectives of the habitat, making clear the multiplicity and diversity of the place, the absence of repetition. Everything here is unique; there are similarities, but no species.

You can't shut it off; silently, relentlessly, the viewpoint keeps showing you more and more, until the inhuman but irresistible beauty of the alien garden or city or machine or mind harrows your heart. It will not let you go, unless you bless it; then, just as you fall into helpless love with it, it expels you, returning you to your humanity, and the dark.

I

Ship Coming In

A GOD STOOD in the sky high above the sunset horizon, his long white hair streaming in the solar wind. Later, when the sky's color had shifted from green to black, the white glow would reach almost to the zenith, its light outshining the Foamy Wake, the broad band of the Galaxy. At least, it would if the squall-clouds scudding in off the land to the east had cleared by then. Gregor Cairns turned his back on the *C. M. Yonge*'s own foamy wake, and looked past the masts and sheets at the sky ahead. The clouds were blacker and closer than they'd been the last time he'd looked, a few minutes earlier. Two of the lugger's five-man crew were already swinging the big sail around, preparing to tack into the freshening wind.

Much as he'd have liked to help, he knew from experience that he'd only get in the way. He turned his attention back to the tanks and nets in which the day's haul snapped, slapped, or writhed. Trilobites and ostracoderms, mostly, with a silvery smattering of teleostean fish, a slimy slither of sea-slugs, and crusty clusters of shelled molluscs and calcichordates. To Gregor this kind of assemblage was beginning to look incongruous and anachronistic; he grinned at the thought, reflecting that he now knew more about the marine life of Earth's oceans than he did of the planet whose first human settlers had long ago named Mingulay.

His wry smile was caught by his two colleagues, one of whom smiled back. Elizabeth Harkness was a big-boned, strong-featured young woman, about his own age and with a centimeter or two of advantage in height. Under a big leather hat her rough-cut black hair was blown forward over her ruddy cheeks. Like Gregor, she wore a heavy sweater, oilskins, rubber boots, and gauntlets. She squatted a couple of meters away on the laden afterdeck, probing tangles of holdfast with a rusty old knife, expertly slinging the separated molluscs, calcichordates, and float-wrack into their appropriate tanks.

"Come on," she said, "back to work."

"Aye," said Gregor, stooping to cautiously heave a ten-kilogram trilobite, scrabbling and snapping, into a water-filled wooden trough. "The faster we get this lot sorted, the more time for drinks back at the port."

"Yeah, so don't stick with the easy stuff." She flung some surplus mussels to the seabats that screamed and wheeled around the boat.

"Huh." Gregor grunted and left the relatively rugged trilobites to fend for themselves in the netting and creels while he pitched in to deal with the small shelly fauna. The vessel rolled, slopping salt water from the troughs and tanks, and then freshwater from the sky hissed onto the deck as they met the squall. He and Elizabeth worked on through it, yelling and laughing as their sorting became less and less discriminatory in their haste.

"As long as they don't *eat* each other. . . ."

The third student on the boat squatted opposite the two humans, knees on a level with his broad cheekbones, oblivious to the rain pelting his hairless head, and to the rivulets that trickled down his neck then over the seamless collar of his dull gray insulation-suit. The nictitating membranes of his large black eyes, and an occasional snort from his small nostrils or spit from his thin-lipped, inch-wide mouth were the only indications that the downpour affected him at all. His hands each had three long fingers and one long thumb; each digit came equipped with a claw that made a knife, for this task at least, quite unnecessary.

Gregor eyed him covertly, admiring the machinelike ease with which the long fingers sorted through the heaps; tangles ahead of them, neatly separated columns behind; the butchering strength and surgical skill and clinical gentleness of thumb and claw and palm. Then, answering some accurate intuition, the saur rocked back on his heels, washed his hands in the last of the rain, and stood up with his part of the task complete.

Elizabeth and Gregor looked at each other across a diminished area of decking on which nothing but stains and shreds of wrack remained. Elizabeth blinked wet lashes.

"Done," she said, standing up and shaking rain off her hat.

"Great." Gregor heaved himself upright and did likewise, joining the other two at the stern rail. They leaned on it, gazing out at the reddening sky in which the god glowed brighter. The highest clouds in the sky—far higher than the squall-clouds—shone with a peculiar mother-of-pearl rainbow effect, a rare phenomenon that had even the sailors murmuring in amazed appreciation.

Behind them the big sail came rattling down, and the engine coughed into life as the steersman took them in toward the harbor. The cliffs of a hundred-meter-high headland, crowned with a craggy castle, the Keep of Aird, rose on the port side; lower green hills and fields spread out to starboard. Ahead the lights were coming on in Kyohvic, the main port of the straggling seaboard republic known as the Heresiarchy of Tain.

"Good work, Salasso," Gregor said. The saur turned and nodded gravely, his nostrils and lips minutely twitching in his species' equivalent of a smile. Then the great black eyes—their sides easily visible in profile—returned to scanning the sea.

Salasso's long arm and long forefinger pointed.

"*Teuthys,*" he hissed.

"Where?" Elizabeth cried, delighted. Gregor shaded his eyes and stared along the white wake and across the dark waves, so much of it there was, until he saw a darker silhouette rise, humping out of the water about a mile away. For a moment, so it remained, an islet in the deep.

"Could be just a whale—" he murmured.

"*Teuthys,*" the saur insisted.

The hump sank back and then a vast shape shot out of the surface, rising in an apparently impossible arc on a brief white jet; a glimpse of splayed tentacles behind the black wedge of the thing, then a huge splash as it planed back into the water. It did it again, and this time it wasn't black—in its airborne second it glowed and flashed with flickering color. And it wasn't alone—another kraken had joined it. They leaped together, again and then again, twisting and sporting. With a final synchronized leap that lasted two seconds, and a multicolored flare that lit the water like fireworks, the display ended.

"Oh, gods above," Elizabeth breathed. The saur's mouth was a little black O, and his body trembled. Gregor stared at where the krakens had played, awed but wondering. That they were playing he was certain, without knowing why. There were theories that such gratuitous expenditures of energy by krakens were some kind of mating display, or even ritual, but like most biologists Gregor regarded such hypotheses as beneath consideration.

"*Architeuthys extraterrestris sapiens,*" he said slowly. "Masters of the galaxy. Having fun."

The saur's black tongue flickered, then his lips once more became a thin line.

"We do not know," he said, his words perhaps weightier, to Gregor, than he intended. But the man chose to treat them lightly, leaning out and sharing an aching, helpless grin with the woman.

"We don't know," he agreed, "but one day we'll find out." He jerked his face upward at the flare of white spreading up the sky. "Even the gods play, I'm sure of that. Why else would they leave their . . . endless peace between the stars, and plunge between our worlds and swing around the sun?"

Salasso's neck seemed to contract a little; he averted his eyes from the sky, shivering again. Elizabeth laughed, not noticing or perhaps not reading the saur's subtle body-language. "Gods above, you can talk, man!" she said. "You think we'll ever know?"

"Aye, I do," said Gregor. "That's *our* play."

"Speak for yourself, Cairns, I know what mine is after a long hard day, and I'm"—she glanced over her shoulder—"about ten minutes from starting it with a long hard drink!"

Gregor shrugged and smiled, and they all relaxed, gazing at the sea and chatting. Then, as the first houses of the harbor town slipped by, one of the crewmen startled them with a loud, ringing cry:

"Ship coming in!"

Everybody on the boat looked up at the sky.

James Cairns stood, huddled in a fur cloak, on the castle's ancient battlement and gazed at the ship as it slid across the sky from the east, a glowing zeppelin at least three hundred meters long. Down the dark miles of the long valley—lighting the flanks of the hill—and over the clustered houses of the town it came, its course as steady and constant as a monorail bus. As it passed almost directly overhead at a thousand meters, Cairns was briefly amused to see that among the patterns picked out in lights on its sides were the squiggly signature-scribble of Coca-Cola; the double-arched golden

M; the brave checkered banner of Microsoft; the Stars and Stripes; and the thirteen stars—twelve small yellow stars and one central red star on a blue field—of the European Union.

He presumed the display was supposed to provide some kind of reassurance. What it gave him—and, he did not doubt, scores of other observers—was a pang of pride and longing so acute that the shining shape blurred for a second. The old man blinked and sniffed, staring after the craft as its path sloped implacably seaward. When it was a kilometer or so out to sea, and a hundred meters above the water, a succession of silver lens-shaped objects scooted away from its sides, spinning clear and then heading back the way the ship had come. They came sailing in toward the port as the long ship's hull kissed the waves and settled, its flashing lights turning the black water to a rainbow kaleidoscope. Other lights, underwater and much smaller but hardly less bright, joined it in a colorful flurry.

Cairns turned his attention from the ship to its gravity skiffs; some swung down to land on the docks below, most skittered over-head and floated down, rocking like falling leaves, to the grassy ridge of the long hill that sloped down from the landward face of the castle. James strolled to the other side of the roof to watch. Somewhere beneath his feet, a relief generator hummed. Flood-lights flared, lighting up the approach and glinting off the steely sides of the skiffs.

Almost banally after such a bravura arrival, the dozen or so skiffs had extended and come to rest on spindly telescoped legs; in their undersides hatches opened and stairladders emerged, down which saurs and humans trooped as casually as passengers off an airship. Each skiff gave forth two or three saurs, twice or thrice that number of humans; about a hundred in all walked slowly up the slope and onto the smoother grass of the castle lawns, tramping across it to be greeted by, and to mingle with, the castle's occupants. The gray-suited saurs looked more spruce than the humans, most of whom were in sea-boots and oilskins, dripping wet. The humans toward the rear were hauling little wheeled carts behind them, laden with luggage.

He felt a warm arm slide through the side-slit of his cloak and clasp his waist.

"Aren't you going down?" Margaret asked.

Cairns turned and looked down at his wife's eyes, which shone within a crinkle of crow's-feet as she smiled, and laid his right arm, suddenly heavy, across her shoulders.

"In a minute," he said. He sighed. "You know, even after all this time, that's still the sight that leaves me most dizzy."

Margaret chuckled darkly. "Yeah, I know. It gets me that way too."

Cairns knew that if he dwelt on the strangeness of the sight, the feeling of unreality could make him physically nauseous: *la nausée*, Sartre's old existential insecurity—Cairns wondered, not for the first time, how the philosopher would have coped with a situation as metaphysically disturbing as this.

L'enfer, c'est les autres.

He turned around resolutely, taking Margaret along with him, and together they set off down from the castle's heights to meet the bourgeois with a smile. Under his left elbow he held the furled and folded flag, the star-circled banner which he'd lowered, as was his custom, at sunset. Behind him the steel rope clanged on the mast, bare against the windy night.

They descended the spiral stair, down steps a meter and a half wide and about thirty centimeters high, each of whose treads had been worn down over millenia into a terrifyingly deep normal distribution curve, as though the stone itself were sagging. The iron handrail around the central well was only centuries old, and at the right height for human hands; the electric lighting, though dim, was tuned for human eyes.

James and Margaret kept close to the wall as they descended. Margaret went first, clattering and chatting merrily; James followed, half listening, the rest of his attention devoted to the many fossils embedded in the stones of the wall's interior cladding, some of which generations of curious or reverent fingertips of successive species of the castle's occupants had polished to a mahogany sheen. He trailed his own fingers across the fragmentary remains of fish and dragons and sea-monsters and other organisms in a bizarrely Noachic, diluvial conglomerate whose ordering had little to do with their evolutionary succession; as always when he climbed up or down these steps, the line he'd used on his children and grandchildren came to mind: this castle had been built by giants, mined by dwarfs, stormed by goblins, and left to ghosts long before people on Earth had laid so much as one stone upon another.

Sounds and smells echoing or wafting from below intensified as the old couple descended. The arrival of the merchant ship might or might not have been expected, but the keep's staff planned routinely for such a contingency. For this first evening nothing much was expected but hot water, hot food, and a lot of drinking and some kind of bed to stagger off to afterward: merchants just off a ship were usually in no condition for formal negotiations or celebrations. The saurs would require even less.

The exits from the spiral stair went past, their numbers as fixed in James's mind as the numerals on a lift's display. He and Margaret stepped out on the ground floor—the stair still had many levels to go, down into the rock—and made their way around several zigzag turns of narrow defensive corridor. Antique space-suits stood in artfully placed ambuscade niches.

The corridor opened to the castle's main hall, a cavernous space hung with retrofitted electric lights, its fifteen-meter-high walls covered with carpets and tapestries, oil-paintings of members of the Cosmonaut Families, heads and hides of dinosaurs, and decoratively arranged displays of the light artillery with which these gigantic quarry had been sportingly slain.

The wide doors stood open; the hall's blazing fire and more practical electric radiators did little to repel the chill inward swirl of evening air. The merchants, their saur companions, and their servants were already mingled with the welcoming crowd that had gathered from all quarters of the castle. Mingled, but easily distinguishable: for this evening at least, the castle's occupants—Cosmonauts and stewards and seneschals and servants—outdid the merchants in the style and spectacle of their attire. In days to come, the most senior of the Cosmonauts and the richest merchants in Kyohvic would be easily outshone by their visitors' youngest child or lowliest page; their present plebeian appearance, though partly dictated by the necessities of interstellar travel, was for all its apparent casualness part of a protocol—setting themselves conspicuously below their hosts—whose invariance James Cairns had observed many times before.

Right now the new arrivals had discarded their protective clothing in a careless heap in the doorway's broad vestibule, and were padding around in woollen socks and likewise warm gear, shaking or kissing hands with all and sundry, smiling and laughing and slapping shoulders. Children scampered and scooted, chased by their own servants, tactfully redirected from the big room's many exits by swiftly posted stewards. Through it all the saurs drifted, their domed heads bobbing in the throng like stray balloons.

Hal Driver, the Security Man, was in the center of the pressing crowd, already deep in hearty converse with a mature, burly man who had "merchant prince" written all over him, albeit he was dressed like a trawlerman. Red hair sprang in a great shock from his head; freckles spattered his broad-cheeked, flat-nosed face; his rich voice boomed above the babble, his asides to Driver now and again dropping to a confidential murmur.

Margaret nudged James with a confidential murmur of her own. "Didn't take them long to figure out who's in charge here."

"Aren't you going up to the keep?" Elizabeth asked.

Gregor finished hosing the scales and slime off his oilskins and hung them in the locker. "Nah," he said, pulling his boots off. "Time enough for that when they have the big bash. Won't be for a day or two yet." He sat on the low fold-down bench, tugging off his thick socks and stuffing them in the boots, then carefully eased his feet into his leather shoes. "Fancy coming along yourself?"

Elizabeth reddened. "Oh, that's nice of you—thanks, but I just don't know if I can."

"Well, the invitation's open," Gregor said, oblivious to her momentary embarrassment, and turned to the saur. "How about you?"

The slow-swinging electric light's reflection made tiny arcs in Salasso's black eyes as the saur waited patiently in the converted hold's low narrow doorway. His clothing needed no cleaning or adjustment. Nor, Gregor suddenly realized with a blush of his own, would it need any possibly expensive alternative for social occasions.

He ducked to lace up his shoes as Salasso said he would certainly come along.

"Don't worry about, uh, dressing up," he called after Elizabeth as she stepped up to the deck. "You know what the merchants are like, they wouldn't know what the fashion is here anyway."

"I'll think about it," she told him, not looking back.

Up on deck the three students thanked Renwick, the skipper, who was making the last check of the boat before leaving it for the night. The specimens, safe in their various containers, would keep until the morning, when they'd be hauled off to the Marine Biology Station.

"Pint at the Bailie's?" Elizabeth asked Renwick.

The skipper shook his head. "Nah, I'll have a short with the crew. Last seen heading for the Shipwright, I think. See you tomorrow, folks."

The harbor was so old it might have been natural, but it was merely pre-human. The quarter-mile–long mole was built of the same hard metamorphic rock as the castle's exterior walls, and was reckoned to have been blasted and lifted from the harbor basin in ancient times, either by the brute force and primitive ingenuity of multitudes, or by the laser lances and gravity sleds of visitors from outer space. It formed one curved arm of the harbor's embrace, the other being provided by the headland's cliffs. Beyond it, the rocky outcrops gave way to a long, white sandy beach, which broke up in the distance to tussocked dunes.

Gregor scrambled up the rusty rungs of the ladder and out onto the mole. A few hundred meters across the water, on the harbor's central docks, a small knot of humans and saurs had gathered around the landed skiffs. Gregor glanced at them incuriously and turned to gazing again at the sky as he waited for the others to join him.

The rainbow clouds had dispersed. Gabriel, the evening and morning star, burned like a lamp low in the west, its light outshone by the god standing higher in the sky, and by the auroral flicker of the starship floating on the sea beneath it. High above them all hung the icy gleam of Raphael and the tiny spark of Ariel, its moon; and—following the ecliptic around to the east—the bright sickle of the new moon, beyond which Gog and Magog, the ringed gas giants of the outer system, glowered like a monster's eyes.

Crossing the sky from north to south, alone in its polar orbit, deserted for two hundred years, went the old ship from home. To Gregor, tracking it with a rapidly blinking eye, the *Bright Star* seemed a stranger and more evocative sight than all the familiar constellations—the Musketeer, the Squid, the Angel's Wing, and the rest—that straddled the sky on either side of the Foamy Wake.

And, ironically, more difficult for humans to reach.

The two humans and the saur walked briskly along the mole and into the waterfront streets of Kyohvic, turning right along a bright-lit, cobbled esplanade to the Bailie's Bar, its sign a jolly, pint-quaffing grandee in plumed hat and lace cravat. Inside, it was long, low-ceilinged, its plastered walls decorated with naive murals and shelves and brackets supporting harpoons and stuffed ichthyosaurs; its tables and bar counters half filled with men just off the boats and ships. It was that kind of place, at this time of the evening; later, the sawdust would be swept up, the tables wiped, and a cleaner crowd would pour in from the shows or the eating-houses; but for now it reeked of sweat and fish, yeast and baccy and hemp, its dim light glinting with the glitter of glasses and pots and the glazed, lidded gaze of men relaxing thoughtfully over their long pipes. The regulars recognized the students with a nod and a smile; others, seamen in from another port, frowned at the saur. As Gregor waved Elizabeth and Salasso to a seat and strode to the bar, he heard hissed mutterings about "snakes." He ignored it; the saur himself turned a black, blank glare in that direction; and, out of the corner of his eye, Gregor noticed the most vocal objector getting an urgent word in his ear from one of the barmaids.

Gregor ordered pints for himself and Elizabeth, and a tall billican of hot fish-stock for Salasso. As he waited for the stout to settle and the thin soup to be brought back to the boil, he found himself worrying again about the unerring aim that so often connected his foot with his mouth. The awkwardness, he was sure, came not from the difference between the sexes but from the perhaps greater communicative gulf of class. Elizabeth Harkness was of predominantly local descent, albeit of good family, some of whose members were prominent in the Scoffer heresiarchy; his own ancestry, give or take a good deal of exogamy with the locals, came from the *Bright Star*'s crew.

From the bar's mirror behind the bottles his own face scrutinized him: the same thin nose and grim mouth and long black hair swept back from a high hairline that he'd seen in generations of portraits. He felt their presence like a weight on his back.

"That'll be five shillings, Greg."

"Oh!" He blinked and shook his head; with that slight start recognizing the barmaid as Andrea Peden, one of the undergraduate students whose work he'd occasionally supervised. Her rippling auburn hair was loose on her shoulders rather than tied back, and he'd only ever seen her in a lab overall, but still. "Uh, thanks, Peden. And, let's see, an ounce of hemp as well, please." Alcohol was not a saur vice—it was a physiological difference; they assimilated it without intoxication—but hemp had definitely taken with the species, centuries ago.

"Another sixpence, then," the girl said. She glanced around. "And we're off-study, so first names, okay, Greg?"

"Ah, sure, Andrea, thanks."

He just knew that if he commented on her working here it would come across as yet another clumsy reminder of the difference between his economic status and that of most other students, so he forbore.

Back at the table he raised his glass soberly to Elizabeth as Salasso nodded almost imperceptibly at both of them and took from a thigh pocket a thin aluminum tube and a long-stemmed bone pipe, its bowl elaborately carved. The saur sucked up fish-stock through the tube and began filling the pipe from the paper twist.

"Hah!" he sighed after a minute, his mouth opening, snakelike, suprisingly wide and showing little fangs. Gregor winced slightly at the momentary waft of carnivore breath. A thin brass rectangle appeared between Salasso's long fingers like a conjuring trick, and he applied its faint flame to the tamped hemp and puffed. "Hah! That's better!"

"Any idea where the ship's from?" Elizabeth asked, as though Gregor might know. But it was Salasso who answered.

"Nova Babylonia," he said, and inhaled on the pipe. His lashless eyelids made a rare blink, and his third eyelid—the nictitating membrane—was flickering more rapidly than usual. "Of the fleet of the family Tenebre." His voice was reedy and harsh. He passed the pipe to Elizabeth.

"Recognize it, do you?" she asked, puffing for politeness' sake.

Gregor was a little disappointed by her seizing on this point. To hell with how the saur knew about it, the ship's origin was what mattered. Ships from Nova Babylonia were rare. From his twenty years, he could recall two such visits.

"Yesss," said Salasso, leaning his narrow shoulders against the seat's tall back. He drew on the metal straw again, hot colors briefly flowing in the gray-green skin of his cheeks. "I have seen that ship . . . many times."

Elizabeth gave Gregor a skeptical look as she handed over the pipe. Gregor returned her a warning glance and just nodded at Salasso, keeping his face carefully expressionless as he sucked the last vile embers of the hemp. He tapped them out on the floor and began refilling the pipe.

"So you might know some of the shore crew?" he asked.

Salasso's shoulders lifted. "It is very possible. If so, I'll find out when I go to the reception at the castle." His great eyes closed for a moment. "Of the family Tenebre, perhaps a few. The human generations pass."

Gregor struck a match on his boot and relit, the cannabis rush roaring in his ears like a burn in spate. He heard Elizabeth's light laugh.

"This I have to see!" she said. "For this, I would come to your party as I am, rags and holes and boots and all!"

"Yeah, you do that," he said warmly. "Come as a scientist."

"Oh, thanks," said Elizabeth indignantly, then giggled. Gregor returned the pipe to the saur, who smoked the rest of it but said no more, his body still, his mind gliding into a typically saurian trance. The two humans watched in silence for a couple of minutes, supping at their pints until the pipe clattered from Salasso's fingers onto the table.

Gregor leaned across and stroked the dry, warm skin of the saur's face. No response was forthcoming.

"He's offline," he remarked.

"Another pint while we wait?" Elizabeth asked.

"Aye, thanks."

No time, or a long time, seemed to pass before she returned.

"Do you think he meant that literally?" she asked, as he settled in again. The saur's head, its great eyes still open, suddenly lolled sideways against her shoulder. She patted it. "Well, that's me here for the duration!"

"About twenty minutes, I reckon," Gregor said abstractedly. "Um, how could he not have meant it literally?"

Elizabeth leaned forward on one elbow, careful not to disturb Salasso, gazing with what seemed like half-stoned fixity into Gregor's eyes. "You know. Metaphorically. Might be that their families, or lines, or whatever, know each other from way back." She laughed. "Do you really think our friend here is that old? He doesn't *act* like it."

"We all know the saurs live a long time."

"Supposedly."

Gregor looked straight back at her, narrow-eyed. "The saurs say it, and I've no reason to doubt it."

Elizabeth nodded slowly. "Aye, well, sometimes I wonder if the saurs are . . . ancient people. That they are what people become, if they live long enough."

Gregor laughed. "It's a nice idea. But the saurs, they're obviously reptilian—or saurian, if you want to be exact!"

"And so? The reptilian genes could still be in us, and only expressed much later in life than people normally live."

"You might have a point there," Gregor conceded, not entertaining the idea for a second. "Nobody's ever seen a saur dissected, after all, or even a picture of a saur skeleton."

He shook the last of the crumbled leaf into Salasso's ornate pipe. That moment when saurs got well and truly whacked by the hemp was the only time they'd open up for a few seconds, and they'd let slip weird things then. But that might just be the drug talking.

"Has anyone ever asked for one?" Elizabeth wondered aloud.

Gregor shook his head. "And I'll lay good money Salasso won't answer any questions we ask him when he comes back to the land of the living."

"Hmm, I wouldn't even try. He'd be touchy about it."

"There you go."

This was an old subject. The saurs' individualism and prickly sense of privacy made humans look like some kind of garrulous, gossiping animal that hunted in packs. They might all look the same to a casual or hostile eye—though here, Gregor had found, familiarity made their distinctions apparent—but their personalities were unpredictably diverse. The few traits they shared included a ravenous thirst for knowledge and a great reluctance to divulge any. Their language, their sexuality, their social relationships, their politics and philosophies—if any—were as mysterious as they must have been to the first terrified savage they'd encountered, many millennia back in humanity's history.

"Well," Gregor said, lighting up, "the least we can do is smoke the last of his weed. He sure won't be needing it."

"Hmm." Elizabeth puffed quickly and returned the pipe. "No more for me, thanks. I want to keep my head clear to write up some notes."

Gods in orbit, his colleague was beginning to look attractive as her merry eyes stared with fathomless pupils into his mind, even though her face and frame were a little more . . . angular than he usually took to in a woman. . . . That girl Peden at the bar—now, she was quite something. . . .

Elizabeth laughed, and Gregor had a sudden suspicion, sobering as a cold wave over the deck, that he'd actually said what he'd just been thinking . . . but no, his dry lips were still stuck to the stem of the pipe.

He licked his lips, overcome by another effect of the weed: sudden hunger. "What?"

"The way you look, Gregor, I wouldn't advise you to bother writing any notes tonight. They won't make much sense in the morning."

Her voice, or the vibration of her laughter, made Salasso stir and sit abruptly upright, blinking hard and looking around. Elizabeth stroked his hand, lightly grasped Gregor's for a moment of what he took to be stoned affection, and rose.

"Good night, chaps," she said, and was gone before Gregor could ask her if she had any plans to *eat*.

2

Resident Alien

I WAKE WITH my ears ringing and a light flashing in my right eye. It takes a licked forefinger to ungum my eyelid enough for the two deliberate blinks that put the incoming video on hold. Then I tug at my left earlobe to take the audio call.

"Yes?" I say testily, sitting up. It's some ungodly hour like eleven in the morning. The bed's a mess and the whisky I incautiously drank while listening to music after coming home from the pub last night is making my head ache.

As soon as I hear the coins drop I know it's trouble. England is the only place outside of sub-Saharan Africa that still has coin-operated payphones. My friends use them not because they aren't bugged—they bloody are—but to signal an unspoken message: Yes, trouble.

"Hi, Matt?" says a familiar American voice. "It's Jadey. Can you meet me at the Market? Say around five?"

Jadey's our local Yank. She has resident-alien status as an exchange student, or something, but spends most of her time running ops for the resistance down south. I've never been sure quite who she really works for, but I've always been happy to modify the software for the hardware fixes she takes with her on visits to London. My little hack for the face-recognition neural net was a rush job, but, like Jadey said, it beats balaclavas.

"Yeah, sure," I say, trying to sound casual. I have a bit of a thing about Jadey; hopeless, given who she probably is and what she probably does, and anyway she's away a lot.

"See you there," she says. The money runs out in a dribble of *bleep*s.

I blink my eye again and patch the other call over to the wall-screen. I peel the phone from my cheek, annoyed that I fell asleep with it on, throw it in the trash and look at the screen. It's an offer from one of the agencies, and I check it out while scratching absently at the weal the phone left.

It looks like another quick and dirty contract job for the European Space Agency; it'll involve digging down several levels of emulation running on top of each other to find a bug in the underlying operating system; which, knowing my luck, will probably turn out to be MS-DOS. I'll have to rope in an old programmer for that, preferably one who hasn't been a paid-up lifelong member of the Linux jihad.

I put in a bid—costing and schedule—making sure to allocate myself about double the time the job should take to do properly. The agency bounces back instantly with a schedule that'll give me about half the time I'd need to do the job properly. But the fee should cover the code-geek subcontract on top of my other expenses and my own day rate, so I take it.

Software project management has always been like herding cats. So I've been told, anyway, by old managers, between snorts of coke in the trendy snow-bars where they blow their well-hedged pension funds. In their day, though, the cats were human, or at least the kind of guys who are now code-geeks. These days, the *programmers* are programs, as are the systems analysts. My job as a project manager is to assemble a convincing suite of AIs—not untried, but not too far behind the curve, either—then let loose marketing strategy webcrawlers to parade their skills before the endless bored beauty-contest of the agencies' business 'bots, take the contracts and ride herd on the whole squabbling mob when a deal comes in.

You need something almost like people skills to do it, but you need to be practically borderline Asperger's syndrome to develop these skills with AI. And when you need code-geeks for the bottom-level stuff, you need to be something of a sociable animal after all. It's a sufficiently rare combination to be worth more than the average wage. I'm an artist, not a technician. It pays the bills.

This contract is for a manufacturing control interface for ESA's asteroid mining project. The asteroid in question is 10049 Lora, a stray piece of junk between the orbits of Earth and Mars, about thirty kilometers long, with a low albedo—currently, I vaguely remember seeing, swinging by within a few million miles of Earth;

detected in the 2020s, reached by an ESA probe about ten years later, and found to be a carbonaceous chondrite. A potential source of immensely useful organics for space settlement, if that ever comes up. ESA's experimental mining station, built around a ship called the *Marshall Titov,* has been running for years, with notoriously poor returns: Think groundnut scheme, think *Mir,* think bottomless pit.

I stare at it for a few minutes, flicking my thumb to tab down the pages, and down: The background info seems excessive, but (I check) it's indexed and searchable. The actual spec is large but manageable. I can handle it, but not before breakfast.

My flat is on the twenty-fifth floor of one of the new Housing Authority high-rises at the top of Leith Walk. The fabric of the place is showing its age—five years, about the expected half-life of new-tech constructions—but for four rooms it's cheap. I traverse all of them, ambling from the bedroom through the living-room to the kitchen via the bathroom. It's in the bathroom that I conclude that I look like shit.

In the kitchen I chew a brace of aspirins and drink coffee and crunch my way through a bowl of cereal. I scroll through the morning's news without much attention, skipping channels. I gaze unseeing through the south-facing kitchen window at the castle and the tall towers of the South Bridge. The sky is blue and the clouds are white, whipping across from left to right, east to west. Their steady procession cools my mind.

The project keeps me busy all afternoon. Whenever I need a patch from outside the E.U.—and let's face it, you do—the connections turn bumpy. At four-thirty, bug-eyed and sore-jointed from jollying the AIs along, I save the story-so-far to a satellite uplink and hit the street.

Waverley Market was a posh bijou shopping-center until the third week of the Ural-Caspian Oil War, by which time Edinburgh was irretrievably enemy territory. A U.S. cruise missile missed the railhead and took out the eastern end of Princes Street, and with it the Scottish government offices which had probably been the real target all along. These days it's a fine example of the role of the flea market in a Socialist Democracy. I browse the electronics and biotech stalls in the late-afternoon, late-summer sunlight, shoulders hunched in a parka—Scottish Augusts have been a bit chilly since the Gulf Stream downshifted—and elbows on guard against the crowds of tourists jostling for the bootleg foreign tech. The Edinburgh Festival is still the biggest in the world, and pulls in tourists from all over the E.U.: I see a Siberian woman pounce on a sliver of nerve-driver memory from Brazil, an Italian couple arguing over whether they can afford a Raytheon eyepatch—months obsolete in America, years ahead of our stuff.

Our stuff... I can smell it on the wind. New tech, wet tech: bioelectronic manufacture, with its whiff of acetone and alcohol, Edinburgh's familiar technology of brewery and distillery and refinery expanded to produce a whole new range of hardware kit, as cheap and disposable and recyclable as paper. All very nice and sustainable, but the old hard tech of America's fossil/metal economy still has the technical edge.

Jadey finds me with her usual alarming ease. I look up and there she is, leaning over the stall. Cropped blonde hair, blue eyes, heat-exchanger tank top, arm-warmers, and a mil-green nylon pod-skirt. She has one of those girlie versions of a rucksack on her back. Her tired smile matches her London-train drained look.

"Border hassles?" I ask.

She shakes her head as she catches my elbow and begins steering me toward a coffee stall. "Nah, but man, I've had hassles." Talking's safe enough, here; the buzz from the gadgetry on sale jams all but the most dedicated surveillance. Most of the street-cameras and other sensors in Scotland and the rest of the E.U. get regularly fucked over by hackers anyway. The arms race between surveillance and sabotage is Darwinian, a Red Queen's Race in which the hackers are usually a whisker ahead. It's a bit tougher down south, where the authorities use heavier, harder apps and hacking is more effectively suppressed by reverse social engineering. Hence my specialist devices for Jadey.

She says, "The gear didn't work—"

"What?"

"Not your fault. Something's changed. Most of the cells down there got the old dawn-knock this morning. It's like, shit, all our codes are being cracked or something. I think they're even on to me—the cops at King's Cross just waved me through with that knowing smile they have."

Jadey lives in the cracks between jurisdictions: U.S.A. and E.U.,

the Scottish Republic and the Former United Kingdom; within the
F.U.K. she plays off the jealousies and incompetences of the contending post-war authorities—the English, the Russkis, and the blue
helmets.

I buy two paper thimbles of espresso and we sit on a bit of
broken wall, sipping.

"You mean the resistance is getting smashed as we speak?"

She stares down, fiddles with the drawstring at her skirt's hem,
looks up sadly. "That's about the size of it, Matt. I gotta get out."

"Okay," I say, with a pang. "What do you need?"

"New ID. Oh, not a retinal job or anything, just a new passport
and history. If they're going for bio checks I'll be picked up before
I've had time to fiddle a DNA hack anyway."

"Hey, don't sound so fatalistic. You're depressing me." I jump
up. "Tell you what. Let me get you something to eat, then we can
hit the Darwin and see what's on offer. I've got a job of my own
to check out there, anyway."

"Great," she says. "McDonald's."

"What?"

She glances back, already heading up the path to the street.

"Last place the cops'll come looking for an American."

As we edge through the crowd in the Darwin's Arms I check the
nasal readout in my left eye. Thank God for smokeless cigarettes—
they make pheromone analysis a breeze. You try pulling that trick
in Turkey, or Azerbaijan, and you get botanical data, not psycho-
logical. The atmosphere's oddly tense, with an undercurrent of brit-
tle hilarity. Now that I notice it on the air, I can pick it up in the
sound as well. Jadey, walking behind me and leaving a spreading
wake of lust (I can see the little red line humping up on the readout), must have caught it too.

"Edgy tonight, huh?"

Her American accent is making me weak in the knees.

"No kidding." I plant my elbows on the bar and finger out a
card. "What you having?"

"Cally Eighty."

I grin my appreciation of her good taste, and order two pints.
"Let's take it easy," I say. "Play it cool. We're safe here anyway,
but . . ."

She eyes me across the rim of her raised glass. "Okay, cheers."

We lean against the bar and scan the room as though looking for seats.

"Bit crowded, too," says Jadey.

"Uh-huh," I reply. "Odd. It's only six o'clock, and the place doesn't usually get jammed until about eleven, our time. That's when the eastern U.S. hits five P.M."

"Yes. And?"

"Well, U.S. office hours are peak time for legacy system problems. Keeps our old guys busy most of the afternoon and evening."

"Thought programming was a young man's game," Jadey says wryly.

"That was in the old days," I say, still idly examining the pub's clientele. I hope that's how it looks, anyway. The old crowd are in far earlier than usual, and so are the new crowd, the young managers; and more of each than I've ever seen in the place at the same time. "Still is, in a way, for the sort of stuff I do. But programming as such is so tied up with legacy systems that it's practically a branch of archaeology. Even the new stuff is something you can keep pace with past your twenties. You've heard of Moore's Law?"

She shakes her head, outstaring some geezer who's looking at her a bit too long.

"Not surprised," I say. "It was the projection that processing power got twice as fast for half the price every eighteen months. That curve went flat a long time ago." I laugh briefly, taking in the sights. "Just as well, or this lot would be as gods."

"Scary thought," Jadey agrees. She looks into her pint, looks up. "Can we talk?"

"Hmm," I haw. The pub's secure, that's its selling point—they put electronic countermeasures in the dust—but I'm not feeling very secure myself.

"You got some reason to be here? Apart from what I want, that is."

"Yeah, sure," I say, realizing she isn't being paranoid. Tradecraft: Always have a legit cover story. I idly ramble on for a bit about the ESA contract, then—

"Wait a minute," I tell her. I've finally caught the eye of the guy I seek, and beckon him. Jason, long and lean, black-clad, hottest cardsharp in the city, picks up his drink and sidles over. "Let's get inside a game."

The three of us amble over to the only vacant games-table and pull on gloves and glasses. The table tunes in and suddenly becomes much broader and a faint, undecided gray. The rest of the pub becomes abruptly remote.

"What game d'you want?" Jadey asks, fingertips poised over the keypad.

"Quantum Pool," says Jason.

Jadey clicks the choice, and the table shimmers to green. The air becomes smoky, layered thick under a low ceiling. Slow light illuminates the pool-table's green baize and colored balls. Outside that light, close by, in a bar that doesn't much resemble the one in the Darwin's Arms, the barmaid is chatting to one of the men who leans or perches at the counter. Somewhere a games-machine jangles, and on a jukebox Jagger sings "Sympathy for the Devil." A little farther away—if you look along certain angles between gaps in the walls and partitions—is another bar, another pool-table, other machines and women and men: the place goes on, repeated as though in mirrors. No windows; but there are doors. Beyond one of them, as though through the wrong end of a telescope, is the real bar we're in. Beyond the rest are bars which I hope are fake, but they add to the authentic Old World atmosphere.

I reach under the table and pull out the Schrödinger box, within which a virtual cat's virtual life is at the mercy of a randomizer linked to a decaying isotope somewhere out there in the real world.

"Dead or alive?"

"Dead," says Jason.

The cat is definitely dead.

"Your break," I say, closing the box. I slide it into its slot under the table. Jason chalks his cue, leans across, sights along it, makes the break. A couple of greens and pinks collide, and each scatters into six blues.

Jadey laughs. She's leaning on something, probably the back of a chair, which the virtuality software has painted up as a garish, brassy bar counter. Jason straightens his back and looks over at her.

"So," he says. "What's your problem?"

She rubs her hand around the back of her neck. "I need a new passport, and new ID and an exit visa. Like, fast."

"Ah." His eyes narrow. "You CIA?"

"If I was," she says, "do you think I would tell you? Or need you to work for me?"

He shrugs. "A deniable non-denial. That'll do me."

It won't do me; in fact this whole question bothers me a lot, but I keep my mouth shut for the moment.

They dicker over the deal's details and the spec while I set up my first shot. I move the cue too fast—almost as fast as the slow light. The Fitzgerald-Lorentz contraction shortens the tip by a foot and I miss completely.

"Damn."

Jason swoops over the baize, leaving me in a tricky position, but not quite irretrievable.

"Why's everyone in so early?" I ask.

Jason grunts. "All the transatlantic connections have been very choppy today."

"Yeah, tell me about it," I say sourly.

"And not much bloody work coming in."

"Aha," I say, chalking the cue. "Interesting."

I pull off a neat relativistic shot: allowing for the contraction, slamming the cue ball hard, cannoning one of the small, light ultraviolets so fast that its mass increases enough to shift one of the greens, which does a slingshot around one of the corner-pocket black holes and sets up a few other balls it collides with to snooker Jason's next. . . .

But he manages a comeback and clears me off completely.

"Again?" I reach for the Schrödinger box.

"Nah." He shakes his head. "Gotta work. Mind if we stay in here for a bit?"

"No problem."

Jadey ducks out into the real world for another round. Jason flexes his fingers. A long, low table trundles through one of the virtual doorways and comes to a halt beside us just as Jadey returns with our pints.

"Don't put them down there," Jason reminds her, just in time. The big table, conjured from his own softwear, can stop his data-gloved hand, but ours—and any other real-world object, of course—would just pass through it. Jadey places the drinks on the real games-table and we watch Jason work. He turns for a moment, frames Jadey's face with his fingers, then places the resulting portrait on the flat and begins morphing it: from passport photo back through employment ID, graduation pic, prom, grade-school group picture, baby . . . Other cards and pictures pop up on the surface of the big table, and he shuffles and slides them around with expert speed. Before our eyes a whole new biography of Jadey comes together, from maternity ward to tourist ticket. He sweeps them up into one stack, taps the edges on the table, and makes them vanish up his sleeve.

Dismisses the table and turns to me, with a broad wink at Jadey.

"Time to make it real," he says. "One for the code-geeks."

Old programmers never die. They just move over to legacy systems.

They even look that way. Early adopters to the last, they don't pop telomere tabs and mitochondrial mixers like the rest of us—no, they have to try out untried biotech, so they tend to look a bit patchy: gray skins–and–smooth beards sort of thing. Jadey, Jason, and I circle cautiously around the edge of a raucous, twenty-strong clot of the old villains, all quaffing beer and talking at the tops of their voices.

"What's with the fucking news?" someone's saying, shaking his head and blinking hard. "I can't get CNN, can't even get Slash-dot . . ."

This particular clique aren't all programmers. Sometime half a century ago, back in the nineties, their social circle overlapped that of the Scottish literary intelligentsia. Neither group's fashion sense has exactly moved with the times. The writers wear variously distressed jackets in fake-prolo denim or fake-macho leather; the coders go more for multipocketed waistcoats laden with the hardware for hardware fixes—Gerber and Leatherman multitools, Victorinox Swiss Army knives, Maglite torches, and over-faded trade-fair T-shirts: Sun, Bull, SCO, Oracle, Microsoft . . . This isn't irony, this is advertising—not of the products or the companies (most of them long gone), but of the skills, not at all redundant, of hacking their legacy code.

I try to look respectful, like some fanboy at a con, but I don't respect this lot at all. The ruling Party considers them unreliable, but as far as I'm concerned this is just the CPEU being its usual stuffed-shirt self. Vaguely left-wing, precisely cynical, they affect a laid-back, ca'canny approval of the so-called "imported revolution" that followed our defeat in the war. It was their kind of crap attitude to quality control that let the Russkis past NATO's automated defenses in the first place.

On the other hand, if you want to hack Unix-based filing systems in dusty metal boxes in schools and hospitals and personnel departments all over the continental U.S., they'll get on your case without asking questions, especially if you pay in dollars. I zero in on Alasdair Curran, a tall nonagenarian with long white hair and boastfully black sideburns.

"The guy who trained me worked on LEO," he brags loudly, "and he was trained by a some spook who'd been at Bletchley Park, so I reckon—"

"Yeah, Alec, and you're still shite!" someone else shouts.

As he rocks back in the general laughter Jadey catches his eye, and I take the opportunity to catch his ear. "Got a minute?"

"Oh, sure, Matt. What you after?"

"Well, I need an MS-DOS subbie—"

Curran scowls, then jerks his thumb at one of his mates. "Tony's your man."

"—and Jason needs somebody with a bit of early-dialect Oracle."

"Ah!" Curran brightens. "That, I can manage."

"We need it, like, now," Jadey tells him.

"Now?" He looks regretfully at his pint, then back at Jadey. She hits him with her best smile, and he has no defense. Hey, it makes my face warm, and I'm not even in the main beam.

Back to the quantum pool-room, but this time we don't even pretend to be playing. Curran boots up some clunky VR database manipulator, Jason sets up his card-table again, and I call up some of my software agents to handle the interface protocols and break the American firewalls.

I get the uncanniest sensation of pushing at an open door. Within moments Curran's up to his elbows in U.S. admin databases, Jason's slipping unlogged updates on Jadey's life story, and I'm keeping the one and only record of the changes and my AIs are booking the new ID an airline ticket.

We back out.

Jason passes Jadey a plastic card.

"That's the lot," he says. "Take it to any copyshop, they'll print and bind it for you. It'll even have the right bloodgroup stains."

I'm shaking my head. "Too bloody easy. It's like all the U.S. codes had been cracked. . . ."

"Shee-it," says Jadey.

Then I remember too. The English resistance network, unraveling.

"Uh-oh."

Curran's looking at us sharply as we move back to his lot's side of the room. "What's up?"

"Oh, nothing," I say hastily.

Then I notice that the whole place has gone quiet and everybody's watching the telly wall. There's that little jazzed-up flourish from "Ode to Joy" that precedes official announcements, and Big Uncle's face appears. CPEU General Secretary Gennady Yefrimovich normally looks appropriately avuncular, jovial, with an underlying solemnity. Right now he just looks insufferably smug.

"Comrades and friends," he begins, the translation and lip-synch software maxing his street-cred as usual in all the languages of the Community. For this particular nation and region, he comes across speaking English with a gravely Central Belt Scottish accent, which I know for a fact has been swiped from old tapes of the Communist trade-union leader and authentic working-class hero Mick MacGahey. "I have an historic announcement to make. The exploration station of the European Space Agency, *Marshall Titov,* has made contact with extraterrestrial intelligent life within the asteroid 10049 Lora."

He pauses for a moment to let that sink in. As if from a great distance, I hear a dozen dropped glasses break, in various places in the pub. He smiles.

"Let me first assure you all that this is no cause for alarm. The alien intelligence is no threat to humanity. These organisms are extremely delicate, and would be vulnerable to attack or exploitation. It is fortunate for themselves and for us that their first encounter with humanity should be the peaceful explorers of the Socialist Democracies, and not commercial companies or military forces."

Something about the ironic slant of his bushy eyebrows gives the message that he's carefully not saying anything that might give offense to the imperialist exploiters, but that we all know whose companies and forces he has in mind.

"Needless to say, we warmly invite the closest cooperation with the scientific agencies of the entire world, including the United States. Great vistas of cooperation are opened up by this astonishing discovery. I now turn you over to the regular news for further details, and wish you well on this historic evening."

Sign-off, with another flourish of trumpets.

Fade to black, with *something* in the middle of the screen . . . and then I recognize some of it and the scale of the rest of it hits me.

I've got chills like water's running down my back; every hair on my body is standing up, and I'm thinking this is the biggest news in human history, this day will be remembered forever. I'm staring at the wallscreen, transfixed like everybody else by the images from space; 10049 Lora looks like a lump of clinker, the space station a tiny filigree on its side. I manfully resist the rising impulse to give a nervous giggle.

"Aliens?" I hear myself squeak. Jadey turns around, almost spilling her pint, as everybody starts yelling at once. She drags me bodily away to a table, past old code-geeks whooping and cheering or, in some cases, just staring slack-mouthed with tears welling in their eyes.

"What?"

She's jammed in beside me in a corner bench, and she looks like it's only our mutually awkward position that's stopping her from slapping me. "Yeah, yeah," she says impatiently, "giant leap and all that, but—"

In one section of screen the Russkis' prettiest newscaster is twittering brightly about "our heroic ESA cosmonauts" and "brilliant scientists"; in another, much smaller window, a reporter outside the European Parliament drones on about a new scandal, some Trot MEP exposed as taking a bigger wage from Washington, or possibly Langley. Any other time, it'd be the hottest item; now it just seems trivial and tawdry, literally mundane. Why are they running it at all?

"Will you fucking *listen* to me?" Jadey hisses. I blink and shake my gaze loose from the screen's hypnotic virtual grip, and focus on her face, tense and pale in the warm light.

"Okay. Sorry." Jesus. I can feel the urge to look back at the screen, like gravity.

"Matt, that ESA station, it's the one you got a job from today."

"Yes!" I say. "That's what's got me so gobsmacked, apart from the . . . uh,"—I replay her cynical words—" '*giant leap*' stuff."

" 'Comrades, this is no accident,' " she flips back. She gives a quick, disdainful glance at the screen; I take this as permission to do the same. In the bottom corner there's a mug shot of Weber, then a clip of him being bundled into a black maria in Brussels, then a quick vox-pop with a shocked constituent on some street where sunshine glares on tin shacks and high-rises and palm trees.

"Where's that?" Jadey asks.

"French Guiana," I answer, unthinking.

"As in, famous for Kourou? That place where they have the *other* ESA launch-site?"

"Yeah, he had a big constituency with the space workers—"

I stare at her, with a wild surmise.

"Another non-coincidence," she says.

We both gaze soberly at the follow-up, an interview with an understandably defensive cadre of Weber's party, the *Ligue Prolétarienne Révolutionnaire*. It's almost drowned out by one of the old programmers.

"Think low-temperature physics, think Bose-Einstein condensates, think quantum computing," he explains at the top of his voice. "Say good-bye to crypto, say hello to the panoptic society. Shake hands with America's missile launch-codes and open the door to the Fourth World War. And that's not the end of it. That's just what the *Russkis* could be doing. What are the *aliens* up to?"

He's a solidly-built man perched on a stool and sprouting curly black hair all over like a burst mattress. He sees us, and a widening circle of others, listening, waves his hands and continues enthusiastically: "That ESA station is a node on the Internet, guys! Who knows what they might have hacked into by now? Hey, if they've been here that long, we can't even trust ourselves, they could've put trapdoors in our fucking DNA back in the Pre-Cambrian . . ."

And somebody else says, "Karl H. Marx on a bicycle, Charlie, aren't aliens *enough*?" and everybody laughs again.

I'll say this for those guys, they adapt to the end of the world we've always known faster than I do. They've seen a lot in their time: the Fall of the Wall, the Millennium Slump, the Century Boom, the Unix rollover, the War, the revolution . . . By the time Jadey and I have got ready to leave they're talking about how aliens that old must have some *really* old legacy systems, and that they must be needing contractors, and wondering what their day rate would be. . . .

Bastards.

3

Bat Songs

E SIAS DE TENEBRE, Magnate and Registered Member of the Electorate of the Republic of Nova Babylonia, exhaled the smoke from his joint and gave a modest and not entirely coincidental cough as he passed the rather insalubrious object to the lady at his left.

"My own small knowledge of terrestriology," he said to the high lord at his right, "is of course"—he waved a hand, as much to clear the resinous air in front of his mouth as to emphasize his point— "strictly that of a dilettante." (This was, strictly, a lie. His interest in news from the home planet was obsessive, and profitable.) "However, I can assure you that as of approximately one hundred years ago—or earlier today, as far as I'm concerned..." (Great Zeus, this stuff was making him verbose; he'd have to watch that!) "... no travelers or indeed, ah, involuntary arrivals have turned up claiming a later departure date than your own."

He wondered if this information would have been worth holding back. Probably not—and difficult to do in any case, if he wanted to trade information at all. This local lord was shrewd; a stocky, tough-looking man with a battered Roman nose, every plane of his face and neck converging to the flat, brush-cut top of his bullet head. His native speech was a dialect of English, grammatically degenerate compared to those Tenebre had heard before, on Croatan. Even the unfamiliar scientific words in its vocabulary could often be interpreted by deduction from the classical roots. But for this occasion he, like most people present, was speaking in Trade Latin, the de facto lingua franca of the Second Sphere.

Hal Driver's broad shoulders slumped slightly, and his features hardened after a passing moment of what Tenebre interpreted as sadness, perhaps disappointment.

"None after 2049, eh? Oh well, I suppose there are two ways of looking at that." He pushed his blue silk shirtsleeves back, planted his bare elbows on the drink-slopped surface of the long hardwood table, cupped his hands to his mouth and shouted for more brandy. Some girl got up from the table and hurried to a distant cupboard.

"Either we've blown ourselves to hell back there," he continued, fixing Tenebre with a blearily jovial gaze, "or we're expanding into a different sphere—a Second Sphere of our own, a *First* Sphere!— closer to the home sun."

"That could well be," said the merchant. He diplomatically did not point out that there were several other possibilities, none of them particularly cheering even compared to *all-out nuclear war,* a procedure which he'd gathered was a faint approximation to the much worse disasters that might by now have been visited upon the Earth.

"But for the present," Tenebre went on, "there's no doubt that you're the most recent representatives of Earth to have arrived in the Second Sphere. So, naturally, we're very interested in doing business with you."

He sounded too eager, but he didn't care. The right strategy for this particular opportunity wasn't to dicker down the locals, play it cool, keep his cards to his chest—it was to get his hands on as much technology and knowledge as possible before any of his competitors turned up.

One of the lord Driver's advisers, the one they called the Navigator—the lord Cairns, a pushy character who'd tried his patience earlier with persistent and barely comprehensible questions about, of all things, *calculating-machines*—leaned into the conversation from a couple of spaces to the high lord's right, vulgarly waving a fork on which a morsel of scallop was impaled. Though evidently old, his cheeks frosted with white stubble, he was vigorous and alert; a lean, muscular man with a bald pate, behind which white hair hung down to his back.

"What I'm still not too clear about," he said, in heavily accented English, "is where you would place Nova Babylonia compared with what you now know of Earth as it was when our ancestors left it. In terms of, you know, knowledge and technology and so forth. Standards of living of the masses, and all that." He popped the fork in his mouth, closed his eyes ecstatically, chewed and swallowed, then brandished the fork again. "According to our records and reminiscences, your dozen or so predecessors over the last couple of hundred years have *babbled*"—he giggled momentarily at the feeble pun—"about great shining cities, beautiful parks, spectacular wildernesses, and, you know, moon-drenched seas . . ." Another self-amused chuckle. ". . . and so on and so forth, and the justice and stability of the mighty and ancient Republic. All very well and good, but they've been as closemouthed as any saur about stuff like, well, what machinery you command, the standard of living of the masses and so forth."

He apparently realized he was beginning to sound repetitive, because at this point he mercifully shut up. But he still looked steadfastly at Tenebre, eyebrows raised in polite inquiry, while absently spearing another marine organism and devouring it with lascivious relish.

"Ah," said Tenebre, feeling that he was on firmer ground, "I can explain that." He glanced around, gratefully accepting the distraction of a refill of brandy and a cigar, which he devoutly hoped was pure tobacco—he needed a clear head. This particular hastily prepared dinner was being held not in the castle's banqueting-hall, but in the servants' refectory, and the servants were joining in eating the various dishes as soon as they'd finished serving them. The table at which he sat held about a score of placings and, like the others, was occupied by a mixture of men and women, masters and servants, guests and hosts. The whole room held a couple hundred people, counting the saurs, most of whom were well out of it by now, gazing vacantly into whatever mental spaces the hemp opened for them. The din of conversation, what with the crowd and the acoustics of the low, raftered ceiling and all the pots and pans still hooked to the walls, was tremendous.

At the table across the aisle he could see a gaggle of women including his first and third wives, a few servant women, and two of the castle's ladies, one of them Margaret Cairns, who was apparently the lord Cairns's number one and only wife. They all seemed to be talking at the same time except when they all screamed together with laughter. This kind of information interchange was one of which Tenebre did not entirely approve, but could hardly prevent. And sometimes, by talking freely, his wives found out things he could never have discovered for himself.

He nodded his thanks to the girl who'd brought the brandy. She handed on the bottle casually to Driver and pulled up a stool, looking at Tenebre all agog. He had an uneasy suspicion that at any moment she might, like some ignorant peasant child, reach out and touch his hair.

"You were saying?" Driver prompted.

"Ah yes, our predecessors. It's very simple. They didn't know about your presence here, weren't expecting it at all, and naturally enough were privately somewhat perturbed by it. A human-crewed ship from Earth is quite unprecedented, and could have foreshadowed all kinds of trouble."

"It could have been the spearhead of an invasion from Earth, you mean," said Driver. The thought evidently amused him.

Tenebre nodded sharply. "That's it, in so many words."

"Now, wait a minute," said James Cairns, scratching a diagram on the table with the tip of a short knife. "We've had ships in from Nova Babylonia via nearer colonies who definitely *had* heard of us, and they were just as closemouthed as . . . Oh, right." He stabbed the knife into the table. "I see now. The point is that Nova Babylonia hadn't yet heard of us when they set out, and whatever response it had come up with in the meantime hadn't had time to reach them. . . ."

"Precisely," said Tenebre. "And therefore the Electorate had not had a chance to discuss it. Now that we have, I'll be quite happy to answer your questions. . . ."

It was a folding lock-knife, the words *Opinel* and *France* still legible on its blade, but long since abraded from its plastic imitation-wood handle. James Cairns fiddled with its locking ring and doodled gloomily with the tip of the blade. Did France still exist? Even as a physical place? How much of French culture could a sufficiently advanced intelligence reconstruct from contemplation of this simple tool's elegant design?

Cairns wrenched his attention away from this futile but seductive line of thought and back to the present. With one part of his mind he began to keep track of the magnate's answers to the questions that flew at him from all sides of the table; with another, he examined the long-sided triangles he'd scored on the table, matching years past to light-years away.

Nova Babylonia, on the planet Nova Terra around the predictably named Nova Sol, was about a hundred light-years distant from Mingulay. The *Bright Star* had arrived off Mingulay around two centuries ago, and the first merchant starship to drop by had been a couple of years after that, so . . .

News of the *Bright Star*'s arrival had undoubtedly reached Croatan, five light-years away, within less than six years, and the more-distant colonies with a proportionate delay. But a ship en route couldn't receive or transmit information—traveling at lightspeed, a starship participated in the timeless, massless eternity of the photon, making the journey subjectively instantaneous. So ships originally from Nova Babylonia, but visiting various ports of call along their trade-route, would come to know of Mingulay's new settlers long before Nova Babylonia—or any ships sent from it directly—did.

This family Tenebre were thus the first merchants from Nova Babylonia to have some idea of what to expect when they arrived on Mingulay. Interesting. He wondered what they wanted, and what they had to offer in return.

Cairns sometimes felt that, deep down in the most adolescent recesses of his seventy-year-old brain, he harbored a personal grudge against the universe for not having turned out the way his ancestors had expected. He could have *lived with* a universe whose interstellar gulfs could be crossed only with generation ships, cold-sleep, or ramscoops. He'd have been absolutely fucking *delighted* with one that could be traversed with some kind of warp-drive or jump-gates or wormholes or similar fanciful mechanism. In much the same way, he could have been quite metaphysically satisfied with a godless universe; or, if he'd ever come across a convincing apologetic, happy to affirm that this one was the work of God.

Instead he'd found himself in a universe where gods swarmed by the trillion, a regular Oort Crowd of them around every star—most of the gods, as far as anyone knew, being convinced atheists. The only thing the gods had ever created for anyone else's benefit was the stardrive. The stardrive could get you to the stars, in an instant of subjective time. At the speed of light.

There were times when he felt like saying to the gods, *Thanks a bunch.*

". . . purchase a great deal of our staple foodstuffs and machinery from the saurs, naturally enough," Tenebre was saying. "Most of our wealth, as you might expect, comes from the profits of trade. Much of the commerce between the elder species is handled by Babylonian business families, who are thus able to support many of the populace through the purchase of various services. The manufacturing and farming classes sensu stricto tend to specialize in luxury production for the saur market. Among the saurs there is quite a fashion for human handicraft products, a taste for certain fruits and vegetables, spices, and, er, herbs . . ."

Everyone laughed.

The merchant leaned back, patting his belly complacently. "All indications are that the popular masses are quite satisfied with their lot; those who aren't, are free to take ship to the younger colonies, and for several centuries such emigration has been at a low trickle."

James grinned to himself, noticing Driver's slow, sober nod. Nova Babylonia didn't exactly sound like a technologically dynamic society. They'd always suspected as much, but it was encouraging, in a way, to have it confirmed. *We could already walk all over them,* he thought, wondering if Driver—to say nothing of Tenebre—was thinking the same. Not that the elder species would allow them to actually do it, but still. . . .

"So," said Driver, "although this is no time for serious bargaining, I find myself wondering just what you could possibly want from our . . . somewhat isolated and backward society." He shrugged, spreading his hands. "Your predecessors have for the most part traded with the other species here, buying little but our poor local copies of gadgets and trinkets originally manufactured in the Solar System. I hardly think our technology is much of a match for that of the saurs."

Cairns noticed frowns around the table, from their own side's more business-oriented types, obviously thinking that Driver wasn't much of a salesman. He wished there was some secret signal meaning, *Give the man credit for being a bit devious,* then realized that these discomfited faces might at some level be a part of Driver's devious design.

"Oh, when we've had a chance to examine what my family and your traders each have to offer, I think we'll all be pleasantly surprised," said Tenebre smoothly. "Products for human use are best devised—if not necessarily manufactured—by human beings. And we have, as usual, much business to do with the saurs and with our cousins of the mines and the forests: pharmaceuticals, certain rare minerals, hardwoods, and so forth." He waved a hand. "Routine trade. But I will tell you frankly that our strongest interest is in what you have brought from Earth. Art, science, technology, history, philosophy—all the knowledge of the home world. Nova Babylonia thirsts for them all!"

"But that's *information*!" Matt said. "And, as we say, information wants—"

Driver's head turned like a striking snake. His swift glare made Cairns pause.

"Information wants to be paid?" said Tenebre. He smiled around at his interlocutors. "We," he told them proudly, "have such a saying ourselves."

The guests had retired, the servants and younger family members had cleared away most of the evening's detritus and gone to their own beds. The few old members of the Cosmonaut Families who still lived in the castle had made their way through to the front hall, and set themselves down in armchairs in a loose arc around the fireplace. One saur accompanied them, old Tharovar, who had welcomed their ancestors, the original crew, on their first arrival. In his long acquaintance with humans he'd acquired a better head for the hemp than most of his kind, and was now relaxed, rather than comatose in the servants' hall like the others.

Cairns nursed his brandy and cigar, in the chair nearest the dying fire. Margaret sat on the floor, resting against the chair's arm, basking in the embers' heat. Tharovar squatted at his other hand. The others gazed unseeing into the fire for a while: Driver, and Andrei Volkov, and Larisa Telesnikova, and Jean-Pierre Lemieux. Those all had partners or lovers who were from outside the notional, hereditary crew—the cosmonaut cadre—and who had tactfully left them to their private thoughts and conversation.

Driver looked around the depleted company and cleared his throat, spat into the fire. Sputum sizzled horribly for a second or two.

"Well," he said, "I got an interesting offer from Tenebre."

"A different one from the ones he was making at the table?" asked Volkov.

Driver nodded. "He picked a quieter moment. . . . What he offered was to pay us well—for shipping. He could make it very advantageous for us to go into the carrying trade."

Low and bitter laughter greeted this statement.

Cairns felt Margaret grip his ankle, and relaxed his own grip, unconsciously fastened on her shoulder.

"So what did you say to that?"

Driver shrugged, a movement exaggerated by the padded shoulders of his loosened doublet. "I . . . temporized, but gave him to understand we'd be interested."

"What?" Cairns almost shouted. The others sat up in their seats, equally agitated. Driver regarded them all with a sardonic smile.

"We always knew it would come to this sometime," he said mildly. "We've prepared for it." He fixed Cairns with a reproving look. "After a fashion. So—what progress do *you* have to report, Navigator?"

James waited for a second or two; Margaret was urgently stroking his foot, and the gentle touch calmed him a little, not much. Tharovar sat tense and rigid beside him; the tendons in the saur's thin neck were like taut wires, and his mouth was, if possible, thinner than usual.

"Come off it, Hal," Cairns said. "For decades now it's been little more than a gods-damned *hobby,* as you well know. It's not easy to interest the younger members of the family in the"—his lips curled—"Great Work, and it gets more tedious with every computer that breaks down and can't be repaired. Every so often somebody shamefacedly turns in a few pages of logic or math. Christ Almighty, I could sometimes swear the paper has had *tears* fall on it, like some kid's exercise book. I put them together in order, I file them, I pass out a few more problems, and they take even longer to come back. People have other priorities, other opportunities, and more as time goes on."

Only the knowledge of how pathetic, how feeble it would sound, made him refrain from adding, *What else can I do?* He hated hearing himself make excuses; it wasn't his manner, not his style at all, not part of the program. *Not done, old chap.* But it was true, and Driver knew it was true, and Cairns knew that he knew.

So he concluded by saying, confidently and aggressively, his oldest excuse of all, a Navigator family joke:

"I'm an artist, not a technician."

That got a laugh—even Driver had to smile—and the tension eased. Larisa Telesnikova took the opportunity to lean forward and speak diplomatically.

"Okay, comrades," she began, as she usually did when talking seriously to any gathering larger than two, "what this means is that we *don't know* what progress may have been made by now. Why don't we use the formal reception for the merchants to invite as many as possible of the Navigator's family, and ask them to bring their latest results, even their latest workings?"

"Better than nothing," agreed Driver.

"That's all very well," said Cairns, "but I don't hold out much hope." He glared at Driver. "As you well know. And what will you tell your new friend Tenebre when it becomes obvious that we can't come up with the goods?"

Driver chuckled darkly, scratching his belly through the bunched cambric of his shirt.

"That's the beauty of it," he said. "I tell him we have technical difficulties, demand a substantial retainer, swear blind we won't cut a deal with any other merchants who may come hurrying to the scene, and ask him to call back on his next trip. For him, that means a wait of a couple of months, maybe a year. For us . . . well, one way or another, it won't be our problem."

Cairns guffawed; the others laughed too, less heartily. Their ages were all in the seventies or eighties, and—even with the medical knowledge that the saurs had long shared with the hominid genera—none of them expected to live more than another few decades. Unless, of course, the secrets of the ancient Cosmonauts could be rediscovered in the meantime—but that was a hope, not an expectation.

Tharovar stood up and strolled over to the fireplace and stood in front of it on the hearth. His silhouette gave Cairns an atavistic pang of unease, like a childish reaction to a familiar person in a frightening mask.

"Have you considered," the saur said in his low, hissing voice, "*accompanying* the family Tenebre to Nova Babylonia and back? You could use their starship as a time machine into the future of this colony, a future in which, perhaps, your mathematical problems will be solved—and your lives could be extended further."

"Yeah, I've considered it," Driver said, surprising Cairns, who hadn't. "I have *no* fucking intention of tearing myself away from my life, my descendants, and my ability to keep up, in order to turn myself into a stranger in a strange time."

Cairns joined in the murmur of agreement.

"Then you could go to Croatan," the saur persisted, "and shuttle back and forth, returning here every ten years. That would surely be sufficient."

53

Margaret spoke up. "You really don't have much of a handle on this 'progress' thing, do you, Tharovar?"

The smile in her voice belied the criticism in her words, and the saur replied with some humor of his own.

"Perhaps not," he said. "I am only an egg."

Gregor hauled himself a meter off the edge of his futon, elbowed his way across the carpet, and slammed down the button to shut off the loud ringing of his alarm clock. Early sunlight rampaged through the narrow window of his room. He lay half in and half out of bed for minute or two, cheek pressed on the rough fibers by the planet's merciless one-gravity pull, while he made a cautious all-systems check. Thankfully, the various aches in his limbs and back were all accounted for by the previous day's work on the boat; minute movements of his head did not result in any explosion. The feeling in his stomach came from an empty belly and a full bladder; no nausea was detectable. His erection, to which one hand had reflexively returned, was comfortingly hard. His mouth was dry, but tasted no worse than neutral.

It followed that he didn't have a hangover and hadn't drunk too much last night. Memory reported in, shamefacedly admitting to a few gaps in the record, but everything seemed consistent with his having shared one more pipe with Salasso, then walked back to his room, fallen asleep fully dressed, woken around midnight from colorful dreams, read for an hour or so, and then gone to bed properly, a mere five hours or so earlier.

Still moving slowly—in part because of the legitimate (as it were) aches in his muscles, and in part because of the remaining possibility of a stealth hangover, the kind that lurked just outside awareness and then sprang on you like a cat from a tree at the first sudden movement—Gregor rolled over and stood up. Everything still being fine, he wrapped himself in a bathrobe and padded down the corridor to the shared toilet to relieve himself. On returning to his room he bent and stretched his way through the calisthenics of the Salute to the Sun, and finished them invigorated. That done, he switched on the electric kettle and made himself a small pot of tea.

The room was just big enough to contain the futon, a table and chair, hundreds of pages of notes, and several hundred books. It wasn't much of a gesture of independence, considering that his father gave him the money he needed for rent, university fees, and subsistence, but it was better than living at home. At the top of a building in Kyohvic's old town, built before his ancestors' ship had arrived, the room gave him peace and privacy and, if he needed it, the easy company of the other students and older eccentrics who lived in its other twenty or so single rooms and shared its decrepit facilities.

As was his habit, he opened the weighty leatherbound volume— a gift from his father—of the Good Books, the words of the philosophers: the Fragments of Heraclitus, the Sayings of Epictetus, the Teachings of Epicurus, the Poems of Lucretius. Their English paraphrases were among the best-loved works of Mingulayan literature; some said they were better than the originals. His glance fell on one of the Fragments:

> *This world, which is the same for all,*
> *no god or man has made.*
> *An ever-living fire it is*
> *whose flames forever flare and fade.*

The book fell open again at another familiar page, from the Teachings:

> *Around the world goes friendship's dancing call,*
> *Join hands in happiness for one and all.*

That would do, he thought, as a devotion for the day. He drained his cup, dressed, and set off to work, picking up his breakfast on the way.

Elizabeth jumped off the clanging tram at Harbor Halt and walked briskly to the quay. The parked skiffs glowed orange in the early light, their spindly legs and lenticular bodies casting long shadows out over the water like tall, striding tripedal machines. The traders' ship squatting in the sound still struck her eye as a startling sight, intrusive, visibly alien, massively out-of-place. High above, an airship from the skyport on the hill behind Kyohvic wallowed upward to meet a southerly air current, and tiny buzzing airplanes made sightseeing circles around the harbor and its gigantic visitor. For a moment, airship and aircraft looked like pathetic, primitive imitations of the starship and the skiffs.

Along the quay baffled seabats squabbled around the well-protected tanks that Renwick and his crew were already lifting off the deck with a creaking crane and screeching winch. Elizabeth mucked in as best she could, helping to maneuver the tanks and crates onto the department's flatbed truck parked alongside. After a while she glimpsed Gregor hurrying up, and her heart jumped like a fish.

"Good morning," he said. "Sorry I'm late."

"You're hardly that," Elizabeth said. "We were early."

She smiled at him, staring and trying not to, trying not to look too long, hoping that he'd notice that she was looking too long. But he just grinned and nodded and grabbed the rope. His hand brushed hers accidentally as they hauled together; she almost jerked it away.

Things might have been different if he hadn't *grown* on her, if they'd met at some student bash instead of in the lab, if they hadn't worked together and become colleagues and good mates before she'd realized what she really felt for him, and had felt from the beginning. Now she felt completely entangled in that easy friendship and close collaboration, frozen by the fear of losing it in a welter of embarrassment and misunderstanding.

He rode beside her as she drove the flatbed, its electric engine whining under the strain, along the coast road to the marine-biology department on the town's westward and seaward edge. There they turned them over to the keeper of the saltwater aquaria, and headed in to the laboratories to begin another day of the research they shared. The frequent fishing-trips for new specimens were almost a holiday; this was their real work.

Gregor, Elizabeth, and Salasso were cooperating on mapping the nervous system of the squid. Its simple structure, relatively large neurons, and—to be blunt—its absence of a hard skeleton made it an ideal laboratory animal for investigating neurophysiology in general, but it was the peculiarities of cephalopod neural morphology that they were concentrating on. The walls were almost papered-over with drawings, diagrams, and readings of pH levels and electrical potentials.

Salasso, as usual, was already there, crouched over a deep glass dish within which a small squid hovered, oblivious to the fine-needle electrode which the saur was slowly bringing to bear.

"Come here, little one," he crooned through barely opened lips. "This is your lucky day."

Tenebre woke beside his number three wife to the dawn's light and the morning chorus of the bats. Somewhere in the roof-space above the ceiling, birds chirruped and scratched as they settled in for their day of roosting sleep. For a few minutes he, like them, huddled in shared warmth, watching his breath fog. The Keep of Aird, like castles everywhere in the known universe, lacked central heating.

Tenebre grunted and rolled out of the low bed, wrapped himself in one of the quilted robes which his hosts had thoughtfully provided, and dragged on the woollen socks he'd discarded the previous night. Thus fortified, he made his way over to the south-facing window—at least it was glazed, even if not double-glazed—leaned on the sill, and looked out across the harbor to the town.

Seeing Kyohvic from the skiff had been his first shock here. The daylight did not diminish the surprise it afforded. He stared for a long time at the buildings, sharp in the long shadows and pink light of the autumn dawn. When he'd last seen it, four centuries in its past and five months in his, it had been a straggle of low houses along the shore, a harbor busy with fishing-smacks, and a scatter of farms beyond. The castle itself had been empty, superstitiously avoided. Now the buildings had climbed to five or six stories and spread miles along the sides of the valley; the fishing-boats still crowded the harbor, but they were dwarfed by much-larger sea-ships, tall masts bristling; the fields were laid out in a dense patch-work—some plowed black, some brown with stubble, others green with the shoots of this spring's winter wheat. At the brow of the hill, airships nudged and bobbed among mooring-pylons, and flying-machines (frighteningly rickety aerial vehicles; to his eyes, little more than motor-powered kites) took off on frivolous or fateful missions.

Tenebre was used to seeing change speeded-up, compressed; it was one of the benefits of life as a merchant—it gave one a long view of history, the closest, perhaps, that a human mind could come to the millennial perspective of the saur. In forty years of life and five centuries of objective time he'd seen Mingulay's parent colony, Croatan, surge upward and expand from unpromising beginnings; he'd seen Nova Babylonia fallen in flames, and risen from the ashes . . . but this was different—this was something new under the suns.

These people whose hospitality (socially warm, however physically chilly) he was enjoying and enduring, were descended from independent human space explorers—"Cosmonauts," they called themselves. He relished the word, with a sort of rebellious vainglory in the human species which he'd never before imagined he could feel. In the great chain of being, humanity had a respected but restricted place: restricted not by force but by circumstance.

The gods wheeled in their million-year orbits, indifferent and inviolate in the spaces between the worlds, much as the terrestrial philosopher Epicurus had supposed, and as the poet Lucretius had sung. The krakens plied their trade between the stars, navigating the lightspeed ships. The saurs steered a shorter course, piloting their gravity skiffs and working in their tropical and subtropical biological factories, their *manufacturing plant*.

The humans . . . ah yes, the humans had a place: inventing and manufacturing, trucking and bartering, farming and fishing, all of it on the surface of land or sea, or as passengers in the older races' craft. The only sentient species with a humbler role were humanity's cousins, the small hominidae digging in the mines and the tall hominidae tending the temperate forests. So it was, in variant proportions, on all the worlds of the Second Sphere, the hundred-light-year radius around Nova Sol. This was the generous limit of the journeys on which the krakens' starships were willing to take humans.

Generous, but still a limit.

Matters were managed very differently on Earth, the home planet; and perhaps on this one, Mingulay, to which humans had come from Earth on their own initiative, and their own ship.

Just before he'd gone to bed, one of his saur crew, Bishlayan, had passed on a piece of information she'd picked up from one of the local saurs. Some of the first crew, the original cosmonauts, were believed to be still alive, somewhere out in the wilds. That ship had brought the secret of long life, as well as of long journeys. *A bright star indeed,* Tenebre thought, turning with a smile to greet the waking mumbles and hungover groans of his third wife. The other two were still asleep beside her.

4

Legacy Systems

OUTSIDE, PRINCES STREET was heaving with the usual Festival crowd, but they weren't behaving in the usual Festival way. A surprising number of people were actually looking up, like they expected some shining mothership to arrive at any moment. Others stood about talking, or grabbing passersby and spreading the news: the number of people discussing it or watching the skies was increasing by the minute. I hadn't seen anything like this since the revolution, when I was a little kid, when we emerged blinking from the shelters and basements and ruins to greet the Russki troops on the street. I remembered the noise of the jubilant car horns. Now, the susurrus of human voices, of feet and bicycle wheels and trolleybuses, seemed eerily quiet by comparison.

Jadey grabbed my elbow as I poised to cross the street.

"Where you going?"

I jerked my head rightward, indicating. "Waverley—run your stuff through the station copyshop, then get a shuttle train to the airport?"

"Na-na-na-nah. We gotta think this through. No rush, it's an open ticket, right?"

"Yeah, sure, but the faster you get out—"

She looked at me sharply. "Hey, who's the expert here? Do I give you programming tips? So, shut up and come with me."

Not much I could say to that. She turned left and we headed down Leith Walk, past the new-tech buildings in the bombed area where I lived and on down to the older part of the street. The crowds were thinner here, the bicycles fewer. Trolleybuses glided down the middle of the carriageway. To the north, the direction we were more or less heading, the sky remained noticeably light: a mere few hundred kilometers poleward, the sun still shone.

After a few minutes' silent hurrying past the software stores and delis and restaurants, Jadey took another left, into one of the side streets in the Broughton area, a canyon of sandstone tenements. Stopped at a door beside a tacky boutique shopfront.

"Won't this place be watched, if you're—?"

Another glare. "Like I said."

She thumbed the keypad, peered into the retinal scanner, and the door swung open. I sidled after her, past tangled bicycles and stacked mail and up a stone stairway. On the third floor she unlocked the door of a flat, using metal keys. Hardware.

Inside, it was chilly and dark. She strolled in, flicking lightswitches. The windows—I saw when we stepped into the main room—were covered by aluminum venetian blinds. There was a sofa, a screen, and a table, and not much else; the wall-posters were tuned to the previous year's bands. Looked like an empty student pad, and probably was.

"Coffee?"

"Thanks. Black, no sugar."

"Just as well," Jadey said.

By the time she came back from the kitchen I had the screen working, with the sound off. Most of the news channels had moved on to talking heads. Jadey sat down at the other end of the sofa, nodded at the screen.

"Countermeasures," she said. "Built in. We can talk."

"So . . . are you really CIA?" I asked. Not the most tactful of opening lines, but it had been on my mind.

"No, of course I'm not bloody CIA!" she answered, almost spilling her coffee. "Statist sons of bitches! They're almost as bad as the goddamn commies, when they're not doing deals with them."

"All right. I only asked. So what *are* you?"

She gave me a serious frown. "You really want to know?"

"Well, yeah. Call it idle curiosity."

"Hah! All right. I'm working for a political organization that does what we think the CIA *should* be doing: stirring up a bit of subversion in the E.U."

"I'd figured that," I said slowly. "It's the bit that came before it that kind of has me baffled. How does it work? Counterrevolution for fun and profit?"

"Neither," she said. "The money comes from . . . well, basically from legacies and trust funds set up by Net entrepreneurs who got rich in the Century Boom, and who thought it might be a good idea to, ah, invest in the future of the free market. As for the fun—"

She put down the cup. Her hands were shaking. "It was fun for a while, down in old England. Making contacts, setting things up, basic agitprop. But the scene's got a lot heavier lately. You know, like, pseudo-gangs?"

"What?"

"Resistance groups set up by . . . whoever—the Russkis, I guess, maybe even the Brits—to discredit the real opposition with the odd terrorist outrage; black propaganda that makes us smell like fascists; spreading rumors that the *real* resistance groups are pseudo-gangs, that the best activists are police agents." She waved a hand. "You know the score."

"The trusting trust problem?" I asked, translating into geek-speak.

"Exactly!"

She frowned again, looked at her nails. One of her thumbnails was bitten right down. "Shit, I thought I'd *broken* that habit. . . ." Looked up. "Let me tell you about last night."

There's a scene in *Battle of Algiers* where the Muslim women of the FLN are preparing to go out and plant bombs in the European quarter, and they're tarting themselves up in immodest European clothes and applying makeup for the first time in their lives, and as they preen solemnly in front of mirrors the soundtrack becomes a relentless martial drumbeat.

Jadey hears that beat as she gets herself ready for the work of the night. She's always liked her complexion, with its natural-blonde creamy smoothness matching her fair brows and pale lips, but now she's covering it all up with blusher and tint, mascara and eyeshadow and bloody-red lipstick. Dye gel turns her hair black and spiky, stains the swirling water as she rinses her hands under the tap.

Her preparations complete, she waits for a few minutes, watching her watch. Time is of the essence. Two minutes until contact. Time to go.

She checks herself in the mirror: lacy white blouse, small black vinyl skirt, fishnet tights, high heels. Subtlety is not the name of her game. She grins at her own unfamiliar features, and jauntily hoists the red leather shoulderbag. She's already checked the gun inside it.

"You go, girl," she tells herself. "Go out there and slay them!"

The air is damp and the light is yellow. It's a dead pre-dawn hour, but not too late for the tarts to ply their trade. Jadey avoids their eyes, outglares the raised brows of lurking pimps and johns. Up ahead, she sees the back of the man she's after, in Russian military uniform. The hardware is soft and warm through her glove, like a wee lump of that stuff kids play with; or maybe plastique, and just as dangerous: Silly Semtex. She slaps it onto a lamppost and walks briskly up York Way, about thirty meters behind the man. A slow, silently counted ten seconds later, the Russki turns off the main drag and into an alley. Jadey follows him without looking back.

Ten seconds is ample time for the hardware to work: for the lump to fasten and flow like a sinister, fast-moving slime-mold, extending its tendrils into the cable of the street camera on the lamppost, and to insinuate its programs into the datastream. By now it should have subtly degraded the image quality to the point where every face on York Way might as well have a balaclava mask over it. With luck, it'll be burrowing into and editing storage as well as input, scrambling the recognition software, but none of that can be counted on. The input masking, however, can—but still she doesn't look around, doesn't give them even that flicker of a chance.

She walks straight past the Russki, who's pretending to examine a window display of dusty plumbing. Her gaze meets the reflection of his for a fraction of a second, then she's past him. He looks smart in that uniform, though he's less a soldier than she is; all the civil servants of the occupation wear military uniform. It's one of those Russki things.

He waits until her heels have metronomically ticked off five seconds, then whistles after her. She turns, swiveling shoulders and hips, clasping the soft leather of her handbag. She grins at him and glances over at a still-narrower alleyway. He nods imperceptibly and strides over and turns sharply into it; she follows, her gait now businesslike rather than professional.

She looks at Josif with a certain warmth and recognition that no caution can prevent. Over the months she has come to quite like the man. Even so, she is surprised when instead of their usual minute of pretended bargaining he catches her by the waist and draws her toward him. His mouth descends on hers. There's a moment of lip and tongue contact and then she hears, as much as feels, a small metallic object being pushed gently against her teeth. She almost swallows, which might not have been a bad idea, if messy in its long-run implications. Then she manages to tongue it between molars and cheek. It's about the size and shape of a small coin, with a rounded rim.

Josif moves his head back with a hushing breath. Jadey nods, almost as imperceptibly. Then his chest slams into hers and she hears a thump, feels an impact, and there's a horrible grating noise. As she takes a forced backward step Josif becomes deadweight in her arms and she has to let go of him. His mouth opens as if to scream. Only blood comes out, and then he's down on the wet paving, head and heels hammering, blood pooling and spurting, bowels voiding.

And she's two more steps back and in the firing position, the one-shot plastic Liberator in her locked hands in front of her.

There's a young man facing her, looking shocked, with a big bloody knife clutched in his right hand. Zip jerkin and jeans and gloves, enclosed from neck to sole in filmy isolation polymer: medical or murder gear.

She could have done with some of that herself. There's blood all down her blouse.

The young man's expression turns to annoyance and puzzlement. "You're not—"

"What you expected?" Her mouth is dry; she tries not to bite the thing in her mouth, or her tongue.

"Not expecting me."

She doesn't look away from his eyes, or from the blade. Josif is terminal; not necessarily dead, yet, but it would take a crash medical team here in the next couple of minutes to save him, and she doubts that she can make this happen.

"Back off," she warns. He flinches, and she strains to keep her voice low. "No, I was bloody well not expecting you. Why should I have been?"

Then she realizes what the guy thinks has been going on.

"Oh, Christ, you thought I was on your team?"

The guy nods. In the dim light she can just about make out his buzz-cut hair, hooded eyes, thin face. She doubts if he's out of his

teens. Exactly the sort of kid who gets involved in nationalist terrorist cells that think luring Russian soldiers into dark alleyways
then killing them is a good way to build an arsenal for the Great
Day. Kids like that are the bane of her fucking life.

"Thought it was all set up," he mumbles. His London accent is
so thick she can barely follow it. "Shit."

She'll let the implications of that pass, for now.

"Run," she says, gesturing with the pistol.

"And then what did you do?"

"Ran in the opposite direction, down another alley. Just a minute
later I'd circled back and crossed York Way again, farther up, and
the cops were like flies on shit around the junction I'd been at.
That's why I reckon your hardware's fucked. Decided not to go
back to my place, headed for a safe house and found it wasn't.
Door was getting the heavy boot just as I turned the corner, so I
turned the other way pretty sharp. Back in the red-light area, I had
a few stashes of spare clothes and ID and shit. Sealed containers
spot-glued inside dump bins, places like that. So I used one of them
to get changed and ditch the tarty gear. Went into my cover job—
it's deliberately a suspicious-looking job, American book import
company—phoned you at coffee break and got the midday train.
And, like I said, the busies were giving me funny looks."

I stared at her, somewhat shaken by this account—for its implied
sex as much as its explicit violence. How long had I known her?
A couple of years, at the outside. She'd wandered into a codeshop
down Leith Walk, where I was working between contracts—this
was before I'd achieved my current high rep as a manager, I hasten
to add—dropped a set of Calvin Klein eyewear on the counter and
asked for a few interesting modifications. *Serious* warranty-voiding
and copyright-violating stuff, and the kind of thing that there really
was no legitimate use for: as blatant and illegal as sawing off a
shotgun. I took it on, without asking questions, and gave her back
the kit a day later. Repeat business was assured, and she'd started
turning up in the sort of places I hung out in. We'd chat, maybe
have a coffee or do some drugs, but nothing more came of it than
that. I wasn't too sure, now, when I'd first become aware that she
was involved in the English resistance; she must have told me explicitly at some point, but I couldn't remember when. We'd never
actually discussed it.

"Do you still have the thing the Russian guy passed to you?"

"Of course." An object appeared in her uncurling palm like a conjuring effect. I picked it up and turned it over.

"It's a datadisk," I said, not surprised but vaguely disappointed, as though I'd been subconsciously expecting it to be a new secret weapon.

"Tell me something I don't know!"

"Maybe I can," I said. "I can tell you what's *on* it."

She shook her head. "I ran it in my reader on the train. It's garbage, or encrypted."

"Feh." I took my own reader from my pocket, patched it to my phone, and slid the disk in. "It's probably not one of the commercial codes, but I doubt it's the latest mil-spec or there wouldn't have been much point in passing it on, would there?"

"You got a point there." Her voice sounded sad. "Josif wouldn't have had access to real hard secrets anyway—this must be important more because it's current than because it's restricted."

I called up my file of thousands of keys and set them to work throwing themselves at it. This wasn't code-breaking as such, just matching the code to keys which, legally speaking, I had no business having, which is why I kept them stashed on a server far away. On the side of the screen a little red line shrank slowly as the program ran.

"Doesn't seem like enough to die for."

"He didn't know he was risking that," she said.

"Or to kill for."

"You think he was set up?" She made a sour mouth. "It's possible."

Ding, went the reader.

"Wah-hey!"

I started paging through the decoded text. Jadey leaned in to look, murmuring interest and appreciation. I paged faster, suddenly suspecting that it all looked familiar. It was.

"This is an ESA spec. Remember—the space station stuff?"

"Can you check it out?"

"Yeah, sure. Can't *do* very much with it on this thing, but . . ." I patched it over to the big screen so we could both follow it comfortably, and resumed clicking through the pages, more or less at random. Some of them were text, with the elaborate numbering system of tech spec—some individual lines within paragraphs had their own version numbers—and some, which took just a fraction of a second longer to resolve onscreen, were deep three-dimensional diagrams and schematics optimized for looking at, and through, with VR glasses or contacts. Most of these were matched either to a photograph or an indistinguishably hyperrealististic rendering of the final object.

"Y'know," Jadey pondered aloud, "I can't claim to be an expert on asteroid mining, let alone whatever equipment you'd need to talk to an alien hive-mind or whatever, but that sure doesn't look like mining equipment, or a scientific research establishment either."

I snorted. "You're right, there. You do need something like a refinery for asteroid mining, but this is more than that. Looks to me like some kind of automated factory cannibalized out of parts that might have passed muster for either that or a research station. They're *building* something out there, or planning to."

"Any indication what it might be?"

"Could be in there," I said with a shrug, "but it would be a devil of a job to find it. There's more data here than in the *Encyclopædia Britannica*."

"Well." She gave me a funny look. "I don't think it's for us to try and figure this out." Scratched her head. "Like, I don't think we should even be looking at it."

"Oh." I clicked it off. "Especially not me, huh?"

"Especially not you. For your own peace of mind."

"That is one way of looking at it." I somewhat resented the idea that I had less business rummaging through possible state secrets than she had, but I realized this was irrational—the E.U. was no more "my" state than it was hers, and I was in my own way as much its enemy. Just not as well-trained an enemy. Not that we had torture to worry about—this was Scotland, a happy little Socialist Democracy, after all, not some Third World client-state of either side—but we both knew what the Federal Security Bureau's truth-drugs could do, and the less we knew, the less trouble we were likely to be in if we were caught.

Jadey fetched more coffee and we sat for a few moments warming our hands on the mugs and not saying anything.

"So," I said at last, "what do we do now? You still want to go to America?"

Jadey stroked her lower lip with the upper teeth, put down the mug and shoved her hands under her armpits, rocking back and forth a little. "Oh shit, I don't know," she said. "If it wasn't for the suspicion that all our codes are crackable in real time now, I'd just zap that lot through on the fast pipe and make my way home clean. Hell, if they pulled me at the airport or wherever I'd still be out in a few weeks."

"A spy-swap? But you're not—"

"Ah, some kinda analogous deal. The private sector has its ways too, okay? But as it is, I have to get that thing back physically, and it has to go separately from me. And you know what? I don't think we can rely on the mail."

"Take it to the U.S. consulate?" I suggested brightly. "Diplomatic bag?"

"I don't know if I want the statists to have it either," she said gloomily. "I don't think my friends in the Russki apparat down south wanted that. They wanted this sent to the people in the U.S. who could make the most use of it. And that means *our* people, not the spooks."

I refrained from asking further who "our people" were, and not just for security reasons. Not having been born yesterday, I already had a shrewd suspicion. One of the arguable advantages of living under the Right-Wing Communist variant of state capitalism was that the official media carried quite sensible materialist analyses, of other countries' affairs, anyway. The split in the U.S. capitalist class was a staple of *Europa Pravda* punditry. At the bottom of it, beneath all the talk about Yankees and Cowboys, Globalists and Isolationists, Old Money and New, lay a material interest that was almost embarrassingly crude—oil.

The U.S. domestic oil producers fueled the New Money forces, and the overseas oil investors lubricated the Old. The latter had taken a bloody nose in the Ural-Caspian Oil War, and the Isolationists had enjoyed a brief triumph with the hasty troop withdrawal and an opportunistic settling of old scores in the "who lost Europe?" / "Greens in the machine" witch-hunts of the early 2030s, but it hadn't taken long for Old Money to rise again to the top. Long-festering hatreds and fresh grievances were now being fought out in a low-level civil war—an assassination here, a bombing there, an angry demo against the posthumous rehabilitation of Janet Reno somewhere else.

Jadey had as much as admitted she was a New Money girl, but

probably had no more idea than I had of who—behind multiple facades of funds, fronts, and foundations—was ultimately pulling her strings.

She stood up, as if having come to some decision.

"Okay," she said. "Let's do the job right here."

"What, *'here'?*" I looked around the bare room, baffled.

"Here in *Scotland*. You've got the kit and the connections to suss out that thing, whatever it is, right?"

"Well, maybe," I said, dubiously. "I'd have to bring some other people in on it. . . ."

"What I said—'connections.' I suspect part of what's going on is a faction fight somewhere high up in the apparat, which means that one side is giving covering fire to our side, at least tactically. Moves and countermoves, you know? Don't know if whoever is behind it knows we're connected, or if someone's just stringing us along in the hope of pulling in bigger fish. But I get the feeling that to panic and run would just land us, or me, and the data, in the hands of the FSB, which in the way of things is likely to be on the wrong side, from my point of view."

"And how do you know that *my* connections aren't the bigger fish they're trolling for?"

She laughed. "I don't. But, come on. You guys. They could just raid the Darwin's Arms if they wanted your connections."

"Hah!" I said. "That's just the old geeks and a few cardsharps. *I'm* talking about Webblies."

"Guns?" she asked, sounding alarmed.

"No, the union. Information Workers of the World Wide Web—the IWWWW."

She looked dubious. "I've heard about that. It was big in the twenties."

"The Global Strike, yeah, glory days. Twenty twenty-six and all that. You should hear the old bros-and-sis talk about how they nearly brought down Big Iron." I chuckled. "And you will."

"You're telling me it's still around?"

"Not as big as it used to be, but yeah. Down to a hard core of aging anarchos and impossibilists and a few young head-cases. Like me."

"Oh!" She gave me another funny look. "So *that's* where you're coming from!"

"What did you think I was, a patriot?"

"That or a totally amoral criminal."

"Thanks a lot."

She grinned, looking happier than I'd seen her in a long while. "Both of them were looking a bit more unlikely as time went on, but I didn't want to pry, just in case."

I leaned back on the sofa, looking up at her. "You should trust me even less now, you know. There's no love lost between us Webblies and your so-called libertarian capitalists."

She waved a hand. "Oh, that." She laughed. "I don't trust you an inch, actually, but trust doesn't come into it—prediction does. I know now which way you're likely to jump."

"We'll see about that."

I jumped up, surprising her and myself by giving her an awkward, one-arm hug around the shoulders, and walked out to the main door. The drama of this was marred by my being unable to actually open the door, Jadey having locked it from the inside. I stepped aside and let her unlock it.

She looked up at me just before the door swung open.

"So where are we going now?"

"Somewhere safer, warmer, and pleasanter," I told her. "The union office."

"Wow," she said. "You sure know how to show a girl a good time."

"You'll be surprised," I told her.

The IWWWW building in Picardie Place, opposite the Playhouse at the top of Leith Walk, was slightly decrepit but still imposing: seven stories of concrete and glass, post-war but not new-tech. I had no doubt it was watched, but I didn't think the surveillance would be more than routine. Officially classified as "hostile and slanderous toward the state and social system of Socialist Democracy," the IWWWW was officially tolerated as a textbook (and, more importantly, *newscast*) example of how tolerant and pluralist Socialist Democracy really was.

As I swiped my union card through the lock, Jadey eyed the slogan chiseled in neat roman capitals above the doorway: THE WORKING CLASS AND THE EMPLOYING CLASS HAVE NOTHING IN COMMON.

"Hmm," she said as the door swung back for us. "What about common humanity?"

"After three world wars? Don't make me laugh."

The entrance lobby was empty except for the guy at the reception desk, who glanced up then returned to his book. I inhaled deeply of the familiar smell of the place—the rubber flooring, the faint waft of sweat and chlorine from the gym and swimming-pool downstairs; the tang of alcohol and herbal smoke from the bar on the first floor alongside the warmer, steamier cafeteria odors; and underlying it all the sharp notes of wire and plastic and fresh cement from the ongoing overhaul of the electronics.

Jadey, too, was sniffing, watching a middle-aged man and a couple of young women, all carrying towels and soft drinks, stroll past and pad down the steps.

"Not what I expected," she admitted as we headed for the lift. "Reminds me of a youth hostel—or the YMCA." She grinned as the lift arrived. " 'Young Militants' Class-War Association,' anybody?"

"Near enough," I allowed, jabbing the fourth-floor button. "We're a sociable lot. You can even stay the night here."

She smiled, distantly, at some point behind my shoulder. The lift doors *thunk*ed shut. We stood for a moment in infinite reflections and varying g-forces, then stepped out. The fourth floor was not as benign and casual-looking as the ones we'd seen. Long, carpeted corridors, heavy doors, everything beaded with cameras. The electric smell was strong.

I ambled down the corridor, Jadey pacing cautiously after me, until I reached the door marked 413. Another card-swipe and we were in. The room was about ten meters by five, windowless, strip-lit, filled with half a dozen long tables with swivel seats, keyboards, and screens. It had the look of a classroom or learning-lab. Nobody else was there, which was a relief. I stepped over to the wall-mounted keypad and hastily booked the room until midnight: greedy, but unlikely to be challenged.

"Right," I said, sitting down and inviting Jadey, with a suitably expansive gesture, to do the same. She did, curling her legs under the swivel chair's seat and giving it a spin.

"God, what a tedious place," she remarked. "Even the walls are bare. No pictures, no screens."

"Yeah, well, there's a reason," I said. "They're *firewalls*." I smirked at my own feeble joke.

I took out my reader and uncoiled some cable, and connected it to the back of the nearest screen. "Could I have your disk again please?"

She spun it over.

I slotted it into the reader, powered up the screen and board, and keyed in a password. The familiar Microsoft Windows 2045 image floated up, to be instantly replaced by a demonically laughing penguin which left the words BUT SERIOUSLY . . . fading on the screen before cutting to the primary interface. I patched through a quick call to the satellite server, asking for an immediate downlink download. That took about a minute—the office, naturally, had roof antennae and bandwidth to burn—after which I leaned back, hands behind my head, legs as close as my precarious balance would permit to putting my feet up.

"That's a load off my mind," I said.

"Great," said Jadey. "Care to explain what I should be feeling relieved about?"

"Depends how much you want to hear about computers," I said, swinging my feet to the floor, my elbows to my knees, and leaning forward earnestly. As usual I felt a little awkward talking about this subject; if I wasn't careful I could easily end up sounding like an old geek.

Jadey waved a hand, generously. "I'll tell you when to fast-forward."

"Fine. . . . Well, basically, we—that is, the biz—have become fairly reliant on what we call the empty-hand model." I waved my reader. "Like this thing. It's a wireless terminal, pretty dumb by the standards of the systems it's accessing, which are usually on hardware a long way away. Makes you overdependent on encryption, for one thing, and on the goodwill of the server owners, for another. That's exactly the kind of thing us Webblies like to avoid. It tends to, shall we say, weaken your negotiating position. We've always been big on the workers controlling the means of production. Result: This building has so much computing power packed in it that you need never go outside it for any program that can be feasibly run at all." I scratched my head. "Apart from ones that need dedicated distributed processors, anyway. What it means is that I've just copied everything I've got, and everything you got, onto the machines in here. And the great thing about them is, they're not accessible from the outside. That download had to go through the equivalent of a series of airlocks and showers before it was stored. Nobody can hack in to them."

"Like, this place is a data haven?" She glanced around, looking more respectful.

"Not quite," I said. "Physically, it's not terribly secure against serious reverse social engineering, but apart from that, yeah—it's pretty safe. We can now work on the data with a fair certainty that nobody's snooping on us."

She cocked her head. "Except from inside?"

"Hey," I said. "This is the union. We have rules against that sort of thing."

"Okay," she said. "What next?"

"I pull together a small company to investigate this thing." I turned back to the screen. "I have a lot of good contacts for this."

"Maybe you do," she said, "but not tonight."

"What?"

She stared at me, then reached out and caught my hand. "Come on. I've had a *murderously* long day. Let's go down to the bar, then I'll take you up on the offer of a bed for the night."

First I knew of the offer, but I didn't refuse.

5

Cosmonaut Keep

E LIZABETH HARKNESS SOUGHT the dress she needed in the back of Ancient Finery, an old shop in the old town, popular with students but hitherto not one of her haunts. Kyohvic, and Tain, and indeed Mingulay in general, had a textile-and-garment industry, but nothing like a self-sustaining fashion industry. Left to themselves, there was little doubt that styles would have changed as slowly in the towns as they did in the villages along the coast: Fashion would have become costume, with mere individual and local variants of cut and decoration. The starships changed all that, their irregular but frequent arrivals imposing a jerky punctuation on that tendency to equilibrium. Fads and fancies, years or decades dead in their places and planets of origin, freakishly flourished in this backwater, until the next arrival of new notions from the sky. The whole relationship, she was pleased to realize, was the precise opposite of what Gregor had thought it was: If the merchants didn't know what the fashion was in Kyohvic, it was because they set (or reset) it with their every arrival.

This wasn't the only relationship Gregor was getting wrong. Elizabeth wasn't sure if he was arrogant or just *blind* or if he just plain found her unattractive or (more hopefully) that he misinterpreted every one of her looks and gestures as part of their relationship as friends and colleagues.

But she had no more idea than he of what would be the Next Big Thing at the merchants' ball, and no way of affording what the better-off ladies of the town would wear to it while they eyed up whatever the ladies of the latest ship were showing off; so the best she could do was to go for something so out-of-date that it wasn't *un*fashionable. Ancient Finery, the best of several such by-products of Mingulay's externally driven style-cycle, was the place to look.

Thus, a couple of days after the ship had arrived, Elizabeth left the lab early—it was a Saturday anyway—hurried to her parents' home in the new town, and hastily changed and showered to remove the lingering taint of dead marine life from her hair and, especially, her hands, and took the electric bus down to the cobblestoned streets of old Kyohvic below the university's fastness.

A pair of chipped shop-window dummies guarded the shop's doorway. The male figure was resplendent in a generations-old braided guard's uniform from a minor estate on Croatan, the female slightly risqué in a chinoiserie chemise off the last-but-one starship from somewhere farther in. Elizabeth considered it for a reckless moment, then smiled at herself and pressed on into the shop's cavernous, brightly-lit interior. The ceiling was at least two stories high, hung at intervals with clumps of long dresses; the walls accommodated two rows, one above the other, of dresses and coats; smaller and shorter garments were shelved or hung on portable rails standing on the floor. The air of the place was a marvelous mélange of the smell of old but clean clothes, cleaning-fluid, phantom scents, patchouli potpourri, joss-sticks permanently burning, and the occasional cigarette surreptitiously smoked by the girl at the till.

Elizabeth took a deep breath and plunged happily in. An hour passed without her noticing. Apart from the—for her—rarely indulged frivolously feminine fun of it all, something about the layered antiquity of the shop's stock appealed to her scientific spirit. There was history here, even astronomy, an almost inconceivably minute particular of the kind of evidence you could find in the fossil record or the shock-shell of an exploded star. Wisps of fabric and echoes of ideas that had moved at the speed of light. . . . She thought about it with one part of her mind, while another part guided her rummaging and considering and discarding.

Nothing here dated back to the *Bright Star*'s arrival, or even to the cultural explosion that had followed hard upon it. Anything that historic was in the museums, not the secondhand clothes shops. But some of the stuff showed traces of influences, radiated out from Mingulay and bounced back—voyages later, decades later—of fashions from twenty-first-century Earth: silly little details that she recognized from the ship's picture files, such as the drawstring hem and the duffel button, these trivial impracticalities betraying their origins like junk DNA.

History, like fashion, was a necessarily disjointed process in the

Second Sphere. New arrivals from Earth were rare, migrations between planets within the Sphere relatively frequent. Any of them could jolt society forward, or at least out of its previous course, as the *Bright Star* had done to Mingulay's.

Approximately six hundred and fifty years ago, Elizabeth's ancestors had arrived on Croatan. About a thousand people: some English, some Indians, a shipload of Africans, and not all from the same place or even (from what later historians had deduced from fragmentary records and traditions) the same time. Others—fishermen, sailors, and slaves rescued from the wild Atlantic by beings that some of them saw as angels, others as demons—arrived in small, bewildered consignments as time went on. The dates of their origin were not necessarily in the same order as the dates of their arrival. Out of two centuries and half of living on this world—newer than the New World from which most of their ancestors had come—and of trying to make some sense of it and of the other worlds with which they gradually came into contact, a sect had emerged that the majority of Croatan's human community called the Scoffers—a name which they eventually claimed proudly for themselves. Their prophetess, Joanna Tain, had preached that the greater universe revealed to them by their displacement, and the strange nature of its other inhabitants, left the Scriptures at best irrelevant ("a Revelation solely to the People of the Earth, as the Law of Moses was unto the people of Israel, and not Universall, as even the Scripture itselfe saith")—at worst, false. The influence of the Stoic and Epicurean philosophies of Nova Babylonia was evident in her doctrines, and deplored.

Blood had been shed, and after urgent appeals from both sides the gray folk had moved in swiftly to evacuate Tain's few thousand followers and to set them down on another planet, which they named Mingulay. They had been there two centuries when the *Bright Star* had risen in their sky, and had brought heresies beyond the wildest rantings of Joanna, and evidence that the universe was even stranger than she had supposed. The ship's library had become the foundation of the university and of most science and technology, and a good deal of the culture and art, in the hands of humans on Mingulay—and on an expanding radius of other worlds.

And hence, Elizabeth supposed, the dress she eventually decided on. She found it in the back of the shop, on the inside of a bundle of frocks on wire hangers suspended from the same wall-hook. She disengaged them carefully, took one look at the last dress, and put the rest less carefully back.

It had a bodice of embroidered leaves, in satin silk and autumn colors; its long, wide skirts of organza over net a darker shade and stiffer texture, fading and fraying to cobweb consistency toward the hems; and to go with it, a long-sleeved short jacket of gold-colored lace. She carried them triumphantly behind the curtain of the changing-alcove, stepped out a few minutes later to do a twirl in front of a freestanding mirror. She liked the outfit so much that she had to make a conscious decision not wear it home on the bus.

If the tall servant just inside the doorway of the Cosmonauts' keep thought her hooded oilskin cape amusing in its practicality and contrast with her dress, his expression as he took it gave no sign. She smiled at him, thanked him, and walked quickly on into the entrance hall. There was no more formal greeting, no announcement or introductions. It wasn't that kind of party; it was assumed, at least as a polite fiction, that anyone turning up already knew enough people present to make such a protocol redundant.

Elizabeth wasn't too sure about that. She felt very much on her own, she would have very much liked some welcoming person to show her in, as she passed from the shadows of the passage to the bright light of the main hall. She felt unsteady on her feet, and not just because the heels of her shoes (borrowed for the occasion from her sister) were higher than she was used to. The only sound that seemed louder than the thumping of her heart was the rustle of her dress, like the sound of walking through a heap of dry leaves.

The great room was laid out for a cold buffet and for dancing, with long tables, chairs, and benches along two of the walls, and tables laden with food and drink along the third, with the musicians—at the moment tuning up their instruments—in the corner formed by that wall and the wall which contained the fireplace. For a couple of seconds, Elizabeth paused just inside the doorway, gawping at the gigantic decorations on the walls; the scale of everything—walls, carpets, animal heads—was about twice what a human scale should have been. Even the portraits were large, and high up. Then she walked firmly onward, relieved to see that about a hundred people had already arrived, so that she wasn't embarrassingly early or late. Several of them—the old Cosmonaut

Cairns, the university's Chancellor, the owner of Mueller's Mill—she recognized as from a distance, and one or two she knew personally. Gregor, so far, wasn't among them, which was also a relief, in a way.

"Oh, hello, Harkness." Mark Garnet, the head of the marine-biology department, hailed her and beckoned her over to the huddle of academics at the drinks table. A small, rather fat man with slicked-back dark hair—he'd always irresistibly reminded her of a seal—Garnet was probably her best friend in the staff hierarchy, always helpful with a knotty statistical problem or an obscure reference.

"What's your pleasure?" he asked.

She glanced over the array of glasses. "Ah, white wine for now, I think."

"Very good, very good." He passed her a glass and waved at a slender, almost skinny woman by his side. "Now, Harkness, this is my wife, Judith."

"Pleased to meet you." The two women bobbed politely at each other. Judith's dress was slim-fitted and elegant, not new but not secondhand either, her hair coiled and stacked.

"I should warn you," Garnet went on, "that she has absolutely no interest in biology, so let's not talk shop."

They took their glasses and sat down at the corner of one of the tables, gossiping idly about the department's office politics while watching the growing throng. More people were arriving: guild-masters and journeymen, industrialists and engineers, heresiarchs in tall black hats and Scoffers in black suits with broad white collars, their swords on their belts. The interstellar merchant and his family and retinue made a particularly grand entrance. The men wore long linen coats with embroidered waistcoats over shirts and knee-breeches, the women loose gowns in various jewel or pastel shades of satin. The dresses' construction was simple, their decoration elaborate, with signifiers of age and status suggested by variations in the length, and presence and absence, of collars and sleeves.

"Not bad," Judith remarked, sotto voce. "Looks like Nova Babylonia is still setting its own styles. For now, at least. Our ancestors really shouldn't have let those costume-history picture books out in the universe. Heaven only knows what concoctions are being contrived right now out of Earth's old dressing-up box."

Elizabeth grinned at her. "Funny, I was thinking along those lines myself, when I was looking for a party dress today."

"Hmm, I don't know," Mark said. "I don't think Nova Babylonia has had time to be influenced. I mean, what's the turnaround time?"

"Shorter than a craze, back there," Judith said. She sounded slightly disapproving. Nova Babylonia had a fantasy reputation, going all the way back to the first contacts with Croatan, as a land of luxury, almost of decadence—an image intensified by the relative rarity of actual contact and reliable information. Hundred-year-old news would be eagerly seized upon at this party, and at trade negotiations, and talked about for years, or until the next ship came along. There was little doubt that the frequency would increase, now that Nova Babylonia's merchants were actively responding to the new developments in the colony, rather than discovering them for the first time. But no matter how frequently it arrived, the news would always be a hundred years old. . . .

"Anyway," said Judith, "you pulled a good dress out of the box yourself. So tell me, where did you find it?"

Elizabeth smiled sideways at Mark. "Now *we're* talking shop," she said. Mark gave them both an ironic wave and wandered off to pick up some food and information.

As he strolled into the hall Gregor felt slightly self-conscious in an heirloom outfit of black velvet jacket, white shirt, and narrow black trousers, but nobody looked at him twice. In the jacket's inside pocket, rather spoiling its drape, was a sheaf of folded-up papers over which he'd sweated all that day and most of the previous night. His grandfather, James, had included the demand, as imperative as a tax return, with his invitation.

He knew the hall, and the castle, from holiday memories of childhood and, more rarely, of adolescence. These days, though still fond of his grandparents, he visited it more often in dreams. His father had—wisely, Gregor thought—done what most descendants of the original crew had done, and moved out and struck out on his own in his teens, several years before Gregor was born. Now the owner of a substantial fishing-fleet, Frederick Cairns was pleased that his first son shared his enthusiasm for the business, and brusquely tolerant of his second son's more academic interest in marine life. Of his father James's far more abstract interests and motivations, Frederick affected nothing but contempt.

Over at the buffet table, Gregor selected a small stack of mollusca and crustacea, a pinch of herbs, a clump of vegetables and a spoonful of rice, picked up a glass of red wine on the sound theory that it was the faster route to intoxication, and looked around rather vaguely for anyone he knew or somewhere to sit. Some of the local children, looking stiffer and more awkward in their formal clothes than Gregor, were staring and nudging each other in response to the saurs. It was rare, in Kyohvic, to see as many as thirty of them in one place, and the opportunity to gawp and murmur was also being taken, more discreetly, by the adults.

Gregor turned away, embarrassed by this rustic behavior, and found himself face-to-face with a young woman whom he instantly evaluated as the most beautiful he'd ever seen in his life. Her skin was the color of amber, her long and wavy hair of jet, her large dark eyes of bright mahogany, all of it set off by the glowing pink of the straight, soft dress which gently skimmed and subtly showed the contours of her body. Hands full, like his, with plate and glass and carefully balanced cutlery, she looked at him with a charmingly helpless but somehow self-mocking appeal. She looked as though about to say something, but hesitating to speak. Gregor felt the same way himself. Something—his heart, presumably—was jumping about inside him.

He smiled (a terrifying rictus, he was sure) and took a quick sip of wine to stop his mouth from going completely dry. "Good evening," he said. "Are you wondering where to sit?"

"Yes, thank you," she said. "Actually"—she laughed lightly, and took a sip of her own wine, white—"I have been most firmly told to mingle with the—the natives?—and practice the language and I'm not sure whom to speak to first."

"Well," Gregor said, "perhaps you might like to sit and speak with me, for a while?"

"Oh yes," she said, suddenly sounding confident. "That would be very utilitarian."

Gregor indicated with his eyes an empty space at a table across the hall, and followed her to it, amazed that everyone in the whole place wasn't attending to her every shimmy and shimmer as much as he was. But then—as some gibbering, scientific, detached part of his mind, the monkey on his back, pointed out—he wasn't actually *seeing* the rest of the party, so the issue was moot.

They sat down, half facing each other on a bench. Another mo-

79

ment of not knowing what to say. Gregor pointed a thumb at his chest. "Gregor Cairns."

"My name is Lydia de Tenebre," the girl said gravely; and then, more casually, "the merchant Esias de Tenebre's seventh daughter, third child of his second wife. I am nineteen years old and I was born"—she waved a hand—"oh, hundreds and hundreds of years ago."

"I must say you don't look it." As soon as he'd said it Gregor was certain he'd just made a stupid remark, the first thing which had popped into his head, but Lydia laughed. She flicked her hair back and at that moment Gregor belatedly realized he was smitten, "stabbed by the arrow of Eros" as the poet had said, and that her objective age was not only the strangest but also the most significant thing about her: the one that hung over everything that might happen between them.

"Now, can you tell me about yourself, and your family?" she asked, as though it were the next item on a protocol.

"I'm training to be a marine biologist," he said. "My father is a fisherman, my mother teaches children. My grandfather—over there—has the more or less hereditary post of Navigator."

"What do those old people do, the ones who call themselves the Cosmonauts? How do they live?" She looked around, at the walls and ceiling. "How do they afford . . . all this? They are not merchants. Are they rulers?"

Gregor rubbed the back of his neck, with a sense of being defensive. "No, not exactly, the real rulers here are the Heresiarchy, although Driver—that's the big guy talking to my grandfather—is a very powerful man. The Security Man."

He scratched his head as she frowned over this. "He runs the police business here. It used to be for the castle and the university, but now it's for the whole town."

"All right," she said, as though comprehending, but probably not, "and what about the rest?"

"They're some of the descendants of the crew of the old starship. Every generation there have been a few people who nominally took the posts that their ancestors in the original crew had held." He shrugged. "It's a tradition. The first crew took over this castle because the local people had left it empty, and because it was, well, a castle! Easily defended. When they came here they were able to sell knowledge and technology to the existing population, and indeed to the saurs and later to merchants from other worlds. Eventually they established the university, which became a research center for local industry and agriculture and fisheries. And not just local industry—we get students and scientists from the nearer worlds, particularly Croatan. The nominal crew still get an income from it, and from other investments, and they oversee it. A hereditary sinecure. Not a very demanding job, but they do it to maintain a continuity with the ship, and with Earth."

"A continuity which is now being lost, then?"

A shrewd question, and not one it would be politic to fully answer.

"Yes, it's being lost. My father has no intention of becoming the Navigator, and nor do I. But my grandfather, I hope, has many years to live, and if I have sons one of them may wish to take his place."

"Or daughters?"

Gregor's cheeks burned. "Of course, yes."

Lydia's dark eyes sparkled, perhaps in amusement at his evident discomfiture. "And what would it involve, being the Navigator?"

"Oh, I'll show you," said Gregor. He fished the folded papers from his pocket and spread them on the table. The papers were covered with crabbed symbols and labored diagrams.

"A few months ago James, my grandfather, sent me this problem. It involves logic and mathematics, neither of which I'm very good at. But I worked at it, on and off, until yesterday evening, when James sent me a message asking me to deliver the solution tonight." He looked down at the paper ruefully. "I've wasted all day on it, but at least it's done."

She poked at the edge of the papers with a perfectly oval fingernail. "You have no calculating-machines to do this?"

Careful now, careful! "We do, of course, have calculating-machines. But not all calculation can be left to machines." It was an ethical platitude throughout the Second Sphere.

"Indeed not," she said solemnly. "But if you are not talented for this, why not give the problem to people who are?"

You've put your pretty little fingernail right on the problem, he thought. "Ah, well, the point of doing this is to keep certain skills alive within the family."

Which was true, though with a different emphasis to the one he gave it. The explanation seemed to satisfy her, and she peered at the pages for a moment and was on the point of reaching to pick them up when James Cairns hurried over. Gregor stood up and embraced him.

"Don't flash that stuff around!" James hissed in Gregor's ear.

"I wasn't!" Gregor protested, into his grandfather's shoulder. He turned to Lydia.

"Lydia, this is James Cairns, the Navigator, my grandfather."

As Gregor introduced him the old man bowed and kissed the young woman's hand, and groped out over the table with his free hand and stuffed the calculations into his pocket. Lydia, looking straight at Gregor over James's head, observed this maneuver with a wry smile. Gregor covered his embarrassment with a wink.

James sat down, one space down from Lydia. At least he wasn't sitting between them.

"So, Gregor, how's it going for you out on the wild ocean?"

"Oh, fine, thanks." Gregor launched into an account of his recent adventures, and minor though they were they had Lydia gazing at him with her lips parted and her eyebrows occasionally twitching up. James listened, and watched with a more quizzical eye.

"Any new information on the squids?" he asked, when Gregor had concluded with an account of the recent evening when the ship—Lydia's family's ship—had come in.

Gregor shrugged. "Nothing but observations, like that one. I'll write it up—well, one of us who were there will. For what it's worth."

"Indeed." James contemplated the small glass of spirit he'd brought with him, and lit up a joint. Lydia's eyes widened as he passed it to her. She sipped at, rather than inhaled, the smoke and passed it on hastily to Gregor. He drew on it deeply and passed it back to his grandfather.

"Actually," James smiled, "I was inquiring about your research on the little fellas. Not the krakens! As old Matt used to say, they are still a fucking fortean phenomenon."

Gregor glared at him, and the old man turned apologetically to Lydia. "Excuse my language." He passed her the joint again, and again she took the smoke into her mouth, puffed it out, and passed to Gregor.

"I understand 'fucking' and 'phenomenon,' " she said. "But what is 'fortean'?"

"I was about to ask that myself," said Gregor, the lift of the high raising him above his annoyance at the old man's vulgarity.

"Ah," said James complacently, swaying back and forth as he finished off the now diminished roach. "According to the records from our starship, the *Bright Star,* the people back on Earth experienced many phenomena which they could not explain—for which they could not, one might say, account—which were catalogued by a man named Charles Fort, and such phenomena came to be called 'fortean.' These phenomena included, I may add, our friends the saurs, and their gravity skiffs, and for all I know to the contrary, the flaming starships. Sorry, Lydia. And strange monsters in the sea. Now, as far as we are concerned, the goddamn kraken or squids or *Archi*-frigging-*teuthys* are still strange monsters in the sea. But perhaps they're more familiar to you and your family, eh?"

Lydia cradled her chin on her interlaced fingers and looked from James to Gregor and back again. The only effect that the weed had had on her seemed to be that she saw the funny side of this blatant attempt to pump her for information.

"Oh yes," she said. "We have . . . communion with them. The saurs are with us to translate, of course, but we believe we are talking to the kraken." She smiled mischievously at James. "They are our real 'navigators.' My father is impressed that you have managed to equal their accomplishment."

"If not their feet!" James's pun was lost on her, to Gregor's relief, and at that moment the band struck up at last. Gregor rose and reached out a hand to Lydia.

"May I have the honor?"

"Of course, thank you." She stood up, stepped over the bench in a pink flutter and curtseyed, a gesture with which he was not familiar but which he found charming.

"Have a good time," said James, with woozy benevolence. He shot Gregor a sharp look, not stoned or drunk at all. "I'll talk to you later."

The first dance was measured and formal, more typical of this kind of reception than of Mingulay's native traditions, and Gregor found himself taking the wrong steps. But if Lydia noticed she didn't seem to mind, and after a few minutes the dance's sedate pace allowed them to carry on their conversation.

"Do you and your family actually live on the ship?"

"Oh no." Twirl. "We rent a villa in Nova Babylonia." Two steps back. "On other worlds we rely on hospitality, or on commercial guest-houses." Step forward, half-turn, raise hand, take hand, turn about. "The ship is designed for the krakens, not for us. Much of the interior is permanently awash." Smile, wrinkle nose. "And it smells." Let go, step back two paces. Hold out both hands, step forward twice. "Of fish." Catch.

Warm caught hands, delicate and bony and fluttery and alarming as little songbats. The music stopped. She curtseyed, he bowed.

"So where in the ship," said Gregor, in a voice which to him sounded rather strained, "do you actually travel?"

"In the skiffs, of course. We ride them out to the ship—which may be on the sea or in space, depending on the locality—and off again, as you saw the other night. Sometimes we have to wade around within the ship to check and secure the cargo. So for the journeys we dress rough, not like this." She plucked at her skirt, smiled. "But that's all before and after. The journey itself takes no time." She snapped her fingers. "Like that."

They sat down again, beside their neglected plates. James had wandered back into the crowd, perhaps tactfully leaving them alone. Gregor was uncomfortably aware that he'd be back, or that he'd corner him somewhere and impart some urgent family message. Lydia began to eat, quickly and deftly, interspersed with chat. Gregor munched more slowly; less used to this kind of socializing, he was for most of the time reduced to gestures and nods and grunts, as he listened to Lydia talking about the other worlds of the Sphere. It had never struck him quite so forcibly before how much similarity underlay their diversity, all their different words written in the same alphabet of DNA. They were no more different, ultimately, than continents on a single planet—or rather, their differences were an extension of that kind of reproductive isolation, as though all their continents and oceans were features of a single enormous world. Their model, and the common origin of their organisms, was distant, unreachable Earth.

Wherever he ate seafood, which was often, the thought that there was something subtly wrong with eating squid—even such as now lay on his plate; tiny, non-sentient relatives or ancestors of the kraken—swam to the surface of his mind. It was almost as bad as eating monkeys. But in the warmer climes and worlds, people did eat monkeys. Lizards, too, for that matter. He decided that this was a thought it would be unkind to share.

Lydia dabbed her lips with a napkin and glanced at her empty glass.

"More?"

"Yes, please. White."

Gregor made his way through the now much-denser crowd and past the now livelier dancing, on the fringes of which earnest discussions were going on between the visiting traders and their local counterparts. He felt a tremor permanently radiating outward from his solar plexus, the arrow's target. Dizzily he contemplated that he had fallen in love, a most unfortunate experience, but one which like any other illness could only be lived through, or died from. So taught the Scoffers, but at this moment—and this itself was a symptom—Gregor was unable to conceive of ever again being anything but a believer.

As he passed one of the tables he caught sight of a third cousin, Clarissa, who sat there unself-consciously suckling her newest baby, and he paused to greet and congratulate her. They talked for a few moments, exchanging family gossip, while Gregor admired the infant.

"What lovely tiny toes she has," he said, tickling them under a lacy hem.

"Why do men always say that?" Clarissa asked, smiling. "And it's a boy. Owen. That's his moistening-gown." She looked up hopefully. "The ceremony's tomorrow, in the North Street Meeting-House. Would you like to come along?"

"I'll do my best, Clarissa," he said, and after some more chat continued on his way to the drinks table.

He'd picked up a couple of filled glasses when his elbow was gripped.

"A moment, Gregor."

"Oh, hello again, Grandpa."

The old man smiled. "Don't go making me feel old. You're old enough now to call me James."

Gregor dipped his head. "I'll remember."

"I see you're in a hurry," the Navigator said, still holding Gregor's elbow like the Ancient Mariner. "So I'll make it quick."

Just as he'd expected, Gregor found himself backed into a corner.

"Yes, go ahead," he said, holding up the two glasses and pointedly not drinking.

"That girl you're talking to—for gods' sakes don't give her any hint about the family business, about what the Great Work actually is."

"I haven't." He thought for a moment. "And I don't know, anyway."

"Good." James grinned slyly. "I've glanced over what you handed me, Gregor, and I have to say it's good work. Damn sight better than anything your uncles and cousins have come up with. Now, we need to get on with it a bit urgently. I know you have research and responsibilities of your own, but is there any chance you could spare some time to help me out?"

"Ah, I suppose so," Gregor said cautiously. James evidently took his assent as much firmer than it was.

"Thank you," he said. "Let's make it tomorrow." Gregor's involuntary look of dismay was met with another sly grin. "And it would give you a reason to come up to the castle."

"Well, seeing you put it that way . . ." Gregor frowned for a moment. "Tell you what. I'll arrange to meet Lydia, if she wants to see me, at some time and then arrive a couple of hours before that to see you. Probably late morning—I'm going to Clarissa's latest offspring's wetting first, if I'm up to it."

"Excellent!" James finally let go of his arm, and Gregor made his escape.

Elizabeth, after tactfully and politely extricating herself from, in succession, the company of the Garnets, a deep conversation with Tharovar and Salasso, and a dance with one of Gregor's cousins whom she'd two years ago had a fling with, finally caught sight of Gregor's progress around the side of the room. She pressed after him, but by the time she saw him again he was back at the table and talking with Lydia, and it did not take more than a few seconds' observation of both their faces for her to realize that she was altogether too late.

She turned away before either of them could see her. Not that there was much risk of that. Seeing no more of the rest of the crowd than they did, she walked out, at first slowly, then with increasing speed after she'd grabbed her coat from the steward at the door. There was no rain and it was not a cold night, for spring, but she shrugged the oilskin on, buttoning it and wrapping her arms about herself as she walked away from the light and music, the coat's heavy length crushing the fragile skirts underneath it, and she didn't care. Her feet hurt in the shoes as she clattered along the castle's long driveway, and she didn't care. The hell with all that, her boots and breeks would be comfortable enough; she wouldn't meet Gregor again in anything else.

The starship shone on the water like a misshapen moon. She didn't hate the girl—too elegant and delicate and innocent a creature to dislike. No, it was Gregor, the unseeing, unfeeling bastard, with her own attention in his face every day, and who responded to it with friendly familiarity, as though she were one of the lads; she hated him.

6

Trusted Third Parties

Y OU KNOW," JASON said, munching fried slice and looking
around the union cafeteria, "this place is not terribly secure.
As in, physically." He waved his hands at the wide windows, one
of which was propped slightly open.

"Tell me about it," Jadey grouched. "Back home, a union office—or anything kinda oppositional like that—would be a lot more
defensible."

We'd set the business meeting up as a working breakfast for
eleven A.M., to which I'd invited Jason, Tony, and Alec Curran, all
of whom had useful skills, were unlikely to betray us, and were
Webblies themselves. Not that there was any necessary correlation
between these three facts, mind you. I had discussed the two old
programmers with Jason first—guardedly, on the phone—and he'd
assured me that they were sound.

The cafeteria was pretty busy at this time in the morning, mostly
with the support staff and Webbly volunteers—the union was proud
to have not a single full-timer or paid official. Those who weren't
engrossed in their own conversations were watching the video wall,
where some daytime TV host had set up a discussion between the
Pope, from his home in Rome, and the Moderator of the General
Assembly of the Church of Scotland, from her home in Harare,
Zimbabwe. The host's attempts to pry open some theological differences on the question of alien life were bouncing off a com-
mendably firm Christian united front. The Church, one gathered,
had always believed that superhuman, but not divine, intelligences
lived in the heavens above us.

Curran made dangerous gestures with his fork, to hold our attention until he succeeded in swallowing. He turned to Jadey. "It's
like this," he said, in a maddening tone of patient explanation. "We

could turn this place into a fortress, but what good would it do? If the state ever decided to crack down on us, it could bring overwhelming force to bear. There's no way we could beat the state at the violence game. Violence is what it's good for. What it's not so good at is spreading ideas around, and it's ultimately ideas in people's heads that make them decide whether or not to use the guns in their hands. The state is good at applying force, but not at legitimizing force. So as long as most people believe we're not doing any harm and should be left alone, we have a good chance of being left alone. Turning ourselves into an armed camp would cut against that, even assuming they'd let us do it."

"I was thinking more about physical infiltration," Jason replied mildly. "Smart dust and stuff."

"Positive pressure," I said. "The windows blow, they don't suck. Besides, the place does not have ECM. Not state-of-the-art, but not bad." I smiled at Jadey. Her toes were exploring the top of my foot, under the table. "Good enough for government work. No, seriously, I think our only problem is reverse social engineering, and as Alec says, that's a political problem, not a physical one. We're as safe here as anywhere."

Jadey looked dubious. "Surely there are places where you can have a bit more privacy? Up in the Highlands, maybe?"

Curran nearly choked; the rest of us just smiled. "The Highlands are the worst," Curran said when he'd got his breath back. "The land reform really bought the Party a lot of support up there."

"Oh well." Jadey dismissed the matter. "I guess that computer room looks safe enough. We're doing it from there, right?"

"Right."

"So what are we doing there, anyway?" Tony asked.

"Basically," I said, very carefully, "We're doing some work on a contract I got yesterday. I need a bit of help from you three, and you're all subcontracted at the standard rate if you want." I waved a hand. "We'll sort out the screenwork later. Okay so far?"

Nods all round.

"Fine," I went on. "However, Jadey here has come across a set of files from ESA. And you all know how important that's suddenly become, and how . . . Well, you remember what Charlie was going on about last night."

I really had their attention.

"I'd like to know what it is. You all warm with that?"

The two old code-geeks responded with piratical grins; Jason nodded soberly.

I looked around. "Okay. Everybody ready?"

We gathered up our final coffees and trooped off up the stairs to what Jadey had called the computer room. Alec remarked how funny that was, how it took him back . . . but it was a thoroughly modern toolkit of readers and VR goggles and contacts that we all deployed as we clustered around the old-fashioned keyboards and screens. I'd already roped in my suite of AIs, had copies of all of them and of my usual software libraries safely corralled in the building's own cores; I'd double-checked with the agency first thing in the morning (over Jadey's mumbled protests; over Jadey's legs . . .) and confirmed that the ESA contract was still valid, even after last night's surprising and historic announcement.

I'd brought in the two code-geeks, Tony and Alec, in case we needed to deal directly with the antiquated underlying software of the ESA system. Jason's specialities, honed in his various ID-forgery sidelines, were in VR work and security systems. VR work looks easy, but without a good grip on indexing and shortcuts and search methodologies it becomes like a physical search for a small object in a large space—not so much a needle in a haystack as a needle on a prairie.

I paused, the goggles on the bridge of my nose. Jadey was sitting on the next workbench along, swinging her legs like a bored kid and doing something delicate to her fingernails with a dispropor-tionately large lock-knife.

"Want to join us?"

She shook her head. "I'll keep lookout."

Hardly necessary, I thought, but if that was how she wanted to play it—

"Fine by me," I said. "Okay, guys, just follow me in."

I slid the goggles up the final quarter-inch and fitted them snugly over my eyes. A blink, and I was in, my viewpoint floating in front of an abstract rendering of the project as a monolithic closed book. The others hung behind my shoulders; I could feel them on the back of my neck, though if I looked behind, I couldn't see them—an odd, uncanny sensation, like being watched by a ghost. My AIs swooped around us like excited birds as I opened the book. Cas-cading dominoes of indexes unfolded across the virtual space.

The real information necessary for a material-requirement planning system was a barely detectable fraction of what was available here. What I most urgently wanted to find out was whether the end product of the process was defined or described anywhere, and if so, what it was. Fortunately, this was the sort of thing that project-management software and skills were ready-made for, so I led my troops into the jungle with a mental shout of *Banzai!*

The refinery-complex arrangements that Jadey and I had seen earlier were the obvious place to start, so I did. Meanwhile I sent the AIs on a trawl of the documentation, using conceptual search criteria to look for any references to output or completion.

The first thing I realized, now that I had time to look properly, was that I had been quite mistaken about the scale—the "refinery" was in fact only a roomful of incredibly fine machinery. I immediately began thinking in terms of the machinery and supplies required to make such machinery—to bore pipes of that diameter to the necessary tolerances, the expense of supplying even a few molecules of transplutonic stable isotopes—rare artificial atoms from the "island of stability" with atomic weights well into the low hundreds—and set up a production process, or at least a supply schedule, whose product would be this machine, whose own product I didn't know. Close up, the machinery looked almost organic—it had that evolved complexity, unplanned and serendipitous, that you can see in electron micrographs of cells and in flowcharts of mitochondria.

"Looks like the fucking Kerbs cycle," Alec muttered, somewhere far behind my right ear. At the same time a flurry of agitation from one of the AIs caught my attention. I zoomed in on it; my companions and the other AIs followed. The excited AI did the equivalent of brandishing a sheaf of papers, and I grabbed them.

The title page read: *Construction Projects 1 and 2—Overview and Recommendations.* It was overstamped with ESA EYES ALPHA and a date: 24 July 2048.

"Bingo!" I said. "Have a look at this on the screen, Jadey."

"Okay." Her voice came from a long way off.

I started paging through it; before long I felt an ache in my chest and a tightness in my throat, and my hands were shaking. The plan for the refinery, or fabrication unit, or whatever it was, had come from the alien intelligences within the asteroid. How this had been accomplished was left unexplained. Two final products were mentioned.

The outcome of Construction Project 1 was referred to as *the engine,* and that of Project 2 as *the craft.* The first instances of the words were highlighted and hyperlinked. I touched them, and the references expanded out into pictures that shone like devices seen in a dream.

The engine—it looked like a model of a jet or rocket engine turned out on a lathe, its fluted surfaces smooth and flowing, but with no visible inlet or outflow, just a peculiar inturning of the surface, unbroken but—as I rotated the view—somehow giving the eye-deceiving impression that there was an unseen opening some-where inside it, like a Klein bottle.

The craft—this was, in a crazy, eerie way, recognizable. It was a shining lens of metal, with—just inward from the rim—tiny rounded protuberances that in a bad light might have been mistaken for rivets. The exploded view showed the ulterior hatch, the tele-scopic legs, the internal controls, and the seats curving around the inside, and at the core something like the machine called *the engine* but differently proportioned and integrated into what superficially might be called the hull of *the craft.* It was blatantly, embarrass-ingly, unmistakably, a flying saucer.

We all backed out of VR and sat or stood looking at each other and talking in a confused, vehement babble. Alec Curran stopped it by banging his fist on the table.

"This is *it,*" he said. "The Rosetta Stone. The Holy Grail. It's like the Majestic Twelve documents."

To my surprise Jadey laughed at this and said: "Remember, MJ-12 was disinformation!"

They bickered rapidly for a minute, slinging references at each other; I had no idea what they were talking about. The idea that flying saucers had been built by aliens, rather than by Americans, belonged as much to the twentieth century as sea-serpents did to the nineteenth. Over the past few decades even sightings had fallen off, the whole UFO cult relegated to white-trash backwoods and the waste, howling wildernesses of the Web.

"Isn't it funny," Alec concluded heavily, "that we get the first proof of secret government contact with aliens the day after the government announces it?"

"Well, we got it the day *before,*" Jadey pointed out, reasonably enough but without making much impression on Alec. They weren't really debating, I realized—they were both so excited at what we'd found that they each wanted to test to destruction the almost unbearably amazing possibility that it was real. Both of them evidently took the UFO mythos more seriously than I did—something I unkindly attributed to Alec's age and Jadey's probable background. The popular base of the New Money faction—the white-trash backwoods, to be blunt—was notoriously prone to conspiracy theories, enthusiastic religions, and such-like eccentricities, according to *Europa Pravda*.

"Guys, guys," Jason said finally, reaching out as though to knock their heads together, "this isn't getting us very far, is it? I mean, the disc shape is kind of logical, in a way, for some kinds of flying machine. Hell, they were used in the war. Doesn't mean anything about the old UFO crap, one way or the other. If this stuff has turned up in a genuine ESA work-docket, I reckon we assume it's there for a reason."

"It could still be disinformation, even if the project is genuine," Jadey insisted. "But you know, I don't think that matters. If the *cover-up* is that it's an alien blueprint for some kind of spaceship technology, whatever it *really* is must be pretty important."

I could see some problems with that theory, but discussing them would be a waste of time. One can twist the cable of paranoia only so many times before something gives way, and not necessarily the cable.

Tony, the other old code-geek—the one I'd pulled in for his MS-DOS experience—was chewing gum with his mouth half-open, his yellow fingers wending through his strands of white beard and his nails making unpleasant rasping noises on his chin. I got the impression that he was a little tense.

He wiped his lips on his wrist.

"So—what you planning to do with this?" he asked, looking back and forth between me and Jadey and then glancing at Alec. "Sell it to the Yanks?"

"No, of course not," I said, indignantly and perhaps too quickly. "We're just thinking of . . . spreading it around."

"Presumably you don't think the E.U. should be the only people with access to this tech, whatever it is." Jadey said.

Tony shook his head. "No, no, but you don't know it will be.

Yefrimovich said last night that they wanted scientific cooperation. How do you know that doesn't include this thing?"

"We don't." Jadey shrugged. "But some of the circumstances around how we got hold of it suggest otherwise."

"Hmm," said Alec. "That sounds fair enough, I suppose. Information wants to be free, and all that." He stood up and grinned at us rather sheepishly. "Excuse me a moment, folks. Nature calls. Back in a few minutes, okay?"

"Sure," I said. "See you then."

He ducked out. It was twelve-thirty, rather to my surprise—time flies when you're in VR. We went on talking for a bit. After ten minutes, Jadey looked around.

"How long does it *take* to take a leak, anyway?"

My phone rang. I tapped the receiver.

"Hello?"

"Alec here. Uh, Matt, I'm in the bar, and from here it looks like the cops are having a very serious argument with Reception. I'd expect them up in the lift in about a minute."

He rang off.

"Alec says the cops will be here in a minute!"

Jason calmly leaned forward and hit the emergency DELETE. Every trace of our morning's work, and the data I'd downloaded the previous night, would be wiped from the cores. Tony's face showed a flurry of conflicting expressions, then he shrugged.

"I won't run," he said.

Jadey jumped up. "They're here for me," she said. She caught my hand and dragged me to my feet. "You go." She slapped the datadisk into my hand. Her lips brushed mine, for a fraction of a second. "Go now! I'll be fine."

Jason was already at the door, looking back at me impatiently. I joined him on the instant, then looked back myself.

"See you in America," Jadey said.

"Where?"

"The Dreamland gate," she said.

Jason hauled me out bodily.

Jason knew the building better than I did. He darted along the corridor, opened what looked like a cupboard door and jumped in. I followed, and found myself in a sort of dumbwaiter lift which immediately began dropping with alarming speed. I braced my hands against the ceiling of the thing just before it came to a jaw-jarring stop that almost buckled my knees.

I was still checking my neck for whiplash as we stepped out into a low-ceilinged, concrete-floored basement. Sagging fluorescent tubes fizzed and flickered. The damp air smelled faintly of motor oil and cement.

"Used to be the car park," Jason said wryly. "Also an emergency exit."

We sprinted across to a ramp which swung us down and around to a wide metal door, apparently sealed shut. Jason slid back a bolt and a smaller door—or vertical hatch—opened, and we stepped through to find ourselves in Leith Walk, under a showery sky. Half a minute later we were sitting at the rear of a trolleybus going down the road toward Leith.

"*Don't* look back," Jason said.

I flushed and hunched my shoulders, then fished out my reader and jiggled my thumbs on its knurled controls. Most of the channels were snow. Jason glanced at it, then his arms seemed to stiffen. He took out his phone, looked at it, then stooped and placed it on the floor between his boot. He straightened up. I heard a crunch and some scuffing.

"Right," he said. He stared ahead with a look of frantic calm.

"What?"

"Look outside the bus, man. It's like the fucking *Invasion of the Body Snatchers*." His voice was quiet, although the only other people on the bus were a couple of old women sitting up at the front.

I swiveled my gaze sideways, scanning the street. The trolleybus had reached about halfway down the mile-long street; rows of shopfronts alternated with rows of residential tenements. The pavements were busy, but not crowded.

"Everything looks normal," I said.

"That's the trouble," Jason said. "This is Leith, not fucking Morningside. Look again."

And suddenly the way he saw it came into focus for me. There were no idlers on the street, no strollers or beggars or hawkers. Everyone walked as though they might at any moment have to explain why their journey was really necessary. A pair of policemen strode along as though they didn't have to worry about their backs. As the trolleybus lurched and jangled from stop to stop the whole thing became even more incongruous—Constitution Street looked as if its notorious squares and boulevards had been cleaned up by some particularly puritanical local authority (which Leith Council, brazenly on the take itself, wasn't).

Even then I wasn't sure that we weren't being paranoid. Perhaps it was just a quiet time of day. I glanced at my watch. It was 13:10.

Only 13:10. Lunchtime. But still. . . .

I had been through so many shocks in the past twenty-six or so hours—Christ, was that all?—that I could be excused for feeling paranoid. So could Jason. Indeed the same applied to the people in the street, who were quite as capable of drawing troubling conclusions from government announcements as any clued-up geek in the Darwin's Arms. Discovering that the superpower in whose comfortably corrupt embrace we lived had an apparently friendly relationship with *aliens from outer space* would be quite enough to get people more than usually anxious not to get on its wrong side. Perhaps they were jumping at shadows, and so were we—but we were jumping more violently, because we knew more.

And because we had already been betrayed. I strongly suspected that Curran had had a fit of patriotic funk at the thought of our discovery's going to the Yanks, or at least at his being mixed up in such a thing, and had taken his chance of nipping out for a slash to call the cops on us. That he would immediately afterward give us a chance to get away was entirely in character.

"We never should have trusted the old geeks," I said under my breath.

"Too fucking right," said Jason. "Now shut the fuck up about it."

The trolleybus jerked and sparked left into Great Junction Road, and clanged to a halt at a stop.

"Go," said Jason.

Rain was falling. I sealed my jacket and followed Jason again as he crossed carefully at the lights and walked briskly but casually along the southern side of the street, a long way down some backstreets and finally ducked into a waterfront pub, the Deil and Exciseman. The place was crowded, as though all the unrespectable people who were no longer to be seen on the street had congregated here. Doubtless every dive in Leith was similarly packed. This was the sort of place where eyes and lenses turned toward the door whenever someone came in—but, apparently recognizing Jason, everyone turned away again. We made our way through the steam and smell of wet coats in the warm, smoky fug to the bar.

"What's yours?" Jason asked.

"Belhaven Export, thanks."

Suddenly hungry, I ordered us a couple of pasties. The microwave *ping*ed at the same time as the beer settled.

"God, that's welcome," I said.

We shifted away from the bar and stood in a corner, where there was a shelf for our elbows and pints. The music was loud enough to make conversation difficult, and eavesdropping very difficult. Still I, leaned in and spoke quietly.

"Is this place safe?"

Jason chuckled darkly. "It's safe for us."

I wasn't quite as sure of Jason's assurances as I'd been in the morning, but I still had nothing else on which to rely.

"What can we do now?"

Jason shrugged. "Get you to America, I guess."

"What?" I forgot to speak quietly.

"Sure. Isn't that what the lady said?"

"Yeah, but I thought that meant as a last resort. Come on. We can do something—I can get a lawyer, go to the media and the embassies, see if they'll get her out, make sure that if I'm pulled I don't just disappear off the street. I might not even be, uh, wanted."

He stared at me. "You don't get it, do you? Jadey can look after herself. It's endgame. This *is* the fucking last resort."

7

The Great Work

S OME SECTS OF the Scoffers still clung to the old ways—to the
Bible, at least as Joanna had interpreted it, and to her early-
industrial materialism, complete with such sacraments as the
anointing with oil, to symbolize the belief that man was a machine
built by the Creator. Others had adopted the dialectical materialism
of Engels and Haldane (and had duly, dialectically, split into further
fractious factions). Most, including the sect in which Gregor had
been brought up, took what they considered a moderate position,
venerating the ancient materialists more than the modern prophets
of religious or political messianism, while of course acknowledging
their contributions (as the tolerant cliché went).

The interior of the North Street Meeting-House was dark with
wood, bright with colored glass. Walking as though balancing
books on his head, Gregor made his way down the aisle to his
family's pew and edged in beside Anthony, his younger brother.
His parents leaned forward—his mother with her usual anxious
smile, his father with his customary curt nod—then settled back.
No doubt they were both grateful to see him; his visits to the house
of philosophy were becoming rarer as he got older.

In fact he had come along out of a mixture of motives, in which
the desire for material enlightenment was the least. He'd vaguely
promised Clarissa, who now sat at the front, her husband on one
side, and on the other a comically regular series of successively
older and taller children. He still had his good suit, relatively un-
wrinkled. And his hangover was too delicately poised for him to
even think about breakfast. So here he was, instead of in bed, at
ten o'clock on a Sunday morning.

The Scoffer stepped up to the lectern and smiled at the larger-
than-usual congregation; it was probably doubled by the younger

members of the Cairns family and their more distant relatives. He raised his arms and in a resonant voice intoned the evocation:

> " 'Self-moving matter,
> mother-maker of all,
> move my small self!
>
> " 'Lend weight to my words,
> vigor to my voice,
> impetus to my instruction!' "

Stepping down, he stood by the font of seawater and waited while Clarissa carried her baby forward. Gently he took the child in his arms and asked:

"Who names this child?"

"I, Clarissa Louise Cairns, his mother."

"What name do you give him?"

"Owen John James Matthew Cairns."

The Scoffer dipped his index finger in the salt water, tested on his tongue that it was indeed salty, wet his middle finger with saliva from his mouth, then dipped his index finger again and with the two waters of life drew a circle on the baby's forehead.

"Welcome," he said.

He raised the baby up for all to see: the small, fortunately sleeping head looking even smaller above the white moistening-gown whose trailing train symbolized the child's kinship with the gods. Then he returned the child to Clarissa, who sat back down and listened to the blessing, formally addressed to the new arrival.

"Owen, you have come to us from the death of stars, and to their birth you shall return. Nothing you knew before, and nothing shall you know after. For a moment between, you will enjoy the gift of life. Your life is now defended by us all." Briefly he drew his sword, swiftly he sheathed it again. "Your blood is our blood. Your life is your own. Enjoy it all your days, and when you must, leave it without fear. Your needs are few and easily satisfied. Understand this, and your life will be a happy one, worthy of the gods. Long may you live, joyous may you live, happy may you live!"

The benediction complete, the Scoffer stepped back to the lectern, opened the Good Books and began his speech. It was an entirely inoffensive and banal homily on the good life, the ethics illustrated with some stretched metaphors from physics and biology, enlivened by brief tales for the children—and, no doubt, all the better for all of that. After about five minutes Gregor's attention wandered to the high stained-glass windows, in which flowers blooming, leaves twining, dinosaurs striding, bats flying, martyrs burning, couples coupling, scientists investigating, and other edifying phenomena of nature, society, and thought, sported in fecund profusion. It was perhaps his bad luck that one panel, for the-gods-knew-what reason, depicted a dark-haired maiden in a pink gown. The pang in his heart brought back the pain in his head, and he was immensely grateful when the discourse ended.

Under cover of the final hymn he made his escape, ducking out of any conversation with his family. The day was fine and blustery; the warm sunshine and cool gusts began to soothe Gregor's hangover as he walked down North Street and up the High Street, on the road out of town and around to the castle. On the way he bought a news-sheet. As he handed over the change and exchanged greetings, he noticed consciously for the first time the romantic novels discreetly displayed in plain covers on the bottom rack at the back of the stall, beneath the eyeline of innocent children and much lower than the racks of books and chapbooks of erotic pictures and fantasies, whose colorful covers were as vivid and public, and as cheerfully explicit, as the stained-glass windows of the meeting-house.

He briefly considered buying one of those under-the-counter love stories, then decided it would be too embarrassing for words.

"Good to see you, Greg. Come on in."

James stepped back, swinging the massive door open, and Gregor entered the study. Dust danced in the sunlight beaming in through the window that occupied most of one wall of the wide, high-ceilinged room. Gregor had known where to find it, from childhood memory. Even childhood memory did not exaggerate the number of stairs to be climbed, or the length and dimness of the corridors to be traversed to reach this room, high in a barely occupied wing of the keep.

But now, the shelves seemed lower, the table broader, the stacks of paper higher and more disorderly, the calculating-machines more eccentric and obsolete. The air was peppery with dust. Suppressing sneezes, Gregor accepted a welcome cup of coffee that the Navigator poured from a vacuum-flask, and sat down on the cleanest-looking chair available. His grandfather relaxed into an old leather sofa from which springs and horsehair sprouted, and waved a hand at the surrounding clutter.

"Well, here it is," he said. "The Great Work, so far. I'd like you to help me . . . finish it."

Gregor's consternation must have shown on his face. The Great Work had been going on for so long that finishing it had never even crossed his mind as a realistic prospect. The task James proposed seemed to loom in front of him like an impossible cliff.

"Oh, don't worry," James hastened to add. "It won't demand much of your time. I just need someone younger and sharper than myself, frankly, to integrate the top level of what we've got, and see if it all makes sense."

"Okay," said Gregor. He sipped at the now cooling coffee. "Just one question. Can you tell me, in confidence if necessary, just what the Great Work actually *is*?"

"Sure," said James. "In confidence, yes—strictest confidence. We're trying to plot a course to take the *Bright Star* to Croatan."

Gregor almost dropped the cup. He had honestly thought that the whole object of the exercise *was* the exercise, a prolonged and ultimately unavailing struggle to keep programming skills alive and within the family.

"All this time we've been doing this *by hand*?"

James nodded.

"Why in the name of the gods haven't we been using calculating-machines, or even . . . computers?"

"The computers the first crew brought down with them from the ship," James said, "were partly organic—'wet tech,' they called them—and have mostly decayed or become unreliable. As to the calculating-machines, mechanical or electronic, well—"

He balanced his cup on the arm of the sofa, spread his hands and smiled disarmingly; then waved vaguely and dismissively at the machines, gleaming or rusty, thick with oil and dust. "You can use them to crunch the numbers, but you can't program a computer *with* a computer."

"You most certainly can!" Gregor protested. "Even I know that."

"So you've looked at the Comp Sci books in the family library," James said, approval and mockery both in his tone. "Well, I've looked at a lot more of them than you have, and I've worked with the old wet-tech computers—oh yes!—and I can assure you that these handy shortcuts are among the facilities we have largely lost. In the early days, two or three generations ago, my predecessors *were* able to do that, and the work went a lot faster. These days, with the work farmed out to all the country cousins of the clan . . ." He shrugged. "It's as you see. Not that we're entirely degenerating. There's good work being done at the university. Someday we'll build our own computers, ones that can handle this kind of task, right here in Kyohvic. But not soon, and certainly not soon enough."

"Soon enough for what?"

"Think about it," said James. He sprang up and strode to the window and stood gazing out, hands clasped behind his back.

"You've seen the beginnings of it," he went on, not turning around. "Out there is the first ship from a Nova Babylonia which is aware of our presence here. In a few years, when their journey carries them to Croatan and other nearby worlds, they'll see our influence on all of them. Compared with Nova Babylonia, we are a new thing in the Second Sphere. All the people in this sector were . . . delivered . . . from Earth or the Solar System after the rise of capitalism. Most of the ancestors of the peoples of the Nova Terra sector come from the ancient world, lifted from lost legions, dying cities choked in the jungle or the desert, wandering tribes. They have become a great imperial republic, a very advanced and enlightened place by all accounts, but we are not like them. We are new."

He turned around sharply, vehement. "And we are weak. If we don't establish some *decisive* advantage, we'll be assimilated into Nova Babylonia's benevolent sway. Our writings will fill their libraries, our thoughts will fascinate their philosophers, our arts will add new colors to their palette. Some might call that a victory of a sort. But *they will not change,* and we will. What makes us unique, what makes us ourselves, will be lost."

"What is it," Gregor frowned, "that makes us 'unique'?"

The old man smiled.

"Instability," he said. "Nova Babylonia has been absorbing new ideas and peoples, as well as generating its own, for hundreds if not thousands of years, and it's a very stable place. We absorb ideas from them, some of which they took with them from Earth, but look what we make of them! The Scoffers' secular christianity is a very different thing from the rather passive philosophy pro-claimed by the ancient materialists in the Good Books, for all that it's hard to make the heresiarchs see that. We change all the time, and I don't want us to change into more of them, and then stop changing. Which, as I say, will happen, as more and more of their ships come in, year after year, maybe month after month. Unless we do something about it."

"What *can* we do?"

"We can build ships of our own," James said. "Ships that don't depend on the krakens and the saurs. We can become *the* trading people of the Second Sphere and beyond. With that power, we will maintain our independence."

Gregor looked up at him, astonished. "Now that," he said at last, "is a *great* work."

"Then let's get to it," James said. He stepped forward and held out his hand. "Welcome to the Cosmonaut cadre."

Gregor was shaken by the casually bestowed honor. The cadre was the core of the Families, the fraction which—by membership in the notional crew of the *Bright Star*—maintained the mystique of a continuity with Earth; with, indeed, its mightiest and most glorious empire, the European Union. Some of the Families had grown wealthy on Mingulay, others poor; but the poorest fisherman or smallholder descended from the original crew felt at least a touch of inherited superiority over his or her native neighbor, and which only the continuity of the cadre with the great union of socialist republics did anything to justify. In the opinion of Family members who'd made it on their own merits, such as Gregor's father, the whole cachet was a hollow tradition.

James ran his fingers through his lanky white hair and tied it back in a ponytail with an elastic band. Then he stalked over to a shelf, tugged out a bundle of papers and spread them on the table.

"Right," he said, leaning on his hands and peering down at them, "this is where we start. The setting of the problem."

The oldest papers, where the task began, were even physically difficult to understand, faded and yellowed, their script sufficiently antique to make reading them an effort.

"It begins here," the Navigator told him, stabbing a ridged fin-gernail on a row of scrawled numbers, "with these stellar parallax observations. They had to work out the distance to Croatan first, obviously. The stellar drift in the intervening centuries is, uh, within the margin of error. *However.* The drive's working is sensitively dependent on mass distribution in the surrounding volume of space, out to several light-years—say, ten, to be on the safe side. So the process had to be repeated for dozens of nearby stars."

He tapped at another page.

"Next, there are readings from the *Bright Star*'s instruments. That's just the top cover, by the way. The rest are over there."

His hand wave alarmingly took in a couple of sets of shelving, all wooden and all bowed under the weight of stacked paper.

"These two sets of information are, fundamentally, the input. The root of the program, the 'algorithm' as it's called, for calculating from them a setting for the drive which will take the ship to Croatan and not to, let us say, the fucking middle of some fucking inter-meta-galactic gulf a billion light-years across is, *we think,* this set of equations here. Deriving a practical program from it to crunch the numbers is a formidable task in itself, which . . ."

And so it went. James spent the next hour or so showing Gregor the barest outline of the task of integration and interpretation he would be assisting with. It still seemed overwhelming, as though he had been appointed an executor of some terrible cumulative will, landed with the job of sorting out the affairs of generations of procrastinators. When the explanation was, as far as it went, complete, it was Gregor's turn to stand by the window and look moodily out.

"Why can't we just *buy* computers?" he said at last. "The saurs sell us instruments and automation for manufactories. Why not for this?"

"The saurs are very careful about what they sell us," James said, still looking down at the papers spread on the table. "They haven't sold us any general-purpose computers. I mean, we've tried cannibalizing and reverse-engineering the stuff they do sell us, but it's like trying to do the same with living organisms before you even have a clue about genetics, let alone genetic engineering. Fucking impossible. Something hard and shiny turns into a smelly puddle."

"Why don't they sell us computers?"

James sighed. "From what old Tharovar deigns to say on the subject, and even he is a bit cagey, it seems that the gods would not approve. And the saurs are gods-fearing, in a way that we are not. The gods may have been involved in some disaster in their past. . . . We can speculate about its being remembered in tradition, even 'race memory,' something in the genes—but that's all. They don't want to talk about it."

"I've noticed something like that," said Gregor. "With Salasso."

"Anyway, relying for our navigation on computers from the saurs would be . . . missing the point, don't you think?" James abandoned the task and joined him at the window.

"Yes," Gregor said. "I see that."

"Good!" James grinned at him and slapped his back. "Now go and see your girl."

He walked slowly along the dark corridors, and slowly down the long—straight or spiral—stairs. The anachronistic fossil assemblages in the walls' sedimentary-rock cladding held a mirror to the confusion in his mind. Still in upheaval over the immensity of the task his ancestors and living relatives had accomplished, still appalled at the scale and complexity of the task to come, he was already trembling at the thought of meeting Lydia again.

This was not the normal and natural passion of sexual desire, or the easy affection that came from its mutual satisfaction—even, at times, from its friendly mutual recognition. This was the madness of infatuation, capable of suspending reason, of destroying lives. His sudden involuntary obsession with Lydia was only made more intense by the improbability of its ever being fulfilled without unhappy consequences. If they were to be together for more than the ship's few brief weeks on Mingulay, one or the other of them would be separated by light-years and lifetimes from all they had hitherto held dear.

Fleeting sexual liaisons between unattached starfarers and locals were to be expected and were, indeed, welcomed on both sides for the new genes thus exchanged. Every visit resulted in a small flurry of pregnancies, and even temporarily broken hearts. The real heartbreaker, the exclusive passion, the mad desire for the one and only—that was neither encouraged nor frequent. But it was what he felt.

Last night he had not told Lydia how he felt. But she must know! They had talked and talked and talked, until they'd noticed how their quiet voices echoed, and they'd looked around and found themselves among the last few people in the hall. And, just before she turned to leave, she'd placed her hands in his, as she had done during the dance; then danced away.

She sat on a bench against the seaward wall of one of the lower levels of the castle, which faced onto a walled garden: a green lawn surrounded by beds in which rhododendron, hydrangea, and dwarf pine ran riot. Honeysuckle and ivy had long since struck their tiny pitons in that wall of the castle and clawed their way to near its summit. Her eyes half-closed against the distant dazzle and persistent breeze, she gazed out at the early-afternoon sea in whose choppy water her family's starship did not float, but hovered, the humming energies of its engines sending visible patterns of distortion across the surrounding surface. Lighters on the sea, gravity skiffs in the air, hurried to and fro, loading or unloading; invisible from this angle and distance, larger submarine vehicles would be doing the same, transacting the starship's real business, which was between the krakens—the trade of saurs and humans being in every sense superficial by comparison.

Gregor approached her from the side, across the grass, enjoying the unguarded moment before she noticed him. Her hair was blown about her face in a breeze to which her knee-length dress, pleated and folded to a sculpted shell of dark-blue fabric, was apparently impervious. As he came into her peripheral vision she turned her head sharply, saw him and stood up, smiling. He stopped a few feet away, not wanting to stop; wanting to walk right into her.

"Good afternoon," she said.

"Good afternoon," said Gregor.

They stood regarding each other for a moment.

"Would you like to take me for a walk?" she asked.

"Good idea," he said, mentally cursing the banality of his words.

They strolled across the grass, toward the far right corner of the garden where a gate opened on empty air. In the sunlight her hair, so wavy it was slightly frizzy, looked different, as did her skin, in endless fascinating ways. The scent that drifted from within the wide high fold of her dress's collar competed with that of the garden's flora: there was something of the animal as well as of the plant in it.

At the top of the stairway she stopped in front of him, looking down at the rough grass of the headland twenty meters below. The steps were of narrow stone, worn and wet, and they descended in one long, steady flight down the outer wall. She put a hand on the handrail and tested it gingerly.

"It's safe," Gregor assured her.

"It looks like an afterthought."

"It is. Bolted on thousands of years after the stairs." He shrugged. "Which themselves are an addition to the original structure. When they were built, safety wasn't a feature." He gestured at the wall's overhang, now a little above their line of sight. "See the slots along there, where the light comes through? For oil. The steps must have been convenient, maybe, for whoever was in the castle, and a death-trap for any attacker who was tempted to use them."

"That's encouraging."

"I'll go first," he said. He stepped forward and held out one hand. She took it, and blushed and looked down.

One hand on the rail and one holding hers behind him, he began the descent. Her shoes were flat and flexible, made of something that wasn't leather and that gripped—as a few quick backward glances showed—better than his did.

About halfway down, something huge and white hurtled hooting out of the wall a meter in front of his face. His involuntary backward jerk slammed the back of his head into Lydia's belly. Their yells and grabbing and stumbling were simultaneous.

The perilous moment passed. He looked up at Lydia's pale face. His own was burning. They each let go of the parts of the other's body they had grabbed.

"Are you all right?" he asked.

"Yes . . ." she said. Her voice shook a little. "What the hells was that?"

He pointed. A few tens of meters out on the air, a white shape with a meter-long wingspan and trailing black claws circled on the updraughts. As it turned, its big binocular eyes seemed to be looking at him.

"Nightbat," he said. "They hunt small nocturnal mammals."

He turned, noticing the dark hollow between blocks from which it had emerged. Faint, indignant noises came from within.

"Wow," he said, awed despite everything. "A nest."

"Could we look at it?"

He stared up at her, impressed, and shook his head.

"No, sorry. The parent might get *really* annoyed. And we don't want that."

She looked over at the wheeling, watchful predator, then back at him with what seemed genuine regret. "No," she said, "I suppose it would be unwise."

She held his hand more tightly until they reached the ground. He didn't let go of it as he turned to face her; he reached out his other hand, and she took it.

"That was exciting," she said with a laugh. "Let's not do it again."

"Sorry about—"

"No, that's all right. You couldn't have known about the nest."

"I didn't. It's years since I've been down these stairs."

Lydia grinned and let go of his hands, shaded her eyes and looked up at the wall looming above them. The nightbat had returned to its nest; around the walls flocks of much smaller bats, with long, sharp wings, swooped and soared with twittering cries, catching insects on the fly.

"They're called swallers," Gregor said. Passing clouds gave him the sensation that the wall was toppling. He looked away, at her still upturned face and the tender flutter in her throat.

"It's an amazing thing," she said. "This castle." She leaned forward and stretched up a hand to the upper edge of the lowest row of blocks. "So huge, so . . . pre-human. But so human too."

"Built by giants," Gregor agreed.

He and Lydia, by unspoken consent, started walking along the path that led up the headland a few hundred meters to skirt the clifftops. "Do you have such keeps on Nova Babylonia?"

"Nova Terra," she corrected him. "Yes, some, on wild shores like this. The city—some of the old temples are like this, but we know they were built by human beings who wanted to feel small."

"Oh." He hadn't thought of that. "What are the gods in the old temples like?"

She shivered suddenly. "I was taken to one, when I was a child, for education. A great empty space, gloomy, lit by oil-lamps with a heavy scent. Sandstone statues in niches, as high as that wall—twenty, thirty meters. But these were of great kings and winged cherubim, not gods. The statue of the god was at the north end of the temple, and it was quite small, like a boulder about as high as a man. It was carved—carved!—from an iron meteorite. It's hard to remember the shape but it was very, very ugly and it seemed to be full of eyes. Not human or animal eyes. It's hard to explain why, but I knew they were eyes. And what looked like rust on it was ancient tracks of blood."

She laughed, and waved a hand as though to dispel the darkness of her words. "I got out of that temple as fast as my little legs would carry me!"

"And ever since have thanked the gods for Epicurus?"

"Yes!" She threw out an arm in a rhetorical gesture, and recited:

" 'Who stormed the flaming ramparts of the world,
and superstition down in ruin hurled.' "

He looked sidelong at her, surprised and pleased. "You know the Good Books?"

"Oh yes, we use the Mingulayan paraphrases to learn the English."

"No wonder you sometimes sound quaint," he teased; then relented. "No, really, your English is astonishingly good."

"Oh, I know," she said. "I hope to use it a lot."

"You already are."

She took this as the compliment it was intended to be. Gregor was glad she didn't notice the pain that lay beneath it.

They walked on up the headland until they reached its point, which rose like a prow higher even than the castle. The path turned around a few meters from the very forward edge of the cliff. They looked at the edge, then at each other, and both laughed.

"I can't," said Gregor.

"Me neither."

She dropped to her hands and knees and crawled forward; after a moment's hesitation he did the same. There was something ludicrously reassuring about the ground's still-upward slope. Rationally he knew it was safe: the cliff was of solid metamorphic rock, not given to crumbling. Irrationally, he vividly imagined it splitting away.

They arrived at the edge by inching forward with their toes and elbows, and peered over—black rocks, white water, and in the stupendous volume of intervening air, the backs of the seabats and diving-bats lofting on the upward rush. Gregor's fingertips were digging into the thin soil. With a deliberate effort of will he un-locked one hooked hand and laid it across the small of Lydia's back. Her body's heat rushed at him through the dry, papery texture of the fabric; he heard its whisper, and found that he was stroking her, higher and lower. She closed her eyes; he felt the muscles in her back relax.

"Mmm," she said, "that's nice."

She opened her eyes, still looking down, and shifted so that her side pressed against his. "To feel in danger, and at the same time to feel held, and safe."

His whole arm was right across her now, his hand in the hollow between her upper arm and her breast. Their shoulders were on the very edge of the cliff, their faces looking down at the sea. They lay like that for what seemed a long time, the roar of blood in his ears and the beat of his heart drowning the sound of the surf and the waves and the high cries of the bats.

They turned to each other. Their faces, now inches apart, were drawn inexorably together as if by gravity. Her eyes closed and her mouth opened to his. They kissed above the void for a long minute, then she pulled away.

"This is not safe," she said; then, in answer to his smile, added: "We might not stop at a kiss, and we might be seen. It would be embarrassing to our families."

She rolled onto her back, sat up, and stood in one continuous fluid movement. A few quick strokes of her hands restored her dress to its ideal shape, leaving not a trace of grass or damp or any wrinkle.

He followed her back to the path, and they walked together back to the keep.

On Sunday evenings the Bailie's Bar was relatively clean and quiet. Its usual clientele of maritime and longshore workers, having an early start on the Monday, left it to the students and the former students who'd settled into casual employment and a student life-style before—in most cases—finding their real profession.

Gregor drank and smoked with Salasso and Elizabeth and with his brother Anthony and two of Anthony's friends, Muir and Gunn. Ruefully he told them a discreetly edited version of his misadventure.

"I can't bear to be away from her," he concluded.

"So why aren't you with her now?" Gunn asked. She was a bright undergraduate with curly red hair.

"She has to help with the family business," Gregor explained miserably. "I might see her tomorrow. She and her father are interested in our work at the marine station."

"Is that allowed?" Anthony asked.

"Of course it's bloody allowed. We're not researching anything secret."

Not at the marine station, anyway.

"I didn't mean sharing the research," said Anthony, smirking wickedly. "I meant you and her spooning about at work. All these pheromones in the air, it'll probably wreck your experiments."

"Oh, shut the fuck up!"

His brother regarded him with unabashed amusement. Anthony had not seen Gregor making such a fool of himself since he'd broken a leg falling out of a tree at the age of eight, and he was making the most of it.

"You've got it bad," he said.

"He sure has," said Elizabeth. She stared at Gregor.

"Come on," she said. "You know what to do. Lucretius, Book Four, lines 1065–1066:

> " *'Oh, ease the pain of love's urgent need!*
> *On other men or women spend your seed!'* "

This helpful quotation from the Good Books was usually offered in a friendly, soothing manner to the lovesick, but Elizabeth spoke them in a bitter tone, for which Gregor could not account.

8

The Dreamland Gate

WALKING IN RAIN across wet tarmac, I felt exposed. My heels lifted with difficulty, and the back of my head felt a backward tug like sleep. Far ahead of me, nearly twenty meters away, a huge rectangular box loomed through the hissing drops. Much farther away, more than two hundred meters, the cranes and container ship bulked like a space station. Jason had got me a travel agent—or "people-smuggler," in *Pravda*-speak—and that entrepreneur had taken four thousand euros cash to put me on a barge at Leith Docks. It had taken the rest of that day and all that night for the barge to make its way up the Firth of Forth, past the busy site of the Grangemouth oil refinery and the abandoned site of the Longannet power station, through the Forth and Clyde Canal, and down the Clyde. We'd reached Greenock, and the Atlantic container terminal.

I walked up to the big box and walked around it, acutely conscious of a Harbor Patrol blimp hanging just below the cloud cover, a few hundred meters out over the Firth of Clyde. In the far end of the container, which just happened to be turned away from the waterfront and to face the other containers so that it could not be seen from a distance, was an iron door. I turned the handle. From inside came a shuffling, scuttling noise. As the door opened, a little light fell on the interior and reflected momentarily off the eyes of a huddle of perhaps a dozen people at the back of the otherwise empty container. Not quite empty; their small bundles of possessions lay at random on the floor. I could think of nothing to say, so I raised my palms to them and stepped inside, closing the door behind me. The darkness settled around me like a hood of felt. Feet moved stealthily. I slipped the goggles on and tuned them to infrared: The people at the back had begun to spread themselves out along the sides, bracing their feet on the floor and their backs to the wall. They moved as though they couldn't see, with much groping and stumbling. I settled myself down the same way that they had.

About half an hour passed. Once or twice a child whispered, and an adult hissed them to silence. Somebody muttered something about a cigarette. Then came the sound of an engine and of fat tires on a wet surface, the jangle and rattle of chains and the thumps and scrapes as some connection was made to the outside of the box. After a moment of increasing strain, the container was lifted off the ground and carried along. More jolting and clanging, shouts—and then it swung, to the now unsilenced cries of the children. I could feel it going up like a lift, and tried not to imagine the height. Down again it dropped, and was eased—at last, gently—into its place.

After so much motion this felt at first like stillness, but after a minute of silent attention it was obvious that the surface on which the container now lay was itself moving, in slight and subtle rhythm. We were on the ship. After a few minutes we could feel the throb of the engine underfoot, and the sway of the floor steepened a little.

We stayed there, in the dark, for another six hours in which the only entertainment was the long buildup of increasingly agitated whispering before one of the kids took a leak. The glow of the puddle's warmth slowly faded. This cycle was repeated more than once.

Somebody knocked on the door, not too hard. The sound still rang out and made us all jump.

"All right," said a man's voice from outside, "you can come out now. I'm gonna open the door real slow, okay?"

A fan of light gradually widened from the door, giving eyes time to adjust. I pocketed the goggles and hung back, letting the others—the "illegals," as I kept thinking of them, patronizingly *not* including myself in their number—go ahead of me onto the deck. They all walked forward. A family—a man, a woman, two small children—and five teenagers and one man who looked a bit older than me. I fell in behind him.

The vessel was so fucking vast that when I stepped out somewhere near the midline of the deck I hardly felt I was on a ship at all. Beyond the ship, as far as I could see, was nothing but white-capped steel-gray to the horizon. The horizon moved up and down a little, that was all. The deck was a low, open area between the bow and stern superstructures, and a maze of close-packed and lashed-down containers.

The man who'd opened the door for us was a short, stout Black-American wearing jeans and a T-shirt and an impressive collection of flashy hardware around his fingers, wrists, and neck. The single obsidian curved band of his wraparound goggles suddenly became transparent, and so non-reflective it was almost invisible. He grinned at us as we stood blinking in the noon sun and breathing the fresh air.

"Hi," he said, "welcome to the free world, and all. You're outside the commies' territorial waters, so you can now do whatever the hell you please." He jerked a thumb backward. "So long as you don't get in the way and the captain don't mind, of course."

People crowded around him, hugging, kissing, crying. The older guy actually kissed the deck. I looked on, bemused. I was relieved, sure, to be safe—safe from the state, and not fallen into worse hands—but my companions' behavior struck me as excessive and unwarm.

Over the next couple of days I realized I'd been mistaken about that. Their reaction wasn't excessive at all. For one thing, the crewman was, literally, right—we had effectively already made it to the U.S., there being no immigration controls whatsoever on entrants from the E.U.

The crew of this huge ship was about the same in number as that of the barge that had taken me across Scotland; the men were more like technicians than sailors. I don't remember their names, and their faces are confused in my memory, but their quick unguarded expressions and loud unironic voices still shine and shout in my mind. Even the way they moved was expansive, uninhibited. On duty and off, their attention flitted and flicked between the real and the virtual worlds so fast their goggles seemed sometimes to strobe between dark and clear. Their hands, when not otherwise occupied, flexed in the flow of the five-finger chording alphabets of the virtual keyboards, and their lips synched in silent conversations.

Not all of them were tall, but each of them seemed to be always at his full height. It wasn't so much (I reflected, as I, too, began to stretch) that we'd had a weight on our backs, as that we had lived all our lives under a low ceiling.

Even my handheld reader and wet-tech goggles seemed to brighten up, and access to U.S. sources to become easier, but that may have been just an illusion. I used my comms and comp gear intensely. Prices on the ship—for food and berths, because our thousands had merely paid for the passage, we were told—made our cash evaporate rapidly. I was luckier than my fellow travelers in that I could start my new work in the brave New World right there on the ship, whereas they had to pile up debts. My serious accounts had always been offshore, and were still valid. I plunged into the New York labor market, holding my nose for the descent into legacy systems. The old code-geeks seemed to be out of the running, and I was in demand. A corner of the ship's canteen made an adequate office, with a convenient bottomless cup of coffee.

I phoned my mother. Her image popped up in the dataspace. She was thirty-five at the time and could have passed for younger than me, except for the wary, weary look she had.

"Yi've got yirsel into some trouble now," she said, in a tone of gloomy satisfaction. "Where are yi?"

"On my way to America."

She looked a bit shocked. She was the most conservative person I knew. She believed in the revolution.

"I always told yi, yi'd get nothing but trouble wi' they anarchists and that Yank spy."

After a moment she relented. "You look after yirsel, son."

"Yeah, I'll do that, Mum."

I'd been looking after myself, I reflected after she'd rung off, for quite some time.

In the minutes between hours-long contract jobs, I dived into the mail and the news, trying to find out what had happened to Jadey, and what was going on back home, and about Dreamland. The answers, not to my surprise, were linked.

I still had the trace of Jadey's original records, which Jason and Curran had so expertly distorted; working back through them, I hit—

"What the fuck are you up to, mister?"

The woman shoved her face into my field, making me recoil slightly. The resolution wasn't good enough to tell if she were real or a repro 'bot, but she certainly looked indignant enough, her otherwise kindly, fortyish features blazing like the henna in her unstylish hair.

"I'm looking for information about Jadey Ericson," I mumbled into the throat-mike. The woman retreated a bit and consulted something out-of-field.

"So what do *you* know about her?" she demanded.

"Last I saw of her, she was about to be pulled in by the commies."

"Oh!" She stared at me. Sheets of data shimmered between us like a heat haze. "You're saying you were *there*?"

"Yeah, in Edinburgh," I told her. "What's it to you?"

Her eyes narrowed, and her expression became calmer.

"I'm going to ping you," she said. "And you just better be who I think you are, else I'll lock you out."

I could feel my kit being interrogated; the sensation was disagreeably creepy. A faint line of light scanned my eyes before I had a chance to blink. Not that a retinal scan was worth much, these days, but it would have been remiss of her not to do it. Meanwhile I sent a crowd of AI agents burrowing past the connection she'd made by opening communications with me. They returned in seconds, flashing up organizational data. A rapid glance before stashing them left me with an afterimage of an organization called the Human Rights Federation, with a stack of letterhead sponsors, each with a string of impressive-looking letters after his or her name: businesspeople, a few token trade-unionists, academics, engineers—your standard-issue New Money think-tank front.

"Man," the woman said, looking a lot more relaxed, "that biodegradable commie gear is the pits."

"Don't underestimate it," I said smugly, scratching the front of my neck. The throat-mike was days old and giving me a rash like a blunt razor. "So was it the HRF sent Jadey to Europe?"

"Huh, smart," the woman replied grudgingly. "Yeah, we're her backers. And you, Mr. Cairns, must be Thin Red. Her hardware source."

"Isn't this," I asked, "getting a bit beyond need-to-know, at this stage?"

She shrugged. "Ah, the goddamn commies have it all laid open like a book now. But yeah, you might have a point. Just gimme a location, and we'll meet up for some serious talk."

"The Dreamland gate," I said.

"Ah-hah. Nice one. Okay, see you there."

"Where is it?"

"You'll find it."

She blinked out, leaving me gazing at a data structure that my AIs had patiently slotted together in the meantime. It was almost too simple to be paranoid, almost simple enough for a professional paranoid like a security apparatchik to ignore, and it went like this:

The ESA launch-site at Kourou in French Guiana had, a couple of years back, been the locus of a minor scandal, much played-up by the protectionist wing of the Party in Europe. One of the fabricators at Kourou had been buying in launch-vehicle components, not from a duly subsidized plant in some godforsaken corner of Angola or wherever, but from an American company. That company, Nevada Orbital Dynamics, had a vice president on the HRF's letterhead and a production facility at Groom Lake, Nevada.

A place also known as Area 51, and as Dreamland.

Kourou's MEP, Weber, had staunchly defended the fabricators, and after the relevant balance-sheets and quality records had been introduced into the parliamentary debate the deal's critics had made a muttering retreat.

Surely, I thought, Weber's suborning—if that was what had happened—couldn't have been as simple and obvious as that. It could hardly be held against him—he and the fabricators were doing what they were supposed to be doing, both commercially and, in the context of peaceful coexistence (the Party line du jour), politically—and he might even be able to use it as a defense against any trumped-up charges of "wrecking," as unprofitable deals tended to be called if any recrimination happened to be required retrospectively.

Another part of my mind thought, *Bingo!*

I turned with renewed hope to tracking down other information about Jadey. She was in the news, in a carefully obscure way: buried in a bottom corner of an inside page of the online edition of *Europe Pravda,* and blazed on the front pages of utterly unofficial American newsfeeds. WHY, they demanded, was OUR SO-CALLED GOVERNMENT doing NOTHING to free this INNOCENT AMERICAN?

The U.S. government, via small paragraphs in the *New York Times* and *Washington Post,* was making obscure and oblique noises about using "the proper channels." Whether this meant they were making frenzied diplomatic representations at the highest level, or passing token queries from the consulate to the constabulary in Edinburgh, was anyone's guess.

The whole issue of Jadey—which in other times could easily have been inflated into a cause célèbre—was completely overshadowed by the fuss over Weber's arrest (the U.S. government's tone on the allegations against him resounded with injured innocence) and the far greater fuss over ESA's alien contact. Over that, the world was collectively and predictably losing its head. Scrolling through the news from the past few days it seemed that every scientist, philosopher, cleric, general, politician, and stand-up comedian on the planet—and off it—had been canvassed for their response. I left the resulting cacophony for a batch of freshly hatched AIs to turn into some kind of digest format, and turned away in some relief to the next contract to bubble up my list.

The soothing relief of routine hackwork didn't last. Twenty-five minutes into the job, the AIs started flashing urgently and the ship's cook, Mr. Nguyen, hurried out of the galley and banged the table. I saved-to-server and switched my attention to both interruptions, the human first.

"Big news for you," he told me. "For us all. Check CNN."

"Thanks," I said. The AIs were urging me to do the same. I followed their advice. The global newsfeed had no doubt what was the most important piece of global news, shoving the alien-contact debate unceremoniously down the stack:

REVOLT ON ESA STATION

Scientists and cosmonauts on the ESA scientific station *Titov* today appealed to the world community to prevent the "militarization" of their historic contact with an alien intelligence. An apparently bloodless struggle has ousted the five military representatives from the station's governing committee. Former station security chief Colin Driver, hitherto regarded as a totally reliable Communist FSB commissar, has spearheaded the move.

In a personal statement, Driver announced:

Tab to a clip.

Driver filled the view. To me, it was as though he were sitting

118

across the table. Behind him, in the back of the field, a half dozen or so people clung at all angles to stanchions and grinned wildly at the camera. They looked like scientists, all right. Driver was a thickset, muscular man in a much-bemedaled uniform. His face could have been Slavic, but his voice and accent (in the undubbed version I was getting) were unmistakably Southern English.

"I'm not much given to public speaking, so I'll keep this short. Three days ago, General Secretary Yefrimovich made an announcement which shook the world. The timing of that announcement, after what many have rightly deduced must have been years of secrecy, has given rise to widespread and alarming speculation. My friends, I have to tell you that some of this speculation is partly justified. Almost certainly unknown to the General Secretary and to the leading Party of the fraternal countries, sinister and reactionary elements in . . ."

Driver paused, and then said, "Oh, the hell with this commie crap!" He convulsively tore the ribbons and badge from his jacket, and took a deep breath.

"Okay," he went on. "Folks, I'll give it to you straight. Some of the hard-line generals in the European People's Army think they can use what we've learned from the aliens to hit the Americans hard—to win the Fourth World War and complete the world revolution at what they consider the acceptable cost of a few million lives. Sooner or later, and better sooner. You do the math—they have. But let me assure you, they don't yet have all the information they need. They've got some—most of your crypto's washed-up, as you've guessed. But they can't yet break the American launch-codes. The announcement was, from their point of view, premature, but that may not stop them from some precipitate action.

"So we—the scientists, cosmonauts, and security staff of the *Marshall Titov*—have decided to do what we can to prevent this. We've put our own militarists in protective custody, and we urge the government, armed forces, Party, and peoples of the E.U. to do the same. Until that is done, not a byte of data leaves this station without going instantly to the public nets.

"We're willing to release the military reps on one condition— that all charges against Henri Weber are dropped, that he is released unconditionally and given the chance to mediate between us and the E.U. government."

Driver smiled thinly. "After all, he *is* the MEP representing this station, via the launch-site at Kourou. As an officer—a *former* officer—of the Federal Security Bureau, I'm absolutely certain that he's innocent of the charges. He's not a CIA agent. This charge has been trumped-up to discredit him, and us, and quite possibly the FSB as well. I know this perfectly well, because . . ."

Another pause, another deep breath.

". . . for the past five years he and I have cooperated closely in feeding disinformation to the CIA and in isolating the real CIA agent on this station, Major Ivan Sukhanov, who is now with his colleagues in the brig."

New York's traffic astonished me. I took a cab from the harbor to JFK and sat back in terrified wonder as it hurtled or idled between and among the biggest, noisiest, shiniest, and smelliest vehicles I'd ever seen in my life. The whole significance of the oil wars suddenly came to life, as well as the difference between the U.S. and the E.U. In the U.S. the internal combustion engine was still dominant; in the E.U., the burning of petroleum fractions was more or less restricted to aviation and the military. The rest of it went straight into new tech. Most civil aircraft in Europe were airships or hybrid vehicles. In the U.S. they were jets. It made air travel faster, but much less comfortable, in ways that you really do not want to know about.

Las Vegas was an exercise in proving that real-life architectural and behavioral excess could still compete with virtual reality; but my strangest moment didn't come from looking out through the vast plate-glass windows of the terminal at McCarran Airport at the vaster plate-glass–and–plastic edifices beyond. I already knew that Dreamland was a place. Standing in the Janet Airlines terminal and looking at the departure board, I felt a sense of untoward excitement and unreality the first time I saw its name spelled out as a DESTINATION.

I walked down the gangway from the little fifty-seater passenger airplane and looked about me with some apprehension as I strolled toward the terminal building, the Base's regular workers striding briskly ahead of me. The flight from McCarran Airport at Las Vegas had taken half an hour. In the early-morning sun Groom Lake's dry lakebed made the airfield's twin runways a blur of dazzling light and dark shadows. A hasty thumbing of the virtuals for my new American-made goggles—spex, they were called here—turned the brightness down and the color and contrast up. The place still looked weird. A flat plain surrounded by mountains, on which the products of human technology stood out like just-dropped alien artifacts.

The former Air Force Base was ground zero for an entire fallout zone of myth and secrecy and suspicion. Between the Second and Third World Wars the region had been used for secret testing—of atomic bombs, missiles, the fabled NERVA nuclear rocket engine, and the U.S.A.'s most advanced and secret aircraft: black projects, from the U-2 through the Blackbird and a series of stealth fighters culminating in the infamous EDSF. The Electro-Dynamic Stealth Fighter had been immensely successful at flying high and fast, at avoiding radar detection, at evading smart missiles, and at generating waves of excited UFO reports. As the Eastern European theater had demonstrated, however, it wasn't at all invulnerable to old-fashioned visual detection and anti-aircraft fire from anyone with the nerve to turn off the aiming computer, look, and trust the force.

After the disasters of the war and the recriminations of the witch-hunts, the whole thing had been shut down—projects canceled, secrets carted off to deep and distant storage—and the remaining facilities turned over to a plethora of private enterprises.

These had included what were, to be kind, nutcase cults—organizations that had wasted years scouring the deserts and the deserted buildings for alloys not of this Earth, for scraps of documentation, for evidence that the pickled corpses of the Roswell aliens had once been here. By now I had stacks of this sort of shit on my reader. It made me wonder—how stupid could people *get*? If unidentified flying objects were seen around secret military aircraft development bases, the obvious inference was that they were secret military aircraft. *But the secret aircraft were secretly reverse-engineered from secretly recovered alien spacecraft. . . .* No, one would think, this particular rescue hypothesis was not going to fly. William of Ockham had shot it down centuries ago—but still it flew, piloted by alien entities unnecessarily multiplied. . . .

More significant, and in the long run more enduring, had been the space companies, some of whose successes were at that very moment making extraordinary maneuvers overhead. Flying triangles and flying discs slid across the sky, shot up and vanished in the heavens.

I entered the terminal past the casual visual and, no doubt, invisible scanning of the camo-clad dudes on the door, and stepped into the air-conditioned coolness. Just across the concourse I saw my immediate destination—an open-fronted airport bar, with its name spelled in flickering, ironic neon:

The Dreamland Gate.

The postmodern tack persisted inside; the walls were papered with ufological and science-fictional posters, and further decorated with battered, rusted metal signs from various sectors of the old perimeter, most of whose legends concluded with the words, USE OF DEADLY FORCE AUTHORIZED. A model of a Gray alien stood in the corner, and obsessively detailed polystyrene hobby-kit flying saucers hung on black invisible threads from the ceiling, swaying erratically in the ventilator breeze. The girl at the bar wore an aluminum fake space-suit and the lad had a Wackenhut Security ID tag pinned to his camos. Behind them, various flavors and colors of vodka were shelved in large flasks within which nauseatingly realistic Gray fetuses floated as though in formaldehyde.

I sat down at a corner table with a Budweiser and a bagel for breakfast, shaded my spex and checked out the scene. About half the crowd that packed out the place seemed to be workers gobbling hasty, preoccupied breakfasts over goggled visions; the more leisurely eaters, chatting loudly or quietly and conspiratorially, were apparently tourists and aging obsessives, with a sprinkle of journalists who had arrived for cheap laughs at their expense. The real alien contact had blown the dust off all the old stories of imaginary ones, freshened them up and revived them to lurch once more through the media landscape like zombies doused with deodorant, and Dreamland was becoming again a mecca for the sad and the mad and—to be fair—the inconveniently inquiring.

"Mind if I sit down?"

A woman loomed over me with a tray and a fixed smile. She was the woman who'd intercepted me in Jadey's records, looking exactly the same, in a most unbecoming fractal-paisley blouse with a floppy neck-bow. I hadn't seen her coming in. She sat down beside me, edging me along the bench and neatly trapping me against the corner wall. Further territorial encroachments were provided by her substantial selection of foodstuffs. Her male companion, tall and heavy in a dark suit and white shirt and darkened spex, sat down opposite, placing an insultingly token cup of Coke carefully in front of him.

"Well, hi," the woman said. She stuck her right hand across to me, for a shake so awkward it must have looked Masonic. "Name's Mary-Jo Greenberg." An eyebrow twitch. "And this is Al."

The big man inclined his head slightly. "From Nevada Orbital Dynamics."

"Matt Cairns," I said. "Pleased to meet you."

"I assume we've checked out each other's credentials," Mary-Jo said. "We know who you are, and you know who we are."

I nodded and glanced around; the inevitable question occurred to me. "Is this place safe to talk?"

Mary-Jo laughed. "Safe enough, Thin Red. Safer than you're used to. Besides our privacy laws and such, there's so much crap being talked here it'd take a damn dedicated processor to sort the wheat from the chaff."

"I'll take your word for it," I shrugged.

"Any news of Jadey?"

"We're working on it," Mary-Jo said. "I mean, we've had a bit of direct contact. The U.S. consulate in Edinburg's on the job, for what that's worth. She's fine. Basically all that has to be done is dicker over the deal. Should be out in a few days, no problem."

"Oh, that's great," I said. This good news combined with an overpowering burst of relief and pleasure at having someone to talk to at last.

"So," I went on, "how much do you want for a flying saucer?"

"Ah," said Al. "I don't think this place is quite safe enough to talk about *that*."

The offices of Nevada Orbital Dynamics were in a long, low, and—most importantly—air-conditioned building. The short walk there had left me somewhat drained. Sweat evaporated before it had time to wet my skin; then, as soon as I'd stepped into the interior, it went all clammy and cold. I sat in a leather-and-aluminum sling chair, gulped a Bud to replace lost fluids, and sipped a coffee to warm up.

The office we were in seemed to be Al's—the name ALAN ARMSTRONG was on the door, and he was familiar with everything within, but he'd not expanded on his introduction. He sat with his feet on the desk, leaning back and sucking a smokeless cigarette. Mary-Jo stood by the window. The painted concrete walls were bare except for a few discreet posters showing cutaway diagrams of obscure machinery and components, cycling through their incomprehensible activities in a distractingly attention-grabbing way.

I told them my story; they acted less impressed than my codegeeks had been. Maybe they'd heard this sort of thing before. When I'd finished, I placed the little datadisk on Alan's desk; they gathered around, looking down at it. For a moment neither of them spoke.

"Do you have something that can *read* this thing?" Alan asked.

"Yeah, sure," I said, amused. I hadn't expected hardware-incompatibility problems, though I should have. I took out my reader, slotted the disk in, peeled out a connection and reached for Alan's desk viewplate, then glanced up at him.

"Do you mind?"

He pulled a plug somewhere—smart guy—then waved.

"Go ahead."

I patched it across, handed him the reader, and stepped back.

"Check it out."

For the next hour or so Alan burrowed through the documentation; as his suspicions eased he added his spex to the interface, keying air and murmuring. Mary-Jo followed him in, but broke off occasionally to give me a reassuring smile or urge me to another coffee. At last Alan came out of it, and pushed the kit away, took his spex off and looked at me. His eyes were blue and mild; the skin around them betrayed tiredness beyond that from examining the specification.

I plucked off the connection, picked up the reader and stashed it.

"Well?" I asked.

Alan nodded slowly, thin-lipped.

"Whatever this is," he said, "it looks damn authentic. The bits I can understand are sound, and the bits I can't are . . . well, *alien* in a way that'd be hard to fake." He laughed briefly. "I've *seen* fake alien flying-saucer specs that were really good—old disinformation, pre-war. They were nothing like this. You always hit some kind of bullshit and hand-waving when you got in deep enough."

"Boron," Mary-Jo said. For some reason they both found this funny.

"Yeah, boron." Alan sighed. "A lot of talk about boron and magnetism and Tesla. Mind you, they didn't have the transplutonics to waffle about back then, maybe that's the equivalent here. There's no 'unobtanium' involved, but the only way this thing can fly is if we are deeply ignorant of the properties of island-of-stability elements. Which, as it happens, we are, so—" He spread his hands.

"Are we talking AG?" Mary-Jo asked.

"Something like that," Alan replied. He rubbed his nose. "I mean, what's a flying saucer without anti-gravity?" He jerked his head back, vaguely indicating the window. "Apart from the ones flying above us, right? *And,* the thing the spec calls 'the engine' looks to me like a space drive."

"Are we talking FTL?" I asked, mimicking Mary-Jo.

Alan shook his head. "No. But fast."

"Could we build it?" Mary-Jo asked.

"Yes, but only in space. That process requires a micro-gravity environment. As for the transplutonics—shit, they're only made in space anyway. By ESA, to be exact. I suppose we could ask nicely."

I stood up, feeling restless; stretched my arms and rubbed my shoulders. "I wonder," I said idly, "if they've already built it, out there."

Mary-Jo and Alan looked at each other. Alan's shrug was not quite imperceptible. Mary-Jo turned to me.

"No," she said. "They haven't."

"How do you—? Oh. You're in touch with them."

"Since the mutiny. Yeah. It's no secret. They're doing everything in the open. Unless they're playing some kind of real elaborate double-bluff, which, given the history of commie intrigues, can't be ruled out; they've given us a general picture of what they've learned. Have you seen any of that, by the way?"

"No, I've been kind of preoccupied with worrying about Jadey, and the politics back home."

"Tell me about it," Mary-Jo grinned. "Looks like all hell's breaking loose in Red Europe, huh? *Anyway*—check out the science data, sometime soon—it's fascinating. Man, they are talking to *gods.* But the *Titov* crew have said nothing about this. Alien space-drives— my God, you'd think they'd mention it."

"Oh." I felt a cold wash of disappointment as the obvious inference struck home. "Do you think this stuff could be some of the 'disinformation' that guy Driver talked about in his broadcast?"

Alan shook his head. "I doubt it," he said. "Look at the time-stamp—last year. Whatever this is, it's been kicking around some-where inside ESA for a while, and if the U.S. government or even the CIA had its hands on something like this, I'd have heard about it. I've been cultivating contacts very busily for the past few days, and if I'm sure of anything it's that nobody on our side knew about the alien minds at all. They were getting stacks of what they thought were bits of valuable scientific information, mainly in Comp Sci and low-temp physics, and all of it true as far as it went, but nothing—I mean *nothing*—of a hint about the full truth. Jesus, these guys did their job well."

"Driver and Weber?"

"Yeah." He rubbed the back of his neck. "Beats me how they stopped the real CIA agent—Major, uh, Sukhanov—from blowing the gaff whenever he was off the station. He managed at least two furloughs on Earth in the past ten years, and he must've had *some* contact on the ground."

"Oh, that," I said. "My guess is Sukhanov's totally innocent, and Driver accused him to stir up trouble in the Army and take the flak off the FSB."

"So who *was* the CIA's—?" He stared at me. "You're kidding."

"Driver," I said. "It must have been. Or that's what the CIA thought! He and Weber were double agents. That's why there was real evidence against Weber."

"If 'evidence' means anything in this context," said Mary-Jo. She sat down on the edge of the desk. "What I wonder about, though, is how the information you've got comes to be on Earth and not on the *Titov*."

"Because it was developed on Earth?" I suggested. "Maybe the design information got passed through without ever having been analyzed, and all the subsequent work was done on the ground, with the intention of not letting anyone on the station know about it until they were sure enough of the security situation, perhaps, to go ahead and build the thing."

"Need-to-know? Yeah, I guess that's plausible." Alan jumped up. "In that case the best thing we can do is get this out to the station. Get that disk, or a copy of it, out there physically."

"Why not just transmit it?"

"Because we don't want the E.U. to know what we're up to,"

Mary-Jo said. "We need someone who understands the system and the programs. Like, that manufacturing-control program? Someone who can handle the interfaces between hard tech and wet tech, and who's physically fit and politically savvy and politically reliable."

She grinned at me. "Like, for example, you."

9

Light-Years Gone

ELIZABETH SAT ON a stool by a lab bench, sipping the day's first coffee, and stared at the diagrams on the wall. The annotated and revised and scribbled-on tracings of the squid nervous system looked as meaningless as a clump of roots in a random clod. Around her the saline aquaria made a continuous hiss as bubbles oozed from the pumice blocks at the ends of the aerator tubes; the little electric pump that powered them all hummed away in a corner of the lab, reliable as a heart.

Getting up had felt like an act of bravery; dressing, like donning armor; boarding the tram like riding to battle. The wise Stoic saws were little comfort when pleasure and pain were what you wanted to feel: anything but this numb sadness. The only comfort, and it was a cold one, was that Gregor would soon feel this way himself. She couldn't see Lydia staying, or Gregor leaving with her—both had too many attachments. Each would tacitly assess that to tear themselves away from their homes would be more painful than to part from each other; but that parting would be painful enough. She was a little shocked to find herself wishing the pain on Gregor, and hoping that he'd turn to her on the rebound.

More likely, the fool would mope for months. The utter perniciousness of romantic love couldn't be more obvious in his case. Or in hers. Gods-only-knew how many opportunities of a good one-night stand or a healthy, fulfilling, longer-term relationship she'd passed up in the time she'd wasted obsessing over this son of a bitch. And because nobody even knew about it, she'd be insidiously acquiring a reputation as a rather cold character, not really interested in sex. There were such people, whose interest in some intellectual pursuit or physical skill or even in business or politics left no time or energy for human intimacy. It was a respectable, if not respected, way of life—not admired so much as wondered at.

She had no desire to be one of them, but there were times when she feared she was. Surely if she were normal, and her desires as urgent as most people's seemed to be, she'd have broken through the awkwardness of the situation, risked rejection and embarrassment and even their existing friendship, just for the sake of grabbing him for once, of surprising him with one hot honest word or thirsty kiss.

She heard Salasso's quick, light step in the corridor and hurriedly composed her expression, looking up with a smile as the saur came in.

"Good morning," he said. He fingered his lab coat from the hook and put it on, oblivious as always to how comical it looked: too long for his height, too short for his arms, too loose for his torso. He reached for the kettle and set it to boil, crumbling a fish bouillon cube into a mug. "You're in early."

"I wanted to think over what we've been doing."

It was hard to make out where he was looking, the corners of his eyes went around so far. He poured the water and stirred.

"Hmm. Ahh, that's better." Salasso sipped the stock and visibly relaxed. His species had a taste for fish, and a distaste for fishing. The arrival of humans on Mingulay had moved fish and fish products from a rare shore-caught luxury to a staple in the saur diet. Nothing could shift their dislike of the sea and fear of deepwater fishing. As far as Elizabeth knew, Salasso was the first saur anyone had ever heard of who so much as set foot on a boat. It didn't seem to bother him at all.

"Yes, we may expect visitors today," he went on. "Is that why you have dressed differently?"

Under her lab coat she was wearing a white high-necked silk blouse and a black linen skirt to midcalf, with dark stockings and light leather shoes. Salasso had never before given the slightest indication of noticing anyone's clothes.

"Yes, that's it," she said. "To look smart for the trader." *And in front of his daughter.* "You never know, he could be thinking of investing."

"Or be willing to share knowledge," said the saur, rather primly. "We have much to learn about the oceans of the other worlds."

"There is that," she said listlessly.

Salasso's head rocked a little. He might have been insensitive to the nuances of human facial expressions but he was quick to pick up tones of voice.

"You are troubled," he said.

"It's nothing I can explain."

"You mean you would not expect me to understand. I think I would." The saur's huge eyes looked down at the floor for a moment, then back at her. "We have such troubles ourselves. But they are more long-lasting."

She stared. This was the closest the saur had ever come to a statement about his personal life, or about relationships within his species.

Then his narrow shoulders shrugged, and he added, "Perhaps that makes it too different to discuss with profit."

Before she could think of anything more to say, the outside door banged open and voices, then footsteps, approached. Gregor opened the lab's spring-loaded door and held it while the trader and his daughter walked in past him. They wore jackets and jumpers and jeans, as though just off a boat. The sight of how Lydia carried this off made Elizabeth feel simultaneously dowdy and overdressed.

De Tenebre's broad freckled face smiled, his voice boomed.

"Good morning," he said, sticking out a hand. "I believe we met at the party."

"How do you do."

"And this is my daughter, Lydia. I don't believe you've been introduced. Elizabeth Harkness."

Good memory for names. She shook Lydia's hand as lightly as possible. At the same time de Tenebre said, or sang, something that made Salasso almost bound forward and bow over his hand, with a response that sounded like the same word/tones, but faster. After a further such exchange, Salasso nodded and said, "I'm honored to meet you."

"And I you."

Looking pleased with himself at his polyglot tour de force, the trader stepped back a little and looked up at the drawings on the walls and around at the tanks and trays and equipment.

"Interesting," he said. "Fascinating. I've seen something like this back home. . . ." He sucked a lip and snapped his fingers a few times. "Ah yes, the Maritime Museum! Remember it, Lydia?"

"Oh yes," she said. "You took me there when I was small. There was this huge glass case, and inside it was a copy of the brain and nervous system of a kraken, done in black glass. It *did* look like that drawing, but bigger."

"Gods above," said Salasso, "somebody had dissected a *Teuthys*?"

"I believe it was a dead one, washed up on a beach," said de Tenebre, still gazing around. "The scientists managed to preserve it before it had time to decay, and later dissolved it in some fluid that left the nerves and brain intact, and dyed them, and made a resin cast, and then drew out a model in glass. Most ingenious technique. That was a few hundred years ago even then, of course."

"Of course," Elizabeth echoed, unimpressed. "And what did they learn from it?"

"Oh, nothing much, dear lady. Very much a natural-history approach back then. Observation and speculation. The experimental method hadn't yet quite caught on. Still . . ."

His smile traveled from Elizabeth to Lydia. "It gave my little girl an interest in natural history which she still keeps up."

I bet she does, Elizabeth thought. *I bet she collects* butterflies, *and* flowers, *and* feathers*!*

"It *was* interesting," said Lydia. "That enormous, complicated brain, so different from our own, with its nerve-trunks thick as ropes, like roots sprouting from a bole. Of course the museum was absolutely stacked with interesting creatures, but," she laughed, "it was the brain that made me think."

"What did it make you think about?" It was all she could do to keep the poison out of her voice.

"Languages," said Lydia. "Is the cephalopod mode of communication via chromatophore display something intrinsic to their neural anatomy? Does it vary within the species like human languages? Is it abstractly symbolic or is it fundamentally ideographic and quasi-pictorial? How is translation possible between it and the verbal and gestural languages of hominids and saurs? That sort of thing."

"Ah." This minimally communicative noise was all Elizabeth could come out with.

"Profound questions," said Salasso. "Our approach to such problems is modest and, as your father suggests, experimental."

"Surely *you're* not cutting up krakens?" de Tenebre asked.

"Gods, no," said Gregor, touching Lydia's elbow and urging her in the direction of a lab bench. "We cut up innocent little squids."

"Aha!" said de Tenebre. "On the hypothesis of common descent! Well, you could say it's a start."

"You could," said Salasso. There was some taut vibration in his tone. "But . . . common descent is not a *hypothesis*. It is an observation."

De Tenebre had started to amble along the side of the room, looking up at the diagrams like a visitor in an art gallery who knows what he likes.

"To your species, perhaps, Salasso," he bantered. "To mine, however, it will remain a hypothesis until we start living as long as you do."

Salasso gave a tinny peal of saur laughter—whether out of genuine amusement or obsequiousness, Elizabeth couldn't tell. Amusement, she guessed. Flattery was not a saur vice. Salasso joined the trader and began earnestly pointing out salient or problematic features of the neural mapping. Gregor and Lydia were already leaning over a preparation on the bench, heads almost touching, talking quietly.

Elizabeth was reminded of how she and Gregor had met. In an undergraduate laboratory demonstration, where the students were randomly assigned in pairs to carry out a classic exercise: the dogfish cranial dissection. The fish stank dreadfully, you had to use great dollops of skin cream and wear rubber gloves if you didn't want to smell of dead shark for a week. The guy beside her had gallantly volunteered to do the actual cutting, letting her concentrate on sketching the brain and optic nerves and eyeballs which were the object of the exercise. She remembered his big fingers gripping the scalpel, the precise and confident way he'd slit through the cartilaginous skull and laid it open, his knowledgeable comments. This wasn't the first dogfish he'd had a good look at: he'd cut them up—for bait, and for curiosity—on the deck of his father's boat.

They'd barely looked at each other—well, he'd barely looked at her, and, after the first few sidelong glances, she'd hardly dared look at him—and that apparent, outward-directed, easy camaraderie had set the tone for their relationship ever since.

She walked briskly to another bench and set to work recalibrating an electrode reader, a tedious, finicky job that had to be repeated every morning, because of overnight changes in temperature and humidity. It absorbed her, letting her tune out Gregor and Lydia's lighthearted chat. The saur and the trader continued their sightseeing stroll around the lab; she could overhear their conversation slide back and forth between English and Trade Latin, and fragments of the saurian speech. She wasn't offended that de Tenebre had chosen Salasso to speak for the team's work; the saur's superior intelligence and honesty would make him, as any trader as experienced as this one was sure to know, unlikely to bullshit. (Salasso had once explained to her, with perfect aplomb, that the qualities of intelligence and honesty were linked: with sufficient intelligence one could see the ramifying consequences of a lie, the sheer cost in mental processing-power of sustaining it, and draw back from it. "Perhaps this relationship does not hold for the hominidae," he'd added, with wounding tact.)

A silence made her look up. The trader stood on his own at the front like a lecturer, Salasso off to one side, Lydia and Gregor still sitting together.

"Well, my friends," de Tenebre began, "this has been most interesting. Fascinating. I have to say it's the most advanced biological research I've come across. I'm sure your ancestors surpassed it, but mine never did. Nor have my contemporaries." He smiled disarmingly. "Unless the academies of Nova Babylonia have shaken up their approach in the past century, of course!"

He stalked to a table and propped himself on the edge of it, leaning forward confidentially.

"Now, I'm a practical man, and I have no idea what practical use this research might serve. But I have no doubt that by the time I return here, some useful applications—in medicine, in industry, in the gods-know-what—will have come out of it. Possibly even in calculating—I understand that the Cosmonaut the lord Cairns is interested in something he calls 'neural nets,' and has been encouraging your work to that end."

Gregor glanced back over his shoulder at Elizabeth, raising his eyebrows for half a second. She allowed herself an almost imperceptible shrug and shake of the head. Salasso, she noticed, had chosen this moment to gaze out of the window.

If de Tenebre observed this brief byplay he gave no sign of it, continuing: "It doesn't matter. What matters is that there'll be money to be made from it, and I'd be delighted to put some money into it now for some share in the returns later."

"Thank you," Elizabeth said, before anyone else could speak. "We would be very interested in that. I believe the next step would be to discuss your proposed investment with the syndics."

Salasso nodded vigorously; Gregor turned around again, still looking puzzled, but pleased. Then he turned back and thanked the trader for his confidence.

"Good," said de Tenebre. "Naturally there are details to be worked out, questions of intellectual property—information wants to be paid, and so forth. And you'll want to ensure that you and your successors don't have their hands tied, about what lines of research to pursue." He held up his hands, palms open. "None of that should be a problem—I really want and expect both sides to benefit. My legal adviser has a standard contract, and we've never had any complaints."

"That's all absolutely fine by us," Gregor said, sounding cautious. "We'd like to be involved in any discussion, as well."

"Of course. But, seriously, if we draw it up properly none of this will affect what you do—you'll just have more resources to do it with, and in a hundred years you or your successors will be paying me a very reasonable portion of whatever gains may be made from it."

Gregor stood up and shook de Tenebre's hand; Salasso and, after a moment, Elizabeth did the same.

"Great, great," said the trader. He took a watch from his pocket and glanced at it. "Well, I'm sure you have work to do—and so have I. Some of my servants are busy up at the university, buying large quantities of books and instruments. We're moving on the day after tomorrow, down to New Lisbon—turns out the meat market's earlier than usual this year. I'll see my adviser this evening, and—"

Lydia sprang up from her seat at the bench, with a loud sob and a sniff, and ran from the room.

"Excuse me," said Gregor, and disappeared after her.

De Tenebre stood looking at the swinging door for a few seconds. Then, flushed and frowning, he stalked out.

Gregor found her outside the main door, facing into a niche in the rough-cast wall, her arm across her eyes.

He put his arm around her shoulder and turned her around. She buried her tear-streaked face in his shoulder and shook for a minute.

"I knew we didn't have much time," she said, muffled and sniffling, "but this isn't *fair*."

He heard the door open, and her father's heavy, hurrying footsteps stop behind him.

"Oh, in the name of Zeus!" said de Tenebre. "Please. Lydia. Stop crying and come and sit down and let's talk about . . . whatever this is about."

Outside the lab-blocks was an area of bolted-down wooden tables and benches, facing the shore, buffeted by swirls of air where the prevailing wind hit the walls and so barely used for its intended purpose of open-air eating. They made their way to a table, Gregor and Lydia sitting at one side and de Tenebre diagonally across from them. At length the girl's shoulders stopped shuddering and she leaned forward, elbows on the table, propping her face and staring at her father.

"We *can't* just leave in two days!" she said.

He scratched the back of his neck.

"I'm sorry," he said. "I can see what's happened. I can't say I really blame either of you. I'm a reasonable man, and I do have your interests at heart. Especially you, Lydia, you're my daughter. I wouldn't do anything to hurt you, you know that." He gave Gregor a dark look. "And I won't *let* anyone hurt you either. I hope this man has not been giving—or taking—any promises."

"No!" they both said, in indignant unison.

The merchant let out a long sigh. "Well, that's not so bad. Hearts mend but words don't, eh?"

The flippant, philistine saying shocked Gregor. He tried to hold back his temper, which he knew would do nobody any good. By this time Lydia had an arm around him, too, and was holding tight. It emboldened him to speak.

"I love her," he said. "I could love her forever."

Lydia's arm tightened around him, and she smiled at him.

"No doubt you feel that way," said de Tenebre, with a sort of cool sympathy. "And believe me, I understand. But—I can't let that affect my actions. We *must* leave." He sighed. "And I have other appointments today."

The early sun slanted across them, the breeze off the sea tugged at them. Not far across the water, the great ship's fields crackled and hummed. Lydia looked down, flicked flakes of pebble-dash from her sleeve, scowled and sniffed.

"Couldn't I stay for a while?" she said. "I could join you in New Lisbon. They have air transport here, after all!"

"Oh, Lydia," said her father, with a mixture of impatience and tenderness. "I wouldn't trust one of these gasbags or kites with a servant, let alone with you. Leaving aside accidents, they're unreliable and unpunctual."

It was true, and Gregor knew he couldn't object.

"I'll come with you," he said.

De Tenebre rocked back and snorted. "For three weeks of trailing around after us? I can think of no better way of prolonging your pain—and Lydia's."

"No," said Gregor, suddenly dizzy with decision. "I meant—"

De Tenebre raised a hand, shook his head.

"No!" he barked. "I will not hear of it. I will not let you say it. Traveling is no life for someone not born to it, and certainly not for you. You have another calling, man. Do not disdain the gifts the gods have given you. And they have not given you my daughter . . ."

He paused, frowning in thought.

". . . or if they have," he continued, "it will be through your own work and your own gifts that you will win her."

Gregor squeezed his eyes shut for a few seconds. He was afraid that at any moment he might start weeping worse than Lydia had. Gradually the trader's words sank in. He looked up at him.

"What do you mean by that?" he asked.

De Tenebre stood up and leaned forward on his knuckles.

"We intend to stay on Croatan for half a year. I can leave you a schedule of our route thereafter, every port of call all the way back to Nova Terra. Your chief, the lord Driver, has told me about your family's Great Work. The lord Cairns your grandfather has confirmed it. They have high hopes in you. If you fulfill them, you can come after us yourself, and meet Lydia again within a few months or a few years of your life and even less time in hers. Bring me a ship. If you do that, Gregor Cairns, you can take my daughter, and I will be forever in your debt."

Gregor felt Lydia's arm fall away. The world became, for a moment, black-and-white and filled with white noise. He took some deep breaths. His first thought was outrage at this challenge, this offer to *trade* Lydia for a ship, or for shipping. Then—

Thoughts tumbled, *click-click-click,* like logic gates. If Hal

Driver and James Cairns had told the merchant the Great Work could be completed in some feasible time—then that explained James's new urgency about it, and at the same time made it difficult to dismiss de Tenebre's suggestion as unreasonable. And if James was interested in the team's research as having something to contribute to calculation, something to do with neural nets, then there was some connection between what they'd been doing and the Great Work—

A chill went through him as he realized what that connection might be. It unfolded before his eyes, the map of the squid nervous system overlaying the data structures of the navigation problem. He understood the architecture of the mind that could understand the problem, and in so doing he understood it himself. He could see, in principle, how the problem could be solved.

He blinked, and the world came back, in full color and high resolution. Lydia and her father were looking at him very oddly.

"I'm surprised to see you look so pleased," said de Tenebre. He straightened up and took a step back. "And encouraged. I was afraid your seniors were bluffing to drive a bargain."

A bargain—Gregor was struck by a further consequence of his train of thought. The deal the merchant had offered to the team would give him a share in all its future outcomes and applications— and if their research was connected to the Great Work, it would give him a share in the grand starship enterprises that James had outlined. A permanent say in all their futures, and in the future of Mingulay, which would thenceforth be tied to Nova Babylonia.

He swung his legs over the bench and stood up, facing the merchant.

"I'm not pleased at all," he said. "I make you no promises, and I don't accept your offer of your daughter because that's for her to decide." He moved behind Lydia, and laid the tips of his fingers gently on her shoulders. "She may be your daughter but her life is her own, not something to be traded between families. I love her too much for that. I knew from the beginning it was hopeless, but it's possible to love without hope."

Lydia reached a hand up and gripped his.

"You're right," Gregor went on, "that I can't and won't come with you. If Lydia feels about me as I feel about her, she'll stay here. If not . . . I'll do my best to come after you. But what Lydia does then, or now, is her choice. What *I'm* going to do now is go back to the lab and urge my colleagues to make sure that your offer to fund our team is politely turned down."

Lydia's grip on his fingers was beginning to hurt.

Then she let go, and scrambled up from the table and stood looking at him, her eyes wet.

"No!" she said. "You don't understand! Coming for me in a ship of your own is how it should be! When my father said that, I felt for the first time some hope for us! You must do it! You must achieve something of your own to win a woman, that's how it is with us. I wouldn't feel traded at all! If you love me, you'll do it!"

How different our worlds are, he thought. *And how alike.* She could have had his. She still could.

"I do love you," he said, and turned and walked away. He didn't look back, but he hoped with every step—across the yielding grass, and the crunching pebbles, and down the echoing tiled corridor to the lab—that Lydia would come running after him.

She didn't.

"It's going," said Elizabeth, from the lab window.

Gregor looked up from a table covered with sheets of paper. White paper and black ink, scrawled with shapes, speckled with numbers. He felt utterly dull, as he had for the past forty-eight hours. Unable to explain the reasons for his objection to the merchant's funding to anyone except James—who approved of it, and had hastily seen the syndics to confirm the objection—he was in bad favor with his team, and with the department. Everyone thought there was something of a scandal behind it, some offense given or taken, something of a cloud.

But still, lured by the primitive primate urge for visual stimulation, he made himself stand up and walk to the window. Another sunny, blustery day. The last of the skiffs were swooping and darting into the bays in the starship's hull, like seabats to their roosts on a cliff. The lighters and sightseeing craft, and the little humming airplanes, were standing or circling well off.

The ship's sides ran with colored lights that scribed names and logos, flags and symbols. The bays and hatches sealed without leaving a seam. Around it, the water bent away from beneath it, until it was obviously not floating but hanging a little above a vast, shallow depression. It began to rise slowly. St. Elmo's fire crackled on masts a mile away. The meniscus of water rose up beneath it, until the sea bulged a fathom above sea level.

Then the water slumped back, setting a swell racing out to rock the distant boats, and the ship rose faster as though released. It began to move forward as it continued to accelerate up, and within a minute was lost from sight in the shining unfathomable blue of the sky.

Gregor realized he was craning to watch, his cheek pressed to the pane. He came down off his toes and took a step backward and turned his back on the horizon. Elizabeth and Salasso faced him, the saur with no discernible expression, the woman with a tentative smile.

"Well, that's it," he said. "They're gone."

At that moment emotion returned to him, flooding his veins and nerves with singing relief. The pain of parting from Lydia, and the pain of not knowing for sure what that parting meant, broke the grip of his anhedonic depression. He felt so much the better for it that he smiled.

Lydia was gone, but he still had friends, and he still had work, and it was suddenly obvious how his friends and his work could yet let him see Lydia again.

"Yes, well..." Elizabeth was saying. Gregor stepped forward and caught her by the shoulders, grinning. She almost recoiled, but her smile broadened.

"I have something to tell you," he said. Her shoulders, under the rough wool of the jersey, were quivering in a way that reminded him painfully of how Lydia's shoulders had felt. He let go with one hand and clapped the saur's shoulder too. "It's about starship navigation."

"Oh," said Elizabeth. Her face fell for a fleeting moment, and then she looked away and looked back at him, interested. "So, don't keep us in suspense."

But keep them in suspense he did, all the long walk to the castle and through its corridors and stairs. Carrying the papers he'd been working on rolled up under his arm, he marched to the Navigator's room. It was unoccupied.

He waved a hand at the sofa. "Make yourselves comfortable— uh, not on that bit, some coffee got spilt."

Elizabeth perched on an arm of the couch, Salasso found some space that was neither stained nor loaded with books and files, then put his hands behind his head and leaned back with his legs stretched out—a human posture he'd picked up, but one which his height, or lack of it, didn't help to carry off.

"So tell us," he said.

"Our family has over the generations been working on a navigational problem," Gregor said. "That much, I'm sure you know. It's no secret. What I've realized is that the actual solution to this problem requires a non-human mind, specifically a squid mind, and that our research in cephalopod neurology can contribute to simulating such a mind—in its barest outlines, of course, but it's the outline, the structure, the *architecture,* if you will, that counts."

Salasso had jerked out of his laid-back pose and now leaned forward, tense.

"I see, I see," he said. "The electrical potentials, the gross and fine anatomy, yes! Yes! But how would you simulate it?"

"In a calculating-machine, of course," said Gregor. "The brain is a computer, and any computer can simulate any other computer."

Elizabeth looked around at the calculating-machines.

"In *these* heaps of mechanical junk?"

"If necessary," Gregor said. "Yes. But I hope, with them and many more, working in parallel."

"It would still take forever."

Gregor's eyes narrowed. "Oh, you know that?"

"Well, I can give you an educated guess!"

Gregor jumped up. "I can see it all in my head, I can see how it could be done. The structure of the problem and the structure of the brain match so exactly it's uncanny, it's like they were made for each other."

He realized what he'd just said, and added:

"Perhaps they were."

Salasso said nothing, but it seemed his lips became, if that were possible, thinner.

"But you're right," Gregor went on. "In theory, yes, one computer can simulate another. But it's just not possible to do it quickly, without far better computers than we've got." His fists clenched. "Now, if we still had the computers the first crew brought from the ship . . ."

"That might be possible," said Salasso.

10

Launch on Warning

S OMEBODY WAS SHAKING my shoulder. I struggled up from a
deep midday doze to find myself sitting on the sofa in Alan's
office. Alan was looking down at me with a concerned expression.

"Sorry," I said. "Didn't mean to—"

"That's all right, you've just had a few tough days catch up with
you," Alan said. "We'd've let you sleep, only—"

He gestured at the wall, and with that wave of his hand the
posters cleared and reconfigured to a patchwork of news-screens.
Most of them showed the same face: Jadey's. I jolted into wake-
fulness.

The picture was recent—no, it was live, the camera tracking her
grim face as she was escorted by two women police officers from
the Sheriff Court in Edinburgh to a police van. I caught passing
phrases. "Remanded in custody." "Extradition hearing."

"Extradition?"

"To the F-U-K," said Mary-Jo, spelling it out viciously. "Down
there she's been charged with the murder of a Russki officer they
say she was having an affair with."

"That's a fucking lie!"

"One would assume so," Alan said, "from first principles. But
how do you know?"

I told them. Mary-Jo's finger's tapped on air all the while.

"Right, right," she said when I'd finished. "Assuming she told
you the truth, and I think she did; it explains why they have a
sample of clothing with that poor son of bitch's blood and her skin
cells. And a bloody knife with no goddamn prints or anything. And
even if your ware didn't work, and the whole thing was taped, there
could still be evidence that there'd been a hack-attack on the street

cameras, which would make any record showing what *actually* happened inadmissible. Shit."

"It gets worse," Alan said in a flat tone. He dug a couple of layers deeper in the news, to the detail behind the headlines. At this level it was practically raw court transcript—nobody'd bothered to summarize this uninteresting minor detail about a mere Brit—and all that leapt out at me was my name and a lot of pictures of me, mostly grainy surveillance grabs but recognizable enough.

"They want you," Mary-Jo translated from the legalese. "They're not sure yet whether they want to subpoena you as a witness or extradite you as an accomplice after the fact. Whichever—the U.S. government is quite likely to cooperate, and even if it doesn't stand up in the courts you're looking at a long legal hassle at best. At worst the INS will have your ass on a plane back to the commies before you can say 'refugee.' "

"Wait a minute," I said, trying to stop a pebble in the landslide of bad news, "I thought people from Europe had automatic refugee status, or something."

"Nah." She shook her head. "It's all de facto. They turn a blind eye, and that's, you know, policy—to waive the immigration controls—but the laws are still on the books. It's a privilege, not a right, and it can be withdrawn at any time and only challenged in court after the fact. Legally you're still an illegal immigrant."

"All right." I sank back in the sofa, feeling drained. "I can handle that. What about Jadey?"

"Excuse me," Mary-Jo said, "but you *can't* handle that. Jadey's situation, we *can* handle. It's what we *do*. No matter what charges they stick on her, it's still political, we can still do deals. It's not like you guys have an independent judiciary or shit. Whereas over here, we do, more or less. Your problem *here* is a bunch of extralegal—official and freelance—people who might come after you. Hell, any of the camo dudes on the gate here might decide to make a bit on the side by turning you in. You don't want to be either administratively dealt with *or* stuck in the courts, believe me."

She stood up and strolled to the window, as though watching out for the camo dudes or the black helicopters. "Y'know," she said, "your credibility as an E.U. citizen who's an oppositionist has just gone off the scale. You could really talk to the mutineers out there. And you are in deep shit here on Earth."

She turned to with me a speculative grin. "Still think going into space is a crazy idea?"

"Yes," I said. I had given them a lengthy piece of my mind on this subject as soon as the suggestion had come up. "But—"

"Good man!" said Alan. "I knew you'd come around."

"That's a *spaceship*?"

I was used to seeing launch pictures from Baikonur, from Kourou, and for that matter from Canaveral. Even with single-stage–to–orbit, flea-on-a-griddle liftoff they resembled everything back to the V2 in their vertical ascent. This black object, out in the glare of the sun on the bitter flat ground, resembled nothing. It looked more alien than any real or imagined flying saucer. It was like a sculpture of some animal native to the vacuum. Just trying to get a perspective on the thing, to form an image of it as a whole, was making my eyes water and my head hurt.

"Nevada Orbital Dynamics SSTA," said Alan Armstrong. (That was his name, he'd finally admitted. He was only the chief engineer—notoriously modest, according to the info my spex were pulling down.) "Single Stage to Anywhere. It's a refinement of the old USAF Electro-Dynamic Stealth Fighter. Our famous flying saucer that the Russkis chewed up so many of in the war. This one can ionize the surrounding air and electromagnetically pulse it to reach escape velocity *in the atmosphere,* then generate its plasma sail and accelerate further. You could go to Pluto with it. I mean, you'd starve first, but your body could get there."

Plasma sail—I checked the ref, found screeds about the system, a vast electromagnetic field enclosing a spheroid of ionized gas that interacted with the solar photon flux like a lightsail. It could take us to the *Marshall Titov* in days, more than half of which time would be spent tacking and decelerating. Final course-corrections by fusion rocket.

"*Fusion?* So why don't you—"

"Use it for everything? It's expensive, that's why. That ship is worth billions of dollars."

I stared at him. "How do you expect to make that kind of money back?"

He shrugged. "The U.S. military is a bit burned-off with flying saucers," he admitted, "and the commercial space operators don't need anything like this—yet. We might flog it to NASA someday, if they ever get their act together, but for now this is blue-sky, foundation-funded stuff for the space exploration which we are certain will revive. More certain now than ever, come to think of it."

"Makes me wonder why we need to bother with alien tech," I said.

"Anti-gravity would be worth having," Armstrong said mildly. "Anyway, you're soon going to find out."

"Jeez." I felt cold inside. Already, trucks were rolling up, in a haze of dust and leaks of pressurized gases, to prep the thing for launch in a few hours.

"Bear in mind that it can get you back just as fast," Alan said. "It's not like you're leaving Earth for months, or anything."

I should have known what to expect when the medical included a few minutes of squirming through a long, narrow, dark pipe, with sensors checking my signs to make very sure I didn't suffer from claustrophobia. It was never something I'd thought about before. The mission psychologist said I would have made a very good cave-diver. I told him I'd bear it in mind if I ever wanted to take up safer hobbies.

The gel-packed g-suit was state-of-the-art. What one wore underneath was a sort of skintight, soft combination garment, and what one wore under that—

"Why the diaper?" I asked indignantly.

"In case this pill doesn't work."

"Can I take two?"

I was told to keep my spex on, and provided with a new, American-made palm computer onto which all my AIs and systems-management programs had been downloaded. It, along with the wet-tech reader and the datadisk, went into pockets on my thigh.

The pilot was called Camila Hernandez. She was several inches shorter and years younger than myself, and I hesitate to estimate how many kilos lighter. Her face might have been pretty if it hadn't been so thin, almost anorexic, and if her hair hadn't been buzz-cut to a five-millimeter fuzz. She shook my hand as we sat facing each other on the back of a trailer that trundled us out to the ship. Beyond that she didn't have much to say. She had a look of fierce concentration and I guessed she was fingering some rosary of flight-checks in her mind, so I kept quiet.

The ship, *Blasphemous Geometries,* was about two meters deep in the center. The entrance hatch was at the center. The cockpit wasn't. Camila climbed in and I followed, to find myself squirming along a long, dark, narrow tube. I emerged in a space less than a meter deep and two meters long and a little under two meters wide. Camila was already lying prone on the couch on the right. I pulled myself up on the one beside her, and at the far end stuck my head into a bubble helmet, which sealed itself around my neck. Behind me, I could hear hoses and nozzles snake out and snick onto my suit.

In front of the bubble helmet, curving around in front of and above and below the two of us, was what looked like a bubble window. There definitely hadn't been a window visible from the outside, so this had to be some scaled-up version of spex, but the illusion of having my head up at the leading edge of the craft was perfect. Above, the blue sky; below, the dusty ground, the technicians going about their final tasks; ahead, the shimmering heat haze and mirage of Groom Lake, the craft's shadow stretching ahead of us in the late-afternoon sun.

Camila's hands rested in front of her head on a control panel. The control panel in front of me was covered with a plastic lid, sealed down; I rested my forearms on it and looked ahead. I absurdly thought of Superman's flying pose, and stifled a nervous chuckle.

"You all right?"

"Yeah, I'm fine."

"Good. Shock-gel deploying."

Camila slid back a bolt. With a loud hiss the space around our legs and torsos filled with some kind of foam which set instantly to a rubbery texture that yielded just enough to make it possible to breathe. It pressed hard against my feet and legs and around my midriff.

"Deployed," she said. Then, in a different tone: "*Blasphemous Geometries,* ready to roll!"

The sound of something disengaging, and a siren outside that brayed for a good two minutes. The air in front of us began to crackle and warp; a deep hum came through the soles of my feet and up through my legs, setting each bone and then each tooth resonating at a separate frequency. With it rose a feeling of tension and oppression and the uncanny sensation that my arms and legs were being tugged and stretched.

The ship began to move, slowly at first, dust and glowing flecks streaming around the curved viewplate, the ground flicking past beneath us, faster and faster until it was a blur of straight lines. I looked up. The mountains surrounding the salt-pan approached in a terrible rush, and then—

—dropped away.

The view around us reddened, then cleared—I guessed the viewplate was correcting innumerable wild distortions and refractions. Despite the gel-suit and the shock-gel, I felt as though my weight were increasing so fast that my bones would crack. Every joint ached. Below, the landscape passed like a panning shot, then it became as blurred as the runway had been, only slowing a little as we climbed. In a shockingly short time we were above the Atlantic; and shortly thereafter, above the atmosphere.

I didn't have much time to appreciate the blue view of Earth. The acceleration dropped, ended, and then, just as my bones were creeping back to their full length, returned, milder but more insistent. Around the craft something bloomed like neon, then faded from view as the correction software reacted like an iris adjustment. Earth's horizon, too, rushed upon us and dropped away.

I stared at space and stars in a sky that went all around.

"That's it for now," said Camila, in a more relaxed voice than I'd heard from her before. "Want to see how we looked from the ground?"

"Sure," I said, reluctant to disengage my view of the stars.

She tabbed a few keys and part of the viewplate right in front of us opaqued and showed, somewhat disorientingly, a band of blue sky. Along that band hurtled an accelerating red fireball; and then, in jerky succession, the view cut to ever-briefer glimpses of our ever-tinier bolide streak across increasingly dark skies.

"Twenty-seven missile station alert-status upgrades," she read off from somewhere, "and two hundred and eighty UFO incident reports logged to date. Not bad."

"What do we look like now?" I asked.

She gave me a sideways glance, doubly distorted by our two goldfish bowls. "Um," she said, "didn't want to worry you, you know? But since you ask, because we have thousands of cubic kilometers of ionized gas around us we're, uh, naked-eye–visible. . . ."

A nighttime view, looking up. According to the Cyrillics scrolling along the bottom it was a patch from a local station in Minsk doing an outside broadcast follow-up of a UFO report or war scare. Above a ragged horizon of new-tech housing-pylons we shone plainly, a bright star.

I never heard the proximity alarm, which was for the pilot's ear. The first I knew was when Camila turned to me and asked urgently: "Matt—are you religious?"

"No," I said, baffled by the question.

"Okay," she said. "Holy Mary, Mother of God, pray for us sinners now and at the hour of our death. Amen." Then, in a different tone: "Right, this is where it gets tedious."

Her fingers played over the control board faster than touch-typing. I immediately, with a mercifully apt reflex, clasped my hands across the back of the helmet and pressed it down as hard as I could into the yielding surface of the gel-couch. The viewplate went black. A moment later we were slammed sideways. It was the first of many such buffetings, giddy moments of free fall followed by brutal bursts of acceleration in unpredictable directions. It actually did get tedious, like a roller-coaster ride that goes on far too long, repeating its thrills to the point where they merge into a continuous dull fear and a wish that you could get *off*.

After what seemed like a long time but, according to my clock in the spex, was only about an hour, the violent motions stopped. All the time the forward acceleration had built up—still nowhere near one gravity, but very noticeable.

"We've outrun them," Camila said. "Every nearby burst gives us more gas and more flux, and lets us run faster. Real neat." She grinned across at me, sweat drying on her face. "Really *soaks up* laser strikes too," she added, worryingly.

I felt absurdly apologetic.

"I had no idea the EPAF would try to shoot us down."

She laughed. "That was friendly fire, bro. Our side. USAF Orbital Defense."

"*What?*"

"Not surprising. Unauthorized launch, overflying E.U. territory—

they had to do *something* to convince the commies we weren't about to nuke 'em. Other politics as well, I guess. The Feds are really worried about freelancers taking advantage of the shake-ups in the E.U. defense and security apparats to start something." Her grin became feral. "Bring down the whole stinking commie edifice."

"God, you sound like Jadey," I said. The thought of her returned like an injury that hadn't hurt as long as the fight continued.

"Jadey Ericson? You mean you *know* her? Wow! Tell me all about it!"

"Shouldn't you be flying this thing?"

"For the next couple of days it flies itself, until I have to start tacking." She frowned. "Now, *that* gets tedious. In the meantime there's nothing to do. We can take our helmets off now, by the way. Twist it *so*—right, then left."

We both breathed deeply, in air that was indistinguishable from what we'd had in the helmets, except perhaps for the faint reassurance of each other's human smell.

"Well, here we are. We can suck glop out of these tubes, water out of that. We can piss, but we can't shit. We can sleep." She jerked a thumb. "That stuff stays around us until we dock. Might as well be in a fucking plaster cast. Best not think about it, huh?" She brightened. "But we can talk. And we can follow the news— we're getting a laser feed, if you want to check your spex you'll see it all." She sucked water. "Talk to me or I'll go bugfuck crazy."

"Or I will." I wanted to see the breaking news, but I knew what she meant.

I told her my adventures, leaving out only the nature of the information I was carrying.

"What I don't get," she said when I'd finished, staring out at the unchanging view of the stars—no speed of ours could change them visibly—"is how you guys *live* with it. All that corruption and controls and shit."

"It's not so bad," I said. "The state's a bit heavier than in America, sure, but let's face it, it does get more things done. More education, less pollution, no beggars . . ." I laughed. "And space exploration—let's not forget space exploration!"

"But the *Party!*" she said. "How can you stand that? I mean, nobody believes in Communism anymore, not even the commies."

"Oh yes they do," I said. "They just don't call it that. They call it 'the sustainable society.' What economists used to call the stationary state. And they think they're getting us there, and that everybody will get there in the end, even the Americans."

"Never!" Camila said. "Maybe the East Coast liberals might go for that, but not the rest of us."

I sighed. "It's got nothing to do with what anybody *believes* in. The falling rate of profit will get you in the end. You can evade it for a while by exporting capital, and follow that falling rate like a star sinking on the horizon, which by following fast enough you can raise for a while, but all that gets you is a fully capitalist—and fully capitalized—world, with low profit rates everywhere, and then there's nowhere else to go but the steady state, an economy just quietly ticking over rather than expanding. In the steady state it's easy for workers to end up employing capital—socialism, near as makes no difference."

She shot me a suspicious look.

"This is Marx, right?"

"Wrong," I said. "It's John Stuart Mill."

"Same difference," she said. "Bloody liberals." Moody silence, then: "Anyway, that's all rubbish because we have space to expand into, forever!"

"*What* expansion? There's no *profit* in space. Nobody's desperate enough to want to *live* there. That gang of libertarians who tried it couldn't stand it, couldn't stand each other—"

"Yeah, yeah," she said. "I know about Hell-Five. But in the long run—"

" 'In the long run,' " I said, quoting another suspect and defunct economist, " 'we are all *dead*.' "

Conversation kept us going for long stretches—we ended up knowing a lot about each other, like pillow-talking lovers—and between that, and sleep, and staring at the stars, there was the newsfeed.

Mary-Jo had exaggerated when she'd said that all hell was breaking loose in Red Europe. But there was no doubt that Driver's message had thrown a spanner in the works of the workers' states. The Party, the Federal Security Bureau, and the European Peoples' Army were maneuvering against each other in an unprecedentedly overt manner: military budgets queried, more MEPs and Party officials under suspicion or arrest, inquiries launched into FSB illegalities, rapid promotions and demotions and cashierings, military exercises proceeding without authorization, unscheduled call-ups of reservists (which, I guessed, added draft-evasion to my crimes).

At this rate it was only a matter of time before the populations, too, would have their say. Whether all hell really would break loose at that point was difficult to predict. Across Europe the peace movement, hitherto a moribund adjunct of official foreign policy, was already organizing mass demonstrations at which Webbly banners were well to the fore. That, at least, was something to count against the (also growing) "patriotic" anti-American demonstrations, which were, with brazen illegality, backed by factions of the Army. The ostensible occasion of these demonstrations was the constant drip of "discoveries" about U.S. links to the "English fascist terrorists" who'd been swept up after the codes had been cracked. Cameras tracked across incriminating caches of weapons.

"That's you guys' problem," Camila informed me confidently. "You're not allowed to have guns. That's why the Russkis walked all over you, and that's why you can't throw them out."

I stared at her, openmouthed.

"Where do you get that from?" I asked at last. "*Everybody* in Europe has guns. Since the revolution, anyway. The Russkis were shocked at the lack of preparedness when they came in, and they set about making damn sure it wouldn't happen again. Unless you're a conscientious objector—you know, a Quaker or something—it's *compulsory* to have a Markov and an AK and ammo at home. I was top of my class team in pistol shooting in *primary* school, I'll have you know. I did my one year's military service from the day after my eighteenth birthday. I could have kept up my training if I'd joined the CDR—Civil Defense and Resistance— but I never bothered. I'm still in the reserves, though."

It was her turn to stare. "So why don't you all just rise up and overthrow the commies?"

"Because hardly anybody bloody *wants* to, that's why! Look, the Party really does get elected! All we have to do is vote them out!"

Camila remained convinced it was all some kind of scam; that guns issued by the government didn't really count, and that elections with bans on rich people buying politicians couldn't be free.

Of Jadey there was no news at all.

·   ·   ·

"Oh-*kay*," said Camila, fifty hours after launch, "helmets on. Time to start work." She sounded much more eager than her earlier talk of tedium might have suggested. We were already far beyond the asteroid's orbital position, and about to start tacking—sunward again—to intersect it.

The viewplate went from black to white, with the sun—I swear—represented as an asterisk in the middle, the asteroid as a constantly changing string of numbers. It looked like one of those primitive ASCII games you find squirreled away, a programmers' in-joke, in the most obscure address-spaces of operating systems.

If the display was like a game, the actual approach it registered was another white-knuckle ride, more violent than the missile evasions. Camila exchanged clipped voice-only transmissions with the station between each abrupt change of course. It went on for hours and ended in free fall. With a flourish Camila toggled the viewplate control, and the asteroid sprang into full-color 3-D view, just as we'd all first seen it, as real as television. The station expanded in the view, its appearance changing from something tiny and intricate, like circuitry, to something huge and intricate, like a factory. At the same time, the general view shifted from traveling toward the asteroid to flying over it. The final fine adjustments became increasingly gentle, from the sensation of a jostling crowd, through a beggar's tug, to the suspicion of a pickpocket's pass.

With a last puff of the retro the *Blasphemous Geometries* settled into a clutch of grapples that clicked around the ship's edges. Banging and crunching noises followed.

"What's that?"

"Airlock connecting." She smiled. "Don't I get any thanks?"

I gave her a high-five. "Yeah, thanks!"

"Keep your helmet on for now," she said. She reached up for a switch. "Clearing shock-gel."

A bluish liquid sprayed in from nozzles at the sides of the viewplate, hosing our shoulders and—as the space cleared—other jets hissed on down our backs and sides. Camila pushed herself up, opening a space between herself and the couch, and I did likewise. The liquid shriveled the shock-gel to dry, rubbery strips, then evaporated in a flush of warm air.

"Wow." I waggled my legs, swiveled my pelvis. "That feels good."

The sudden physical freedom made me all the more anxious to escape the remaining restrictions. For the first time I actually did feel something like claustrophobia: the space around me was too small, and the air didn't satisfy my lungs.

We both looked as though covered with ragged bandages—the robot from the mummy's tomb. Camila brushed at the sticky rags of dried shock-gel. They hung annoyingly in the air, drifting.

"Extractor fan in the next model!"

Something clunked and made grinding noises. Camila cocked her head, listening to the voice in her ear.

"That's it," she reported. "Airlock sealed." She waved me past her. "You go first. I get to turn off the lights."

With fingertips and toes I propelled myself backward along the narrow tube to the hatch. Just before my feet touched it, its cover plate slid smoothly aside. Even in the suit and helmet, I could feel the change in pressure, and the draft. Light shone up from beneath, or behind, my feet. I continued on in a direction that now felt like "down," though not from any effect of the asteroid's microgravity, of which I felt nothing. Down, then: down past the locking rings and down another long but wider tube, and then out.

For a moment I hung there, hands braced in the exit of the tube, feet just above the metal mesh floor. The receiving-bay with which the ship had docked was large, about three meters high below the airlock tube, twenty long, and ten wide. Crates and bits of equipment were tethered or taped to stanchions and I-beams. Fluorescent lighting flickered over the garish color-coding. Across from me was a heavy door in front of which a small, crop-haired man in multiple-mission–patched cotton fatigues floated, holding on to a crossbeam with one hand, the other resting on the butt of a standard-issue 9-millimeter Aerospatiale Officier stuck in a webbed waistband.

He let go of the pistol and gestured to me to remove my helmet. I let go of the airlock rim and did so, beginning to tumble over in the air. Camila emerged from the shaft, and did the same with more grace.

The place stank: rank, organic stenches of human and plant and animal combined with the harsher reek of hot metal, burnt plastic, old machine-oil. I almost gagged; Camila just wrinkled her nose. The man favored us with a wry smile.

"You'll get used to it," he said. He stuck out his right hand, empty. "My name is Paul Lemieux. Welcome to the Revolution."

Even looking up at him, one hand holding the mesh of the floor where I'd drifted, I could grasp his meaning—if not, at that moment, his hand—and think:

Oh shit!

11

Manufacturing Plant

Here, at the top of the hill, the wind off the sea was una-
voidable and constant. It gave airplanes a little extra lift as
they bounded and jolted down the runway taking off, and permitted
a lower approach speed as they landed—also bounding and jolting.
If the pilot cut too close to stalling speed, when the wind dropped
so did the plane.

The wind moaned in the tall bamboo pylons, and made them
flex, and made the airships sway at their moorings like bait on a
trolling hook. Others, released from the moorings but tethered to
the ground, strained and rippled. Gangs of workers used ropes and
windlasses and main force to haul and steady the craft for the passengers and crew to get in or out. Tankers of water for ballast and
kerosene for fuel (the former conveniently doubling as fire engines)
hurried back and forth.

Gregor sat in the glassed-in waiting area and watched, fascinated
by everything he saw. He hadn't visited the airport since he was a
small boy, and it was somehow galling that all the exciting activity
he remembered from childhood had ever since been within such
easy reach.

Beside him sat Salasso, then Elizabeth—each, like him, with a
traveling-bag at their feet. Salasso's was small and made of something that looked like flexible aluminum; Gregor's was bulkier but
not much heavier, of dinosaur hide. Elizabeth's was a laminated
suitcase just within the weight limit. She had dressed rather well
for the flight, in blouse and skirt and long leather coat. Gregor and
the saur were in their usual working clothes, though in Gregor's
case, at his mother's insistence, freshly cleaned.

Elizabeth saw him looking, and smiled.

"This is just great!" she said. "What an amazing place, and so close."

"Just what I was thinking myself," he said. He grinned. "Maybe the people who work here never visit the port."

Salasso said nothing. His thin mouth was turned down at the corners, and his shoulders sagged. His eyelids blinked and his nictitating membrane flickered more than usual. His long fingers dug into his bony knees.

"Will somebody please fill me a pipe?" he said.

"You don't want to fall . . . asleep just now," Elizabeth chided.

"I do," said Salasso. "I wish I could. I wish you could *carry* me on board, unconscious. But I realize that would be undignified for all concerned. So please, fill me a pipe. I don't trust my own hands to do it, and I want to at least have it ready as soon as we board."

"Is smoking allowed? I wonder." Gregor asked, as Salasso passed him the pipe and pouch with a visibly shaking hand.

"Yes," said Salasso. "I checked that most carefully. Nothing but potent drugs could keep me calm through a journey on one of these devices."

"Ah, we should have hired a gravity skiff," said Gregor. "Now, why didn't I think of that?"

Salasso's eyes swiveled around, the pupil a deeper black within the black iris.

"*I* thought of that," he said. "But we couldn't afford the expense."

"To tell you the truth," said Gregor, "I never even imagined it was an option. Where can you hire them?"

"Oh, some saurs will do it, if you know who to ask. But usually only to other saurs. It is, as I said, expensive at the best of times, and at the moment it's completely out of the question because all the skiff owners on the planet are making a fortune down south, driving dinosaurs to the meat market."

"That must be quite a sight," Elizabeth said.

"It is. If a little distressing."

"They're just cattle," said Gregor. "*Big* cattle, yes."

Salasso shook his head. "I am not what your people would call sentimental," he said. "Few of my people are! But we all feel . . . some respect, some kinship, with the noble if ignorant beasts on which we prey. Needs must— We are a carnivorous kind, far more than you. But still—we were hunters before we were herders, and before that, we were hunted. We retain some of our past nature."

"And you're saying we retain less?"

Salasso leaned back. "I am not saying that."

A warning frown from Elizabeth stopped Gregor's impulse to pursue the matter further. It didn't stop him from turning it over in his mind. It was generally accepted—on what evidence, he wasn't sure—that the saurs had been civilized for millions if not tens of millions of years. Even allowing for their longer lives, and greater intelligence, there was something anomalous and disturbing in the suggestion that they retained some traditions from the savage state.

And for humans, Nova Babylonia represented continuity and antiquity! Even the Keep and the harbor, pre-human though they were, stood shallow in the depth of evolutionary time which for the saurs was *history*.

He finished filling the pipe and passed it back.

A bell sounded and a message flashed on the projection screen announcing the imminent departure of their flight. They picked up their bags and trekked out onto the field with the other fifty or so passengers, into the shadow of the hundred-meter-long semi-rigid dirigible. Salasso ascended the stairladder to the gondola without further demur, headed for the smoking section at the back, and had passed out before the craft had taken off.

"Well, so much for the supercivilized," Gregor remarked, after he and Elizabeth had stowed their bags and sat down on opposite sides of a window table a couple of rows forward of where Salasso sat slumped.

"I suppose to him it's like—I don't know—going out on the ocean on some ramshackle raft would be to us. And some humans have a fear of flying as well, you know."

The airship lurched and the floor tilted upward as the cable at the bow was released a second before that at the stern. Gregor grabbed the edge of the table, Elizabeth threw her arms across it. The engines roared to bring the craft to a level keel.

"Fear of flying, eh? Who'd have thought it?"

She laughed, and they both turned their attention to the view as the airship ascended. How broad the sprawl, how small the ships.

"Wow," said Elizabeth, "you can see our shadow."

"Where? . . . Oh, right." There it was, rippling across street and field and river like a black fluke, paced by the flashing glint of the sun on pool or mire. Then the coastline like a map; clouds from the side and from above.

But after the airship had reached its cruising altitude and had followed the coast southward for a while, even this fascination palled. Gregor and Elizabeth turned away from the window and settled down like seasoned travelers. Salasso was still sleeping off the effects of smoking an entire pipe by himself.

"Still keen?" Gregor asked.

"Oh yes. Should be interesting even if we don't find any of them. I mean, I know that would be disappointing for you, but . . ."

"Aye, I know what you mean." Gregor sighed, looking around the cabin. Most of the passengers seemed to be on business, and either drinking spirits in a rather forced attempt to relax, or toiling over sheets of paper and hand calculators.

"You know what this world needs?" he said. "A *Beagle* voyage. Somebody to sponsor some long-range travel just for exploration and sampling."

"And to come back with a theory of evolution?"

She smiled, he laughed.

"An account of it," Gregor said. "We already have the theory; what we need is a better idea of how it's gone, here. The planet's story."

Elizabeth looked down at the crawling coastline for a moment, then back at him.

"It would be difficult," she said. "How many incursions have there been? We can't even guess at the number of major deliberate introductions of species, let alone the accidents. I swear it must happen every time a starship comes in—"

She laughed suddenly.

"What?"

"I just remembered. Talking to a lighter skipper down in the Bailie's. He said that if you get to one of the ships up close you can see *barnacles* on them."

"Tough little critters, barnacles."

"Uh-huh. But these must be able to survive at least hours, sometimes days, in *space*."

"Vacuum barnacles!"

She nodded. "There you go, that's one new species right there. And I bet they've spread here."

"Okay," he said. "We'll call the ship the *Barnacle,* and get it sponsored by a manufacturer of anti-fouling paint."

She rubbed an eye. "I think that's a saur product, actually. But, yeah, something like that. Shipowners. Fishermen."

"Hey, don't look at me. My father isn't much of a one for pure research."

"How about the castle?"

"They've got enough on their plate with the Great Work."

They'd continued the conversation without taking it seriously up to this point.

"What?"

"If we succeed," Gregor said, "the Great Work will be done. Over. And the castle, the crew, and the families will be rich. So they might well have more money to throw into research."

He looked out, and down. The coastline had swung inward, and they were now crossing the east-west leg of the L-shaped stretch of ocean, Cargill's Sound, that divided the northwestern subcontinent from its larger neighbor. Mainland was saur country, dinosaur country.

"You know, I could get excited about that," he said. "To sail around the world just to *find out more* about the place."

"That would be wonderful," Elizabeth said, in an uncharacteristically dreamy tone.

"Even if we never did get the planet's story straight?"

"Yeah, even then."

She didn't seem to want to talk any further, hauling down a book from her coat pocket. Gregor looked out of the window for another while, then decided to emulate the business travelers by doing some work.

Paper was the heaviest part of his luggage. He tugged out a double handful of notes, fingered a pen from an inside pocket and began going over them again. They represented the best part of a week's work by him and his companions. How much previous work lay behind it, he hardly dared to fathom. Even then, it was probably inadequate. *If* they tracked down one or more of the original crew, and *if* they still had their hands on some still-functioning hard-tech (as Salasso had claimed), and *if* they were willing to share and cooperate—then *maybe* the figures and data structures summarized here might be the basis for the outline of the model he'd imagined. And even then, the navigation problem itself would have to be formulated and formatted appropriately before it could be entered.

If, indeed, it could. His ideas of the capability of these ancient machines were based on little more than family legend. Even if the most enthusiastic and incredible accounts were true, very likely the machinery had deteriorated over time.

Enough. He could only do what he could. He worked steadily for a couple of hours, pausing only for a coffee brought around by the air-steward, and then noticed that Salasso was stirring. He got up and joined him, leaving Elizabeth nodding off over her book.

"Feeling better?"

"Yes," said Salasso. He looked out of the window and blinked. "One gets used to the most astonishing things. I think I can fill my pipe myself now."

That he did, lit up and toked and passed it to Gregor. After they'd shared two pipes and the saur had passed out once more, Gregor returned to his seat and found that the figures no longer made much sense. Or rather, they made a completely different kind of sense. They'd begun to resemble the physical structure of the squid brain which they mathematically modeled.

Some time after that, he woke to find himself leaning forward over the table and sideways against the window, and Elizabeth having done the same. They each had a forearm across the table, and Elizabeth's hand rested on top of his. He eased his head back gently, wary of cricking his neck. His hair and Elizabeth's had become entangled. As he was easing the strands apart she woke up. She blinked and looked at him, bewildered but beginning to smile. Then she woke up fully and pulled away.

"Ouch! Sorry." She combed with her fingers, freeing their hair finally, and sat up straight. "You fell asleep stoned then I fell asleep reading. Right on top of you!"

"Ah, it's all right," Gregor said. "What are friends for?"

"Good night," said Elizabeth.

Gregor looked up from his stack of paper and cup of coffee.

"Good night."

She tugged her overnight satchel from her bag, picked up her book and walked to the end of the cabin where a small stair coiled up to the interior of the hull. Salasso turned from gazing at the night, or at the reflections, and raised a floppy hand. Most of the rest of the passengers had already gone to bed.

Up the stair, two turns. Did gravity *increase* as you rose above the surface? It seemed so. Inside the creaking, tough fabric hull was a warren of narrow, low-lit passages between the translucent plastic bulges of the gasbags. She used a tiny washroom and made her way to a cabin—little more than an enclosed bunk—of laminated wood. Balsa for the walls, aluminum for the bed; thin foam mattress and down covering. There was room to stand, and undress, and hang her clothes. The top of the bunk was too low to sit hugging her knees. She lay on her side, hugging her knees.

Gregor had seemed a little surprised, and pleased, that she wanted to come at all. Really, he'd insisted, it wasn't necessary. Salasso had to come because they had to track down saur rumors— rumors so obscure that even old Tharovar had never heard them. Gregor had to come because they'd then have to track down people, maybe in tough places. She didn't need to put herself to this trouble and possible hazard. Why not continue the labwork while they were away?

She'd told him she had no intention whatsoever of staying behind. She wouldn't miss this for anything. She'd pay her fare herself if she had to. James had assured her that the castle would pay her way, no problem. Research expenses.

So here she was: huddled in a narrow bunk, a few meters away from Gregor, on a journey to find what just might help Gregor catch up with—and catch—Lydia. Her only consolation was that its success was unlikely.

Wonderful.

The thousand-mile journey took two more days and nights. They spent the days much as they had the first one; the nights in their separate cabins in the hull, between the plastic spheres of the gasbags.

On the third morning, at breakfast, Salasso called across to Elizabeth and Gregor.

"Look down," he said.

The ship had descended to what seemed to Gregor like a couple of thousand feet. Beneath them, in a glaring low sun, lay the northern fringes of the manufacturing plant. Here, it was still sparse, but startling nonetheless. Clumps and stands of trees, their green branches angled out then straight up like those of decision trees or clade diagrams, cast long shadows. Some had leaves in the shape of inverted umbrellas; others, diamond-shaped.

"Like giant cactuses," said Elizabeth.

The saur had wandered over and leaned in beside them, his breath smelling of kippers.

"Correct," he said. "The cactus plant was one of the sources of the original genes. Of course, much has been edited in since."

"Such as the pipelines between them," said Gregor. He'd just begun to grasp the scale of what he was seeing. Some of these things were a hundred meters tall. The airship was still descending, and he could see dots moving on the ground. At first he'd thought they were saurs, but now he could see they were vehicles.

He swallowed to ease the pressure on his eardrums. The scale jumped again—the vehicles were chemical tankers. He saw a road and his gaze followed it south . . . to even taller structures, well over the horizon now and rapidly approaching.

"Docking at Saur City One in twenty minutes," the steward announced.

Salasso said something.

"What?"

The saur's lips twitched. "Its real name," he said. "Some of the syllables are outside the range of human hearing."

"Ah," said Gregor, who had been mentally trying to pronounce it. "Fine. Saur City One it is."

As they drifted closer it became obvious that the city was of the same stuff and shapes as the manufacturing plant, but expanded and contorted into towers and gantries, platforms and plazas, aerial roadways and walkways. These structures were clothed and foliated with dense, decorative overgrowths of smaller and more colorful, more vegetation-like versions of the plant.

One tall tower loomed, a helical twist of three trunks supporting a platform that bristled with masts.

"Docking in two minutes," said the steward. "Please return to your seats."

Gregor followed the others down a ladder, made—almost reassuringly—of something like mutated bamboo. The platform, too, was wooden, but without planks or other divisions, and it swayed slightly. Two saurs sat in a saddle out from the edge of the platform, operating levers which seemed to control the snaking vines of the airship's tethers. A steady breath of oxygenated and cooled air from stomata in the wall at the far end of the platform did little to relieve the heat and humidity.

"Over here," said Salasso. The other passengers, disembarking or just stretching their legs before the next part of the journey south, had trooped off through a double-glass doorway. Gregor and Elizabeth lugged their bags after Salasso, through an arched doorway off to the left. Inside, they found themselves in a green, smooth-sided corridor which expanded to a circular room, its walls dotted with yellow-green lights and broken by further doorways. A ring of low seating, like some fungoid growth of cork, occupied the hub of the room.

"We wait here," said Salasso.

"At least it's cooler," said Elizabeth, sitting down. "What are we waiting for?"

"A lift," said Salasso.

Other saurs passed in and out, most busy and incurious, a few exchanging words and gestures with Salasso.

"Why here and not with the other passengers?" Gregor asked.

Salasso shrugged. "They'll be here to make deals, in the human quarter. More comfortable accommodations. We are going deep into the city. Perhaps deeper." He hesitated. "Forgive me. You may wish to stay with the other humans? I can very well go on alone."

"Not a chance," Elizabeth and Gregor told him.

"Good," he said. "You can, however, leave your luggage here."

In one of the apertures something settled with a thud, filling the space behind it. Then it, too, opened up, revealing a small, bright chamber just large enough for a few people to stand in.

Salasso stood and walked toward it; they hurried after him and joined him inside it.

"What's this?"

"Like I said," Salasso explained. "A lift."

A section of the wall slid across the opening. Then, quite without warning, they dropped. Gregor felt his body become lighter for a few seconds, then briefly heavier. The sliding door opened again, to the open air.

They stepped out, onto grass, and then Gregor and Elizabeth stopped and stared. At the foot of all the towers and silos they were as mice in a forest. Sunlight, shining down between the trunks and reflected off their polished-looking surfaces, fell shadowless, filtered to green. Across all the grassy space that they could see, saurs strolled between towers or sat or ran about on the grass. Most of the saurs here looked quite unlike those Gregor had seen before. They wore a diversity of clothing and ornament: loose, flapping trousers and jackets, robes and gowns, cloaks and daggers, in colors vivid and various. Their height, too, varied from taller than Salasso to so short they had to be infants. High-pitched, fluting cries filled the air like batsong.

Salasso looked back from a few meters ahead, and returned a couple of steps.

"I had forgotten," he said. "No human has been here before."

He beckoned, and they followed him to where three saurs sat on a low hillock a little way off the path. Two were of normal height, one in black pajamas, the other in a loose robe. The third, the two-foot-high one kneeling on the grass gazing intently at a wheeled wooden box it pushed along with both hands, was covered in what Gregor at first took to be a fluffy yellow one-piece outfit.

Then he saw how the covering became sparser at the nape, and realized that it was all the infant's own downy feathers. Elizabeth saw it at the same moment and immediately squatted down a couple of meters away from the infant, looking at it intently. Salasso was talking to the adults; Gregor hung back, not wanting to scare anyone. His own knees were shaking. No human had seen a saur infant before, not even in a photograph. He'd heard half-joking, edgy speculations that saur infants hatched from eggs in hot sand and lived like beasts, unparented until they proved their capacity to survive; that saurs didn't even have offspring, that they were as sterile as they were ancient; that they were all constructed like robots by the manufacturing plant . . .

He wished he'd thought to bring a camera, to document the evidence of this close encounter.

The child turned to look at Elizabeth, then stood up. The head was more disproportionately large than that of a human baby. Upon some reassuring sounds from the adults, the young saur ran across the grass and tumbled into Elizabeth's arms and lap. She crooned over it, tickling and stroking; it reached up its clawed fingers to her hair and whistled.

"Her name is Blathora," said Salasso. "She is two years old."

"She's just so cute," said Elizabeth. "Super cute. Such big eyes. Aren't you just the sweetest thing. Wow. What a tiny mouth."

"Sharp teeth," warned Salasso, as Elizabeth's fingers teased around the high cheekbones. "And a taste for mammal blood."

"Oh." She drew back a little. "Gregor? Do you want to hold her?"

"Oh yes."

Dandling the saurian child, drowning in black pools deep as the past of her species, Gregor had one of those moments when time stops. The rarity of the moment, the privilege, stunned him. How many human parents would trust their baby to the hands of even another hominid, to one of the tall hairy men of the high snows? He found himself responding to the saurs' trust, in a rush of affection and protective feeling toward this small but significant life.

He returned Blathora to the adults, and found that she'd left a spot of snotty, chalky guano on his thigh.

"Where are we going?" Gregor asked, after half an hour of walking on the floor of the city.

Salasso looked back.

"This a very safe area, outside the industrial processes. Like a park, but safer. It's used for relaxation, play, and teaching. I expect to meet one of my old teachers."

"Teachers!"

"Why do you laugh?"

"It's funny to think of saurs having teachers."

"Did you think we hatch knowing everything?"

"Some people do think that," said Elizabeth. "Seriously."

"No, it isn't that, it's just—" Gregor shrugged. "I suppose I imagined you taught by machines, or something."

"Machines!" Salasso hooted. He paused to let them both walk beside him, and continued in a lower tone:

"We have a policy, an agreement. It is not enforced, but . . . nearly all of us see the wisdom of it—not to share much information with you, and especially not about ourselves. We are a very private people, and cautious. But when I hear things like this, I wish we could be more forthcoming."

He hissed through his teeth, a sigh. "But we cannot. Our societies would become less distinct, and the stronger one would absorb the weaker."

Gregor looked around and upward yet again at the biotechno-logical complex, shining and alien. Spectacular though it was, it held no attraction for him.

"I don't think you need worry about us being absorbed," he said.

"That," said Salasso, "is not what we worry about."

Oh.

"How many people are here?" Elizabeth asked.

"Saurs?"

"Yes. In Saur City One."

Salasso shrugged and waved his arms. He was walking ahead of them again, pressing on, eager. The shadows had shortened, and the light and heat become more intense.

"A million or so. At a guess. We do not number each other."

"Hm," said Elizabeth. She glanced from side to side as she walked, her lips moving, her thumbs moving along the tips of her fingers.

"What are you doing?" Gregor asked, in a low voice.

"Population stats." She looked sidelong at him. "There seem to be a lot of kids . . ." She laughed. "Whatever—chicks? squabs?—anyway . . . young saurs about. But if you actually count them, as in per hectare, and see how each of them is getting serious adult attention . . . it looks like a very low reproduction rate. High K/R strategy."

"Goes with the long life," said Gregor lightly.

Elizabeth shook her head firmly. "No! Not necessarily. They're limiting their population, maybe keeping it just ticking over. No growth."

"While we—"

She smiled crookedly. "Us humans. Yes. How many cousins do you have?"

He waggled his fingers in front of her. "I'd have to take my boots off to count them, unless you have a clicker."

Salasso stopped walking and looked back. His mouth stretched to the sides.

"There she is!" he cried, pointing. Fifty meters away, a saur in a long blue coat was sitting on a cork chair in front of a dozen smaller and younger people, in the shade of a metallic umbrella.

Then he did something they'd never seen him do before. He ran to the adult saur, who stood up and embraced him.

"Gods above," said Gregor. "The little bugger has feelings."

"I knew *that*," said Elizabeth.

Something in her tone made Gregor turn to her, but she was looking away. Salasso waved to them and they joined him.

Up close, neither the greater age nor different sex of the other saur were apparent, at least to them. The features were as smooth as Salasso's, the body—naked where the coat fell open—as neutral and neuter in its external anatomy as that of the male, whom they had once or twice seen swimming, very badly.

"My friends, meet Athranal, my venerable teacher," said Salasso.

They introduced themselves.

"Good day to you," she said, in a stilted, sibilant Trade Latin. "We welcome you here."

"We are honored to meet you."

She laughed, wheezily, for the first time sounding old.

"Indeed you are. I was young when this tongue was new."

Gregor felt his nape hairs prickle. They suddenly felt as stiff as the pinfeathers of the infant saur he'd played with. He preferred to think he'd misunderstood, or that her grasp of the language was rusty. He nodded politely.

"We seek our own . . . old folk."

"So my best pupil has told me," she said. She laid a hand on Salasso's shoulder. "Salasso, Salasso! How good to see you again!"

Turning to the younger saurs—adolescent, Gregor guessed— who were standing politely back, she launched into a declamation in the saurian speech which had the pupils sinking to their haunches and staring at Salasso, who after a time squirmed his shoulders and looked down. Had he learned the body language of embarrassment from humanity? Gregor wondered.

After about five minutes, Athranal stopped. Her pupils thumped the ground with their feet.

"And so we say good-bye," she concluded, clapping Salasso's back and turning to the others.

"Good-bye, and good fortune," said Salasso.

Gregor and Elizabeth stumbled the same salutation.

"We must go," said Salasso.

He almost grabbed them, almost swept them up in his arms as he shot past them, then sprinted to the base of the nearest shaft without a backward glance. With one hurried look over his shoulder at the old teacher, now placidly returning to her seat, Gregor raced after the saur, with Elizabeth's footsteps thudding on the turf behind him.

They tumbled over each other into a lift. The door slithered shut. Their knees buckled as it ascended, then they were pulled sideways as it accelerated horizontally.

"What's going on?" Elizabeth asked. "Why didn't you wait for her to tell you?"

"She told me," said Salasso. His breathing had become deep and rapid. "Into that . . . oration, she worked an account of where they are. The old crew. Not so that the young ones would understand, but I understood."

"How?"

"A code." The lift swung around some corner, and shot upward again. "Something like what you would call an acrostic."

"A what?"

"Initials of words, spelling out a word," Elizabeth explained.

"Many words," said Salasso.

"You did all that in your head?" asked Gregor. "And she must have—"

"Improvised it on the spot. She is clever."

"Why not just tell you straight-out?"

Salasso passed a forearm across his forehead, in a curiously inhuman gesture, like a fly cleaning its eyes.

"If the children understood it, they might tell their parents, and some might think that the gods would not approve."

Well, that clears that up, thought Gregor.

"And where are they?" he asked.

"In and around New Lisbon," said Salasso. "At the dinosaur drive and the meat market. We must catch the flight. There is not another for days, and by then it will be over."

The lift slammed and buffeted them and spat them out into the circular hall. They raced through, barely remembering to snatch up their bags, and out onto the platform just in time to see the airship vanish behind the most distant of the city's towers.

12

Orbital Commie Hell

T HE STATION, LEMIEUX gleefully informed us as he led us
through its crowded, cluttered spaces, was no longer called the
Marshall Titov. It was called (deep breath) *The Darker the Night
the Brighter the Star;* after a volume of some obscure biography
of Trotsky, I gathered. I wanted to suggest that *The Prophet Stoned*
would have been snappier as well as more apt—the people we
passed were certainly high on something, maybe the pervasive acetone and alcohol vapors of degrading wet-tech—but I forbore.

I began to get the hang of moving in microgravity, with the
occasional shove from Camila to correct my mistakes. Beyond
the heavy rubber-sealed door of the receiving area the smells of
the place were stronger and more various. The air-circulation system made a lot of white noise but didn't seem to make the air
any fresher. Hardly a light source was without its huddle of hydroponics. Rabbits and chickens—the mammals better preadapted to free fall than the birds, oddly—floated or dived in airy
spaces fenced off with fine plastic netting that contained their
droppings but not their odor. People in grubby fatigues or quirky,
scant selections of clothing and tools worked at all angles in
every available cranny. As they glanced up—or down, or across—
at us, they looked pleased enough to see us but returned without
reluctance to their work.

At a corner of two corridors Camila took advantage of a momentary collision and entanglement to ask me, sharply under her
breath, "Why aren't they *saying* anything to us?"

Lemieux glanced back. "Because they don't know who's listening."

"That's us told," Camila muttered, as she pushed me on.

I didn't believe Lemieux's explanation for a moment. These people didn't look as though they were worried about saying something that might be held against them by whoever came out on top of the power struggle. They looked like people who had something better to think about than that.

Driver looked much as I'd seen him in his announcement, but thinner, with a few days' growth of stubble; eyes bloodshot and sleepless. Patches of his cheeks had been scratched almost raw from the itch of overused wet-tech. He'd angled himself in between a work surface and a wall as though sitting at a desk. A net bag tethered to the surface bulged with crushed smokeless filters and crumpled sets of waste goggles and phones. Shelves of transparent containers, toolracks, computing equipment, and surveillance gear covered the walls behind him and the ceiling. Postcards of landscapes and seascapes—almost pornographic in the circumstances—decorated them.

Lemieux crouched in an upper corner of the inadequate space, watching us at a disconcerting angle. Camila and I looped our arms through some webbing opposite Driver's desk and relaxed in the air.

"Well," Driver said, "I got a warning from Area 51 that a flying saucer was on the way. Kind of amusing. Didn't say why you were coming, though, or who you were." He grimaced. "We've been announcing you as the first American researchers to accept Big Uncle's kind invitation to join us. So who are you really?"

Camila came close to standing to attention.

"Camila Hernandez, test pilot for Nevada Orbital Dynamics. This is Matt Cairns, a systems manager from Scotland who has some information for you. That's all I know."

Colin Driver's attention switched over to me. "Hey, I've seen you on the news somewhere. The defector, right?"

"You could say that."

"Well, what have you got?"

"I've brought back some information you downloaded to ESA," I said. "It's been ramped up into project designs. It'll drop out a complete manufacturing spec, once I've done some more work on it."

"A spec for what?"

I glanced at Camila and Lemieux and then thought, the hell with it, this was something that everybody needed to know.

"You know, for the anti-gravity vehicle and the space-drive."

Camila turned and stared at me.

"The *what*?"

Lemieux guffawed, from his simian perch. Driver contained his amusement not much better.

"First, I've heard of it," he said. "You're telling me it came from *here*?"

I nodded. "Via the ESA planning-system, yeah."

"Well, it *can't* have," Driver insisted. "Everything—the legit info to ESA, the disinfo to the, ah, other side—all went through my desk." He thumped it, in ringing emphasis.

"Perhaps," Camila suggested, "some of the scientists transmitted it independently?"

Driver held up and swirled his hands. "It's possible, sure. Nothing to stop somebody setting up a pirate rig somewhere. But there's no way they could have hacked the ESA planning-system, or my desk, come to that."

"Not even with that alien code-cracking math you got?" I hazarded.

"Uh-huh," he said. "The math came from here, all right, but the resources for applying it are way beyond anything anyone here has, or has access to. They had to grow honest-to-god *forests* of new tech to generate the computing capacity on Earth. Besides, we aren't relying just on encryption. Basic security measures—" Driver shrugged. "You should know."

I nodded. "Okay. You know Alan Armstrong?"

"Nope."

"Heard of him," Lemieux said.

"Check him out any time," I said. "Call him up, if you like. No need to go into details. Just ask him if he thinks what I've brought is gen."

Driver's fingernail worried at his earhole. "All right," he said. "Let's see what you've got."

"Are you the right person to evaluate it?" Camila asked.

"No, but Paul here is. And if any of it really came from here, I can find it in my audit trail."

"That'll take awhile," I said. "We're exhausted, we need some proper food and sleep and a wash."

Driver glowered. "And we don't? We're *all* exhausted here." He slid his fingertips across his closed eyelids. "Oh, the hell with it.

You're right. Whatever it is, it can wait another few hours. Okay, Paul, you take them out and I'll catch some kip right here."

Lemieux unfolded himself from his corner of the ceiling, drifted past us and opened the door. "Come on. Let me show you some hospitality."

Chicken, mashed potatoes, runner beans, all stuck to the paper plate with a glutinous gravy; and a squeezable plastic bulb of orange juice. It was the best meal I could remember having. When I'd eaten enough to start thinking again I slowed down and looked around. The servery was a narrow room with one long aluminum table at which the diners could approximate sitting by hooking their knees around the railing half a meter down from each edge of the table. A slow queue shunted past the hatch at the far end of the room. The illusion of being in a normal gravity field must have been important to the room's designers and users—nobody left the table by floating over it, though it wouldn't have inconvenienced anyone.

People ate fast, and talked, and kept their spex on and often shaded. Hardly anyone wore new-tech goggles. At any given time there'd be about twenty people around the table.

"How many people are there on the station?" I asked.

Lemieux looked up from a sticky apple-pie–and–treacle dessert. "Twenty-one with cosmonaut training, including ten science or technical officers—that's me—the five security staff and three military liaison officers—two of whom are currently in the brig, guarded by the third—plus fifteen civilian administrators and two hundred and seventy-two scientists and technicians."

"That's *a lot,*" said Camila.

"There's a lot to do," Lemieux said. "As you should know, if you've looked at the science data we've already released."

Camila shook her head. "Seen some stuff on the news, that's all."

"Nor me," I admitted. "I've been too busy running."

"Well," said Lemieux. "We have been in contact for over five years. There is much work. The scientists"—he waved a hand at the oblivious company—"are totally obsessed with it, now that they have freedom to investigate and share and publicize. It was very difficult when it was a big secret."

"Difficult to keep secret," I said, "with that many people here, and I suppose hundreds more on the ground, knowing it."

Camila and Lemieux both laughed.

"Your friend here is laughing," said Lemieux. "She is right. Big secrets can be kept for a long time by many people, and the bigger the secret, the easier it is. As your Area 51 showed, and the Manhattan Project, and our Operation Liberation."

"What are the aliens like?" I asked, smiling to show I recognized how stupid a question it was.

Lemieux leaned forward, elbows on the table, letting his fork float from one hand to the other, catching and releasing it precisely with finger and thumb.

"They are *like* the microorganisms that produce the calcareous mats which build up to stromatolites," he said. "Except that what they build are not stacks of stone, but something between a larger organism and a computer, to put it crudely. To put it delicately, they build quasi-organic mechanisms of incredible beauty and diversity. The basic unit, the builder, is something *like* an extremophile nanobacterium. Obviously these are not the seats of consciousness, any more than our neurones are. Collectively, though, they build something greater than themselves." He smiled, and added: "As our clever English comrade Haldane mistakenly said of the ants, they are 'the smallest communists.'"

Camila made a snorting noise. "Communism sounds just fine for *germs*," she said witheringly.

"You would not think it so funny when you see what they have achieved. They are not a collective mind as a whole—there are more separate minds in this asteroid than there would be in, let us say, a human Galactic Empire, if such a thing could be."

"And you're in communication with them?" I asked, anxious to avoid any political argument.

Lemieux's eyes narrowed and his lips thinned, as though in momentary pain. "We are," he said. "It is a theoretical scandal, but it is the case."

"What's the scandal?" I asked. "That you can . . . translate? Or that they can?"

"It is worse," said Lemieux. He scratched his head. "There was no need. They know our languages."

"Like, they learned them from television?" Camila asked.

"Impossible," said Lemieux. It sounded more definite like that, in French. "It is simply not theoretically possible for a genuine alien

to learn a language from television broadcasts. A language cannot be learned without the . . . interaction."

I had scant respect for linguistic theory, particularly when delivered in a French accent.

"Can you be sure of that?" I asked. "Perhaps, I don't know, something in their code-cracking, something we don't understand yet, some mathematical underlying structure, Chomskyan deep grammar—"

Lemieux caught the fork at both ends and began to bend it.

"That is conceivable," he said. "Barely. We may be all wrong about the theory. That is not the scandal. The scandal is that they understand languages that not only have never been televised or transmitted, but that have had no living speakers since before the invention of writing. *That* is the scandal."

The fork snapped.

We've washed ourselves with wet sponges in cylindrical stalls through which air flows and water flies. We've dried in the same stalls, with hot air. We've been given much-laundered underwear and stiff, fresh blue fatigues and soft plastic boots. Lemieux has left us together in a cubbyhole behind a clipped-on curtain, with a shrugged apology that it's the best he can do. The walls of the little space are hung, like many walls in this place, with loose webbing. We look at each other and laugh. I have three days' worth of stubble and our faces are flushed and puffy with blood that's no longer pulled toward our feet. We hook elbows and ankles through appropriate holes in the webbing and fall asleep against the upper and lower partitions, facing each other a half-meter apart.

I dream. Lemieux's words and worries combine with scraps of pictures I've glimpsed of the interior spaces of the asteroid, the alien city or computer or garden, fractal and crystalline and florally organic. I'm falling on it from a great height, like in an airliner descending on a lighted city, like a parachutist's view of onrushing grass, and every dandelion is a clock. Inside it, tiny green men the size of ants are watching television, laughing in thin high voices, and scribbling notes to each other in cuneiform and Linear B.

I fall onto something and wake to realize I've drifted and been snagged by the webbing. Camila's snoring, openmouthed, a few inches in front of my face. I shrug back into the webbing and sleep again.

And fall again, but this time more gently, onto a bed. Jadey's face, troubled, as in the last shot I saw of her, looms above me. Then she smiles, like she did the last time she was in this position, and our faces and lips meet.

Sometime after that I hear a voice telling me to wake up, and I feel—for a few dozy seconds—happy and comfortable, before I wake to find that Camila and I have worked our limbs out of the webbing and are now huddled and cuddled like frightened monkeys, and that I have a quite obvious erection pressing against her.

She disengages and smiles at me in a friendly, *We're all adults here* kind of way, and rattles the curtain back and pushes herself out. Bending over awkwardly, I follow.

Back in Driver's office we all took the places we'd had before. He didn't look more than marginally refreshed.

"Right," he said. "You ready to show me what you've brought?"

It was easier to walk Driver and Lemieux through the material than it had been with the Americans. The tech was compatible, the protocols familiar to both of them—the ESA-specific ones more familiar, indeed, to them than to me. They tabbed about in it, finding links and paths I'd missed, taking it all in quickly, with rapid-fire, cryptic remarks to each other. Camila hung out on the edge of our shared dataspace, not commenting apart from the occasional murmur of "Holy shit!"

We backed out and looked at each other, blinking.

"Hmm," said Driver. He looked at Lemieux, eyebrows raised.

"Interesting," said Lemieux.

Driver fiddled with the datadisk then slotted it in his desk. "Let me run that past the audit trail."

He put his goggles back on and sucked at a smokeless. Lemieux relaxed into a meditative posture; we fidgeted.

"Shit," said Driver. He peeled off the goggles and flicked his filter into the net bag. "Shit." He looked at Lemieux, then at us.

"It's there," he said. "All spelled out. No way could I have missed it, not back then. Last year, hell, Paul, you remember. We double-checked everything. You and me."

"I didn't double-check the disinfo," said Lemieux. "Obviously."

"Yeah," said Driver, in a dangerously calm voice. "But I'd have known about any disinfo, because anything that wasn't totally innocuous, bland, censored shit about low-temperature chemistry and so forth, *I fucking made up myself*. Not from the whole cloth, sure, but you can bet I read every bloody line of the real stuff that went into it. And I did *not* send disinfo to ESA! You'd have seen it, mate."

"That," said Lemieux, "is not in question."

The two men looked at each other; some unspoken understanding was reaffirmed.

"Okay," said Driver. "So what *is* in question?"

"Who, and how," said Lemieux. "Which of the civilians managed to hack this datastream, and how did they do it?"

"I don't believe it for a minute," said Driver. "They don't have the skills, and they don't have the balls." He considered this for a moment. "More to the point," he added, "they don't have the motivation. I mean, anyone who'd found this would have been all too keen to tell us. And why send it to ESA, if they weren't loyal? Why not send it to the other side—they knew about the controlled datastream going to the West, and it would have been easier, if anything, to slip it in that."

He closed his eyes and scratched his eyebrows. "Or maybe not. Maybe I do need more sleep."

"You do, Colin," said Lemieux, with an odd, affectionate, personal note I hadn't heard in his voice before. "But you are right. It makes no sense."

"What about your CIA spy?" Camila asked.

Driver dismissed this with a wave of his hand.

"That was all bullshit. Sorry." He looked at us fiercely. "I've apologized to Sukhanov about the slander. It was necessary."

Aha! I thought. "So the CIA must have—"

He glared at me, glanced at Camila. "Leave it."

"All right," I said. "You're all making one assumption, which is that someone on this station hacked the datastream and downloaded the 'flying saucer' stuff to ESA."

"Well, no," said Driver. "I've just found the *evidence* that someone—" He blinked, then gave me a sick-looking smile. "Nah! Come on."

"What's so unlikely about it?"

"About *what?*" asked Camila, sounding exasperated.

Enough dramatics, I thought, and said flatly: "The datastream was hacked by the aliens."

Everybody tried to reply at once. Driver banged the desk.

"Paul? What do you think?"

"It's possible. That is to say, it is not theoretically impossible and it is not simply improbable, like the scientists' doing it would be. So, yes, we should consider it."

Driver sat silent for a moment.

"Hell," he said. "If they've done it, it's something that has never happened before." He scratched his cheek. "Intervention."

The word hung in the air like the pieces of Lemieux's broken fork.

"Like all the information they've been feeding you *isn't?*" Camila asked.

"I don't think the scientists would call it 'feeding,' " Driver said. "The aliens are pretty selective about what questions they'll answer."

"Oh? And what *do* you call giving the E.U. a massive military intelligence advantage?"

"They didn't necessarily know that," Driver protested. He looked at Paul Lemieux, as though for support. "There's no evidence the aliens even understand the politics of Earth, let alone take sides in it. Nor is there any evidence that our presence is being dealt with at any kind of high level in the alien . . . community. For all we know, we may be in contact with nothing more than their equivalent of the *Encyclopædia Britannica*—and the children's version, at that."

Lemieux was shaking his head. "I know that's what you'd like to think, Colin," he said, "but you know it would be disputed by every scientist on this station, and by me too." He moved his teeth as though nibbling at his lower lip. "Is it not time we—explained the situation?"

"Ah, I guess so," said Driver, and suddenly looked much more cheerful. "It's that or stick them in the brig, and I don't want to do that. The publicity might be bad." He grinned at us. " 'U.S. hostages in orbital commie hell,' sort of thing."

We laughed, with nervous politeness.

"Wait a minute," I said. "Have you any idea about, you know, whether we're going to *build* this thing? Because that's why we came here."

Driver disengaged himself from the desk and reached for the door.

"First things first," he said. "Time to meet the aliens."

"He means, the scientists," said Lemieux, on the way out. Driver heard him.

"Same thing," he grunted.

The scientist took off his spex and blinked at us. In a literally laid-back position—and pose—he hung across the end of a small corridor or long cubbyhole, surrounded by more cables than an intensive-care patient. Some of them were fiber-optic, others insulated metal; most, however, had the fibrous, quasi-organic look of new tech. None of them, as far as I could see, actually went into his body, but many of them terminated in the equipment slung around it. His faded sweatpants and baggy T-shirt barely contained his beer gut, and his hair and beard looked as wild and coiled as the cabling.

He waved, in an airy, notional handshake all around.

"Hi, guys. My name's Armen Avakian. And your names have been all around the ship's intranet. Welcome aboard. Have our two politicos here clued you in yet?"

"We decided to let you do that," said Driver. "Including about the *politics*. So far we've only discussed security issues."

"So I'm not on the hook, whatever they were," said Avakian. He let out a laugh that made me want to cover my ears. "Great! So—you got spex? Right, sure, okay. Now just a moment while I tune in to them and call up a consensus space. . . ."

Blankness surrounded us, a shadowless, pearly light. Avakian's voice murmured, somewhere behind us:

"Ready?"

It was somehow obvious, and disturbing, that the question was not addressed to any of us.

The bright monochrome bubble burst, throwing us into color and complexity. More color, more complexity than I'd ever seen or imagined or dreamed. The pictures shown of it in the newsfeeds were a quite inadequate preparation for the real thing. We hung in a vast interior space. Distance and perspective were impossible to judge, the shapes difficult to cohere in the eye. At one moment it made sense as the interior of a vastly magnified, non-human brain; the next, as the view of a city from a height; or a cathedral, made

177

entirely of stained glass; then again, as some multifarious botanic garden in whose gargantuan greenhouse we were as fruit flies.

For a long time the only possible response was silence. The place filled the mind, and the eye, and the mind's eye.

My entranced, meditative moment was shattered by Avakian's laugh. The view collapsed, back into white light, like waking to a dash of freezing water after some warm and vivid dream.

"So much for the big picture," he said. "The actual interface has a bit less bandwidth."

I hung in the air, shivering, blinking away tears behind the spex.

"Just as well," Avakian went on, "because the interface is addictive enough as it is. If we were working in the big picture we'd do nothing but hang around with our mouths open."

He laughed again, the sound even more manic and hideous than before, and even as I resented it and shrank—no, *cringed* from it—I realized that he was doing it deliberately, and in our interests: Without that iconoclasm we would be lost in idolatry. Or worse—our adoration of this celestial city might be the closest any of us would ever come to devotion to real gods.

With an audible *click* the interface appeared—a wide, wraparound screen this time rather than a full-immersion view. If we hadn't seen the latter we'd have been almost as stunned by the former, crowded as it was with still and moving images, depth, and *text*.

"It's what you might call 'feature-rich,' " Avakian said dryly. "This is what all of us—the scientists—are hanging out in, every moment we can."

The image vanished and we became again four people hanging in the recycled air of a smelly, confined, and cluttered space.

"So," he said, "what can I do for you?"

I was about to tell him when Lemieux interrupted.

"No, no!" he said. "First, you will please tell them what you and the other scientists have found, and what your consensus is as to what is to be done—the politics, if you will."

"Oh, yeah, that," said Avakian. He ran his hands through his springy hair, making no discernible difference to its condition. "Well, this place here is unique, right, but it's not *alone*. You know, when Big Uncle made the announcement? That was a bit of an understatement, comrades and friends; old Yefrimovich was a tad economical with the truth."

His fingers rampaged across his head again.

"The truth is there are *billions* of the fuckers. In the asteroid belt and the Kuiper and the Oort. There are more . . . communities . . . like this around the Solar System than there are people on Earth. And each of them contains more separate minds than, than—"

"—a Galactic Empire," said Lemieux.

"Yes! Yes! Exactly!" Avakian beamed.

"How do you know this?" Camila asked.

Avakian hand-waved behind his shoulder.

"The aliens told us, and told us where to look for their communications. Their EM emissions are very faint, but they're there, all right, and the sources fill the sky like the cosmic microwave background, the echo of the Big Bang."

"Sure it ain't just part of that?"

"Nah, it's comms, all right." Avakian sucked at his lower lip. "The point to bear in mind is that our cometary cloud's outer shells intersect those of the Centauran System, and, well—"

"They're everywhere?"

He shrugged. "Around a lot of stars, yeah, quite possibly. Trafficking, communicating, maybe even traveling. They have conscious control over their own outgassings, they have computing power to die for, and it only takes a nudge to change their orbits. It might take millions of years between stars, sure, but these guys have a *long* attention span."

"And what do they actually do?"

"From the point of view of us busy little primates, they don't do much. Hang out and take in the view. Travel around the sun every few million years. Maybe travel to another sun and go around that a few times. *Bo-ring*." He put on a whining, childish voice. " 'Are we *there* yet? He's *hitting* me. I want to go to the *toilet*.' "

He laughed, a genuine and humorous laugh this time, and continued briskly: "But from their point of view, they are having fun. Endless, absorbing, ecstatic, and for all I know, *orgasmic* fun. Discourse, intercourse—at their level it's probably the same fucking thing." He underlined the obvious with a giggle. "They're like gods, man, and they're literally in heaven. And in all their infinite—well, okay, *unbounded*—diversity they have, we understand, a pretty much unanimous view on one thing. They don't like spam."

He looked at three puzzled faces, and at mine.

"Spam," he said. "Tell these good people about spam."

I flailed, literally and metaphorically. It was an obscure issue, difficult to explain to people outside the biz. But I tried.

"Spam is, um, sort of mindlessly repeated advertisements and shit. Junk mail. Some of it comes from start-ups and scams, some of it's generated by programs called spambots, which got loose in the system about fifty years ago and which have been beavering away ever since. You hardly notice it, because so little gets through that you might think it's just a legit advertisement. But that's because way down at the bottom level, we have programs to clean out the junk, and they work away at it too." I shrugged. "Spam and anti-spam waste resources, it's the ultimate zero-sum game, but what can you do? You gotta live with it. Anti-spam's like an immune system. You don't have to know about it, but you'd die without it. There's a whole war going on that's totally irrelevant to what you really want to do."

"*Exactamundo,*" said Avakian. "That's how the ETs feel about it too. And as far as they're concerned, we are great lumbering spambots, corrupted servers, liable at any moment or any megayear to start turning out millions of pointless, slightly varied replicas of ourselves. Most of what we're likely to want to do if we expanded seriously into space is spam. Space industries—spam. Moravec uploads—spam on a plate. Von Neumann machines—spam and chips. Space settlements—spam, spam, spam, eggs, and spam. "

"How about asteroid mining and comet farming?" I couldn't keep my face straight, but Avakian looked grim.

"Don't even *think* about it," he said. "Um . . . Where this all gets political is that it didn't take long for us to realize that the ultimate engine of spam is capitalism. Endless expansion is the great capitalist wet dream, and it's totally incompatible with the way the universe really is. It's certainly incompatible with what the overwhelmingly dominant form of intelligent life in the universe is willing to accept. Quite frankly, I'm no Party hack myself but the fact of the matter is that the Party's aim of a steady-state society with a bit of sustainable, careful, non-invasive space exploration is the only kind of society that the aliens are likely to be happy with." He made an ironically sad face at Camila. "The dream you guys have of treating the Solar System as raw material for orbital mobile homes, guns, and beer cans is *right out.*"

"And what," Camila asked, "are they going to do about it?"

Avakian's thick eyebrows twitched. "With control over cometary and asteroid orbits, you can, oh, engineer mass-extinction events." He spread his hands. "Just a thought."

"Now wait a minute!" Camila exclaimed. "With that kind of threat from outer space, hell, we could all pull together. There'd be real backing for the big stuff—lasers, nukes, battle stations, a proper space-defense system at last! Hey, we could even pull in the commies, once they understood what we're really up against. And with the political will, we could get the heavy stuff in orbit real fast! These aliens of yours couldn't react in time to stop us. And if they tried, they'd find a few extinction level events coming *their* way. Shit—did these guys ever pick on the wrong species to keep cooped up in a keg."

Avakian looked away from her and at me and Lemieux and Driver, who were listening to this little rant with expressions of amusement and disbelief.

"Ah," he said. "You begin to see the problem."

"Don't patronize *me*," Camila said, shoving her face in front of his and forcing his attention back to her. "Anyway, if the aliens don't want us to go into space, why the hell have they given us the plans for a flying saucer and a space-drive?"

Avakian blinked slowly. "Tell me more," he said.

13

Gravity Skiff

GREGOR GLARED AFTER the departing airship, his fists clenched in acute frustration and annoyance. He turned to Elizabeth and Salasso, who like him were leaning dangerously out over the platform's parapet, as though that would help.

"Can't we ask the tower to call it back?"

"No chance."

"So why the hell didn't you—"

"Listen," said Salasso patiently, "I did not at all expect the people we are looking for to be in New Lisbon. The last I heard, they were rumored to be somewhere else." He waved up at other airships drifting in to dock. "Somewhere reachable by one of those flights. I only sought out my old teacher for confirmation, and for more detail as to the location. If I had thought for a moment they might be in New Lisbon, we would not have walked."

Their stroll along the city floor and their encounter with the saur child now seemed like a futile waste of time, something to recall with regret instead of delight. At the same moment, the mention of New Lisbon made Gregor's heart jump. Lydia would be there.

"Wait a minute," said Elizabeth. "You said New Lisbon's where the gravity skiffs are right now? They can't be working *all* the time. Why not call in and see if any pilot is willing to nip up here and nip straight back, with us?"

"That is a—" The saur's tongue flickered along his lips. "That is a very good idea. I should have thought of it myself."

Gregor dropped his bag and flung an arm around Elizabeth's shoulders.

"Yes!" he shouted. "Brilliant!"

"You anticipate," said Salasso. "Let us see."

They followed him again into the circular room. He marched up to a flat gray plate on the wall and started poking at some small rectangles outlined along its lower border. After a moment the plate glowed dimly, and Salasso began an animated, gesticulating conversation. Gregor watched from one side with a feeling of vague resentment. Television, or the lack of it, was something of a sore point.

Saur display-screens worked outside the human visual spectrum, and even when corrected for that, they didn't make much sense, most of the picture being lost in a blizzard of additional information which the saur optical system filtered quite differently from the human brain. Mingulay's industrial capacity didn't extend to mass production of cathode-ray tube monitors—let alone anything more advanced—and this deficiency was one which the saurs seemed in no hurry to supply from their manufacturing plant.

What made this a sore point was the distinct impression their traders gave that this was entirely to the humans' benefit.

The dim glow faded. Salasso stepped back.

"I have arranged it," he said. "The skiff will be here in an hour."

Two automatic glass doors *thunk*ed open as they walked toward the entrance. Looking from one side to the other rather warily, Gregor and Elizabeth stepped through. Salasso hesitated for a moment, the doors began to close, then opened again as he jumped through. He glanced back at it suspiciously.

The room was quite large, with a counter along one side, fluorescent tubes suspended from the high ceiling. CRT monitors displaying flight information were mounted on the walls, as were long vertical loudspeakers playing indistinct and undistinguished music. Varieties of padded plastic seating and laminated plastic tables were scattered and clumped on the broad floor, some of which was polished wood, the rest carpeted. A few businessmen were sitting about, some still negotiating with saurs, others sipping drinks and looking blank.

"This is bizarre," said Gregor. "Like something from outer space."

Salasso climbed onto a seat by a small table. "Luxurious, anyway," he said, swinging his legs. "Much better than our facilities."

"Speaking of facilities . . ." said Elizabeth.

Salasso pointed. Elizabeth looked at the sign and shook her head.

"Just as well I'm not wearing trousers. . . . By the way, is anyone else hungry?"

The girl at the refreshment counter wore a pink-and-white-striped dress that didn't seem to fit properly, and an apron over it that looked prettier and more valuable than the dress it was supposed to protect, and a similarly frilled band on her head that didn't actually keep her hair out of her eyes. Gregor was troubled by a vague puzzlement about all this, the uneasy feeling that everything here was a copy of something that was itself not the original and not quite right in the first place. He paid for the coffee, sandwiches, and fish-stock in Kyohvic coin, reluctantly accepted change in a handful of New Lisbon hole-punched lira, and returned with the tray.

"Didn't realize humans worked here," he remarked. "Must be boring as hell."

Salasso's mouth twitched.

"They tend not to stay long."

"Hmm," said Elizabeth. "I'd find it interesting. Fascinating. Working in Saur City!"

"The novelty palls," said Salasso.

As Gregor drank his coffee the stimulant rush made him vividly aware of the queasy, fluttery feeling in the pit of his stomach. He realized he was actually nervous and excited at the prospect of traveling in a gravity skiff. In truth, more nervous than excited.

"Salasso," he said. "Would you mind, perhaps, sharing a pipe?"

"You're welcome."

Elizabeth drained her coffee and stood up, taking her half-eaten sandwich with her.

"Excuse me, chaps," she said. "I'd rather not partake, right now. I'll just go and watch the airships."

"Fine," said Gregor, squinting at her around the lighter flame. "See you."

She walked off briskly.

"What's eating *her*?" Gregor asked.

Salasso shrugged. The man and the saur smoked in companionable silence for a while, the saur taking far less than half the puffs. He accepted the final toke. Then he put down the pipe and fixed Gregor with his gaze.

"Perhaps I should not say this," he said in a barely audible voice, leaning forward. "The hemp makes one relaxed and emotionally expressive. Elizabeth wishes to keep very close rein on what emotions she expresses."

"Oh. I see." Gregor frowned. "Is she worried about something?"

Disturbing possibilities flashed through his mind—an ill parent or grandparent, an injured sibling, student debt, some medical trouble of her own—

"Is it something I can help with?"

Of course she wouldn't want to *ask*. Her prickly dignity would get in the way.

The doors banged open as another lot of passengers came in. Salasso fiddled with the pipe, tapping the ash into an ornamental glass dish on the table before Gregor could remind him to use the floor.

"I don't know if you could help," he said. "But—"

He closed his eyes for a second, then looked up at Gregor.

"You must know this. Elizabeth is in love with you and is distressed that you are in love with someone else."

Gregor felt a chill go through his belly like a cold blade. The fuzzy cloud of the hemp dispersed instantly, letting everything else crash in. Never had he felt so surprised, so embarrassed, so wrong-footed; and at the same time, so painfully pleased, and so satisfied—as everything that Elizabeth had said or done in his presence was seen in its true, and now obvious, significance.

But it was his dismay that told in his voice.

"Oh, gods above. I never knew."

"I am sorry I had to tell you," said Salasso, the double edge of his words as polite as ever. "But it may be important for our expedition that you know this. It would be good if you were considerate of what she feels, and if you took great care not to give her any opportunity, in a moment of danger, for recklessness on your behalf." Some humor returned to his expression. "Or against you, come to that."

"Oh, gods, yes," said Gregor. It came out as a groan. "I think I need another coffee to pull myself together."

"Bring two," said Salasso, gazing out through the glass doors. "Elizabeth is heading back."

Fetching the drinks served as a small distraction for Gregor's mind and enabled him to face Elizabeth with some restored equanimity when he returned to the table.

"Oh, thanks," she said.

"How did you find the airships? Or has the skiff arrived?"

"We have about ten minutes," said Salasso.

"I wasn't watching the airships much," said Elizabeth. "The city itself is actually more interesting. More going on, all the time. And I kept getting the scale wrong, it's—"

"Fractal?"

"Yes. Like the waves when we were above the sea. You can't tell how high you are, just by looking down."

"I can," said Salasso. He rolled his eyes from side to side, and they all laughed, and drained their cups, and went out to wait for the skiff.

Salasso spotted it first, and pointed southward, upward, and tracking. Gregor could see nothing but blue sky for half a minute, and then he saw a tiny point of light racing to the zenith, where it stopped. The silvery fleck enlarged above them until it became obviously a descending disc. Other people began looking and pointing, gathering in a small, excited crowd. At a thousand feet above them the disc went into a bravura display of falling-leaf motion, finally swooping around the platform until it came to rest a few meters above and a meter out from the safety rail. Close up, the silvery surface was streaked and splashed with brown muck that looked like dried mud, dung, and blood. Bits flaked off as the hatch opened and the stairladder extended to the platform.

Salasso hefted his case.

"Let's not keep them waiting."

Gregor gestured to Elizabeth. "Let me take your bag. After you."

"Oh, thanks!"

She ascended the ladder rather grandly, raising the hem of her skirt, wrinkling her nose at the faint farmyard pong. Gregor followed, clutching their bags and trying not to look down where the stairladder passed beyond the edge of the platform. As soon as he'd stepped inside, the stair folded in and the hatch closed.

The interior was in apparent daylight, from a window that went all around and which had been invisible from the outside—a screen, he guessed. Around a central fairing was a circular seat, at the far end of which a single saur was sitting in front of a panel, looking back at them over his shoulder, his hands resting on a sloping panel under the window-screen.

He exchanged greetings with Salasso then said in English, "Hi, grab a seat. Doesn't matter where you sit. Or stand if you like."

But, moved by the impulse to avoid being thrown about by acceleration, Elizabeth, then Gregor, crowded up to sit alongside Salasso who had taken the place beside the pilot.

"I've turned the view to your vision," said the pilot. "Hope I got the colors right."

Gregor looked around. Where the screen wrapped behind him he could see people waving from the platform, standing back.

"Looks perfect," he said.

"Okay," said the pilot.

He turned to face forward, and his fingers rippled on the panel. The view tilted away from the tops of the city's towers to the sky and clouds. For a moment it seemed stationary, then the clouds began to grow visibly larger. Gregor looked around to the back, and saw the city tipped at a crazy angle, dwindling behind them. There was absolutely no sense of motion or that the craft was anything but horizontal. He felt Elizabeth clutch his arm as she leaned around him. They shot through a cloud in a white blink and then the view tilted again, revealing nothing but a very dark-blue sky.

Still unable to make his reflexes believe what he saw, Gregor stood up. Elizabeth, hanging on to his arm, rose too. Looking down from the upper side of the screen they could see the ground—or rather, the surface of the planet, the horizon discernibly curving away on either side.

"Oh, gods above!" breathed Elizabeth, letting go of his arm and leaning on the yielding material of the screen's sill, peering downward, then tilting her head sideways and looking up. "You can see *stars*! We're practically in *space*!"

"Welcome to the stratosphere," said the pilot. He leaned back and took his hands off the panel, revealing what looked like shallow imprints of his palms. "Makes a pleasant break for me too, I must say. I've been dodging sauropod shit for weeks."

"Not always dodging," said Elizabeth.

"Nothing a good tropical rainstorm won't wash off. It's their tails you have to watch out for, even in this crate."

He clasped his hands behind his head and stretched out his legs. Gregor guessed that, like Salasso, he'd been around humans for a while.

"Why do you get close to their tails in the first place?" Gregor asked, returning to the seat.

The pilot laughed. "I might have to give you a demo, on the way in to New Lisbon. Don't worry—never lost a skiff yet."

On the area around the palm-prints, tiny rectangles of dim light appeared, flickering back and forth. The pilot leaned forward and scrutinized them.

"Oh good, Coriolis storm ahead. Time for a wash."

He laid his hands on the panel again and the view swung down to a blue ocean surface and, some way ahead of them, a roiling mass of cloud. Within seconds the craft had plunged into it, swooping out of its dive and into level flight. Rain-lashed darkness, a glimpse of blue sky, a rollover in another wet and dark space, then out the other side and up to the stratosphere again.

"If you pull something like that again," Elizabeth said, "you're going to have some cleaning to do on the *inside*."

"If I have to do that again I'll ask you to close your eyes first," retorted the pilot. "It's the dissonance between eye and inner ear that—"

Salasso hissed something and the pilot shut up.

Gregor, now that everyone understood that no motion of the craft could throw them about, was careful to sit clear of Elizabeth. He edged around the seat until he was looking directly behind, to the north and east. The seatback and the faintly vibrating, quietly humming, dimly glowing truncated cone of the engine-faring was between him and Elizabeth, a far more dangerous body. The hurricane, typical of the band of equatorial ocean between Mainland and Southland, receded over the horizon.

As this flight in its turn passed from the magical to the familiar, what Salasso had told him returned in all its novelty and force. He remained at once flattered and appalled. As he reviewed and re-evaluated their three years' acquaintance and friendship, he found himself wishing heartily that Elizabeth had made her true feelings known from the start. He couldn't know if he'd have reciprocated, but at least things would have been resolved. He had never thought of her in a sexual context, apart from an undercurrent of approbation of her as a good-looking, healthy woman, hardly more erotic than the sort of admiration he'd feel for a fit and handsome and intelligent man. It was possible, he supposed, that in their work relationship—inevitably close and sometimes physical, when they sweated together on the boat—he'd unconsciously masked off any such thoughts as no more appropriate for fellow scientists than for fellow soldiers.

Now—breaking through that screen—the knowledge that she was in love with him was in itself enough to make her suddenly enormously attractive and exciting, in a way that was both natural and perverse.

Lydia still shone in his mind in a way that made him feel guilty about even enjoying the thought of Elizabeth . . . and yet Lydia had turned back from throwing in her lot with him; instead making it conditional on his meeting her father's extravagant requirement. His own requirement of her, he knew, was perhaps more exorbitant. The fact remained that Elizabeth had chosen to accompany him, and Lydia had not.

He wished that Elizabeth and not the saur had told him of her feelings, but he could not blame Salasso for doing it. The thought of what infelicities and blunders—even perils—his ignorance of the situation could have brought about, made his sweat run cold.

The sea behind them gave way to the long white beaches of the northern coast of Southland, then a broad fringe of manufacturing-plant which in its turn merged almost imperceptibly into the natural rainforest. Gregor stood up and moved around again to the front. When Elizabeth looked up as he sat down, he returned her a smile more gentle, more inquiring, than he perhaps intended.

Again the landscape below tilted upward, almost filling the screen, and they hurtled down to where the rainforest thinned out to grass-land. Interrupted only by outcrops and mountain ranges, the sea of grass stretched all the way to the permafrost below the ice cap. Vast herds of gigantic beasts browsed the prairie; from this height, they appeared as stains on the land, irregular patches the size of counties. Untroubled by anything except the packs of predators and hordes of parasites that harassed their every moment, the dinosaurs of the northern reaches paid the high-skimming skiff less attention than they would a fly.

Someday, they might learn a different response.

With a gleeful yelp the pilot took the skiff upward again, skip-ping over a ten-thousand-meter mountain range like a saucer sent spinning across water. And down again, to the southern plain.

Here, the herds were not patches but rivers, flowing north in their annual autumnal migration away from the oncoming snows to the approaching rains and lush growth. Most of the streams were moving in the direction of gaps in, and passes through, the mountain range. Others had been diverted onto a path that would take them parallel to and south of the mountains, toward the western coast.

A saur voice, distinct from that of the two in the craft, sounded in the air. The pilot made a long, low noise in reply, lifted the craft again and sent it yet farther south, and then down in another swoop until it was skimming along at a hundred meters. Gregor felt his fingers dig into the screen's sill—the forward rush was terrifying at this height, the grass a green-and-brown blur beneath them.

A blemish on the horizon resolved in seconds into a great tide of animals moving along in a cloud of dust and a haze of insects and bats. The craft flew straight toward the herd and then, five hundred meters in front of its leading edge, stopped.

And dropped until it hung a meter above the grass. The herd advanced like a striding forest, the swaying necks of the adults reaching fifteen meters into the air. Gregor could see the ground in front of them actually shake, dust particles jumping above the tough stalks of rough grass. He could see the dappled patterns of their hides, brown-on-green for the most part, their undersides yellow and white. The younger and smaller animals seemed almost to dance along, dodging around the mighty legs of their elders. And darting between them, the dark slinking shapes of the bolder predators. When the compact leading group was a few steps, a few seconds away, the pilot took the craft up and at them. A head that looked bigger than the craft itself loomed in the screen, sending Gregor and Elizabeth into a futile instinctive backward lurch.

At the last moment the pilot veered to the left, jinked about and took them in again at the herd's leaders, from the side this time. They dived directly at a huge rolling eye, then up and over the tossing head's flailing wattles; swung up and away, much farther to the left, to the east, and paced that edge of the herd, setting beasts shying and rearing, shit flying by the steaming ton as they lurched sideways, shouldering their fellows.

Then again in at the group at the front, this time coming at them from behind and to the left. And around at the flank again, and

then to the front again, until—the fourth time they approached—
the leading bulls and cows broke into a run, veering off on a course
that now leaned to the west. At that the pilot pulled the skiff back,
zooming skyward and halting at a few thousand meters, surveying
the success of his deflection of that whole miles-long torrent. Slight
though it was, he seemed satisfied.

"That's enough for now," he said. "I'll be back. I've staked my
claim on this lot."

With that he leaned on the indented panel and set a course
straight to the west. In the next few minutes they passed to the
south of several herds now trudging in the same direction that the
craft flew. Other skiffs attended these, chivying them on, blocking
any breaks toward the north. Such attempted breaks became more
frequent as the mountain range ran down into isolated peaks and
foothills. Long-necked carrion-bats, circling on thermals, were
thrown into screaming downward spirals by the skiff's wake. Predators and scavengers feasted on the bodies of beasts that had refused
to turn back, and had been—as the pilot explained—decapitated
by skiffs flown straight through their necks.

"Isn't that dangerous?" Elizabeth's face was white, her hands
tight, her lips thin as a saur's.

"Oh no," the pilot said. "Edge-on, it's no contest. It's the tails
whacking you from above or below that you have to watch out for.
Or getting crushed underfoot, for that matter. You have to be gods-
cursed stupid or unlucky to do that, but it happens."

Ahead of them the western sea appeared on the horizon, and as
they flew toward it they could see the herding become more intense,
skiffs buzzing the great beasts like bees, to the point where entire
herds were being panicked into stampeding for the final few kilometers and minutes of their lives.

To the slaughter cliffs.

The skiff hovered, hanging in the air a hundred meters above the
level of the top of the cliffs and a few hundred meters out from the
beach. The cliffs themselves at this part of Southland's western
coast, the reach called by the humans Gadara, rose about two hundred meters above the beaches.

Any sauropod that shied at the edge was pushed implacably forward by those behind. So by the dozen, by the score, the huge

animals plunged to their deaths. Any that survived for a moment, their impact softened by the bodies already fallen, were swiftly crushed by the next to fall.

The bodies were given no time to pile up further. For miles around this primitive mass slaughter an industrial process of butchery and preservation went on. Specialized vehicles waded in the bloody surf, dragging and cutting, pumping and hosing. The sea close to the shore thronged with great iron ships, from which hooks and cables and cranes were deployed to haul the hacked meat away. Half a mile to the south an installation the size of a small town stood on stilts in the sea. Clouds of steam and smoke drifted above it.

Above everything, above the beach and the inshore fleet and the processing-plant, the air was filled with the white-and-gray wings of seabats, the surface broken by their diving in a million places like raindrops on a lake.

Gregor found himself gazing at the process with a kind of nauseated fascination. He was very glad that he could not smell any of it. All he could bring himself to say was:

"Isn't this a bit inefficient? Doesn't it contaminate the meat?"

"And," added Elizabeth, likewise transfixed, "isn't it *cruel*?"

"Good gods, no," said Salasso. "Death is swift, perhaps swifter than any other method of killing such large beasts would be. As to efficiency, we use every part of the animal. Contamination, well—it is actually not difficult to hose away the excreta."

"Anyway," said the pilot, "It's traditional. We did it on a bigger scale in ancient times, and less efficiently."

Another unfelt jump took them farther back and higher up, to show a wider view of the coast's black cliffs and miles of white sand.

"See the beaches we no longer use," he said. "Their sand is splintered bone."

The craft spun about again and flew a few more miles to the south. The cliffs sloped away to shingle shores bordering the grassy plain, and a straight road and railway line crossing the prairie and terminating in a kilometer-long causeway came into view. At the causeway's end, New Lisbon hunched in the sea, a rocky island crusted with streets and fringed with quays. Its harbors were crowded with ships and boats. A mile out to sea, attended by the usual fleet of small vessels, the starship hung on the water.

The pilot set them down at the end of one of the quays, and flew off, back to the dinosaur drive. Gregor stood on the boardwalk watching it disappear, and took a deep breath. The breeze carried no taint of the gruesome work being done beneath the cliffs. The meat handled here, being transferred from the shuttling factory ships to the refrigeration tankers for the long haul, was already processed and packaged for freezing, or salted and smoked, boiled and canned. Some of it would be due for a longer haul than an ocean crossing. What delicacies, Gregor idly wondered (eyeballs? tongues? sweetbreads?), would be worth shipping to the stars?

He turned to the island town and to his friends. New Lisbon loomed before them on its volcanic plug, its buildings dense and high, its streets narrow and steep, a haystack of needles.

"So where do we go now?" he asked.

Salasso lifted his case and set off along the echoing boards with dauntless step. Gregor and Elizabeth hurried after him.

"We find a lodging," the saur said. "Then we split, and search. I have a list of places. Simple."

14

Revolutionary Platform

T HE DELEGATES BRANDISH their weapons."
  We were sitting on the edge of a rickety stage. Driver and Lemieux—their avatars shabby-suited like Bukharin and Zinoviev—sat behind the table, frowning over data in its illusory depths. Camila, her head seamlessly edited to the body of a bandy-legged horsewoman, propped her cutlass on the shoulder of her yak-hide coat and looked at the gathering throng with nervous amusement.

"What's this based on?"

Avakian, robed as a mullah, looked up from a grubby notebook, his virtual visual display.

"Baku Congress of the Peoples of the East," he said. "Nineteen nineteen, I think. Swiped the details from an old film about John Reed, to tell you the truth. Last week we did the Petrograd Soviet, but there's only so much fun to be had with muddy trenchcoats and Lenin's trousers."

Remember the Twenty-six Commissars of Baku, I thought grimly, as my virtual leather jacket and trousers—Bolshevik chic—creaked around me. My hand tightened on the realistically rusty Afghan-workshop copy of a Lee Enfield which represented my say in decisions. Pathans and Mongols, Turks and Armenians, Kazakhs and Kalmyks and many other nationalities—all in traditional costumes with swords and rifles and fierce expressions—were filing in and taking their seats in a semicircular auditorium under a flapping marquee. The scene and our accoutrements might be testimony to Avakian's warped sense of humor but the meeting was as seditious, and as fraught with consequence, as its original.

Even if none of us ended up shot by the British.

It was the day after our arrival, the day after we'd shown the project data to Avakian. *He* hadn't needed any walk-through from me. After zapping through the whole thing faster even than Driver, he'd come out raving and raring to go, hand-waving wild speculative explanations of the implied AG physics, from which all I could extract was that the density of the transplutonic nuclei generated a quark-gluon plasma at the nuclear core which, when set in cyclical motion, interacted directly with the quantum foam of the space-time manifold, after which matters got complicated and arcane. He also had a few ideas about "the engine," about which he was even more excited and less comprehensible.

"Think fusion bombs compared to atomic bombs," he said. "It's the same physics, but ramped up several orders of magnitude to something that has *no practical limit*. You don't just *control mass*. You *become light*."

And then his frightening laugh.

Driver had told him to spread the word around the station's intranet, and while he was off doing that, Driver and Lemieux had explained the mutinous crew's brilliant plan for the Revolution.

They were busy releasing the alien mathematics, the basis for completely ripping open any kind of prime-number–based encryption, to as many nodes on the Internet as the station's powerful and highly directional transmitters could reach. With this, it would not take long for the distributed processing-power and collaborative ingenuity of the world's hackers and geeks to pry open the secrets of every military and security establishment on Earth. The people would shortly thereafter have the goods on all the deceptions practiced by the powers of both sides, and . . .

And in this way, we will build the Revolution!

It struck me as the kind of program that could only have been dreamt up by scientists, disillusioned security men, and code-geeks, and exactly the sort of naive, apolitical suggestion that got laughed out of enthusiastic young information-techs at their first IWWWW meeting. Knowledge is one thing, and power is something else.

But I didn't tell them I thought that. Their program wouldn't bring down any states—maybe a few governments—but I couldn't see it doing any harm.

Driver stood up and addressed the assembly.

"Comrades and friends," he said, with only a little irony in his voice, "I know you're all very busy and I know you all know what this meeting's about, so I won't waste time. We've already decided on our revolutionary strategy—"

He was interrupted by a murmur of approval and a shuffle of opposition, both of which Avakian's VR software, getting into the spirit of the thing, translated into a pounding of rifle-butts and a tumult of cries of *"Allah-hu Akbar!"* He smiled and continued:

"—so all we have to do now is decide whether to incorporate the Nevada Projects—as we're calling them—into the program. I can see arguments for and against it. One obvious argument for it is that if the devices perform as some of us seem to think, we'll have an extraordinarily effective means of defense. Against it, there's the obvious point that developing the machines might be a diversion of time and resources from more-urgent tasks. I don't consider myself in any way competent to decide this at present— it's partly a technical question. Over to you."

He sat down, to a jangling quiet. One of the scientists immediately stood up. Her name was Aleksandra Chumakova—a small woman with an intense gaze. She must have hacked her avatar, because she appeared as wearing ordinary uniform fatigues.

"This is a farce!" she said. "Let's stop playing at being revolutionaries: we're scientists. You uncovered some illegal actions by Major Sukhanov and his connections on the ground—well and good. You moved decisively, appealed to the people and the proper authorities, action is being taken. . . . Excellent! And then you went and ruined our moral position by starting this campaign of subversion—"

About two-thirds of the assembly flourished their weapons and flashed their teeth. Chumakova glared at them and continued:

"—which many of us deplore, and which could easily destabilize the military balance on Earth—"

Driver raised a hand.

"We had this discussion last week," he said. "We've taken our decision and reconsidering it is *not* on the agenda of this meeting."

"Very well," Chumakova said. "Let's look at what is on the agenda. You now suggest building obviously dangerous devices, the plans for which have been brought here by an American agent and a renegade! Why not just blow us all up and be done with it?"

The one in three who seemed to agree with her probably just

nodded and "hear, hear!"ed in real life, but the VR translated their response as before.

"This could get old real fast," Camila said under her breath. Avakian glanced at her and frowned, but thereafter the responses were less tumultuous.

A man called Angel Pestaña stood up, leaning on the butt of his long rifle. His avatar's black burnoose looked North African.

"I think my colleague Chumakova exaggerates a little. Comrade Driver is not urging us to build the machines, he is asking us to discuss it. Very well, then, let us discuss it! First, the issue of safety is a diversion, as is the notion that this is some kind of American sabotage operation. Those of us who've taken the trouble to check have confirmed that the science data did indeed originate in the interface with the aliens. I can give you the references, Aleksandra!

"What's far more important is for us to understand why the aliens gave out this information, and why they bypassed us to do it. Once we understand that, we can decide whether or not to prioritize building the machines."

"That might delay the construction for a few million years," said Driver. "I take it that's not what you propose?"

Pestaña shook his head. "I suggest asking them."

Laughter.

"Hmm, yes, there's always that," said Driver. He looked around for someone else waiting to speak. Louis Sembat rose next.

"I've been running some calc overnight," he announced, waving what looked to everyone else like a scroll covered with curlicued calligraphy but was probably a hand reader, "based on the work begun by Mr. Cairns here. It looks feasible—we aren't making much use of the fabs for the information campaign, after all. The basic inputs and materials are available. We have enough transplutonics in the labs to build at least prototypes of the craft and the engine. It really is not a big deal. I say go for it. Going by the Cairns documentation the first construction should only take a couple of weeks. The engine might take a bit longer, but the experience gained in building the craft could even speed it up."

I signaled frantically to Avakian, who gave me the floor. A few hastily keyed macro commands got my avatar clunking over in its tall riding-boots to stand in front of the table.

"I just want to make one point following the last speaker. I'm not a scientist or technician, I'm a systems manager, and I know for a fact that any time-estimate you may have found in the documentation will be worthless. So please don't count on getting this thing flying in a fortnight."

My avatar delivered this modest contribution as though addressing troops from an armored train. As it strode or staggered back I told Avakian to stop messing around. He just grinned.

More arguments followed, some of them quite technical, and by the end the two obvious groups in the meeting were themselves divided: Some of those who'd supported Chumakova were in favor of going ahead, perhaps because it was at least something to do other than the information war; some of Driver's supporters opposed it explicitly, for that same reason. The division was looking very close indeed when Driver beckoned Camila. She shot me a surprised glance and strolled over to stand behind the table, looking skinny and vulnerable and fierce.

"Friends," she said, "I'm just a commercial test pilot. I don't know much about politics but I do know about aircraft. If these machines do what Mr. Avakian thinks they do, then you can change the world from right here. You can make it available to anyone you choose, or no one. Above all, you can win a lot of respect if you're visibly handling the most advanced technology we've ever seen. This could break a lot of logjams; it could make space an attractive prospect again—even the stars! You could hold out the promise of the stars! Okay, okay, maybe the cometary minds already own most of the real estate, but we can work something out. I mean, come on, guys, you're scientists! You can do it, and you . . . you know . . . I think you should."

She returned to the edge of the stage in an eerie silence. Avakian, master manipulator, was letting this response take its course.

"God," Camila whispered, "I blew that one, I just let it run into the sand."

"You were great," I told her.

The vote went three-to-one in favor.

"God is great," said Camila.

The delegates brandished their weapons.

As soon as they'd dispersed into the heat haze Avakian shut the display down, and once more I was hooking a leg around an angle-bracket in Driver's crowded office. He, Lemieux, Avakian and

Camila and I all looked at each other, blinking and shaking our heads—the usual uncertain moment after coming out of full-immersion VR.

"That went well," said Driver. "No thanks to you, Armen. I'm surprised there wasn't a complete walkout by Aleksandra's mob about the way you were stacking the deck."

"Hey, I cooled it later on, and I'll tread lightly in future, okay?"

"Fine. Matt, how much more work do you need before you can turn the project plan over to production?"

I tried to give an honest estimate. "Couple of days at the most. But I can't promise there won't be bugs cropping up when we actually try it."

"Yeah, sure, no plan ever survives . . . et cetera. Okay. Go for it. Get a material-requirements list—even crude aggregates—together as fast as you can. If we're missing any actual *elements,* we're buggered, but components can be cobbled up in the fabs and there's still a fair bit of raw stuff, from volatiles on up to iron, that we can dig up and refine if we have to. I don't want to find a bottleneck after we've started. If there are any, I want to know about them ASAP."

He turned to Lemieux. "Paul, you get a team together, liaise with Matt and the scientists, pull in Sembat, keep Chumakova's lot on board, get Volkov and Telesnikov to keep the cosmonauts up to speed, and make sure you get their input—the craft won't be much bloody use if the controls are for, I dunno, *tentacles* or something."

Avakian laughed, and interjected: "It's okay, I've seen the panels, they're for hands. Maybe not *our*— Ah, forget it. But definitely, no tentacles."

"All right," said Driver, as though thinking his joke had been taken too literally. "Maybe you could help Matt with systems integration and science data, okay?"

"Yup."

"You square with all that, Paul?"

Lemieux nodded.

"Fine. Camila . . ." Driver studied her for a moment, frowning. "Can you keep us in touch with Nevada, and maybe work with our engineers on your own, uh, flying saucer? I'm sure it needs a bit of turnaround maintenance. No security problems there?"

"It's open tech," Camila said. "Yeah, that's warm."

"Great!" Driver gave a most uncharacteristic wide grin and a clenched-fist salute. *"Per ardua ad astra,* then. Latin for 'Get off your arse.' "

We did.

My first task was the mundane and tedious one of porting most of my software from storage in American hard tech to implementation in European wet tech, and integrating the lot with my reader and the American spex. Fortunately, the station's intranet had an entire library of hacks and kludges for doing just that, but I could have done with an old geek at my elbow. When the crossover had been completed, my sense of triumph was muted by the thought that already half a day's slippage had thus been added to our notional schedule. But worrying about that would only lose more minutes, so—

I sucked a coffee, keyed the spex, and got busy on the real job.

In Avakian's Baku Congress scenario my reflexes, already adapting to microgravity, had been thrown off balance by an environment where virtual objects behaved as though they had weight and my real body didn't. It was a pleasure to get back into my own VR, where everything meshed. I'd never thought of it before, but the dataspace in which I usually worked had zero-g virtual physics. My viewpoint darted about in it like a minnow, now that it wasn't subconsciously contending with my inner ear.

Furthermore, the entire project was now embedded in its original context, from which the ESA documentation sent to me had been abstracted. Concepts and details and reasons that had been leaden and flat the first time, now twanged with resonance. Understanding far more of what I was doing, I did it faster. The AIs also brightened, their suggested solutions often surprising me, going beyond the bounds of their conceptual thesauri. Didn't make some of their suggestions any less stupid, of course, but weeding these out was where I came in, and I was doing it better. You can do a lot with a good dataset, but there's nothing to beat on-site, hands-on problem-solving.

After I'd got the first-cut list of raw material inputs completed and zapped off to the relevant departments I called up Avakian, who merged his workspace with mine and then, increasingly, with the scientists who'd taken an interest in the project. Hours passed, fast—it was like my earlier experience of moving from the hobbled environment of E.U. dataspaces to the U.S., but with even greater freedom because everybody was free to share. It was a style of collaborative work I'd not encountered before, and it was as addictive as a well-designed game.

Eventually Avakian noticed that our rate of errors, misunderstandings, and frictions was creeping up.

"Knock off," he said. "Call it a day shift. See you all in eight hours."

After we'd dropped out of the shared space I hung in the VR for a while, channel-hopping the station's news-servers. In Europe the crisis seemed to be easing off a little, the street demonstrations hanging fire while assorted commissions and committees attempted to hammer out compromises. At the same time, high-level scandals and low-level protests had erupted in the United States. The governments of India and China had lodged with the U.N. some unspecified complaints about allegedly unfraternal dealings by the E.U., putting some strain on the great anti-imperialist alliance. In the background to it all, in both blocs and in the independents, leaks and rumors and speculation about the scale of the alien presence in the Solar System was spreading.

Of Jadey's plight there was no news at all. I sent her a message, care of the Sheriff Court, but without much hope that she'd see it anytime soon. Then I went to the refectory and ate mashed potatoes, grilled carrots, and curried rabbit.

Yum.

I rattled back the curtain of the place where we'd slept, to meet Camila's glare as she wiped her naked body with a damp cloth.

"Jeez! What *is* this, Privacy Central?"

"Sorry," I said, moving to slide the curtain back.

She beckoned. "Hey 's warm, come on in."

I looped in and hung opposite her as she hung herself out to dry. She didn't look as skinny in microgravity as she had in the spacesuit, her breasts full above the bony cage of her ribs. She looked back at me in that shamelessly direct American way that, like the accent, had always excited me.

"Do you want me to find somewhere else?"

She shook her head. "It's as bad everywhere. I'd still have to share with someone, and I'd rather share with you than with one of the commies. Especially the women."

"They're not commies."

"Yeah, yeah, I know. Russkis, French—same thing. Weird. Wacko. Not like us."

"Us Anglos, Ms. Hernandez?"

"Like I said. You know what I mean." She dismissed the question. "You look tired."

"Knackered. But we're making progress." I told her about it, briefly. "What have you been doing yourself?"

"Oh, talking to engineers. Wandering about in the real world. Checking over the old *Blasphemous*. Raiding the commissary."

She rummaged in a bundle of clutter behind her.

"Managed to score some dope," she said. "Want to try some?"

"How do you get *that* on a space station?"

"All that hydroponics, someone's gotta put it to good use. And it's hardly like there's a fire risk."

She busied herself with a ten-centimeter roll of plastic and a battery-powered steam-pipe.

"Oh, all right, thanks. My head's buzzing anyway."

She sucked in the fragrant steam and passed me the apparatus. I inhaled gratefully and passed it back, riding the rush. Her dark eyes shone.

"Buzzing with what?"

"When I shut my eyes," I said, shutting them, "I can still see the data structures, the critical paths, the exploded views, the lot, and the craft and the engine at the end of it all, sort of glowing in the dark."

My eyes snapped open. "And the news from home."

"Ah." She pumped the steamer until it hissed and bubbled again. "Jadey. No news of her?"

"Nope."

"Sorry about that." Her pupils widened, her eyelids narrowed. "Really. You and her. Shit. Bad luck for—"

She laughed and passed me the pipe. The air-conditioning roared in my ears.

"Bad luck for who?"

"Ah, for her." She closed her eyes, drifting. "No, to be honest, I meant for you and me both."

I could see where this was going, I hadn't been born yesterday.

"Why?" I asked, as though I didn't know.

She stared at me, drifting closer, her breasts and eyes looming like approaching ships.

"We were real close on the flight," she said. "Talked about every-thing. Never talked to anybody like that."

I dizzily recalled our conversations. They hadn't seemed so in-timate to me—more like . . . I didn't know . . . finding a friend you could talk to about anything that took your fancy. She'd talked about childhood, her grandparents' voyage from Cuba on an inner tube, her education, her training. She had talked about guys, with nostalgia, even sentimentality, sometimes crudity. With both of us clad in shock-gel, it had seemed like time-out from sexuality.

The loneliness of her rare talent and reckless courage hit me.

"I never knew," I said.

"Ah shit, you did—you were listening. Hell, when you were asleep it was all I could do not to kiss you."

"I *love* Jadey," I said. "Christ, I *miss* her."

"I got no problem with that," she said. "And I don't think you have."

Our mouths docked before I could answer.

"Christ, man, you were supposed to get some sleep," Avakian said. "What the fuck you been doing, steaming dope all night?"

"Something like that," I mumbled. I rubbed my bleary eyelids and slid on my spex. "Hard to sleep after all this."

"Yes, isn't it just!" he agreed, as one by one the rest of the team clocked in.

We ran a match on the lists of available and required materials. It took awhile—the trees of acceptable substitutions were multi-branched, intertwined, close to a combinatorial explosion, chal-lenging even for the AIs.

"Chug-chug-chug," Avakian muttered.

The display flared into green.

"Yee-hah!"

"Okay, now for the Leontiev matrices . . ."

A program capable of running the economy of a minor socialist republic or a major multinational corporation clunked through its iterations and punched out the complete production plan. We hung there for a moment, just looking at it. For that moment it seemed accomplishment enough. If I'd done this back home I'd have taken the team out for Chinese.

"That's it," said Mikhail Telesnikov, the cosmonaut. His phantom presence radiated impatience. "Let's run the sim."

The simulated production run uncovered enough glitches to keep us busy for hours, tweaking and rerunning it. Eventually the VR models of the fabricators did their spidery work, and spun out the disc.

It floated in the center of our dataspace, a silvery lens that focused all our attention. Doubly unreal, a simulation which we could not in our hearts believe; an original too cheapened by endless fake reproductions and false reports to produce the effect it must have had on its first viewers, or the intent of its craftsman.

"*Numinous Geometries,*" I thought, mentally christening the device. Telesnikov switched to a full-immersion avatar and stood in front of it, looking back at our—to him—invisible viewpoints.

"Well, come on," he said. "It's only a *ship.*"

Avakian, silent for once, flipped us all in and we walked up just as Telesnikov reached up and touched the shining rounded edge of the thing. I had a flash of recollection of a Festival preacher in Princes Street Gardens going on about some biblical widget—the arc of the covenant, I think it was called—that could strike you dead if you touched it.

But all that happened was that from the seamless structure a tripod of legs extended, a hatch opened, and stairladder of child-sized steps unfolded. Telesnikov boldly ascended, then Avakian; I cheated my way to the front and followed. The others, not quite so quick off the mark, made do by switching back to non-immersive viewpoints and tabbing straight through the hull.

Inside, the craft was almost familiar—at first disappointingly so, then uncannily. A smooth central casing over the engine formed the back of a circular bench, facing the viewscreen which likewise ran all around the craft. Beneath the viewscreen was a sloping shelf, one section of which consisted of an incomprehensible display of unreadable instruments and a panel in which the shapes of two small, long hands were recessed, as though someone with three fingers and one long thumb had pressed their palms into the material before it had set.

I'd seen very similar arrangements in documents and accounts in the decades' worth of rubbish I had scanned from Dreamland. Just about everyone who'd ever claimed to have been taken inside a UFO, or to have reverse-engineered one from crashed specimens had come up with something like this.

"Devil take this," said Telesnikov. "They're laughing at us."

"Maybe they aren't too clear on the concept of *fingers,*" said Avakian.

"No, that is not what I mean. This is ridiculous! This is copied from some shoddy piece of USAF disinformation."

His words set off an agitated babble from our colleagues, swirling around the cockpit like invisible but angry bees. Telesnikov and I seemed to be the only persons present who had more than the vaguest notion of the details of the UFO mythos. The others inclined to Avakian's more charitable interpretation, that it was a simple error in the aliens' grasp of human anatomy, a suggestion which those with the longest experience of interfacing with them seemed to find a lot more believable than I did.

"They think and see on a different scale from ours," Louis Sembat insisted. "There are gaps in their knowledge, blind spots. Imagine us conversing with bacteria! How could we know that certain cilia were significant?"

Avakian brought the discussion to an unceremonious halt by dumping us all back to an abstract workspace where we faced each other around a table.

"Enough already," he said. "Whatever the reasons for this glitch, we know our friends are perfectly capable of providing us with a suitable interface because they've already done it once. It's just a matter of getting into the restricted view and letting them know our requirements."

From the comments and laughs that greeted this I gathered it wasn't likely to be as straightforward as he made it sound.

"We could also have a crack," he continued, unperturbed, "at hacking out some kind of control interface ourselves. We've got some way to understanding the physics of the thing; the controls shouldn't be beyond us. Meanwhile we bash ahead with building it and running the project analysis and so on for device number two—the space-drive."

"Hang on," I said, "if we're looking at a different outcome, even if it's just the controls and the displays, the changes could be feedback to anywhere along the production pathway."

Avakian looked at me. "Yes," he said. "They could indeed. But that's the sort of thing you and your AI menagerie are supposed to be good at finding out."

"Oh, thanks," I said sarcastically. "I thought I might have time on my hands over the next few days."

"Don't worry," he said. "I'll help you, and we can call on a lot of other help." He waved a hand at the others around the table. "If we can't, I seriously doubt if anyone else can, except— Hey!"

He theatrically smote his forehead.

"*And* we're in touch with the only other place that could maybe do better, on the practical side. Your Mr. Armstrong's engineers in Nevada. Make this a *real* Nevada project, huh? I guess that means we'll have to get non-Comrade Hernandez in on the team. Maybe you could persuade her."

His horrible laugh was echoed by enough sniggers for me to realize that in a place without privacy, some news traveled fast.

At the end of the evening shift Driver called me to his office. I saved-to-date and arrived to find Lemieux, Camila, and Avakian with him. We still seemed to be the self-appointed project committee.

"Not bad work today," said Driver. He'd been scanning reports skimmed off by our VR activities. "I seem to remember you saying something yesterday about *hands,* Armen. Why didn't you raise it as a problem?"

Avakian shrugged. "I had only a suspicion, from a few obscure diagrams that might not have been definitive. Besides, I wanted to see what would eventually come out the other side rather than get bogged down in arguments first."

"Fair enough, I suppose," Driver allowed. "Still—anything else like this turns up, and you let me know absolutely clearly, okay?"

"Now that you mention it," Avakian said, "there doesn't seem to be any control interface *at all* for 'the engine.' The big engine. The space-drive."

"Hmm." Driver's eyes almost lidded over. "That could be a problem. We should add that to the list of things we want the aliens to clarify. If we can; or they can."

"What's this problem with getting answers from the aliens?" Camila asked. "I thought you guys had got a lot."

"Yeah, we have," said Avakian. "Trouble is, it's mostly high-level stuff: mathematics, quantum computing algorithms, and so on.

Not so much on the concrete, as we'd see it. Nothing on Earth or Solar System history, though we have asked."

"There were some things that Man was not meant to know," I said.

"Not so much that," Driver said. "My own impression from outside the science circus here is that there are some things that Man was bloody well meant to find out for himself."

He reclined in silence for a moment. "Speaking of which . . . When you think it necessary, Armen, I think the people to make the first inquiries should be you and Matt."

"Me?" I said. "But I've no experience—"

"Experience with the interface is valuable," Lemieux said. "But it is not necessarily of value in formulating queries, and in understanding answers. You at least know what kind of answer would be useful. And it is something you should become familiar with anyway. You are very good at cross-platform integration, and this is perhaps the ultimate in that."

"I can't wait," I said.

I suspected that they just wanted me to do it because they feared exposing themselves more than necessary to the seductive, addictive effect of the alien interface, and they didn't entirely trust the scientists who already had done so to come back with anything meaningful.

We dealt with some of the more mundane details of tomorrow's team deployment and then prepared to leave.

"Before we go—"

Lemieux, up in his corner perch, drew something on a physical notepad, tore off a sheet and let it flutter in the air among us. I caught a glimpse: It was an oval, with a single horizontal line a little above the sharp end, and two tilted ellipses on its small axis; the iconic, ironic ideograph of the mythic Gray alien.

"I hardly dare say it," he said. "But as a solution to the problem of how they know our languages, and of the strange design of the craft's controls—I wonder, Camila: Is there anything you might know, even a rumor about . . . the old rumors?"

But Camila was already laughing, giggling an explanation to the still-baffled Avakian. She reached out and grabbed the sketch and balled it up and stuffed it in Driver's trashbag.

She shook her head. "Sorry to disappoint you, guys, but I've been through all that; I've spoken to people who'd know if anyone would. The only Dreamland the little Gray folk have ever been to or come from is the one in our heads."

She smiled around at us. "Come on," she said. For a moment she looked puzzled, as though startled by a sudden thought, then she shook her head even more firmly.

"Nah."

15

The Space Shore

T HIS PLACE WAS smaller than Kyohvic, but it felt like a city—or how she imagined, from what she had heard and read, that a city felt. Kyohvic, for all its half a million inhabitants, its university and houses of philosophy, its ships and trade, had "small town" written in its genes. New Lisbon might have but a tenth the population of her hometown, but the people were so much more diverse. It was on the shore, not just of the sea, but of space: Other worlds were in the air, in the smells, in the surprises around every corner; in the attitude that everybody knew everything, but didn't know everybody.

She walked briskly but carefully down a sloping cobbled street, if you could call something three meters wide a street. Gregor walked beside her, having firmly rejected Salasso's argument that it would be more effective for them to search separately. It felt strange to be alone with him. She hadn't realized the extent to which she'd become used to Salasso's presence when they were together. Not that it had ever bothered her. Any inhibition she felt had been entirely her own doing. But still.

Buildings rose to three or four stories on either side, black and narrow as dominoes, and as dependent on each other's support. Overhead, a cable car fizzed and sparked, laboring up the incline at just the right height to barely avoid knocking a tall hat off a man on horseback. (Municipal regulation, she'd been told.) A gaggle of small blue-and-red-mottled dinosaurs which shared the size, shape, gait, and probable fate of geese, slithered and skittered past them, honking in protest at their casual herding by a ragged little girl with a big stick. The street was so steep that Elizabeth could see the ocean when she looked straight ahead. Which was not advisable, because of the dinosaurs, because the cobbles were uneven, and because out there on the sea squatted the starship.

Yes, it was the de Tenebre ship. Everybody knew that. She had cherished a faint hope that it wasn't. Gregor had said very little about the prospect of perhaps seeing Lydia again; she had rather expected him to prattle on about it, but he seemed to be focusing his attention and excitement on the possibility of tracking down some of the old crew. Which was, she supposed, all to the good.

Salasso had scribbled a list of thirteen waterfront dives ("for a start"), and drawn an elegant and precise street map of the relevant district.

"You got all this from your old teacher?"

Salasso had looked at Gregor as if he were being stupid.

"Of course not," he'd said. "This is my own deduction, from what I know of this place. I have been here before, and it doesn't change much."

Salasso himself had set out to prowl the saur hangouts, from the skiff pilots' bars to the more refined haunts of entrepreneurs in the butchery business. Listening for rumors, he'd explained; he was reluctant to actually ask around, and advised them, too, to be cautious, and to dress rough. And to remember that they were marine biologists, here to scout out possible lines of research, maybe hire a boat to watch kraken, something like that. Near enough the truth.

"You know," Elizabeth said, as the small dinosaurs waddled off down a side alley, "our cover story might turn out to be the only thing we get out of this trip. It's actually a *good idea*. This is a far better place to study the kraken than out of Mingulay."

"You don't hold out much hope of nabbing one of the old buggers, then?"

"We don't even know what they *look* like!"

"I do," Gregor said. "Or I bloody should—I've seen their portraits often enough. Cairns, Lemieux, Volkov, Telesnikov, Driver . . ."

A hairy gigant lurched around a corner and up the street, almost blocking it as he swayed back and forth, singing in a basso profundo whose sweetness made her shiver, drunk though he was. They pressed their backs to a wall, ducked under his arm as he passed.

"But will they still look the same?"

Gregor glanced at her sidelong.

"So the story goes."

At the foot of the street they turned left, past the cable-car terminus and on to the main drag, the street which ran all the way around the island and debouched to the causeway at the shoreward end. Built along a thirty-meter-wide shelf, it sometimes passed behind the pillars of elegant esplanades, sometimes dived behind outcrops of rock, sometimes overhung the sea. Every couple of hundred meters a jetty fingered out from it, on stilts or stones.

Much of the traffic consisted of carts laden with meat or fish, being hauled toward the railhead by petrol-engined tractors or by massive, plodding quadrupeds. Their drivers, and the pedestrians who crowded the sidewalks, were a roughly equal distribution of saurs and the three most widespread hominid species: humans, gigants, and pithkies. Elizabeth had seen few members of the last two before, and it was hard at first not to stare. The gigants stood about three meters tall, naked but for their shaggy reddish body hair and their belts of tools and weapons. The pithkies, slim and lithe at a meter and a half, wore human styles of clothing over the silver or golden fur that covered all but their sharp faces.

"I thought the pithkies were kind of stockier than that," she remarked in an undertone to Gregor. "All the ones I've seen before were, you know, heavily muscled."

"That's because they were all *miners*," he said. "But mining's just as unnatural to them as it is to us."

"So how come it's their specialty, huh?"

"Maybe the saurs gave them the mineral rights," he said. "Or the gods did." His glance indicated the god, clearly visible in the early evening sky. "Who knows?"

"But one day we'll find out?"

He turned a warm smile on her.

"Yes!"

His arm moved up and sideways, as though to fling around her shoulders; fell back. Awkwardly breaking stride, he fished in his pocket for Salasso's list, quite unnecessarily she thought; she and he both knew at least the first few names by heart.

"There it is," he said, pointing at a tavern sign ten meters away. "The Headless Chickadino."

"*Bad* taste," she said.

"No, no," he said. "Tastes like chicken."

Her yelp and skelp followed him through the door.

The tavern was high-ceilinged, bright and airy, with tall windows, seafaring scenes in their stained glass. Perhaps it once had been a house of philosophy, and later desecularized. The landlord was a gigant, the barmaids pithkies, the crowd mostly human and taking a break. For many people work here went on through the evening; at this time of year, through the night.

"What do you want to drink?" Gregor asked.

"Maybe guava juice, for now."

"Aye, I guess so," he grudgingly allowed.

They sat on stools at the bar, sipping the iced drinks and chatting idly as Gregor eyed the crowd. Most of them were local: sun-darkened men in workclothes, still grubby from cart or quay; a few sailors from Kyohvic, identifiable by their lighter skin and softer accents—one or two of them nodded to him. He presumed they recognized him no more than he did them.

But there was one man, sitting by the window talking to some old seamen or dockworkers, who did look familiar. Gregor couldn't place him at all. Red-haired, pale and freckled like a northerner, very relaxed. Very openhanded—after a few minutes Gregor saw him wave and nod for another round, and pay for a tray laden with tall and short glasses.

"What are you doing?" Elizabeth asked. "Ogling pithkies?"

"They do look a bit sexy," Gregor admitted, grinning. "Foxy ladies . . ."

Elizabeth kicked his shin, not very hard.

"Don't look around," said Gregor, stoically ignoring the sharp pain. "Count to thirty in your head and look in the bar mirror at the young bloke with the old men at the window."

When she turned to the mirror she rather cleverly faced straight ahead, as though at herself, flicking at a stray strand of hair.

"I've seen him before," Elizabeth said, turning back.

"Me too, but where?"

Elizabeth shrugged. "Some guy we see every day without noticing—a docker, someone at the university . . ."

Gregor was shaking his head. "Nah, I'd remember that. We must have both seen him once—"

"The party!" Elizabeth said. "At the castle. Remember?"

Gregor did remember him, in a very similar pose but splendidly dressed, listening to some Kyohvic merchants.

"Oh, right. Yeah, that's it. He's a trader. So much for that mystery." He looked at her, puzzled. "You were at the party after all?"

As soon as he'd said it, he realized he shouldn't have. He could all too clearly imagine how the party had gone for Elizabeth. He also realized that he couldn't let Elizabeth know that he did realize, because she didn't know that he knew.

She looked away, her cheek reddening, sharp and sudden as though slapped. Then she looked back at him with a forced cheerful smile that raked his heart.

"Yes, I was!" she said. "I guess we just missed each other in the crowd. I doubt you'd have noticed me anyway—that was where you met Lydia, wasn't it?"

"Yes," he said. He drained his glass and stood up.

"Time to wander on? And we could get something to eat at the next one if the name's anything to go by."

"The Hot Squid? Yeah, okay, I'm starving."

Out on the street the crowd had thickened. The next place was a few tens of meters on, its sign a lurid scene of cephalopodan coupling, the artist's interpretation of the relevant anatomy owing nothing to marine biology. It was, however, genuinely a bar and grill, much smokier and noisier than the Chick. And larger, with more than one room, impossible to take in from a single vantage.

Stuffed swordfish and sea reptiles hung among the lamps on low rafters. Seafood sizzled on a broad hotplate; mussels, squids, scallops, and fillets of fish were flipped and turned, doused with sauce and sprinkled with herbs in seconds or minutes by a gigant whose long, strong arms made him seem preadapted to the job. Very little grease was involved in the cooking, so the air was fragrant rather than heavy—the smoke came from hemp, not burnt oil, and the whole combination made Gregor's mouth water and belly ache with hunger. Pithkie waiters and waitresses yelled orders in rapid contralto Trade Latin or English; the short-order cook rumbled his responses and grumbles back. In a raised alcove at the back the saur manager or owner, clad improbably in a black business-suit and white shirt, clattered and fretted over a calculator, looking as though he'd be tearing his hair if he'd had any. The crowd was likewise mixed, saurs and hominidae rubbing shoulders, drinking and talking loudly, some half listening to a pithkie soprano at a microphone, her silver satin shift flowing over her silvery fur, her Latin torch-song keening above the babble.

"Bet *she* incites a few cases of hopeless love," Elizabeth said, with a kind of vehement flippancy. Gregor, swinging into a seat at a small table covered with sticky plastic, chose to take her literally.

"Gods, do you really think—" He shook his head with an exaggerated shudder.

"It's no crazier than what people really get besotted with," said Elizabeth, facing him boldly, then turning to wave at a waitress.

"Think we can risk a beer or two with this?" asked Gregor.

"Wouldn't dream of drinking anything else."

"How about white wine?"

She brightened. "Yes, thanks. A small one."

There was a moment of awkward silence after they'd placed their orders. The waitress returned with a brace of beer bottles.

"Do you think we have much of a chance?" Elizabeth asked. "Of finding them."

Gregor scratched at his beer bottle's damp label, then stopped as though catching himself doing something obsessive.

"Salasso seems very confident, and I think—"

"What?"

"He's not just blundered into this. Our squid research, for example. I'll have to check through the university's admin when we get back, but I suspect he had something to do with initiating the project in the first place. And he's a bit odd, for a saur."

Elizabeth laughed. "They're all odd."

"Yes, but he's a lot more open to humans than most. Maybe the ones on the ships, and old Tharovar in the castle, are as friendly. But not many."

"Hmm," said Elizabeth. "He seemed to know a lot about the First Crew, how they went to the saurs to help them hide."

"Maybe he was there at the time," said Gregor. "Why not?"

The waitress arrived with a tray of food and a bottle of wine. Elizabeth put down her half-finished beer as the glasses were filled.

"Speculation," she said. "Let's eat."

They ate and drank for a while, too hungry to talk much.

"Why," Elizabeth asked, "did the old crew go off to live incognito in the first place?"

"I don't know. My guess is that they didn't want to hang around and become a focus of resentment or undue respect. Not much fun being ageless if everybody envies or worships you."

"Or if you have to watch your children growing old and dying . . . but why couldn't they have used whatever it is they had on the rest of us?"

"Perhaps they didn't have the technology to reproduce it for anyone else."

"They could have left us some lines of research!"

Gregor shrugged. "Maybe they did. We're on the way to developing a worldwide biotech industry, eventually."

"Yes, eventually! And the saurs have one already! Why not get them to work on it?"

"Ah," said Gregor. "That's a different question: What the saurs are and are not willing to do for us, and share with us. I'm sure if the saurs wanted to, they could have given us everything they have, from a cure for aging—if they have it—to gravity skiffs. But they don't."

"It might have something to do with what Salasso said; that they don't want to merge our societies."

Speculation seemed fruitless, and Gregor had no wish to take the conversation further in that direction, well aware that he as much as Elizabeth was evading what they really wanted to talk about.

"Finished?"

"Yes." Elizabeth sighed contentedly and wiped her lips. "Let's circulate."

They stood up.

"Together, or separately?" she asked.

"Oh, together," Gregor said. "People are more likely to talk to us that way."

Elizabeth smiled at him defiantly. "We could pretend we're a couple."

"I'm sure everyone will assume we are anyway."

They had reached the third room in the place, and talked to a few men off the boats about their idea for scientific expeditions, without attracting much interest.

"It's like fishing without getting a nibble," Gregor was grumbling, when somebody slapped his back.

"Hi, Matt, what are you up to?"

Gregor turned to see a tall man in seaman's garb, a grin slowly fading from his ruddy face.

"Sorry, mate," the man said. "Mistook you for someone else." He frowned, shook his head, smiled apologetically and walked off through the crowd to the next bar counter.

Elizabeth caught Gregor's arm. "Let's ask him!"

Gregor shook his head. "Wait a minute. Don't want to warn them off."

He took a minute or two to finish his half-pint, and raised the empty glass to Elizabeth.

"Same again please?"

"Okay."

"Back in a tick." She turned back to order the round, her mouth narrowing.

Gregor edged his way between swaying bodies and balanced, brimming drinks, and walked blinking into the brighter light and thicker smoke of the next lounge. The man who'd accosted him was back at a table with some pals, evidently fellow seamen, with three young women wedged in between them. All were talking loudly, and being listened to by the trader Gregor had recognized earlier.

It wasn't that recognition, however, which made Gregor stop and turn away to lean his forearms on the bar and gaze into the mirror under the thin pretense of eyeing the inverted bottles of spirits racked above it. He'd recognized one of the seamen.

Unless he was making the same mistake as the back-slapping chap had done, he was looking sidelong at the mirrored image of the crewman and Cosmonaut Grigory Volkov. The broad features might be a family resemblance, but the blond buzz-cut seemed a little too distinctive for that. The man's face had acquired a few creases and many faint scars, but otherwise was just as it appeared in the paintings, and in photographs in old books.

Gregor felt as though he needed a stiff drink from one of those racked bottles. His knees were rubbery. Taking a deep breath, he steadied himself and returned to Elizabeth. She regarded him quizzically, a little sourly, and shoved the half-pint along to him as he sat up beside her.

"Found one," he said. "One of the crew."

"Seems to have shaken you up a bit."

"Yes." He put down the glass, more carefully, and smooched a splash of beer from the back of his hand. "Grigory Volkov. I was named after him. Famous cosmonaut in his own right. There were *books* written about him."

"Never heard of him, myself."

"Ah, well." Gregor smiled. "Being the first man on Venus probably didn't seem such a big deal after he got here. Anyway, there he is, talking to the trader we saw earlier."

"Any bright ideas about what to do next?"

"No. I can't think of a way to approach him while pretending not to recognize him."

"Well, I can! Come on."

She picked up her drink and slid off the stool. Gregor decided that he might as well take his turn at following. Again the drinkers' walk, threaded with subtle moves and etiquette, like an elaborate dance. As soon as Elizabeth was in fair view of their targets' table, she waved with her free hand and called out a bright hello. Gregor sidled and dodged after her, as all the people at the table turned to look at them.

Elizabeth made straight for the trader and leaned over the table and shook his hand, grinning into his baffled face.

"Well, *hi!*" she said. "I'm *so* pleased to see you again! I didn't get a chance to speak to any of you before."

The trader blinked and half rose, half bowed over her hand. His expression of confusion was swiftly replaced by a puzzled but polite smile.

"Your pardon?"

"The party in the castle at Kyohvic, remember?"

"Ah, of course." He nodded briskly, sweeping his hand to indicate that they should sit and everyone else had better make room for them. "Your dress and hair, so elegant then, I didn't recognize you. Forgive me."

Gregor wasn't sure if this claimed memory was genuine, but as he perched on the end of a bench he had to admire the man's quick thinking and aplomb as much as he did Elizabeth's. She was sitting down beside the trader on the end of the opposite bench, patting her hair and smoothing her grubby jeans.

"Marcus de Tenebre," said the trader. "And now you have the advantage of me."

"Elizabeth Harkness. And this is Gregor Cairns, my . . . um . . . friend. We're marine biologists."

217

The man he'd recognized as Volkov was jammed up in the corner of Marcus's side of the table, and had been looking at Gregor with a slight frown all the while. On hearing Gregor's name he flinched away, facing one of the women opposite him and initiating or resuming some quiet conversation.

Gregor hoped that his own reaction to the trader's name wasn't as obvious. That man had given no sign of recognizing his; perhaps he was a sufficiently distant, or preoccupied, relative of Lydia's not to have heard any family gossip.

"You've arrived here very quickly," said Marcus.

"Oh yes, we took a skiff," said Elizabeth, as though it were quite the done thing. "We wanted to visit while the meat market was on."

"Why, if I may ask?"

"Oh, it's to do with science," said Elizabeth. "We're wondering how all the meat processing, the factory ships, and so on affect the local sea-life, and maybe in setting up some possible future research. Have a look at the kraken in their home waters, stuff like that."

She glanced around the table. "Anyone interested in some off-season boat hire?"

A lot of head-shakes and shrugs.

"There's no off-season," one of the men said. "The meat processing keeps us busy in the autumn, the meat shipping keeps us through the winter, there's whaling in the spring when the pack ice breaks down south, and the rest of the time it's the fishing. Doesn't mean you couldn't squeeze something in, mind, or maybe get a berth on a trawler or a whaler. You'd have to speak to a skipper down at the docks, or the company offices."

"Plenty of kraken to be seen on the whaling," someone else put in.

Elizabeth smiled tentatively. "You never hit them by mistake?"

That raised some laughs.

"Not a chance," the first man explained. "Clever buggers, they are. Smart, you know?"

"Smart enough to fly starships," Gregor said.

"Aye, but that might not be enough to keep them out of the way of harpoons. Krakens can hunt whales. I've seen ones that got away. Sucker-marks this size on their flanks."

He spread his hands a meter apart and everyone laughed except

Gregor and Elizabeth, and Marcus and the man who might have been Volkov.

Gregor asked Marcus: "What are you doing here yourself?"

The trader smiled disarmingly at everyone. "Oh, just relaxing, enjoying the company. I've had a long day. And to be honest, it's beneficial to us to get to know folk."

He turned to Elizabeth. "And your kind interest in me was . . . ?"

"Oh! Well, traders are always interesting! But I just have a quick question, just wondering if you've ever noticed. Do the ships ever . . . change pilots, when they're on a planet's ocean?"

"Ah." Marcus looked puzzled by the question. "I believe they do, though not very often. We understand that the pilot takes some recreation off-ship. We presume it's the same one that swims back! To be honest, it would be hard to tell."

Gregor noticed the recurrence of the phrase, and wondered if the trader *was* being entirely honest. He also noticed that most of the glasses at the table were depleted, and stood up to offer a round. Marcus demurred, Gregor insisted. He left as Elizabeth launched into a detailed query about vacuum barnacles.

At the bar he was joined by someone else from the table.

"I'll help you carry them," the man said. His accent was hard to place.

"Thanks . . . Ah, I didn't catch your name."

They looked at each other sidelong, while the pithkie barmaid met the order with more-than-human efficiency.

"Grigory," the man said. His voice dropped, barely audible above the music. "And between you and me, Gregor Cairns, my surname is what you think it is, but Antonov's the one I wear now. What are you after?"

Gregor fumbled the unfamiliar coins and notes, hesitated to lift any glasses for fear of dropping them.

"We're looking for members of the old crew," he said. "Especially Matt."

"So's our friend Marcus," said Volkov gruffly. "Just pricking up his ears, making idle-sounding inquiries. He suspects, but I don't think he's sussed me out yet, so watch your mouth."

"I will," Gregor promised.

"What do you want from us?"

Gregor hoped their talk could pass for light barside banter. He accepted a tray and began loading it, passing the lighter drinks to Volkov, to have something to do.

"Nav tech," he said. "Comp."

"Ah." Volkov's eyebrows twitched. "Interesting."

They returned to the table and distributed the drinks. The people sitting on Elizabeth's side had crowded the space where Volkov had sat; he took the seat where Gregor had been, and Gregor squeezed in by Elizabeth, suddenly acutely conscious of her warm body pressed against him. Her conversation about barnacles had spread into a free-for-all about invading species, about which everybody had a loud opinion.

Gregor met Volkov's sardonic gaze.

"You a fisherman yourself, Grigory?"

Volkov shook his head. "Engineer on the factory ships, most of the time. I come and go."

Marcus leaned past Elizabeth, his face curiously intent.

"Grigory Antonov—before it slips my mind—perhaps we could have a private word tomorrow? We're interested in marine engines; we have some supplies and techniques that you may find worth a look. Fine lubricants and such."

"Sure, sure," said Volkov. "You can drop by the company office—third block, Quay Four. Ask for Ferman and Sons. Opens at nine. I'll be there."

The conversation moved on; people came and went with drinks, changing places until after about half an hour Elizabeth and Gregor found themselves together against the wall. The place had become more packed, the music louder. A gigant was singing now, in a voice deep but definitely female—strange. Elizabeth began to worry about all the other places they were supposed to visit.

"Think we're doing all right, or would you like to move on?"

Gregor considered this for a moment.

"I think we've found . . . the people we're looking for," he said. The phrase stabbed her. Gregor indicated Volkov with a glance. "Confirmed, by the way."

"Oh. Good."

She looked down at her glass. "But we should move on, because we still haven't found anyone to hire us a boat."

"We can do that in the morning," said Gregor. "Company offices or down at the docks, the man said—talk to a skipper, remember?"

"Oh. Sure. But I'd still like to move on."

She turned to him. His face was close to hers, flushed with the drink and the heat, his eyes a little glazed from the smoke they'd shared. His swept-back hair was rough and stringy after several days without a proper wash. Their hips were jammed together. As she turned, her arm slid behind him and she brought it up around his waist in a sudden reckless moment. The thought went through her mind that here was a chance that might never recur. If he didn't respond the way she hoped, she could pass it off later as part of the pretense that they were a couple.

So she brought her arm up to his shoulders and placed her other hand on his cheek.

"Come on, Gregor," she said, smiling. "Let's go somewhere quieter."

His eyes widened and his mouth opened. He touched her cheek very gently. Her fingers were—she suddenly realized—exploring the back of his head, his hair lapping her wrist. Whether she pulled him forward, she wasn't sure. They were kissing before they knew what had happened, hot and forgetful, their tongues sliding and twining over each other like mating dolphins.

Then they pulled apart and looked at each other. Gregor held her shoulders as though she might break.

"I've wanted to do that," she said, "from the first time I saw you."

He looked happy, but more confused than surprised. Maybe— she thought hopefully—maybe he had suspected.

"I wish you had," he said.

"I never dared."

"You dared there."

"Yes!"

Before either could say anything further there was a small commotion at the table as Marcus de Tenebre climbed out of the middle of the bench and stood up to greet Lydia.

Gregor, his hands still on Elizabeth, looked up at Lydia with a strong wish that the ground would open up and swallow him. She looked back at him with a very odd expression, not indignant or shocked, but concerned. Her face was shiny with sweat. Her long black hair was tied back with a purple ribbon and she was wearing the same cleverly folded dress that she'd worn on their walk.

She said something urgent to Marcus and then stepped past him and stood at the end of the table, still looking worried.

"Gregor . . . Elizabeth. I'm so glad I've found you so quickly. Can you come with me, please?—with me and my cousin. You'll be all right, we can go—"

She stopped, as though out of breath.

"What's wrong?" Gregor said.

"Your saur. Uh, Salasso. He's in trouble."

Gregor found himself standing in front of Lydia and beside Elizabeth with no very clear idea of how he'd got there.

"What kind of trouble?"

Lydia put her hands over her ears for a moment and gave him a reproving look.

"With other saurs. You must come at once."

"Of course, right away. Elizabeth, can you—"

Go and tell Salasso, he was about to say.

"I'm coming with you," said Elizabeth.

Gregor blinked and shook his head.

"Yes. Thanks. Okay."

Thoroughly unimpressed with himself, he followed the others out. Getting through the crowd was like wading through thick mud. He glanced once over his shoulder, and met Volkov's watchful gaze. The cosmonaut raised a hand as though to wave, then very deliberately clenched it into a fist.

16

Cool Stuff

R EADY?"
    "Yes," I said; but—as before—the question was not addressed to me. Avakian flicked a datagloved finger and the screen encircled us. We could see ourselves, and each other, and the interface, and nothing else. With spex and gloves I could see and touch the screen at a comfortable arm's length; it tracked my glances, its features brightening and magnifying wherever I looked.

"We reckon it's indexed," said Avakian. "In an unknown alphabet, alas. Use the search engine. That's it—the slot on the left."

I grabbed the schematics, highlighted the control system, tabbed in a complex Boolean query we'd sweated over for the previous couple of hours, and stuffed the lot in the slot. The surrounding screen instantly shimmered. All the streaming pictures and words which were its icons vanished, to be replaced by a black background on which the flying saucers shone. Arrays of discs stretched to infinity in every direction. I stared at them, fascinated by their endless subtle variations. By focusing on a column, I could glide along it, exploring the possibilities of a design path to its limits and beyond. . . .

"It's like being in the middle of an invasion fleet," Avakian said. "Opening scene of *Mars Attacks!*, with facing mirrors."

His cackle jolted me out of my trance.

"Huh?"

"Forget it. Look at the thing *critically*, dammit! To me that looks like the least-helpful reply I've seen since my first inadvertent outer join."

"Maybe that's what we've done."

It's a common and easy mistake to set up a query which returns vastly more than you're interested in, which in fact returns every-thing *except* what you really want. If you're clever or stupid enough, you can fire off a query whose reply links everything in the database to everything else, and eats every system resource you've got while doing so. Lights going out is a clue.

"Nah," said Avakian. "The syntax is sound, I checked that first."

Of course he had, as had I.

"Well, this sure isn't a response to the question we asked."

"Or we aren't looking at it the right way. . . . Look, can you restore it to how it was before you went off on your little expedi-tion?"

"What?"

Avakian gave me a spex-masked stare.

"You were out of it for *ten minutes,* man. I thought you had *found* something, but I gave up on that when the drooling and heavy breathing kicked in."

"Shit."

I looked around in the array, realized I'd got hopelessly lost.

"Let's just launch it again," I said.

I pulled the schematics and the query out of the search-engine slot like clogged hair from a plughole, and shoved them back in. This time I took great care not to move, and not to look at anything but the nearest disc, the one right in front of my eyes. I reached out and touched it. The tactile feedback was chill and smooth. That disc expanded, the rest blinked away.

"That's better," said Avakian. "Let's tab in."

We looked around.

"This is getting almost familiar," I said.

"Better rendering," said Avakian. "But lookee here."

The control panel had been ripped out, as though for hot-wiring, and the hundreds of sprouting cables labeled. I peered at the tags, then pulled in a few aerospace-engineering handbooks off Camila's palmtop.

"Shit," I said. "They've done it to U.S. military spec."

"By now," said Avakian, "I could believe they wrote it in the first place."

"Dreamland, huh?"

We laughed and saved the ship to our own systems and backed out.

· · ·

"Let me get this clear," said Driver. "You're telling me we can just rip off the panel and patch in a joystick?"

"Um, no," I said. "The whole control system on this disc is different from the one we have the production plan for. It's not at all obvious how to merge the two."

"Anyone had a look at the control system in the first one?"

"Yeah," said Camila. "I have. It's solid-state all the way down from about a millimeter below the palm-print thingie. I've lowered a viewpoint through that millimeter thickness under high-res, and my best guess is it's some kind of pressure-sensitive pad combined with something that responds to changes in the upper surface's conductivity. For all I know it could be tuned to patterns of heat and sweat."

"Sweaty-palmed aliens," said Avakian. "What a creepy thought."

"And from there," Camila went on, spreading her arms out and upward, "it branches all over the craft, especially to the engine. Nothing as crude as wires, either. It's completely different from the one Matt and Armen have pulled out."

"But you could put a joystick and a viewscreen on that one?"

"Oh, sure." Camila nodded vigorously. "No sweat."

She looked puzzled when we laughed, then joined in.

"The only problem with that is we don't have a plan to build *that* ship."

"Would it be possible to reverse-engineer one?" asked Lemieux.

"Give me a few years," I said. "Mind you, merging the plans would probably take longer."

"Which inclines me to wonder," said Driver, "why they didn't give us the plans for one with human-compatible controls in the first place."

"We could always ask for one," said Avakian.

"Worth a try," I said.

Driver glowered at us.

"Don't hang about," he said.

We ducked out of the office and dived into Avakian's cubbyhole. After ten minutes of discussing the details of the query we dropped into the interface, fired it off, and got nothing but a blank screen for our pains.

"Hmm," said Driver, when we reported back. "Why does this not surprise me?"

"You mean it's some kind of initiative test?" said Camila.

"No," said Driver. "They ain't playing games. They must think they've given us the answer."

Camila poked about in the air in front of her spex, examining our results.

"Something's bothering me here," she said. "The conventions are U.S. mil-spec."

"So?"

She flicked her fingers and looked up.

"You guys—I mean, you can tell me, right? They're not exactly secret, they're in the goddamn public domain. So was it you that passed them on to the aliens?"

Driver and Lemieux frowned at each other.

"Nobody passed anything on," said Lemieux. "We have not been *entering* information in the alien interface. Well, we can, but there isn't much point."

"So how the hell do they know it?"

"That seems an awfully trivial question," I said. "Seeing as we don't even have a clue how they know our languages."

"It is not trivial," said Lemieux. He rubbed his stubble. "And it is not something they merely tapped from our own communications, because we use ESA conventions and we have had no occasion to refer to yours."

"I'm willing to bet," said Camila, "that the only place on this station that spells out U.S. mil-spec conventions is in the handbooks stored right here."

She held up her palmtop.

"And the only thing built to them," she went on, "is the *Blasphemous Geometries*' onboard systems."

"What about our spex?" I asked. "I mean, face it, everybody here uses them."

Driver shook his head.

"All civilian," he said. "Commercial."

"The U.S. military uses them!"

"That," Camila explained patiently, "is because the kind of spex you can buy in any American hardware store or military-base PBX, for that matter, is better than the fucking clunkers that the Army uses. Even your commie biodegradables are better than—"

"What are you getting at?" I said, not patiently.

"What I'm getting at," she told us, "is that the aliens can read every bit and byte of data on every computer on this station."

"Ah," said Lemieux. "Since we identified the earlier datastream hack, that has been our default assumption."

"Well, that's that little mystery cleared up," said Driver. "Now, as we were saying—"

"No!" said Camila. "Wait a minute."

"I'm waiting," said Driver.

Camila, Armen, and I all started saying much the same thing at once. Driver held up a hand.

"Camila."

"You were right a minute ago," she said. "They think they've given us the answer, and they have—they're telling us to build the controls and the engine into the *Blasphemous Geometries*."

There was a moment of silence.

"All right," said Driver. "Nice idea. But if the thing is modular enough to do that, why isn't it modular enough for a merge of the two alien discs?"

I shook my head. "No, no, it's a totally different problem. Just a minute. Camila, could you zap me through to a spec of the *Blasphemous*?"

She tugged a cable from her palmtop and plugged it in the port of my spex.

"All yours. Remember not to share this information with anyone from a Communist country."

"I'll keep that in mind," I said, diving in.

First, I checked that the controls on the new disc were compatible with those of our own ship. They were, as was the instrumentation. Then I overlaid the two disc renderings and set tracers on the cables in the new one. They did indeed match up with clearly defined nodes on the engine of the first. When I isolated that engine and backtracked it through the production plan, I found that the plan had a concealed modularity—it was possible to build the craft's engine independently. It meant a lot more work, but I could see how to do it.

When I'd tried to do something similar with the two craft themselves, I'd bogged down with the problem of not knowing which parts were redundant—the solid-state control system—and which weren't. This one, however, slotted together perfectly.

"So, let's go for it," said Driver.

The only problem that bugged me, as I checked off at the end of that long day shift, was the question Driver had raised earlier:

227

why the aliens had first given us a plan for a craft we couldn't fly; a craft designed for another species. Was it their answer, I wondered, to a question we hadn't asked?

"Do you think those two are queer for each other?"

"Who?"

Camila looked at me as though from a much longer distance than the half-meter between our faces, as we hung, each with our heels crooked around the other's buttocks, in our companionable cubbyhole. Then she put her elbows on my knees and leaned forward to speak quietly.

"Driver and Lemieux."

"What?" I laughed. "Can't say I've noticed any flamboyant mannerisms from either of them."

"Lemieux—"

"—is French. They all talk like that, except gay men, and *they* sound like Americans. *Très, très* fashionable, I'm told."

"Well," she persisted, "these two have something going on. I'm sure of it."

"Well, what if they are?" I said. "It's not like it's a big deal. Not in sophisticated Socialist Europe, anyway."

"Okay, okay," she said, sounding a little defensive. "What I mean is, if they're not, what are they up to?"

"Now, that is a good question. But come on. They're conspirators, who may have been at it for years. They've just carried out a coup here, one which isn't one-hundred-percent popular on the station. Chumakova's lot are no doubt plotting against them as we speak. When things settle down back home, one way or another they're gonna have a lot of explaining to do. Driver was regarded by the CIA as an asset, and he now claims to have been a double agent all along, but the book's always open on these situations."

"Yeah, tell me about it," she said gloomily. "What are we?"

"In what context?"

She kissed the tip of my nose. "Politically."

"Oh." I thought about it, rubbing my chin, almost surprised at its smoothness; Camila had brought me an electric razor from the commissary, and had been quite insistent that I use it.

"Well, I'm a good European and you're a good American, but not everyone back home might see it that way."

"You said it. I can't begin to list all the laws I've broken just by being here—technology export and trading with the enemy and shit—and you're being called a defector. So—"

She let out a long sigh, and reached sideways for the steam-pipe and the packet of grass.

"So?"

"So it's time we started looking out for ourselves. Making sure we don't get shafted when all this is sorted out. Offered up as a sacrifice to the powers that be, you know."

I shivered in the humid warmth: the phrase "powers that be" seemed strangely inapposite for governments, now that we knew what other powers there were. But I knew this wasn't what she meant.

"I don't see Driver as likely to shaft us," I said. "And not your bosses either."

"It might not be up to them, by then."

She bubbled up the pipe, sucked it, and passed it to me. I inhaled, looking around our den with a sudden surge of paranoia.

"Is it safe to talk here?"

"Sure." She shrugged, reached behind her, and waved a small device like a torch. "There were the usual bugs when we came in, but I've swept them."

"What's that thing?"

"Classified," she grinned, stashing it again. "Take it from me, though, it frazzles millimeter-scale wet tech."

"All right," I said. "What do you suggest we do?"

"Some real spying. Get some information that we can trade with, something that either side might find useful. For a start, find out what Driver and Lemieux are really up to."

"Oh, great." I returned her the pipe. "And how do you propose to do that?"

She grinned ferally at me.

"We listen to them," she said. "Through the alien interface."

I woke and found it was morning in the station's day cycle—not just from my watch, looped by its strap to the webbing a few inches away—but by the increased light around the edges of the curtain and the increased sounds of busyness from the corridor. Listening further, I guessed it might even have been a cock-crow that had wakened me. Someone was filling the food-hoppers at the nearest chicken run.

Camila was still asleep, and we were still wrapped around each other. One advantage of microgravity is that you can sleep in a cuddle without waking to find that one of your arms is trapped under your lover and has itself gone to sleep. I nuzzled her shoulder with my chin, now scratchy again, and stroked her short black hair, which had lengthened by a millimeter or two since launch and now had a very pleasant, furry nap to it. She stirred and mumbled and snuggled closer. We'd had more sleep this night than the night before, though not from any loss of interest in each other, having had sex before and after our conversation and having wakened up to some kind of dozy mutual stimulation in the middle of the night. Right now, if her sleepy strokings were anything to go by, Camila was warming up for another session before breakfast.

As I floated there in her arms, all of that erotic intimacy stood vivid and real in my memory, and only our conversation seemed like a dream. But later, after we'd stickily separated, and gone to wash and dry and dress, it all crashed in on me again like a cold shower. Her assessment of our situation was more realistic—or at any rate further thought-through—than mine had been, caught up as I was in the fascination of the work.

Camila was showing herself to be cool and clearheaded, like not many other people I knew—Charlie, maybe, among the old geeks; Jason; one or two Webblies; and Jadey. The thought of Jadey brought a pang, but not guilt. Basically I was working my way back to her, the fastest way I could. Much as I loved her—and I did—I had no illusions that she wouldn't do the same sort of thing; whatever was necessary to get her through.

And to get through here, and back to Earth, and Jadey free, I needed Camila. And I needed to think like her, to think like a spy. As I pulled on my jumpsuit I felt the familiar shape of the hand reader in my pocket, and beside it, the datadisk.

It was at that point that I did my first bit of thinking like a spy, and what I thought was: *There's something wrong here.* I unzipped the pocket and ran my fingers around the edge of the datadisk, and as I made for Driver's office I pulled it out and looked at it, and realized that it was the piece of the puzzle that didn't fit. There was no place for it in the picture I'd been shown.

I almost shouted, as around that anomalous object the pieces of a quite different picture clicked into place.

・ ・ ・

"Ready?" I said.

A word floated across my spex:

Yes.

The interface surrounded me.

I'd spent most of that day finishing the modified production plan and handing it over to the people running the fabs, and liaising with Camila, who was working with the engineers—Volkov and the rest—on the *Blasphemous Geometries*. In one slack period I'd jaunted into Armen's workspace and asked him for access to the interface. As though surprised I didn't have it already, he zapped the key-code to my spex. Betweentimes, I'd checked the news channels, forced myself to ignore them, and worked on a query.

Now, my day's work complete half an hour before the usual late-evening debriefing in Driver's office, I had time for a little experiment.

Fighting off the interface's hypnotic distractions, I slotted the query into the search engine. It was a very simple query, for a set of data I knew to be unique to my own handheld reader because I had made it up myself, very laboriously: Test data for a job I'd done several months ago. The sort of low-level programming that really should have been beneath me, and I'd cursed the limited budget that had made me do it myself at the time. "An artist, not a technician," et cetera.

But I was glad of it now. I had to restrain a whoop when the screen returned a blank, almost the instant my thumb left the virtual switch that fired off the query.

Next I scanned around for a data-input port, and found one—eccentrically but appropriately—at 180 degrees around from the search-engine slot. I zapped the test data in, rotated my viewpoint, and repeated the query.

The data I'd just entered scrolled before me, like another boring chapter in the Book of Numbers.

The sight of it sent chills down my back.

With a sense of satisfaction alloyed with a certain sadness, I said: "Finished?" and the interface said yes and went away.

I joined Camila on the way to Driver's office. Her hand brushed mine, like a wing in flight.

"Hi, Matt." Warm smile. "Did you have time to—?"

"Yes," I said, quite truthfully. "Didn't find anything though."

"Ah. Shit. Worth a try though, anyway. Guess they're being real cautious. Smart guys."

"Yes," I said. "They'd have to be."

But not as smart as you, Camila, I didn't say.

"So that's it," said Driver, after taking the reports. "We can start production tomorrow."

"Hell, we can start it now," said Avakian. "For this job I'd be happy to pull an all-nighter."

This meeting was bigger than our unofficial cabal; the various team leaders were patched in through their spex and ours, filling the cramped room with an unreal crowd and forcing the graphics into surrealism. Driver, probably unwilling to let Avakian show off his skills in yet another frivolous and manipulative manner, had declined the offer of a full-immersion conference space.

The overlapping phantom shapes of Sembat, Telesnikov, and Chumakova all became simultaneously agitated at Avakian's remark.

"We can't do it," Sembat said. "Be realistic. The team is exhausted, we've been prepping the fabs all day—"

"And we've been on EVA hauling materials," said Telesnikov, on behalf of the cosmonauts. "Anything more, and we'll start having accidents. Out there, that means possible fatalities."

Driver took the last point with the bored skepticism of a manager listening to a union rep, but he raised his hand and nodded, glaring for a moment at Avakian.

"Okay, okay, Mikhail, there's no question of working further tonight. It's hardly a matter of urgency. Paul."

Lemieux, shaved and spruce again, smiled down at us.

"However," he began. "There is a growing urgency to the entire project, which I'd like to impress upon you and urge you to communicate to your teams. You've all heard the news today, unless you have been even more dedicated than you appear to have been."

Solemn nods all round. Chumakova looked as though she were about to say something, then thought better of it.

"I must thank all of you for your discipline in continuing to work, regardless of the . . . distraction and anxiety and indeed indignation which the news has doubtless provoked. We must hope that our political intervention will help toward a political solution,

232

and in the meantime we must work harder to demonstrate that much of the political and military conflict is now obsolete, as Camila said."

This seemed to soothe and impress most of the people present and telepresent, but it only made me wonder further just what game he was playing. The day's events were a savage reminder that we weren't playing games; that the strategy of releasing the code-crackers and flooding the world with secrets was not without consequence. People no longer knew what to believe, and a lamentably large number were ready to believe anything.

The news reports I'd put firmly from my mind throughout the day replayed themselves in flashback. Only yesterday it had seemed that the political crisis in the E.U. was easing off into negotiation. Despite—or perhaps because of—this, a rash of riots had broken out across Western Europe. Mostly in the poorer areas, the ones where the mafias had more influence than the Party. (Parts of Leith, I'd noticed, were literally in flames.) Apolitical, apocalyptic slogans accompanied the trashing and looting; a lot of people seemed convinced that the governments, all governments, were somehow in league with the aliens. Not just our aliens, but the aliens of popular nightmare, the sinister, satanic Grays.

"Matt? You with us?"

Avakian's nudge brought me back to the moment. The others had gone, and we were back to the small cabal. I took off my spex and rubbed my eyes, looking around at Armen, Camila, Driver, and Lemieux. We didn't seem such a cozy little clique anymore, now that I knew a bit more about what was going on.

"You're very tired," said Driver.

"Yeah," I said. "And worried. I know a lot of people in the area of the rioting in Edinburgh, and Jadey's still in a jail just a couple of kilometers away from it."

Driver nodded. "We all have worries, we all have people back home. There's nothing we can do, except get on with the job."

I considered confronting him then and there, but decided against it. There was Camila to consider, and I didn't quite have her angle figured out yet.

"Okay," I said. "Let's get some sleep."

Sleep was not on my mind, though it was on my brain. As soon as we'd secured the curtain Camila started climbing out of her clothes, and I did likewise. We bumped and rolled, laughing. She caught me and held me.

"I need this," she said. "I need you. Otherwise I'd get very tense."

"Well, thank you," I mumbled. "So would I."

For a while I forgot about whatever reasons she might have for being tense. Then, as we hung in a contented, conjoined orbit of our own around the sun, the question came back.

"Have you swept up?" I whispered.

"I do that as regular as brushing my teeth," she said. "Why?"

I pulled my face away from her shoulder.

"Could you put some music on?"

She fished out a player, and I adjusted the volume carefully so that it would cover our voices against direct eavesdropping.

"You took a risk," I said, "playing that little game with the mil-spec stuff."

Her arms tightened, her legs clenched for a moment, then she relaxed again. She frowned at me.

"What 'little game'?"

"You ported the specs across yourself, zapped your handbooks into the interface, right?"

She screwed up her eyes and shook her head.

"What makes you think that?"

"I found out today that the interface doesn't actually have access to all the data held on this station."

She pushed me away, herself back. We fetched up on opposite partitions of the space, facing each other.

"Shit," she said. "This is serious. Don't you trust me?"

"Yeah, I *trust* you," I said. "But I don't expect you to always tell me everything. I'm just letting you know that I've figured out what you're doing, and to warn you—because I do trust you, see— that at least one of our friends will have figured out the same thing. Driver or Lemieux knows it."

She closed her eyes again, then stared at me.

"Let's take it from the top, okay?" she said. "How did you find that the interface can't access every computer here?"

I told her about my little experiment.

"And you concluded for that, that I must've zapped in the mil-spec data myself?"

"Uh-huh."

"Well, I didn't! I really don't believe in lying, Matt. Not like this. Why would I do that, anyway?"

"To get first dibs on testing the AG engine, and maybe . . . taking it home?"

She laughed. "It's a neat idea. Wish I'd thought of it."

"All right, so how d'you explain how the interface knew U.S. military conventions for labeling diagrams?"

"No idea at all," she said. "I'm as baffled as you are. What made you wonder about that, anyway? Was it because you found you couldn't eavesdrop through the interface?"

"No." I omitted telling her I hadn't even tried out her suggestion. "No, it's because I realized that Driver or Lemieux or both of them were bullshitting us the day we arrived. They told us there was no way the project data could have got to ESA without them knowing, and I thought this meant that the aliens had hacked the datastream. But I wasn't thinking properly. There was something I hadn't taken into account."

"What?"

I fumbled behind the webbing and in the pocket of my fatigues, and pulled out the datadisk that the Russian officer had given to Jadey.

"This," I said. "It was passed to Jadey in very dangerous circumstances. Now, I can just about believe that was the result of information being inserted in the data outflow from this station, with an ESA address attached, and that it just sort of rattled around in various automated systems. But getting this thing out would have required deliberation, decision, organization. This was no accident—as the commie saying goes."

"Okay," she said. "Go on."

"Which does rather strongly suggest that it was released deliberately from here, and not by aliens either. By Driver, Lemieux, or both of them, in liaison with whatever organization on the ground they're working with—probably the same one that got the disk to Jadey."

I grinned at her, across that five-foot gulf.

"And Jadey is connected to an organization financed by—among others—Nevada Orbital Dynamics. Your employer's company. Which means you and I, my dear, have been connected all along. Now, isn't that sweet?"

Camila smiled back at that.

"And of course the company sent us here," she said. She described a circle with her finger. "It's all a big chain, and it's all come back to here."

"Yes," I said. "And we know what's at your end of it, the American end, but we don't know what's at the European end—this end. We don't know who's pulling it. We don't know who's hauling it in."

The following morning the news was slightly better, if shots of gutted buildings and talk of firefighting and arrests and casualties counts as "good." The damage ran into billions. The rioters were duly denounced, or carefully *not* denounced, and analysis of the nuances of such pronouncements kept a lot of heads talking. Camila and I were called to Driver's office for a pre-work meeting.

"Just stand by," he told me, "and keep channels open to the fabs. No doubt there'll be glitches when it comes to actually running it. Just keep out of the way the rest of the time, maybe get started on the big 'engine' plan when you have a chance. And Camila, you hang out with the crew working on your ship, make sure they know what to take out and what to leave. Armen, stick close to the production teams. Give them anything they need on the science front, and keep track of progress on the second project."

"Fine," said Camila. "That's what we were going to do anyway."

"Before you go," said Lemieux. "And you too, Armen, please stay."

He glanced over at Driver.

"We have something to tell you."

Camila clapped her hand over a giggle.

The two men looked so serious and embarrassed, I could for a moment almost believe they were about to declare their long-standing love for each other.

"We've been listening to you," Driver said. "Sorry about that."

"How?"

"Camila," Lemieux said, "I know you are not a spy, because if you were, you would know that your anti-surveillance device works very well against E.U. wet-tech bugs, but not, unfortunately, against the latest U.S. microbots."

"The Federal Security Bureau," said Driver, "never uses anything else."

"Well, I hope you had fun," I said.

They exchanged another embarrassed glance.

"We are sorry to have violated your privacy," said Lemieux. "But it is the political and not the personal element in your conversations which was of interest to us. We think misconceptions may arise if we don't take you into our confidence, and we can't afford that."

He looked over at Armen. "And you, too, are clever enough to figure things out eventually, and clever enough to get them wrong. We all have to trust each other, because the next few days are going to be very dangerous indeed. Matt, you spoke of a chain of links, and you were right. You said you did not know what is at our end of it. It's time you did."

17

Judgement of Krakens

NIGHT HAD FALLEN, with the suddenness characteristic of that latitude, while they had been in the bar. Lights marked out the long street around the shore. Gregor hurried through the now denser crowd on the esplanade's pavement, and fell in beside Lydia. Elizabeth and Marcus walked quickly ahead of them.

Lydia smiled and caught his hand, swinging it as she strode along.

"It's good to see you again," she said. "Even in such a difficult situation for your friend Salasso."

"How did you come to find out about it?"

She took a small rectangular box from a deep pocket in the side of her skirt, then slid it back.

"Radio. On shore, most of us carry them. I was out shopping this evening when I got a call from Bishlayan, one of our saurs. She knows Salasso, and they were talking when the trouble started. She lent her radio to Salasso, who gave me a list of places where I might find you."

"What kind of trouble is Salasso in?"

"Nothing violent. The saurs are not like us—they do not *brawl*. As to what it is, best you see for yourself. It is very tense. I'm really glad I found you as quickly as I did. It was such a relief to see you and Elizabeth."

Gregor couldn't hear any hint of irony or reproof.

"Uh . . . About Elizabeth, she and I—"

"Yes," said Lydia, "I see that you like each other."

Again the same uncomplicated note. Gregor frowned.

"You're not . . . upset?"

She gripped his hand tighter. "Why should I be? I could see that she liked you back in Kyohvic, that day at the lab. I'm pleased that you have someone to be with."

"I still don't understand."

"It's possible to love more than one person at once," Lydia said earnestly. "My father does."

"Yes, but that's *different*—"

She shot him a look. "Don't be so naive."

Before Gregor could collect his confused thoughts, let alone say anything, Marcus turned sharply left, leading them up a narrow stairway of worn, wet stone. The doorways of small taverns and shops interrupted the mossy walls every ten or so steps. Gregor concentrated on keeping his footing and following Lydia's heels; an upward glance, dangerous but interesting, showed the walls going up like the sides of a canyon, the street- and window-lighting obscuring any strip of sky above.

After about a hundred steps they reached a final flight, broader and less slippery but no less worn, which ended at a street. Halfway up that flight, Marcus stopped. He indicated a door to their left, a few steps farther up.

"This is the place," he said. The door was half-glazed, the windows dim, the sign brightly lit but indecipherable. It might have made sense, to other eyes; Gregor could see only swirls and blocks.

"What kind of place is it?" Elizabeth asked.

Marcus grimaced. "The saur equivalent of a tavern, or a . . . place of assignation. Been in one before?"

Gregor and Elizabeth hadn't.

"It's quite safe to go in, but it is very important to be polite, not to stare, and not to make loud noises or sudden movements. Otherwise we may be thrown out. Clear? Right. Elizabeth, maybe you should stay beside me, and Gregor with Lydia. If there's any trouble, let us do the protecting. Follow me."

Marcus held the door open until they were all crowded behind him, and Gregor let it swing back behind them as they went in. It took a moment for his eyes to adjust to the low lighting. The air was rank with fish and meat; the sweetish whiff of hemp only made it more sickly.

It was the eyes he saw first, slanted obsidian ellipses reflecting the faint glow of the suspended lamps. Then he made out the shadowy shapes of saurs, sitting on chairs at wide circular tables. There was no bar, just a darker opening at the back, a source of clattering noises and strong smells. In front of that opening two saurs in belted robes faced each other, hands raised, in crooked, edgy postures. They were moving very slowly, as though in dance or ritual combat. Dishes and cups lay on the tables. Glowing pipe-bowls moved up and down and about, like mysterious lights in a dark sky. Saur conversations went on quietly, a background hiss rather than a murmur. Above it and behind it, some rhythmic sound he couldn't quite hear worried at the sockets of his teeth.

Lydia clutched his hand. Together they followed Elizabeth and Marcus—also holding hands, he noticed—toward a corner table at the back. From behind the table, five pairs of eyes observed their approach. As he got closer he recognized Salasso, who nodded. He was sitting beside a saur who wore a dark but shiny gown. One of the other saurs stood up and indicated four vacant chairs on the near side of the table. Following Marcus's lead, the humans sat down. The chairs were of the same corky substance as they'd seen in Saur City One. The table, made of a single block of the same stuff, had a sharp inward curve from the top to the base to make room for knees, though not quite enough for human knees.

"Bishlayan," said Marcus. The saur in the black gown ducked her head briefly.

"Salasso," said Gregor. "Are you all right?"

"For now."

Of the other saurs, the two to Salasso's right were in the familiar one-piece coveralls, the one to Bishlayan's left in what looked curiously like one of the bulky leather jackets favored by airplane pilots; almost comical on his—or her—slender frame. A fur collar added to the impression, and the incongruity.

"Let us introduce ourselves," said the saur at the opposite end of the group. "Gregor, Lydia, Elizabeth, Marcus, your names and sexes and occupations are known to us. Salasso and Bishlayan you know. The one beside them is Delavar; he is, as you may surmise, a local skiff pilot. My name is Tharanack, and I am of the male sex. My female comrade is called Mavikson. We are citizens of New Lisbon and are employed as what the humans call 'peace-keepers,' and what we call 'fighters.' "

He spread his hands, splaying the four digits on each. "You may ask for our documents, or you may call for peacekeepers of another species if you wish. No? Very well. I cannot ask Marcus and Lydia, but I must ask you, Gregor and Elizabeth—are you armed?"

Gregor turned to Elizabeth and felt heartened by her wry smile. "No," she said. "Apart from our knives, of course."

"You are well-armed," said Tharanack. "That is good. We would not want you to feel intimidated."

Gregor didn't believe for a second that the sturdy, sharp lock-knife in his pocket would make much difference in a fight with saurs, but he reckoned the whole significance of the question was symbolic anyway. This preliminary palaver probably wasn't even saur custom, just police procedure in the multispecies municipality of New Lisbon. He realized that his companions were looking at him, waiting for him to speak.

He laid his hands on the table and rolled them, palms up. As a gesture of peace and open-mindedness it probably came across as theatrical to the saurs, but he was acutely conscious of the need to err on the side of caution. If that meant doing the equivalent of throwing himself on his knees and baring his chest, so be it.

"What seems to be the problem?" he asked. Out of the corner of his eye he noticed Marcus's slight nod of approval. The pilot Delavar leaned forward sharply, hissing some epithet; Mavikson silenced him with a glance.

"The problem is this," the female peacekeeper said. "Delavar, Salasso, and Bishlayan have a relationship of long standing. Salasso and Bishlayan, of course, have most recently met in Kyohvic. A certain tension arose when Salasso turned up here, while Bishlayan was with Delavar. In order to reassure Delavar that he was not here in competition for Bishlayan's attention, or some other ulterior motive, Salasso explained his real purpose. Delavar, and others here who, ah, quickly became aware of the conversation, were even more disturbed by this than by his initial jealous suspicion. Assistance was called for. So here we are."

The irritating background rhythm stopped. Behind him, Gregor heard four bare saur feet slap into a different position. A different, but still subtly annoying rhythmic sound began. Off to the side, he could see a lot of black eyes watching him, and a few, apparently, on the dancers. The sight brought him out of his astonishment at the idea of a relationship, or a rivalry, that had spanned centuries.

"Ah," he said, fixing his gaze on Mavikson. "And what would you say was Salasso's true purpose?"

"You know that as well as I do, Cosmonaut Gregor Cairns."

Gregor bowed slightly, acknowledging his error. The saurs weren't given to verbal games.

"Very well," he said. "But what I truly am not certain of, and what I ask your indulgence to explain, is what the objection is to this purpose."

Delavar's right hand shot forward and down, clawing into the table. The two peacekeepers hissed sharply. Bishlayan laid a hand on his forearm, and stroked it, and said something in his ear. Slowly, and with a body-language of bad grace that easily jumped the species barrier, the pilot sat back.

"He understands your language," said Bishlayan, still stroking his arm. "But he is too angry to speak it. I will speak for him, though I do not have an opinion on the matter, myself."

Her other hand was plucking and stroking her chest, claws now and then snagging the gown's fabric. Gregor had a strong impression that for a saur this indicated almost unbearable distraction and distress. He raised his hands, palms open and bent back, as though offering her his wrists to slit.

"Please," he said.

She seemed to recover some composure.

"My lover Salasso has angered my lover Delavar, and others here, with his idea of helping you, the . . ." She said something he couldn't catch.

"Hominidae," said Salasso.

" 'Monkey-fuckers,' " translated Mavikson, in a tone of weary honesty.

". . . to become navigators," Bishlayan continued. "He believes that this will anger the gods. Salasso was surprised at his opinion, which he referred to as . . ."

Another saur phrase.

" 'Perhaps irrationally conservative.' "

" 'A steaming pile of stinking dinosaur shit.' "

". . . because they have long been friends, and he had thought they were of similar views. The argument became extremely heated. They were both doing *this*."

She drummed her fingers on the table, then made quick flopping gestures with her hands to emphasize that she hadn't really meant it.

"When that happened I asked the keeper of the house to call the keepers of the peace, and called up my shipmate Lydia, and let Salasso speak to her on the radio to fetch you."

She sat back, sliding her hands into her wide sleeves, Gregor could see under the cloth each hand's fierce grip on the opposite elbow.

Salasso leaned forward and turned to Mavikson.

"I do wish," he said, "that you would not translate our idioms so literally. And I urge our human friends not to take offense."

"None taken," said Lydia, speaking up for the first time. "Apart from that, would you both say that Bishlayan has given a true account of your quarrel?"

Salasso and Delavar glanced at each other, turned sharply away, and nodded.

"Good," said Lydia. "Gregor, Elizabeth, I have a suggestion to make. May I?"

Elizabeth shrugged; Gregor, who had no idea what do next in any case, nodded. Lydia smiled at them both and turned back to the saurs. She turned her head farther, turning her shoulders with it, then put her hand under her ponytail and lifted it to display to the saurs the back of her neck. Gregor stared, fascinated by the fine wispy curls on her nape. The saurs all inhaled at the same moment.

"As you see," she said, facing them again, "I am very young. I have little experience and no wisdom. How could I know what may or may not anger or please the gods? And I see that you yourselves, who are so much older and wiser than I, cannot agree. So I ask you to consider for a moment taking your disagreement to someone who was old and wise when everyone here was less than an egg. One who has talked to gods. Would you accept such a judgement, and remain friends whichever way that judgement fell?"

As though unconsciously, artlessly, her hand had crept again to the back of her neck, lifting the tuft of the ponytail to the top of her head. She held the pose for a moment.

"I only ask," she said.

Her hair fell back.

Gregor realized that his fingernails were digging into the table. He relaxed them hurriedly and rolled his hands over again, but no one had noticed. They were all staring at Lydia.

Delavar reached across in front of Bishlayan and took Salasso's hand, tentatively at first, then in a firm mutual grasp.

"We would," he said.

"Good," said Lydia briskly. "Let us go to the ship, and consult the navigator."

For a giddy moment Gregor misunderstood her, then realized she was referring to the kraken.

Delavar was willing to accept one of the peacekeepers as a fair witness, and was in any case anxious to resume his interrupted tryst with Bishlayan, so it was only Salasso and Tharanack who left with the four humans. Salasso, very conscientiously, stayed close to the peacekeeper and said nothing. Lydia and Marcus led the way. Rather than go back down the steps, they turned into the street at the top, which, like most streets in the city, sloped down to the shore and ended at a convenient quay. Gregor and Elizabeth brought up the rear.

Gregor drew a deep breath, trying to drive the smell of the saur dive from his nostrils. People streamed up and down the street, free of any traffic but the overhead cable cars.

"It's good to be out of there," he said.

"What the hell's going on?" said Elizabeth.

"I still have no idea why Marcus was after—"

"That's not what I'm talking about. What's going on between you and Lydia?"

"I don't know."

"I saw her walking along, holding your hand and chatting blithely as if she'd never seen us back in the bar. I didn't like that—it was as if I didn't exist."

"She saw us, all right. She didn't mind; in fact she seemed quite pleased about it."

"Did she indeed? How very enlightened of her. How philosophical. I'm sure she's very happy that you have someone to ease the pain of love with until you and your family have got your bloody ship up there ready to go haring off after her."

She stared straight ahead as she said this. Gregor felt himself actually trembling as he walked beside her. Their kiss in the bar had made what Elizabeth felt for him real in a way that Salasso's report of it had not. It had shaken him, and Lydia's arrival before they'd had time to talk had left his own feelings in upheaval. His conversation with Lydia had only made it worse. The tense minutes in the saur hostelry had come as a relief and distraction.

There, he'd admired Lydia with a curious detachment, unclouded by adoration; her tactical, tactful skill in talking to the saurs was, perhaps, what he should have expected of a space-merchant's daughter but it had astonished him nonetheless. It recalled the un-expected understanding she'd shown of the deep questions about the kraken, when she had visited the lab, although then he'd sus-pected she was showing off. This time she'd shown herself capable of thinking on her feet.

"Elizabeth . . ."

"What?"

Still looking straight ahead and walking fast.

"Can we stop for a moment?"

She stopped and faced him. He had a second of sharp and clear perception of her, a sudden sum of his knowledge of her. She was taller and stronger and older than Lydia, and not as pretty, but at that moment she looked far more vulnerable and far more beautiful. It stung him and stunned him that he had not seen her like this from the beginning.

He held her shoulders, as before.

"I love you," he said. And as he said it, it became true, all his tension and confusion resolved, became sharp and straight and sing-ing, a bowstring that still twanged from sending an arrow on its flight.

"I've always loved you," she said.

When they unlocked from the embrace he was still shaking, and they had to run.

The reflection of the starship's lights smeared across the water like spilt petrol on a puddle. Up close, it was too vast to be strange. It could have been one of the factory ships or the bulk carriers in the harbor, apart from its size, which dwarfed all of them. Water lapped its sides, but it definitely was not floating; if it had been, Gregor vaguely thought, it would have had to be lower down, with a greater displacement. The fields smoothed the sea around it, replacing the waves and swell with complex racing ripples, and made hair prickle and ears hum.

Above the hull's overhang, the occasional skiff flitted in or out of long, narrow rectangular openings, their lens-shapes flashing re-flections of the lights within. At one end—whether fore or aft Gre-gor could not guess—a slanted, rounded opening on the lower side gaped like a mouth, partly in the sea and partly just above it. The water around it and below it was brightly lit, greenish, swirling with kraken whose full-spectrum chromatophore communications sent flickering rainbow flashes through the upper levels of the water.

Their own point of entry was more modest: a wide doorway in the lower curve of the hull, with a pontoon of wood and old rubber tires and tubes moored to its sill. The boatman throttled back the petrol engine, hove to and made fast, and the two saurs and four humans climbed off the boat.

"You'll wait for us?" said Marcus, as he paid for the outward journey.

"I'm not going anywhere," the boatman assured them, settling back in the stern and firing up a smoke.

They walked along the swaying planks, Elizabeth and Gregor more confidently than the rest, and stepped over the high threshold into the ship.

Elizabeth glanced downward as they entered, nudged Gregor.

"Barnacles," she said. He grinned back at her.

A young crewman sitting on the mooring, reading a book, glanced up and nodded as they arrived. Behind him, a large receiving-bay, planked with wood and slopping with seawater, was almost filled with crates. Marcus led them past the crewman and turned right, into a corridor along the side of the ship, in the direction of the circular opening they'd passed in the boat.

"We're all related here," he explained, over his shoulder. "Don't stand much on ceremony. This way."

There was no other way. The corridor went on and on, for hundreds of meters, or so it felt. White-painted metal plates with big rivets, caged electric lights overhead, the occasional hatch on their left, and bulkheads every ten meters or so. They might have been in the bowels of any large ship. Or an airship built of steel, Gregor thought, this corridor passing along the space between the outer and inner skins.

After about five minutes they reached the end of the corridor, and stepped out onto a wide, wet metal shelf that rang under their feet. Three saurs stood at a railing about ten meters in front of them. Beyond it, the opening to the sea lay like a small lake, about a hundred meters across, lit from below and from the sides as though for some extravagant festivity. Two krakens floated there, their twenty-meter tentacles extended. From that lake, on their left,

246

a channel fifteen meters wide ran back into the interior of the ship. The sides of the vessel curved up around the pool, to meet a convex floor of glass high above it. Above the glass other lights shone, and two other krakens swam, among darting shoals of fish and drifting weeds. From the far side of that gigantic aquarium, a glass column extended down to beneath the far edge of the pool. Inside the column, a lift—or the piston of a pump—was gliding slowly upward, carrying a kraken holding a vertical position, its tentacles curled to its head, its mantle rippling in powerful pulses.

"That," said Marcus, pointing upward, "is the navigator's cabin and bridge, and this is his private mess-hall, where he meets and entertains his guests. Channels and sluices of seawater connect it to other parts of the ship."

He indicated the channel beside them, and then led the way to the railing. Leaning over it, Gregor found himself looking into the largest pair of eyes he'd ever seen. Even thirty-odd meters away, they still seemed uncomfortably close. The thought of the size and complexity of the brain that must lie behind them was even more disturbing to contemplate; apart from the gods, *Architeuthys extraterrestris sapiens* was the largest intelligent species, and almost certainly the largest intelligence, that humanity had ever encountered.

It was also, considered merely as an animal, frighteningly large. The thought that it was a mollusc was not especially comforting.

"Let us consult our navigator," said Lydia.

"How do you know which one it is?" Gregor asked.

"We have to ask," said Lydia. She spoke to one of the ship's saurs, who led them over to the corner between the main pool and the channel where a sloping display-screen and control-panel was mounted on the railing. His long fingers danced across the panel, and complex patterns of light flowed on the screen.

While the saur was doing this, Marcus leaned over the railing and pointed downward. When Gregor and Elizabeth leaned over, too, they could see a much-larger version of the screen, about four meters by seven, shimmering directly below them in the water and obviously repeating the patterns displayed on the screen above. One of the krakens had sunk beneath the surface, and after a minute or two resurfaced, facing in the opposite direction, its tentacles away from them and its broad back toward them. The eyes regarded them as before.

Patterns of light played briefly across its back.

The saur at the screen turned to them.

"That is our navigator."

"Well, that's lucky," said Lydia. She gestured to Salasso. "Please ask your question, as you wish, in your own language. Tharanack will translate it—and any answers—into ours, and Voronar here will translate to and from the language of light."

Salasso stepped up and asked his question. Voronar recoiled slightly, glancing over at Lydia and Marcus as though appealing for support. They both nodded firmly. The saur bowed again over the panel, his fingers unsteady at their task.

"Salasso has asked," said Tharanack, "whether the navigators appointed by the gods know if the gods would be angered, and if they themselves would feel at all offended if some of the, ah, hominidae were to take it upon themselves to guide ships between the stars."

The effect of the question, once Varonar had transcribed it into the colorful ideoglyphs and displayed it on the underwater screen, was like lighting a fuse to start a fireworks display. The krakens in the pool, and others now visible in the sea beneath, and those in the overhead aquarium, burst almost simultaneously into rapid-fire exchanges of racing, flashing colored light.

Gregor felt Elizabeth's arm clasp his waist, and clasped hers in response, but more firmly. He felt that they needed to cling to each other to remain on their feet. Lydia and Marcus and the saurs were gazing at the display with almost as much amazement.

"It's rare to see anything like this," said Lydia. "So long, and so intense. The volume of information being exchanged must be enormous."

Eventually, after about five minutes, the lights died down and the navigator's body darkened. Then, quite slowly, a much simpler series of patterns scrolled across his back. Varonar began to speak, and Tharanack translated into English.

" 'The gods are all around us, and care little of such things. It is their felicity to contemplate the universe as it is. Nothing can anger the gods which does not threaten the variety and beauty which they see in it. Others, not the gods, lifted our ancestors from the seas of Earth long ago. These others incurred the anger of the gods, and we lifted the ancestors and relatives of the saurs from the lands of Earth, to escape that anger which destroyed the others. The saurs have lifted the hominidae and other species. Recently some of the hominidae have lifted themselves, and traveled here without us and without the saurs. We must assume that the gods approved of their coming, and will approve of their further traveling.

" 'As to ourselves, we are happy to be navigators, but would be as happy to be passengers. Our home is the great ocean that spans the worlds. If we lost one specialization, we would find others. Species change, the niche remains. If the hominidae can fill our niche at a lower price, we will only gain from it, as will all the other intelligent species. Peace and trade to you.' "

Salasso spun around and embraced his two friends.

"I knew it!" he said. "I knew it!"

"It's not as simple as that," said Varonar, the translator. "The navigator just told you that he and his kind will not fight you, and neither will the gods. But they will compete. And so will we."

Gregor smiled at him over Salasso's head.

"Peace and trade," he said.

He gently disengaged himself from the saur and from Elizabeth, and stepped back and looked at Marcus and Lydia and their crewmates.

"We have a navigator to find," he said.

Marcus said good-bye with a swift handshake and a thin smile, Lydia with a sudden kiss. Then they walked with Tharanack back along the long corridor to the floating pier and the waiting boat.

Tharanack parted from them at the end of the quay.

"I will take the navigator's judgement to Delavar," he said. "By morning it will be all over town. By noon, all over the world. Nothing will change. The humans still have to work things out for themselves."

"Of course," said Salasso. "But at least they will not face ignorant opposition."

"We may hope so," said Tharanack, and left.

Salasso waited until the peacekeeper had disappeared in the crowd, then struck a pose like one of those assumed by the saur dancers. After a moment he stood straight again, and looked away as though embarrassed.

"That was undignified," he said. "But still, it is good news. Better news than Tharanack imagines, but he will soon find out. He'll repeat the judgement word for word, and others of us who are not so concerned about the question of humans will hear a different message in the answer, a message about our past."

"What message?" asked Gregor.

Salasso's nictitating membranes flickered.

"That the gods were not angry with us in the deep past. They never were angry with us, but with others. This is very good news. I feel like climbing onto a roof and shouting it. I will tell it to everyone I meet."

"Don't," said Elizabeth. "Unless you want to end up nailed to a cross."

"Your pardon?"

"Thrown from a cliff," said Gregor, making a guess at the likely mode of saur martyrdom.

"Such a thing has not happened in many thousands of years."

Aha.

"But I'll consider what you say." Salasso dismissed the matter. "Meanwhile we have to decide what to do next. Have you found any of the old crew?"

They told him about Volkov.

The saur's eyes narrowed.

"So Marcus, and possibly others from the ship, are searching for them too. That is alarming."

"It is indeed," said Gregor. "How come the merchants know about the First Crew at all?"

"I told Bishlayan, back at Kyohvic, that some of them were alive. She knew that Athranal, our old teacher, would know where they were. So she took a skiff to Saur City One en route, and asked her."

"Did Athranal tell you this?"

"No," said Salasso. "Bishlayan told me tonight."

Gregor stared at the saur, then shrugged.

"They're probably just hoping to cut them some kind of deal. After all, the original crew must know how to navigate."

"Cut them a deal and cut us out?" said Elizabeth.

"Quite possibly," said Salasso. "I think they may also want them for something much more valuable—the knowledge of the long life."

"They may not have it," said Gregor. "They have the long life, all right, but that doesn't mean they know how to give it to anyone else."

"They don't need to know," said Salasso. "They carry the information in their bodies. And if there is one place in the human societies that could extract that information, it is in the academies of Nova Babylonia."

Gregor was getting impatient hanging around.

"I doubt it," he said. "Remember what Esias de Tenebre said? That our lab was more advanced than the academies of Nova Babylonia? Let's just go back to the Hot Squid and find Volkov."

"Yes," said Salasso, "and as quickly as possible. You said Volkov arranged to meet Marcus at nine tomorrow. We have to meet him first, or we'll be left out in the cold."

"Marcus could offer an inducement to the old crew that would be enough to make them cut us out?"

"Oh yes," said Salasso. "He could indeed."

But back at the Hot Squid, Volkov and his companions were nowhere to be found. By the time they'd checked all the other likely places along the front, it was well after midnight.

"Let us try to intercept him in the morning," said Salasso. "In the meantime, let us return to our lodging and go to bed."

Elizabeth and Gregor looked at him and at each other.

"What a good idea," said Gregor.

"Yes," said Salasso. "We all need some sleep."

"Yes," murmured Elizabeth, as they followed him out, "but not all of us will get any."

18

Social Engineering

I FLOATED ALONG a dim-lit corridor, propelling myself with occasional touches of my hands or feet against the sides. The green fronds of plants now and then brushed against me. In the spex I kept the view constantly shifting back and forth between the reality in front of me and a three-dimensional diagram of the layout lifted from the station library. The only sounds I could hear were the constant sigh of the air supply, and my own breathing.

Over the past two days I'd explored the station like a scuba diver sounding out an undersea cave system. I didn't make it obvious— whenever anyone met me, I was plausibly on my way somewhere, or plausibly lost. I was on call all the time, and often had to visit the fabs, in real or virtual space, to help sort out some discrepancy between the plan and the practicalities of construction. The rest of the time my work consisted of rehashing the procedure we'd gone through for the craft, this time for the second project: the engine.

In a way, the second project was easier. I'd already met most of the bugs in the project plan while working through the details for the craft; and the engine itself was a simpler construction, more straightforward and robust, less finicky, than even the stripped-down version of the craft currently taking shape in the fabs. It would require more actual material, including such exotica as black-hole atoms, but it might take less time to actually build. Consulting the interface had become easy and habitual, and that, too, clarified matters and speeded things up.

At the end of the corridor I heard voices. I caught a stanchion and let my bending arms take the strain of my sudden halt. Listening more closely, I could make out two voices speaking in Russian, too low to quite make out and too fast for me to follow. One of them sounded male, the other female. A tab to the station map

252

showed a big storage depot off to the right; although pressurized, most of the handling required in it was robotic, and it didn't seem a likely place for people to be. Especially as one of the depot's features was that it was a big metal box—a Faraday cage, impervious to electromagnetic radiation, and hence to our spex' comms.

I kicked off again, aiming for the doorway. The door was, for good safety reasons, unlockable. I swung the lever to open it and gave what I thought was a convincing impression of blundering in, arms windmilling as I drifted across several cubic meters of empty air before snagging the upper edge of a lashed-down plastic crate with my foot.

Snugly braced by their feet and backs between rows of crates, side by side and face-to-face, were Aleksandra Chumakova and Grigory Volkov. They looked up at me guiltily, as if I'd caught them in some clandestine assignation, then instantly recovered their composure, covering their confusion with indulgent smiles as I covered my own with more newbie flailing-about.

Aleksandra I'd seen before, leading the opposition at the mass meeting and later speaking for her team at Driver's debriefings. I'd never seen Volkov, but I recognized him at once. His Slavic cheekbones and crew-cut fair hair had made him the most photogenic cosmonaut since Gagarin. The first—and last—man on Venus, who'd risked his life for the glory of a landing that was about nothing but glory; and, of course, a CPEU member, one of the Russian hard core, a CP loyalist and E.U. patriot.

"Hi there, Matt," he said, in English with a perfect Voice of America accent. "Are you lost, or have you come here for some peace and quiet?"

Chumakova was fanning a hand by her ear and shaking her head. "I know how it is; sometimes you can't hear yourself think back there."

I grabbed an edge and maneuvered myself into a better position, out of reach and a bit above them.

"Yeah, that's it," I said. "But as it happens I'm very glad I found you."

"Problem in the fab?" said Volkov, shading his spex, then clearing them. "Ah, I see your difficulty. We've been working offline."

My spex had gone offline as soon as I'd entered the room. The only way you *could* work inside this metal sheathing was offline.

"Ah, it's not that kind of problem," I said, making myself more comfortable. "I've been thinking about what you said at the meeting, Aleksandra. You remember, the Baku one?"

"*That* circus? I remember it very well."

"Well," I sighed, "you seem to have been right about some things. This so-called information campaign is costing scores of lives back home every day."

Chumakova nodded. "*Of course* people riot when every rumor comes across as a just-cracked state secret!"

"Yes," said Volkov gravely. "Even where the stories are true, they're very misleading when they're taken out of their proper context."

"Provocations," I said. "I've seen what they've done to my own city, Edinburgh. But apart from any, you know, personal concerns, what worries me is that the unrest will actually strengthen the militarists on our side, and the extremists on the American side."

Volkov was nodding and smiling. "Of course, of course," he said. "It's only to be expected that the excesses of the so-called 'left' play into the hands of the right, both in our Party and in the capitalist world. Don't get me wrong, Matt, I totally agreed with exposing the militarist plotters, but this anarchistic campaign is just the kind of excuse the real hard-liners need for a crackdown, and perhaps a foreign adventure . . . some confrontation that might be symbolic at first—the Siberian concessions, perhaps—but such things can get out of hand, and turn real, and ugly, real fast."

Chumakova gave me a sort of friendly frown. "But Matt," she said, "this is something of a sudden conversion for you, is it not? As I understand it, you are a member of an anarcho-syndicalist union yourself."

"Oh, I haven't changed my views," I said. "I know they're not the same as the Party's. You know how it is—in my line of work you get your nose rubbed constantly in the few areas where U.S. tech is still ahead of our own. It's impossible not to be a bit critical of official policy."

"That's very understandable," said Volkov. He took his spex off and smiled wryly. "We know how you must feel. A good worker appreciates good tools."

"Exactly," I said. "But, well, it's good to talk over a few worries with people who, you know . . ."

They both nodded and smiled at that. Like many Russians, they were unshakeably convinced that most sound, ordinary working people were basically loyal to the socialist brotherlands, even if some of them did vote for parties other than the Party or go to church or dye their eyes in funny colors.

But Chumakova persisted in her caution, still sounding me out.

"You seem to have plenty to talk about with your Yank pilot," she said. "Of course, that is your affair, so to speak. And according to the newsfeeds, you had some kind of relationship with the American spy."

"Yes," I said, squirming a bit, "I feel very guilty about Jadey. Not because of Camila, she's . . . a friend, and you needn't worry about her, she doesn't have a political bone in her body."

"As I'm sure you would know," said Volkov.

We laughed.

"So why do you feel guilty," Volkov went on, "if you are not being moralistic about it?"

"It's . . . Well, I suppose it *is* moral, or maybe political. Jadey Ericson is in jail because of me. Not just because she was arrested while I got away—and you must remember, we had good reason to be afraid at that time—but because she's being held on trumped-up charges. There's already a warrant out for me—contempt of court because I didn't come in as a witness—and I can't help wondering if she isn't going to be used at some point to put pressure on me."

"To do what?"

I shrugged. "I don't know; that's what worries me. Anyway, I've been assured the Reform faction is doing what it can to get her out, so for the moment I can't afford to antagonize Paul."

"Lemieux is in the Reform faction?" Volkov asked.

"Oh, sure," I said. "I didn't know he kept that a secret. Shit. Don't let him know I told you!"

"No, no, of course not," said Volkov.

"Aha!" said Chumakova. "So *that's* why Driver's made such a big deal about that bastard Weber."

"Who?" I asked.

"The Trotskyite MEP, the one who was arrested—"

"Oh, yeah, right. I remember, but— I'm sorry, I don't see the connection."

"The Reform faction are a bunch of Trotskyites, basically— rights posing as lefts," said Volkov, with the confidence of a man confirming a long-held prejudice. "Look at how they renamed the station: *The Darker the Night the Brighter the Star*. After a book about Trotsky! Ridiculous."

"It does seem to have annoyed a lot of people," I said. "After all, Marshall Titov was a real Soviet space hero."

"First space-walk, yes," said Chumakova, with a sidelong glance at Volkov. "They can't take that away from us."

"No," I said. "They can't. And we can still do some great things here."

"We already are," said Chumakova. "First Contact, my God! And building an anti-gravity vehicle! What the Yanks would have given for that."

I pushed up and rolled over.

"Ah well, screw the politics, the project's still worth doing. I better be getting back to it before Driver gives me an earful. Catch you later."

"Yeah, see you soon," said Volkov, as I sailed to the door. Urgent messages blinked up as soon as my head passed the jamb.

"Where the fuck have you been?"

I clipped my belt to the webbing and resettled my spex.

"Ah, I just needed to get away for a while," I told Avakian. "Sometimes it just feels a bit crowded in the living-quarters."

"Yeah, I guess some people find that," he said, in a tolerant but uncomprehending tone. "You gotta watch it, man, maybe get some meds."

"No, I'll be fine now," I said. "Now I know there's places on the station where you can't be reached."

"Well, don't go to them without letting someone know," he said.

"Okay, okay, it was a bit irresponsible; I'll let you know in future. Now, where were we?"

"Have a look at this," said Avakian.

We patched in to a shared space.

"Oh wow," I said.

" 'Wow,' fuck indeed," said Avakian. "I've done it. Well, to be honest, we've done it, but I just realized that what I've just done had actually finished it, and I wanted you to be the first to see it."

It was the engine. Only in VR, of course, but it meant that the entire production process had been run through successfully in simulation. It gleamed on its smoothly integrated pedestal like an anvil from another dimension, or a mounted rocket-motor from some museum of the far future. I'd seen the sketches, the 3-D diagrams in the plan, but this was different: a hyperreal rendering of how it would look when built. It was about four meters long, less than a meter across at its widest diameter, and its maximum height was about two meters. I could reach out and touch it, and I did.

"Thanks, Armen," I said. "What a sight."

"Yeah," he said. "Fundamentally it's a weirder sight than the craft. See the four small holes in the corners of the base? I reckon what you're supposed to do with it is fucking *bolt it to the floor.* Just one little problem though."

"Control system?" I hazarded, thinking: *Not again!*

"As in, there ain't one."

"Wait a minute," I said. "There is on the plan."

I rummaged the pages up. "There, that plate—it's obviously a control system, it's covered with switches, even if we can't use it without—"

"Yeah, take a look at how that turned out."

He rotated the view and zoomed on a completely featureless blank rectangle on the pediment.

"Shit."

"For all we know," he went on, "that could be a goddamn name-plate, and what looked like switches in the plan could be just the equivalent of a company name engraved in brass."

"Okay," I said, "there's no reason the aliens would have given it to us like this. Maybe if we take the question to the interface, they'll come up with something we can use."

It took us the rest of that day to formulate the query. What it came up with was not an answer, but a picture and a set of coordinates on three axes, which pinpointed to the nearest centimeter a place within the interior of the asteroid.

"I reckon they're telling us to go and get the answer there," I said.

"You first," said Avakian.

"Oh hell," I said generously. "There must be somebody here who'd be a lot better than me at getting around in the big picture."

"I wasn't talking about that," said Avakian. "I meant you can be the first to tell Driver."

Driver was too tired to explode. He didn't even seem particularly annoyed.

"We never expected to actually test the big engine straightaway," he said. "It's the craft that's something we can hope to actually use. Even an unusable but unarguably real version of the engine would be enough to get people excited. I mean, don't get me wrong, it's great you've got this far, and you can see if you can sort out this control-system problem if you like, but don't let it delay the other stuff."

"Okay," I said, relieved and a bit disappointed.

"Tomorrow's the big day," he said. "We shift the little engine from the fabs to the receiving-bay, and then maneuver it into the *Blasphemous*. That'll require some EVA. Mikhail, how are your boys and girls?"

Telesnikov, physically present, gave him a thumbs-up.

"We're ready to go," he said. "In fact, we're quite keen on doing the whole shift as an EVA—take it out of the fab's door and lug it around to the *Blasphemous* directly, instead of maneuvering through the corridors. It'd be more straightforward, for one thing, and for another, we know the engine can handle vacuum—it's in vacuum already in the fab—but we don't know how it'll cope with exposure to biologicals."

"That's not a bad idea," said Driver.

Telesnikov grinned. "Yeah, it's so obvious I wish I'd thought of it myself."

"Who did think of it?" I asked.

"Grigory Volkov."

I swallowed hard.

"Uh, can we just discuss this further for a minute?"

Driver raised his eyebrows. "A minute."

"Okay," I said, "I know I'm not an expert on space-working, but I do know that machine we've built as well as anyone can without understanding it, and I'd swear it's totally robust against biological contamination. I mean, come on, every moving part is sealed. The control systems are our own kit, and we know how tough that is. Whereas, uh, no offense to your team, Mikhail, but the longer something's being handled in EVA the bigger the chance of an accident. One slip and we could send the thing spinning off into space and lose it for good."

Telesnikov waved a hand.

"It'll be in a mesh, tethered all the way," he said. "There's no question of its being unsafe."

"Ropes can break," I said.

"Not these ropes," said Telesnikov. He gave me a reassuring grin. "NASA spec. And we have the most experienced EVA operator in the Solar System—as far as we know!"

"Who?"

"Grigory, of course." His eyes widened suddenly. "Oh, I see! You may have heard that ESA just assigned him here for reasons of prestige, but that's the kind of envious rumors that spread around in the bureaucracy. No cosmonaut believes them. Grigory is far from just a pretty face."

"But—"

Driver raised his hand. "You've had your minute, Matt. We do it as EVA all the way. Next business."

Camila was shaking my shoulders.

"Matt! Wake up!"

"Wha'?"

"Your *bleep*'s going off. Can't you hear it? Everybody else bloody can!"

I woke and fumbled for my reader and spex. When I thumbed off the *bleep* it became obvious it wasn't the only one sounding in the vicinity. They fell silent one by one as I slid the spex on over eyes grainy with tear-salt.

"Patch me in?" said Camila.

"Yeah, sure." I opened a channel to her spex as the report floated up in front of me.

PERSONAL PRIORITY NEWS:

Opening shot of someone being bundled up the stairs of a United Airlines 777. Zoom and track: Two Scottish WPCs holding Jadey. She seemed to be struggling, but in a theatrical, pro forma way. At the top of the steps they let go of her and just pushed. She stumbled, caught the doorframe, and turned.

She raised an outstretched arm and extended index and middle fingers and a thumb, the current version of a defiant salute.

"Death to Communism!" she yelled, and backed into the aircraft.

SURFACE:

The American spy Jadey Ericson was released at midnight tonight and is now on a plane to the United States. The murder charge against her has been dropped in the light of new evidence, and she leaves a full confession exposing the anti-European, anti-socialist conspiracy in which she was a pawn.

DEPTH:

The subversive Human Rights Federation, financed in part by the military-industrial company Nevada Orbital Dynamics, which recently sent aid to the mutineer-held space station *Marshall Titov,* is linked to the fascist and nihilist gangs behind the violence of the past few days, and with the CIA agent and space mutineer Colin Driver. Driver's partner in the cabal that has temporarily seized the station, to the dismay of its honest scientists and cosmonauts, is Paul Lemieux, long identified with the so-called "Reform" grouping in the CPEU, who was a member of the Trotskyite LPR in his student days at Lausanne. Further CIA influence on factionalist elements in the CPEU and on the Trotskyite LPR have been clearly established by the investigations into the connections of the former MEP Henri Weber. The motivation of the current campaign of disinformation and claims of access to "alien spacecraft technology" appears to be to strengthen the self-styled "Reform" faction in the CPEU, which parades itself in the E.U. as a popular, democratic current and internationally as the only Communists ready and able to "do business with" the United States. The demagogic and contradictory nature of this "platform" should be obvious.

ANALYSIS:

At that point I switched off. Camila's arm was around my shoulders.

"That's great news, Matt! Jadey's free! Wow!"

"Aye, thanks," I said. "It's brilliant, it's a big relief. But, shit, they're saying she confessed all that stuff. . . ."

"Ah, crap," said Camila. "Nobody'll believe that! Especially when they said she was a pawn. How could she possibly have known all that?"

"She couldn't," I said. "And as far as I know, she didn't."

"It's all commie paranoid gibberish anyway."

I took off my spex and rubbed my eyes and stared at her in the dim light of our alcove.

"It isn't," I said. "Modulo the comical prose of the Party press release, it's exactly what Driver and Lemieux told us the other night."

"It *is?*"

"We get used to doing translations."

I grabbed her and hugged her, for no other reason than comfort.

"You don't seem very happy."

"I'm happy," I said. "God, I'm so relieved I could cry. But we're still in a very dangerous game."

"Yeah, you said it." She stroked my back. "Go back to sleep. Jadey should be home by morning. I'll wake you up when the news comes in."

I slid the spex back on and flexed my fingers in their infrared feedback.

"No need," I said. "This thing will."

Before I could take them off and go back to sleep, an incoming message flashed. I accepted it and Grigory Volkov's handsome features filled my view, like a poster on a teenager's bedroom wall.

"I think congratulations are in order, Matt," he said, smiling. It was a canny sentence; nobody listening in could have guessed that he was asking, rather than offering.

"Yes," I said. "Congratulations all around. Thanks, Grigory."

By the time the reader woke me with news of Jadey's debarkation— at McCarran Airport, Las Vegas, much to my relief—Camila had gone. She was due in the receiving-bay under the *Blasphemous* from the beginning of the day shift. Slightly miffed that she hadn't even said good-bye, let alone roused me with her usual morning cuddle, I washed and dressed and made for the refectory. Over breakfast (salted rabbit meat and fried-egg sandwich—not recommended) I scanned the news with the thought at the back of my mind that I'd got very used to Camila's morning cuddle. But it was Jadey who was at the front of my mind. As soon as she'd got out of E.U. airspace she'd put out a statement repudiating the confession, denying she'd made it, and ridiculing its contents as summarized.

Most comments I tracked seemed to agree with her there, but disagreed over whether it was a complete fabrication or whether it was based on some encrypted information the FSB (or some random hacker) had managed to crack, and were releasing in this way so as not to compromise their real sources. To add to the tortuous confusion of the whole labyrinthine affair, the smartest analysts— whether on *Europa Pravda* or the *Daily Web*—were pointing out that the FSB itself undoubtedly favored the Reform grouping, and that the CIA usually kept well clear of backing violent opposition in the Socialist Democracies, being far more likely to try to exert its influence on the FSB . . . which, of course, itself . . .

I switched off. The world has become one big grassy knoll, crawling with lone gunmen who think they're the Warren Commission. My own take on the matter was that my heavy hint to Grigory the previous day had led him to believe that Jadey was being held as a bargaining-chip by the Reform faction, and that releasing her would help his cause—that of the straight-down-the-middle centrist faction, conservative but not outright reactionary like the militarist hard-liners. We would see.

I routed a phone message for Jadey through the station's mailbox. She wasn't online, but it went through to Nevada all right. After a good jolt of coffee, and with my breakfast settling in for a protracted stay in my stomach, I headed for the fabs.

The fabrication units occupied a separate wing of the station. This was my first visit to them outside of VR; for which, after slogging through a dozen airlocks and blast doors and decontamination bays, I was quite grateful.

The control room was crowded with at least twenty people, apart from the five operators, who were mercifully able to ignore it all in their spex and full-body rigs. Most of the people here were familiar to me only as names that had popped up in my workspace, or called me into theirs, with a construction problem. Driver and Lemieux were at the front, Chumakova beside them. Avakian hovered at the back. I jostled in and managed to find a position with a clear view ahead.

The fabrication unit itself lay beyond a thick partition of diamond-laminated glass. The multiple, multiply-subdivided robotic arms of the fabricators—the closest anyone had got to a Moravec bush robot—bristled and sparkled. In the tips of their toughest fingers they held the engine and control system of the craft.

Despite all my familiarity with it in VR, there was something of a thrill in seeing it in reality, with actual photons that had just reflected off it entering my own eyes. I greedily absorbed the sight, which in truth was nothing more than a smooth metal bulge with a flat base, attached by three meters of electric cabling to a block of polystyrene cladding which I knew contained an instrument panel and a racked array of levers.

The outer door of the fab was already sliding up, to reveal a ten-by five-meter rectangle of black. This frame was quickly filled by two cosmonauts in EVA suits, deploying a barely visible net around the doorway. Cables trailed behind them. The movements of ropes and net in vacuum and microgravity were different enough from the familiar to give me a sense of unease.

Or to provide a focus for the unease which I already felt. I tuned my spex to the comms channel and listened in to the cosmonauts and the control-room crew. They were speaking Russian and neither my own language skills nor those of the spex were able to make much of it.

The mechanical fingers flicked, and the thing sailed out to be caught in the net. The net was closed at the mouth with a simple drawstring, and was hauled off to the right, out of view.

I patched to an outside camera, and watched the mesh bag and its contents being lashed to a basic sled, the free-fall equivalent of a forklift truck. It consisted of several cubic meters of crate with a fuel tank underneath. At each end, fore and aft, were mounted four jets, a set of controls, and a step for the pilot to stand on, with the jet nozzles safely behind. The bag was now free, except from the sled. The sled, with the kind of belt-and-braces caution alluded to by Telesnikov, was itself tethered. A long, loose cable with one end fixed at the fab and the other just beneath the half-kilometer-distant

Blasphemous Geometries passed through two sturdy metal half-rings projecting from the sled's side. Five cosmonauts, the tubes of personal rocket-packs curving from their shoulders like the outlines of cherubic wings, were spaced out along the sled's path.

The sled's pilot fired up the jets briefly and the tug moved forward in a straight line at a low speed. It had passed two of the cosmonauts and was halfway to its destination when something went wrong.

The rope snagged and stopped playing through the loops. The abruptly-halted sled swung around and at the same moment its forward jets began to flare, far more intensely than the rear jets had done. It shot backward and away from the asteroid's surface, stretching the rope instantly to a flattened V. As I racked the view into close-up it became evident that the rope had stuck not just along the side but around the front of the crate. As suddenly as it had stuck, the rope broke at both sides of the sled, which soared away at an angle, jets firing for a few more seconds. By the time they stopped, the sled was beyond even the swiftly tracking camera's zoom.

Everybody in the room was either yelling or shocked into silence. The cosmonauts' comms channel remained calm. Discipline was holding. I heard the tug-pilot's voice in crackly, halting Russian:

"The sled's fuel is exhausted and the sled is tumbling."

Volkov said, "We have you on the radar. Jump clear, stabilize with your own rockets, kill as much outward velocity as you can, and we'll pick you up."

"*Nyet.*"

"For the love of God, Andrea! Abandon it now!"

The reply came through, still crackly, in English.

"This isn't Andrea, this is Camila, and I'm not going to abandon it."

I yelled out at that, a completely futile howl because I was unable to transmit to the comms channel. Even its discipline seemed to be breaking up, in a sudden babble. Through the camera I could see cosmonauts jetting about, toward or away from each other.

Camila's voice broke through again, fainter.

"Stand by," she said. "I'm bringing it in."

I tabbed frantically between camera viewpoints until I found one directed outward. In the starfield a point glowed like a blue nova, slowly brightening and becoming fuzzy. Within seconds it was in full view, hurtling straight toward us. The camera back-zoomed and stabilized and I could see the sled and its pilot within the blue nimbus.

She brought it right up to the door and then to a dead halt. In her hands was the engine's control panel. Chunks of shattered polystyrene swirled around her as though in atmosphere, a sight as flagrantly impossible as her spectacularly non-Newtonian arrival. She waved, and skittered the sled off to the side, to bring it to another abrupt stop beside her own ship.

"EVA transfer complete," she said. "Unscheduled flight-test complete. Engine and controls nominal."

By this time the arrests, too, were complete.

Lemieux squatted in his habitual upper corner, practicing a new and irritating and dangerous stunt: He'd place his Aerospatiale 9-millimeter in the air, and then tap the end of the barrel sharply down, making the weapon spin in front of him, and letting it drift away a little. Then he'd grab it from orbit. Over and over again. He seemed to pay attention to nothing else. Short of trimming his fingernails with a combat knife and whistling through his teeth, he couldn't have come up with a less subtle display of instability and menace.

Driver, meanwhile, was hamming the soft-cop role, complete with occasional worried glances at Lemieux. He reclined behind his desk, in front of which Chumakova and Volkov looked as though they were standing to attention, their arms looped through the webbing. They weren't tied; it was all very civilized, apart from Lemieux's routine.

I hung off to one side of them, jammed against some shelving; Camila floated by the door. Almost everybody else on the station, including the forty-seven in detention at various improvised places, was watching the show on their spex.

"Come on, comrades," Driver said. "If this was a goddamn NASA accident inquiry, I could maybe believe that what happened was an overdesigned safety system going wrong. Some chemical deterioration in the cable that made it sticky and easily broken, an unpredictable sloshing of fuel in the tug's engine, a burnout. These things happen, right?"

Volkov shrugged. "So we are told. Sometimes it's a mistake to rely on U.S. tech and NASA procedures instead of our own skill."

"Yes," said Driver. "But it was your idea, wasn't it?"

"There was nothing wrong with the idea," said Volkov. "If you are suggesting sabotage, it is ridiculous. I thought it was Andrea Barsova on that sled. I wouldn't risk a cosmonaut's life. You know that, Colin."

"But you weren't risking anyone's life," said Driver. "Barsova is an experienced sled operator, and you would have expected her to jet clear at the first sign of trouble."

"This is all speculation," said Chumakova.

"It isn't," said Driver. "We know you're in touch with elements in the Party and government. After Matt spoke to you, you relayed the conversation to a contact in Brussels. Someone quite high up in the administration. Within hours, Jadey Ericson was released and a fake confession was in circulation, calling me a CIA agent and so forth. I don't think that was a coincidence, and I don't think the people you immediately contacted within the station just happened to be colleagues."

"How do you know—?" Volkov stopped, and glared at me.

"All right," he said. "So Matt told you, and then you followed every contact we made afterward. What of it? It's not a crime."

"Some of your people have talked, and they admit it was more than talk," said Driver.

Volkov laughed. "You won't catch me with that one."

"Maybe not," Driver allowed. "But we'll catch you with the recordings."

Chumakova made a convulsive movement. Lemieux stopped spinning his pistol, and cocked it. Driver gave him an anxious look.

"Easy, easy, Paul," he said. "Aleksandra, you were saying?"

"Nothing that we did was a crime! We value our work, and we will not let you hand it over to the Americans! You're a spy and a filthy traitor, Colin Driver, and when order is restored you'll be shot."

"I'll take my chances on that," Driver said. "Now, I'll ask you to step outside and accompany the detail to the brig."

Volkov shot me another look of disgust, then shrugged and nodded.

"Very well," he said. "It's an honor. We won't have much time to enjoy it."

"What do you mean by that?" said Lemieux.

"Look at the news, everyone," said Chumakova, over her shoulder. "Order is being restored."

19

The First Navigator

Elizabeth, straddled across his hips, leaned forward, hair swinging, cheek catching the dim light, and teased his nipples with her fingertips. "What are you laughing at?"

He reached up, returning the favor. The breasts so soft and smooth, the nipples so hard and rough, and so much bigger than his two tiny tips. He wondered, in a kind of detached way, whether her pleasure at this manipulation was greater in a similar multiple. If it was, he envied her.

"I'm laughing at me," he said. "I've been a fool."

Her hair made a broad brush-stroke down his chest.

"That you have, Cairns, but not as big a fool as me."

His hand was in her hair, another marvel. He wished his response could be as inexhaustible as the stimuli, so many of them, so much jungle and ocean, mountain and hillock, the long white beach of her back, the whole unending planet of her body, the blazing dark sky of her mind. A world that he had explored for hours, and which had explored him right back.

"I don't know if that's going to work, this time," he said.

Her tongue did something shockingly clever with his foreskin, by way of reply; an experiment that refuted his null hypothesis. She was a biologist, and she knew her subject well.

Third block, Quay 4, Ferman and Sons. At eight in the morning the quay was a vile place, the wind off the sea carrying the stench from the killing-cliffs and the closer, chemical reeks from worn refrigeration and harsh disinfectants on the factory ships. Bone-chips underfoot and a slippery mixture of mineral and animal oils. Haulage vehicles creaked and rumbled on the cobbles. Among the dockers and sailors the saur and the two humans were inconspicuous. They found a waterfront cafe opposite the office building's entrance, and lurked around a table by the steamy window. Elizabeth and Gregor munched their way through smoked-fish sandwiches; Salasso picked at strips of brackie beef. Gregor kept lookout, wiping the window every so often with his sleeve.

"Lipids colloidally suspended in water droplets formed around smoke particles," he said. "You could write a whole thesis on this place without even starting on the biology."

"Have another coffee," said Salasso. "Your brain is undergoing early consequences of sleep deprivation."

Gregor yawned and nodded, smiling at Elizabeth as Salasso raised three fingers to the waitress. The cafe was full of manual workers having a late breakfast and office workers or business owners having an early one. Most of them were human, apart from a gigant docker and a couple of saurs.

"This man Volkov," said Salasso after the waitress had brought the refills. "You got the impression he knew Matt Cairns?"

"Oh, definitely. He was with a man who mistook me for Matt, from the back, anyway."

"So we know your ancestor has hair similar to yours, and perhaps a similar stance and build," said Salasso. "That may be helpful, but I wish you had spoken more to that man."

"To tell you the truth," said Gregor, "I was so shaken by meeting Volkov that the other man seemed less important. And I was being cautious, because we know *they* are cautious. Didn't want to ply him with questions."

"Even so—"

"Look," said Elizabeth, grinning across the table at them both, "the fact is I distracted Gregor from his research. Don't be too hard on him."

"I'm pleased for you both," said Salasso, "but this liaison has happened at an awkward time. And now you are both suffering from sleep deprivation."

Gregor didn't take his attention away from the blurred view through the window. The memory of his night with Elizabeth seemed imprinted on every part of his skin, and all her curves and angles remembered in his hands.

"I wouldn't call it 'suffering,' " he said. "And while we're on the subject of awkward times, you yourself were . . ."

"There is that," said Salasso. "But the consequences of my personal entanglement were *fortunate*."

To Gregor this sounded uncharacteristically defensive. Whatever emotions were involved in Salasso's evidently centuries-long affair could only be intense. He decided not to press the matter.

"Anyway, about Volkov," he said. "He wasn't at all eager to let Marcus know who he was, so I don't think he'll be selling any secrets to the merchants."

"Then why's he coming here?" said Elizabeth.

"Assuming he is. . . . He didn't say right out that he would. Maybe he does just want to set up some deal involving marine-engine lubricants."

"There is more going on than that," said Salasso. "I am irrationally certain of it."

Gregor laid his cheek against the damp glass, not sensually—the greasy feel was quite unwelcome—but to see farther up toward the street end of the quay. The clock on the cafe wall showed half past eight.

"That's one of the things I like about your people," he said idly. "Humans don't call their certainties 'irrational,' especially when they are."

"Rationality is a worthy aspiration," said Salasso. "For your species."

Gregor was still chuckling when he recognized a man walking slowly along, a bit farther up on the other side of the quay, pausing occasionally to peer at doorways and signs.

"Don't all jump," he said, "but I've just spotted Matt Cairns. Wait here."

He stood up and was out the door before anyone could object, and barely remembered to look both ways before crossing the road.

The man stood on the pavement by the third block's doorway, looking at the names of businesses listed beside their bell-switches. He was just raising a tentative finger toward them when he noticed Gregor's approach, and turned.

Gregor stared at him, transfixed. The only thing about him that looked old was his jacket, its dinosaur hide worn so soft it hung like cloth. Despite what he knew, he'd subconsciously expected his ancestor to look ancient, the image of the young man in the castle

269

portrait gravitating toward the lined features of James. Even seeing Volkov hadn't dislodged the assumption. This man's face looked younger than the one Gregor had blearily seen in the shaving-mirror a couple of hours earlier. It betrayed no recognition or surprise.

"Can I help you?" the man said.

Gregor blurted the first question on his mind. "Did Volkov send you here?"

"Volkov? Shit!"

The man immediately turned away and walked off, up the quay toward the street. Gregor hurried to catch him up.

"Excuse me," he said. "My name's Gregor Cairns—"

"I know your name," said the man. "And I'll thank you not to say mine."

Gregor almost missed his stride. "What?"

"Shut up and keep walking and we might just get out of this trap."

They'd reached the junction of the quay and the street before the man relaxed a little. He stood with his back to the corner of Block 1, where he could watch all three of the possible approaches.

"Okay," he said. "What's this about?"

"I was going to ask you—"

"All right. Last night I heard about your inquiries, and the merchant's." His gaze kept shifting as he spoke, with unsettling effect. "And I heard the merchants would have someone at Ferman's about nine. I didn't know Volkov was behind me hearing it. Somebody's going to get a good kicking for that little omission."

"Volkov—"

"Fucking hates my guts. Not like he'd stick a knife in them, but anything he sets me up for is unlikely to be much fun." He met Gregor's gaze full-on for the first time. "What are you after?"

"We were hoping you had some old tech from the ship."

"What for?"

"Navigation."

The response was a rude laugh.

"What's so funny?" Gregor was finding the man's manner as annoying as his shifting gaze, and was beginning to glance around uneasily himself. The street was unfamiliar in the daylight, the traffic light, the pavements cluttered with the flapping canopies and bare tables and detritus of the market winding down. The quay was loud with the squeal of metal and the hiss of rubber on cobbles.

"I'll do the watching," the man said. "You look at me, and tell me what you see."

"I see Matt C—"

"Like I said. Shut the fuck *up* with that name. The second one. Yes, I'm Matt. Matt Spencer. Side branch of the family. Interesting resemblance, isn't it?"

"You mean you're *not*—"

"Yes, of course I'm the goddamn navigator. That's worth far more to the merchants than anything to so with navigation. They have navigation. They don't have this."

"Ah," said Gregor. "That's what Salasso said."

"Your saur pal figured it out, did he. Good for him. If I know Volkov, he thought the same, and made fucking sure that if anyone turned up for the meeting with the merchant, it wouldn't be him."

"Would meeting the merchants be all that dangerous?"

Matt's gaze fixed on him again.

"Would you like to find out?"

Gregor walked back down the quay in a dino-hide jacket from whose pockets an interesting collection of weapons had been removed. Imagining that extra kilogram's weight on his shoulders helped him get Matt's walk and stance more or less right. He resisted the temptation to glance across at the cafe.

The sheet-metal door of the block stood open, to a concrete passageway ending in a spiral stair. Beyond the stairwell another door stood open to a narrow lip of quay. He checked the faded labels pasted beside the doorbell buttons:

Ferman & Sons, 3rd Flr. Marine Engnrs.

He bounded up the three flights of stairs and arrived a little dizzy. A big door with the firm's name on a brass plate stood slightly ajar. It swung back on a gentle push. Across a couple of meters of stained carpet was a heavy wooden desk. The female pithkie behind it looked up and smiled.

"Good morning," she said. She glanced down at an open diary. "Are you expected?"

Gregor's head lowered and his shoulders hunched involuntarily as he stepped into the office, a warehouse conversion, open-plan, partitioned at head height. Keyboards clattered and conversations hummed. Narrow floor-to-ceiling windows overlooked the harbor. Nobody waited at either side of the door.

Still looking around, he stopped in front of the desk.

"Good morning," he said. "I'm not expected, but I'm here to meet Grigory, uh, *Antonov*."

"Engineer Antonov should be along in a moment," the receptionist said. She picked up a pen. "And your name?"

"Cairns."

She noted the name, then rippled her long-fingered, long-nailed hand to indicate a leather sofa to his left.

"Please, take a seat."

"Thank you."

He sat on the edge, fists in empty pockets, and then willed himself to sprawl, if not relax. After a minute Volkov strolled in. He was walking past when he must have noticed Gregor out of the corner of his eye, and turned around sharply. The edges of his hands came up like knives in front of him; his knees crooked. Then he straightened and backed off. Gregor had jumped up to meet the expected attack, for all the good that would have done.

Volkov laughed and stepped forward, hand extended. Gregor shook it gingerly.

"Good morning," said Volkov. "My apologies—for a moment I mistook you for our friend Matt." He looked pointedly at the jacket. "I see you've met him."

"Yes," said Gregor. "And if you hadn't been mistaken?"

Volkov shrugged and smiled. "He might have tried to attack me. He's a bit paranoid, as you'll have noticed."

"Uh-huh," said Gregor, in as neutral a tone as he could manage.

"I suppose he expected the people from the ship to shanghai him or something, and that I'd somehow set him up for it." Volkov shook his head. "And why did you come here in the first place, before you ran into Matt?"

Gregor looked around.

"Uh, can we talk privately?"

"Of course," said Volkov. "This way."

Behind the maze of partitions was a corner office on a raised concrete dais with two glass walls. From its convenient supervisory vantage Gregor could see about a dozen people within the partitioned spaces, working at drawing-boards or keyboards or calculating-machines. Volkov spun a well-worn castor chair over to Gregor and sat behind the desk.

272

"When are you expecting the merchants?" Gregor asked.

"Any minute now, so make it quick."

"I'm here because we're after the old computing-tech for navigation, as I mentioned, and quite frankly we think the merchants are after the same thing. We're also concerned that the merchants just might find it very tempting to take one of you with them and, uh, extract the life-extension tech from you one way or another. For that they might make you an offer you couldn't refuse."

"And Matt thought I'd set him up for that? Well, well." Volkov shook his head again. "As for your other concern, I doubt if anyone has any functioning tech from the ship. I certainly don't."

He stood up and stepped to the glass wall. "If I had it, I would use it—secretly, of course—to get an edge on my competitors, instead of paying people to crank out calculations on the clunking monsters down there."

"This firm is yours?"

"No, no. I have this office, various contracts with the staff—I do most of my work at sea. I'm genuinely interested in what the de Tenebres have to offer. Speak of the devil, here they are."

He left, to return a minute later with Marcus de Tenebre and one of his crewmen. Marcus gave Gregor a raised eyebrow, and Gregor moved to leave.

Volkov raised his hand. "Gregor, I'd like you to stay. This is not confidential. I want you to report on this meeting to Matt, and to your colleagues, and to the Families." He shrugged. "And the news-sheets and the radio if you like."

Marcus took the chair Gregor had vacated, Volkov sat back down at the desk, and Gregor followed the crewman's lead and slouched against the wall.

"Gentlemen," said Volkov, "am I right in thinking that you aren't here to sell fine-grade lubricants?"

Marcus nodded.

"Good. So let's not waste time. I gather you intend to leave shortly. I would like to leave with you. In return for my passage, and obviously for some hospitality and initial assistance in Nova Babylonia, I offer you my full cooperation in rediscovering the medical procedures which have enabled me to live as long as I have."

Marcus's face remained impassive. The crewman simply gaped.

"That's a generous offer," said Marcus. "It seems almost too generous. You offer us the long life, in exchange for your passage? a house? some help in finding a *job*?"

"I ask more than that," said Volkov. "I ask for a guarantee of my freedom." He waved a hand. "I'm not afraid of being of being cut up in a laboratory—I've met enough Nova Terrans and emigrants over the years to know that I have nothing like that to fear. But I don't wish to be tied to your family, or to your ship, though of course you will get the first benefits of any success we may have. And I offer less, by the way—I have no guarantee that the research will be successful."

"That's reasonable," Marcus said. "How do you expect to hold us to this?"

Volkov slid a piece of paper across the desk. "I have a contract. Naturally, it's not explicit as to the nature of the knowledge, but it's watertight enough. I know it's in your interests to honor contracts, because for you repeat business depends on a *very* long-term good reputation. Copies have been lodged with my solicitors, and young Gregor here can witness it and take one too."

Marcus scanned the document and nodded.

"I'll sign," he said.

Volkov signed, Gregor witnessed. Then they all signed the copies.

"You have no one you wish to take with you?" the crewman asked.

Volkov's lips compressed. "No," he said. "The long life can be a lonely business."

"And your practice here?" Marcus glanced around the busy office, evidently impressed.

"I'm happy to leave it." Volkov stood up. "Are we ready, gentlemen?"

"In a moment," said Marcus. He rose, propped himself on the edge of the desk, and turned to Gregor. "You are skilled in the life sciences, perhaps more than our philosophers. You could help us in the research. In Nova Babylonia, you could become a great scientist, a man of renown. I know of your conversation with my uncle. I can assure you that he would regard this both as a proper use of your gifts, and a gift worthy of his daughter."

Gregor didn't doubt a word of it. He could imagine it all, clear and vivid, glowing and glorious. He shook his head.

"What I want is here."

Marcus extended an open hand.

"Your friend Elizabeth can come too, if she wishes. Or if you prefer to depart without good-byes—our skiff is on the quay out the back."

"No," said Gregor. He felt slightly dizzy. "No, thank you."

He picked up the document, and paused a moment until his mouth was no longer dry.

"Perhaps it would be best if I leave before you, gentlemen. Give Lydia my love, all the same. If I see her again, it'll be in one of our own ships."

Marcus nodded, Volkov smiled skeptically, the crewman stood aside.

It seemed a long walk through the office. As he came around the partition into the reception area, he saw Elizabeth and Salasso sitting on the sofa. Elizabeth jumped up.

"Everything all right?"

"Everything's fine," he said.

"We were keeping an eye on you," said Salasso. "Matt told us it was a bad idea, but we disagreed."

Gregor clapped them both on the shoulders. "Thanks. It wasn't necessary, but thanks. Where's Matt?"

"Still in the cafe, I hope."

"Good," said Gregor. "I have some questions for him."

"Well, that's it," said Matt. "Nothing to be done about it now."

They had left the cafe and walked to the end of the quay, and had conducted most of their conversation sitting around on bollards, out of earshot of anyone. The ship was about to lift. Their hair prickled. Odd currents of wind whirled scraps of news-sheet and fishwrap into small vortices.

"Nothing to be done about what?" Elizabeth sounded edgy.

Matt gestured at the ship, rising above a bulge of water. The last of its skiffs scooted to the long slits in its side.

"Volkov," he said. "You've done Nova Terra no favors, letting him go. Nor your friends the merchants, for that matter. Nor us, in the long run."

"He seemed a reasonable-enough man to me," said Gregor.

"Of course he fucking did! When you've lived as long as I have, you'll know that anyone can seem reasonable if they want to."

275

Yes, but why would anyone want to seem like a paranoid git?
Gregor felt like asking.

"You," said Salasso, "do not seem very reasonable. Is that because you don't want to?"

"Maybe I will when I've lived as long as you," said Matt. "Or maybe not. Us monkeys don't get any better from living longer. We learn nothing and forget nothing. We get worse. My way of getting worse is a lot better than Grigory Volkov's, believe you me."

The ship floated upward, like the airship it so blatantly wasn't. High in the sky it began to move forward, on a horizontal line that would soon take it out of the atmosphere, and which much sooner took it out of sight.

"Gone to Croatan," said Salasso. "I know the course."

"What do you mean, you're better than Volkov?" said Gregor, in a sudden gale of disappointment and rage at his ancestor. "Volkov's a successful businessman. You're a bum."

"Volkov's been a bum in his time," said Matt. "And I've been rich. *C'est la* fucking *vie*."

He stood up, still staring after the ship. "The point is, Volkov could be a successful politician. What a man who doesn't age could do to the politics of Nova Babylonia is a bit worrying. Still. What's done is done."

He turned around. "Now, what can I do for you?"

"For a start," said Elizabeth, "you can tell us whether you do in fact have any of the old tech."

"Yeah," said Matt. He dug into a deep pocket and pulled out an aluminum case that Gregor had seen already among the knives, pistols, and key-rings. "Come and have a look."

They gathered around the bollard he was sitting on.

He opened the case and passed a pair of wraparound sunglasses to Gregor.

"Go on, try them."

Gregor's hand shook a little as he opened them. The earpieces had tiny speaker-grilles at their curved ends, and still-bright copper and optical connections at their hinges. He slid the glasses on. When he looked at the sea it sparkled with tiny, perfect reflections of the sun.

"Wow," he said. "They really cut down the glare."

"Exactly," said Matt. He held out his hand for them. "That's all they do. Anyone else want a go?"

"What happened to them?"

Matt shrugged as he folded them away.

"Accumulated errors, radiation damage, general fouling-up of the directories . . . in short, everything that didn't happen to me."

He stood up. "Look, we didn't know," he said, sounding defensive. "We didn't know how well the fucking treatments worked. They hadn't been running long enough, I mean, sure, the biotech companies made big boasts, but they always do. The telomere tabs were one-shot things, right, most people got them in their early twenties. Fix and forget. We didn't have them on the ship, and we didn't have the spec for them. It's not like we kept something back from you."

His face was bleak.

"It's all right," said Elizabeth. "We'll get there ourselves."

Matt grinned at her. "That's the spirit. Speaking of getting there ourselves, when can I see this navigation solution of yours?"

They walked up the quay, back to the city.

It was a small window, and the light came through it in a narrow beam. They followed its hot yellow pool around the floor, shifting position unconsciously as Gregor talked Matt through the calculations that summarized the Great Work. Elizabeth and Salasso filled in details of the model of the squid nervous system.

A last sheet of paper lay on the floor: the bottom of the stack. Gregor slashed a pencil line below the last line of figures, and rocked back on his heels.

"That's it," he said.

He stood up. His knees hurt a little. Matt rose more quickly, and walked to the window. The sun, low and orange, threw his dark shadow back.

"Well," said Elizabeth, "what do you think? Have we cracked it?"

"I don't know."

"What?" Gregor heard his voice crack. Salasso silently handed him a chill bottle of beer—the local stuff; tasted of chemicals. He gulped gratefully.

"You must know," Gregor said. "You're the first navigator. You navigated the ship across ten thousand fucking light-years. You set the problem. You must know if we've solved it."

Matt stepped away from the window and sat down on the bed. It was still rumpled, as Gregor and Elizabeth had left it. The One Star Hotel, aptly named, didn't do room service. He reached for his jacket and fished out a pouch and some papers.

"Thank the gods you people had this," he said. "I never could have stood it otherwise. I'd have gone bugfuck crazy."

His hands shook a little as he wrapped the leaves.

"Knowing that the baby in your arms will get old and die before you. Knowing that your grandchildren will die before you. We made a choice, see. We were scientists, on the whole we were civilized people. We didn't want to become gods, or kings. So we had to disappear, and keep on disappearing, generation after generation, decade after decade. Some of us took ship to other suns. The rest of us . . . well. Enough self-pity. Let's just say, it's been tough, and the dope and the drink help, and they don't even kill us, like they should."

He inhaled deeply. Gregor resisted the impulse to clout him, and accepted the joint. The soothing smoke dissolved his rage.

"All right," he said, after Elizabeth and Salasso had partaken. "You've got all of us mellow, Matt Cairns. Now tell us why you don't know."

"I'm an artist, not a technician," said Matt. "I'm a mathematician, a systems manager, a programmer. I've followed every step of your reasoning, and I have to say it strikes me as sound. I set up the problem for my descendants to solve, yes. I'm good at that. I think you've solved it, but I don't know for sure, because . . ."

He looked down, then up. "I'm not the first navigator."

"So who *was* the first navigator?"

"There was no first navigator," said Matt. "But there is now. You are the first navigator."

20

Blasphemous Geometries

C HUMAKOVA WAS RIGHT. Order was indeed being restored back in the European Union. While we were dealing with Volkov's abortive conspiracy, a rather better-planned coup was being launched in Brussels and the regional capitals. Oskar Jilek, a Major-General in the European Peoples' Army, popped up on screens, goggles, and desktops to announce the formation of an Emergency Committee and the honorable resignation of General Secretary Gennady Yefrimovich. Firm action would be taken against rioters, provocateurs, military-adventurist elements, revisionism, dogmatism, and corruption within the Party and state apparatus, and agents of imperialism within the state security organs. Urgent negotiations would be opened with the United States over *genuinely* collaborative access to recent advances in space exploration.

Rather cleverly, the Emergency Committee rescinded all "administrative measures" against members of elected bodies. Weber and other MEPs and councillors who'd been arrested were immediately released. This eliminated one democratic grievance and instantly clogged up the elected bodies with Party-initiated procedures to get rid of them through proper channels. It also distracted attention from a swift roundup of less well connected citizens, mostly for offenses that had long been winked at. Import controls and safety regulations shut down hardware and software bazaars like Waverley Market within hours. Corrupt officials who'd lined their pockets by allowing black-market racketeers to endanger the livelihoods and lives of E.U. citizens were exposed and arrested with a great show of shock and indignation.

"They'll be overthrown in a few days," said Camila. "It's 1991 all over again, you'll see."

"Not this August," I said.

One more news item was given a lot of play: a ship was being readied at Baikonur to rescue the scientists and cosmonauts of the *Marshall Titov* from the small rebel cabal currently holding them hostage.

Shots of boosters lifting heavy equipment and a large number of personnel to orbital rendezvous with a large craft. It had to be large because it held a complement of about a hundred.

Two were ESA cosmonauts. The rest were EPAF Special Forces: space marines.

I looked up from my plate to see Driver moving crabwise behind the long table. He squeezed in opposite us with a plate of tonight's sticky rice-and-meat concoction and a liter plastic bottle of red. It was the first time I'd seen him in the refectory; now that I came to think of it, the first time I'd seen him outside his office.

He pressed the plate to the table and passed the wine across.

"Help yourselves," he said.

We ate for a while, pausing occasionally for a squirt of wine. Driver drank rather more than we did.

"You're looking very relaxed," said Camila.

"Oh, I am," said Driver. "The anti-gravity actually works! Weight off my mind, know what I mean?"

We laughed politely.

"Nah, it's actually getting Volkov's little conspiracy lanced that did the trick," he said. "Christ, it does get tedious knowing people are plotting against you, and not knowing when they're going to make their move. Tomorrow I'm going to shove all the responsibility for running this station onto whatever committee the scientists see fit to elect. Let somebody else take the strain for a while."

"You'll still be managing the projects?" I said.

He shrugged. "If they still want me to."

"I hope so," I said.

Camila was looking from one to the other of us.

"I don't *believe* you guys," she said. "There's just been a goddamn *military coup* in your own country, and you're carrying on like something good has happened."

Driver crushed his plate and glowed up a smokeless.

"It's not good," he said. "But it's not as bad as it looks. It's still the Party that's in power, not the Army, and not the FSB, thank God. And it's the Party centrists, not some ideological dingbats."

"Huh!" she said. "That commie gibberish that Jilek came out with sounded ideological enough to me."

Driver and I both laughed.

"That ain't ideology," said Driver.

"Well, what is?"

"Do you believe," he said, "that human beings are endowed by their Creator, or by their nature, with certain inalienable rights?"

"Sure I do!"

"Why?"

"It's, well, like the man said, it's self-evident. You get it, or you just don't get it."

"Fine," said Driver. "Now, *that's* ideology. What the Major-General appealed to in his serious little talk is *vocabulary*. It's just a structure of ideas and symbols and organizations that helped the Russkis get their act together a generation ago, and helped the Europeans to unite shortly after. What our people really believe in isn't microwaved Brezhnevism but the Party's *real* ideology, which is something a good deal more insidious."

"And what's that?"

He shrugged. "Protectionism, I reckon. Anyway, fuck it. The coup's a bit of a relief. It's like we're not waiting for the other shoe to drop anymore."

"It's you that's gonna drop," said Camila, "when they come out here."

Driver shook his head, narrowing his eyes as though against imaginary smoke.

"Nah," he said. "We don't do hanging. Nor shooting, not even for spies and traitors, despite what Aleksandra said. Nor your horrible Yank electric frying." He made a chopping motion. "Guillotine. Quick and humane—at least, nobody's ever complained afterward."

I folded my plate over the remains of my dinner and took a quick squirt of wine. Asteroid 2048. Rough, definitely not a good vintage.

"Do you really think—"

"Let's not kid ourselves," Driver said. "You guys should be all right. Camila, you're an American just doing your job, they can't touch you. Matt, well, maybe if they throw the book at you, but I don't think so. Emigration isn't a crime, even if you did it illegally. As for the rest of the crew—"

He sat back, and at that moment I realized that everyone else in the refectory had stopped talking and started listening. No doubt this was all going out on more than one set of spex. Driver pretended not to notice.

"Most of the scientists should be all right, they can claim they didn't have much choice. At worst they'll be taken off the station and given other work. Even my good mate Paul—well, hey, they don't want to hand a martyr to the Reform faction. Five years, tops, in a temperate climate." He grinned and winked at me. "I hear the Highland lumber camps aren't too bad, apart from the midges. I've seen guys who'd sweated out a tenner up there, no bother. Paul has the connections. I don't."

"Is that because you're English?" Camila asked.

"Yeah. My parents were English lefties. We were on holiday in the south of France that summer the Russians rolled over the Yanks in the Urals and just kept on coming. Didn't see any reason to go back to London. I got a good education and I've done all right in the FSB, but, you know how it goes. If there was ever anybody who'd make a perfect candidate for the chop, it's me."

He stood up and stretched. "Still, it's been a good run. No complaints. See you tomorrow—we'll skip the debriefing tonight and have a general meeting in the morning. Make sure the teams know, okay?"

He was off before either of us could say a word.

Not much work got done that evening. People hung in the station's intranet, talking or watching the news. The Emergency Committee was making frantic efforts to mend bridges: with its own populations, with China and India, and with the United States. They made hostile gestures at Japan. As Avakian pointed out, it was safe enough to annoy a country about which nobody gave a shit.

I was following the arguments in a fairly desultory way when a call from Nevada blinked up.

"Well, hi there, Matt," said Jadey. She smiled, bright across the light-seconds. I felt a surge of joy; and a pang of guilt, which I had not expected.

I propped my reader where its camera could see me and replied.

"Hi," I said. "It's great to see you! Are you all right? You're looking well."

After forty-odd seconds' delay her answer came back.

"Yeah, I'm fine. It's great to see you too, Matt! They treated me all right, apart from that pack of lies they put in my mouth—I'm still mad about that. Thanks for your messages, though, they did get through and they were a big help. You know, this is more like instant messages than phoning? Like, it's *not* instant? So I'll just keep talking and then let you come back, otherwise we'll be talking across each other all the time. You're not looking too hot yourself, Matt."

"Ah, I'm all right, just knackered. We've been busy. You heard we got the flying saucer to fly?"

I watched her waiting.

"Uh-huh. Camila Hernandez has been in touch with Alan. But look, Matt, you're not getting this, you have to talk for longer than that, otherwise we spend half the time waiting. So give me your news, and what you make of this commie coup and so on. And while you're thinking about that, I can tell you things are getting a bit hot over here too—all kinds of legal hassles. The Feds are accusing us of stealing the alien tech from the commies without authorization, *and* of giving it to the commies. It's like they got us coming and going."

When she stopped I was still thinking over the implications of Camila's having been in touch with her home base. Not that there was anything wrong with it, but she hadn't told me about it; not that she had to, but . . .

"I've been missing you," I said. "I think it might have been me who got you out."

I recounted my social engineering with Volkov, and what he had been up to.

"And," I continued, "your so-called confession was a fake, sure, but basically I think it was more or less true. Your Feds—the CIA or whatever—and some factions in the E.U. have been using us, and they must have some plan to wrap it all up."

"Yeah, yeah." She nodded impatiently. "They all dream the same dream—a stable society with themselves on top. Statist shits! Full marks to you guys for splashing the code-cracking math all over the Net, but they're already talking about ways around that: keep secrets on paper or in people's heads, use trusted messengers instead of electronics. I can tell you, the nukes are now invulnerable to cracking, they moved real fast on that one, which is a good thing, I guess. But they're gonna try to keep the alien tech in safe hands—

theirs! Think about that, Matt. Uh, I've gotta go, this is one of the few secure channels we've got left, and there's a queue. But keep sending the voicemail, and I'll reply when I can. And thanks for getting me out. Try and get yourself back in one piece, okay? Just for me?"

"I'll do that," I promised. "And you look after yourself. Watch out for the black helicopters."

"You're tense," said Camila. She was massaging my shoulders, her thighs gripping my hips.

"Yeah." I laughed. "I've been talking to Jadey."

"Jeez, is *that* what it's about? Hey, come on. This isn't hurting her, and it's helping you. And me, I have to say, nothing's changed. So give the conscience a rest, okay?"

"It's not just that," I said. We rolled around and I began returning the favor. "It's all the stuff that's coming up. Not that I ever expected the information campaign to change the world, but I expected it to do something better than make the governments even more paranoid than before. And—God, this sounds so childish—I didn't ever expect us to get in trouble for what we've been doing."

"Ah," she said. "Don't let that bother you. This is endgame, sure, but we ain't beaten yet, not by a long way. And come on, Matt, today I near enough flew a goddamn flying saucer! *Nothing's* gonna make me feel down after that!" She shifted her shoulders under my hands and sighed. "Just you keep doing that for a while longer, and see if I can't make you feel a lot better real soon."

The amphitheater at Ephesus—not a bad place for a meeting. This time Avakian had resisted the urge to fiddle with the dials. The scan was recent: ruins, scrub, litter, and lizards. Everyone appeared in their own avatars, a small crowd in a space built for a large one. Aside from that, and the site's subliminal implications of elite democracy, the virtual venue seemed neutral enough.

"It's like a football game," Camila said, sitting down beside me and gesturing at the people taking their places on the worn tiers.

"No, that would be in a *stadium*."

She punched me, her avatar's fist swiping through my avatar's chest.

"I won't do that again," she said. "Makes me queasy."

"Me too," I said. I shut my eyes. It was something like travel-sickness.

When I looked up again I focused on the stage down at the front, where Driver had taken his position. When he looked up, he held out one hand, palm uplifted like a classical orator. I couldn't guess whether the imitation was deliberate.

"Okay, comrades," he said. "We all know why we're here." He looked around. "Okay, some of us aren't here. I've given the, uh, comrades in detention the opportunity of taking part. None of them have.

"Right—we can assume the marines are on their way. Those shots yesterday of the ships being prepped wouldn't have been released before launch. Trouble is, we don't know when they actually were launched, but we have a minimum of eight days, a maximum of thirteen. We have to decide now what we're going to do, because we have quite a wide range of options, starting with unconditional surrender and working up from there.

"Up until now, you've all had the option of claiming that you did what I told you, and you obeyed me for whatever reason—coercion, or the belief that I had some constitutional authority, or for want of any alternative. That option ends here. As of now, I'm stepping down from provisional command of this station. What you decide to do about the, ah, rescue mission, and what to do about me, is entirely up to you."

He then literally stepped down, to take a seat a few rows up from the stage. For a moment everyone looked at each other, uncertain what to do next. I glanced over at Avakian, hunched over his virtual keyboard. He shrugged and shook his head. It wasn't like Driver to leave something like this to chance; I was certain he'd have sounded out someone else to step in at this point. Lemieux, also sitting near the front, stood up without taking the stage.

"For different reasons, I take the same position as Colin."

Out of the uneasy silence that followed, the scientist Louis Sembat jumped up and bounded to the speaker's dais.

"For the moment, unless there is any objection, I will chair this meeting."

No objection.

"Very well." He pointed. "Angel, you wish to speak?"

Pestaña stood up, turning around as he addressed the crowd rather than the chair, though he maintained the formalities.

"Colin must know," he said, "that his comments last night were widely discussed. Nobody, other than some of those in detention, is going to let him take all the responsibility. We are certainly not going to see him executed, or Paul imprisoned. Above all—let us be quite frank about this—we are not going to have our work taken away from us."

"You might be given the choice," said Driver, from his seat. "Let them have me and anyone else tagged as a ringleader, and keep your work."

Pestaña shook his head. "It wouldn't be politically possible to condemn you for inciting us to do something that we would still be permitted to do. Also, you have done nothing that we have not done. Replacing us would be difficult. I say there is room for serious negotiation."

The mathematician Ramona Gracia spoke next.

"I would not be too sure of that," she said. "They could retain our colleagues who are not present, and these could train a new influx of scientists. Some work would be lost, but it might be considered worth it for a reliable crew."

Jon Letonmyaki, a Finnish cosmonaut: "Perhaps I could ask what it is we—or indeed Colin or Paul—have done that is illegal? We are acknowledged to have prevented a very dangerous move by the militarists. We have released some information to the public domain, but the General Secretary—the former General Secretary— had already called for international collaboration. Colin resigned from the FSB and, I presume, from the Party in a rather demonstrative manner, but that is not a crime! So what have we done?"

Driver raised his hand. "May I?"

Sembat nodded.

"Okay," said Driver, clambering to his feet. "Let me tell you what I've done, and what you've done. I deliberately transmitted the news about the alien contact and the crypto-war plans to the Americans. That was conscious and deliberate treason, which I took care to conceal from my friend Paul Lemieux. He's only up for trying to exploit it politically. As for the rest of you, you've all collaborated in releasing mathematical tools that have made most existing forms of encryption useless, and destabilized most of the governments of the world. That may not get you jailed, but you can bet it'll get you off this kind of work—or any potentially security-sensitive work—for the rest of your goddamn lives. If the

286

E.U. authorities regain control of this station, your careers are over."

There was no rush to speak next. Most people here, I guessed, had figured this out already, but at some level they'd still clung to the kind of hopes so naively expressed by Letonmyaki—and, less naively, by Angel Pestaña. A lot of them seemed to acquire a sudden interest in the realistic rendering of crushed Coke cans and hardened chewing-gum on the steps, or the haze and cypresses in the middle distance.

Telesnikov, whose card I'd long since marked as Driver's man within the cosmonaut cadre, stood up and strode to the front.

"Enough of this!" he said. "We are not helpless, we do not have to sit and wait for the marines. We can elect a committee to represent us in negotiation with ESA and if possible this new EC. We can appeal to the world public, preferably along the lines that Jon Letonmyaki suggested: do our best to sound innocent and reasonable. And while we are doing that, we can prepare for the worst.

"We have the most advanced aerospace vehicle in the world, just awaiting completion. We know that it works, and we have only the beginnings of an idea of its capabilities. Avakian has told me he believes it can reach Earth in a matter of hours. There is much we can do with a machine like that!

"We also have the space-drive, which we can construct in perhaps ten days. It is just possible that we can complete it before the marines arrive. And if we do . . ."

He paused, and looked around, daring us.

". . . we can use it, and when they arrive we will be somewhere else!"

This time, so many people wanted to speak that Avakian could barely fend the rush.

The Bengali astrophysicist Roxanne Khan had the strongest objection, after most of the obvious what-ifs had been argued into the ground. If the thing didn't work, we were no worse off. It was unlikely to blow up, or otherwise destroy us, unless the alien intelligences had some very warped motives indeed; and if they did, we were safer dead than at the mercy of murderous or suicidal gods.

"The problem, as I see it, is one of navigation," Khan said. "Mikhail speaks of making a small, controlled, jump of a few light-minutes—a proof of concept which would indeed be quite sufficient to give us the whip hand in negotiation. But we already know that the information we are given is sometimes ambiguous, difficult to interpret. What if we make a mistake? Let us leave to one side morbid thoughts of ending our jump inside a sun. What if we find ourselves halfway across the galaxy? Or halfway across the universe?"

Telesnikov had an answer for that. I suspected he'd been thinking about this for some time.

"There are about three hundred of us, about equally divided between the sexes. That is not a bad number to begin a colony."

"Using what?" somebody shouted, through a clamor of more ribald comments. "Cometary resources?"

"Mine the gods," said Avakian, as though under his breath, but so that everyone heard, and most laughed.

"Not all the small bodies in the Solar System are . . . inhabited," Telesnikov went on, unperturbed. "We have no reason to think this is exceptional. So in principle, yes. We could."

That didn't exactly end the discussion, but somehow it took the edge off it. From what I picked up afterward, most of us were glad to have something to do other than wait to be arrested, and the knowledge that if negotiations failed we had an outside chance of escape.

There was also the strangely comforting consideration that at worst we might die, but we would not *die out*.

"I'm ready," I said.

My breath was loud in the helmet. Ten meters away from the faceplate, in a direction I refused to think of as "down," was the surface of the asteroid—the nightside, at the moment, its clinkery detail faintly visible in the dim light from my suit. In every other direction were the stars, sharper than frost. I couldn't think of them as a destination. The Copernican hypothesis seemed absurd. These scattered points of light could not be suns.

"Turn the light off," Armen said.

In front of me now, nothing but black.

"Pull very gently on the ropes, and stop when you see it."

The paired ropes, one for each hand, were stretched between two tall masts a hundred meters apart. I'd moved along them about forty-five meters, sliding the clip of my tether under one hand. I tugged myself farther, peering into the black. Beneath me—in front of me—I saw the alien apparatus. It glowed just enough to be visible. It looked like a bush, or a bush robot, just big enough to fall into.

"Now," said Armen, "just pull the ropes toward you and let go, and let yourself drift into it. Don't worry about missing it, you won't, and remember you're still attached to the ropes. Turn the radio off."

I did, then tugged as gently as possible, and let go, and sank forward between the ropes. In the seconds it took to traverse those few meters, the apparatus looked ever more crystalline and fragile, as though I were about to crash very slowly into a snowflake chandelier.

When Avakian had shown us what he called "the big picture" of the asteroid's interior, I'd assumed we were seeing a direct view of it, of something that was relayed to us in a vastly diminished, user-friendly form through the interface. Actually, what we'd seen was recordings from previous encounters such as the one I was about to have. The interface aside, there was no ongoing direct view of the interior. The interface was fed by a fiber-optic cable as thick as my arm extending from the bush down the side of the asteroid to the station, but for the real live action we had to use this other interface, constructed—or grown—by the aliens themselves. For what reasons, the gods only knew; and for once that flip phrase was a literal truth.

The apparatus didn't shatter as I collided with it. Some of its branches moved and parted, others gathered, to mesh at their tips into shapes like huge petals. It absorbed my momentum and held me. One of the flat shapes covered my faceplate. For a second of complete darkness I felt, quite irrationally, as though that covering would suffocate me. Then I found I could still see the coordinate readouts on the faceplate, printed on the upper left corner in faint red digits. That display, and an input jack on the helmet, and the orientation controls under my splayed fingers, were the only interactions with the apparatus which the aliens had deigned to allow.

There was a small increase of light, or perhaps my eyes adapted. I saw obsidian walls passing on either side, then faster and faster the viewpoint rushed me down endless branching corridors, each one slightly wider than the last. The red numbers on the readout flickered. It occurred to me that I might be seeing the branches of the crystal bush, from inside. The sensation of movement was inescapable. I closed my eyes, and found that I still saw the black corridors down which I helplessly hurtled. By means I could only guess at, this scene was being played directly on my retinae. Only the readout vanished from my sight. When I opened my eyes I saw it again, the numbers a red blur.

Down one final straight, smooth shaft I went, and was sent flying out of it into the asteroid's interior space. Beauty flooded my brain. If closing my eyes could have stopped me seeing it, I would have grudged a blink.

This time I didn't have the chill splash of Avakian's laughter to save me. It took all my mental strength to turn my attention to the three long numbers of the coordinate display, and to press my fingers against the apparatus to take control of my virtual flight. And once I had, the temptation to use it to play, to swoop and soar, was almost irresistible, but not quite. I moved until the numbers matched the coordinates we'd been given, and found my viewpoint hovering inches above an intricate, floral, fractal pattern like a bank of moss.

My viewpoint was being provided by an icy chip wafted by molecular gusts, transmitting information back to the apparatus and thence to the input jack. So it was supposed. My face plunged into that minute and perfect garden, and some plant in front of me was ripped out by the roots. The sense of damage done filled my eyes with tears as fast as the structure repaired itself. I blinked, and the view vanished. The apparatus pushed me away with as much force as my arrival had delivered to it. As I drifted backward, it was all I could to grab the ropes.

"That's it," said Avakian. "Do you want to have a look?"

I shook my head. "Just tell me."

"I'll show you," he said, waving from his spex to a screen stuck to the wall, and tapping his thumb.

In the hours since returning from my encounter I'd been unwilling, and possibly unable, to go into VR. Even the interface, on recollection, struck me as unbearably clunky. Avakian had assured me the effect would wear off: "It's like a drug—burns up your endorphins, or something. You'll bounce back."

With a dull pretense of interest I watched as a diagram and sheets of data appeared on the flat screen. High-res, but to my jaded eyes it was crude, as if I could see the pixels. The engine was displayed, subtly changed. I couldn't see the difference at first. Avakian threw a laser bead on the screen.

"There," he said. "A control system, and it looks like a human-oriented interface. The data columns underneath are *settings*. We're in business, man. All we have to do now is build it."

All I could think of was the tedium of churning through the project plan yet again, tweaking it bit by bit to bring this changed result.

"Good," I said. "I'll get on with it."

"You will not," said Avakian. "We may be going to the stars, but *you* are going to sleep."

"Will that help?" The notion sounded vaguely intriguing, but irrelevant.

"Trust me," he said. "I'm a doctor."

"Did I wake you?"

Camila had climbed out of her overall.

"Yeah," I said, "you must have bumped into me. What's the time?"

"Midnight," she said.

"So I missed the meeting."

She hooked a foot through webbing and pulled me to her, wrapping her arms around me.

"You didn't miss much," she said. "The new committee's still getting the cold shoulder from ESA, not to mention the junta. The good news is, we've got the *Blasphemous* fitted out. I take it for the first proper test flight tomorrow."

"Hey, wow! That's great!"

She caught my shoulders; her own shook with restrained laughter.

"Matt, wake up properly! That was routine, we knew we were going to make it. Everybody was talking about what you did."

"What I did . . . Oh!"

The memory of what I'd done came back, but it was like the memory of a dream remembered not on waking, but later in the morning, already breaking up into elusive, colorful fragments. At the same time I felt a surge of well-being. My endorphins, or whatever, were onstream again.

"The data you got back, what Armen calls the settings, Roxanne and Mikhail have checked them over and they definitely are for a short jump, just like you asked for. And you went right in among the aliens to get it!"

"Yes, I did that. I can hardly believe it now. And, oh hell—"

I laid my forehead on her shoulder for a moment.

"What is it?"

I swallowed. "I can see why they were so keen to volunteer me to do it. If you've done it once . . . you'd never want to do it again."

A shiver shook her warm body. She pushed back and looked into my eyes.

"Is it *that* horrible?"

"No! No, it's beautiful. It's the most beautiful thing I've ever seen."

"More beautiful than me?"

"Yes," I said, without hesitation. "It just ravishes the mind, like a packet storm overloading a buffer."

"My, what an evocative vocabulary you've got."

I had to laugh.

"But I'm forgetting it," I said. "And I want to forget it. The beauty I'm seeing now is a lot more real."

"Now you're talking," she said.

Some synergy of Camila's excitement at flying the *Blasphemous Geometries* with its new engine at last, and my endorphin overshoot, and perhaps my last shreds of memory of that garden of intelligent machines, filled us with energy and invention and affection, and kept us awake most of the night.

I didn't feel at all sleepy in the morning; indeed I felt immensely refreshed. I followed Camila to the receiving-bay where we'd first arrived, so few days and such a long time ago.

A small crew of cosmonaut techs was waiting for her. Roxanne Khan was nominally in charge as chair of the recently elected committee. Colin Driver hung about in a purely advisory capacity.

Camila dragged her g-suit from a mesh crate.

"Is that necessary?" Driver asked.

"Maybe not," said Camila, sliding into it with a neat somersault. "But just in case."

Helmet under her arm like an astronaut posing for a pre-launch photograph, she drifted toward me and parked the glass bubble in midair before giving me an unexpectedly firm hug.

"Wish me luck," she whispered.

"You'll be fine," I told her. "You're the best. Good luck."

"You too," she said, and turned away like a fish. She vanished through the hatch. Her routine checks and messages began to come through on the comm, until they were complete.

"All systems nominal."

Driver glanced over at a tech by the wall. "Shut the airlock," he advised. "Okay, everybody out of the bay."

"Why?" asked Kahn. "It's safe enough."

"We don't know that." He scratched his throat, making noises in the mike. "There might be some, uh, electromagnetic phenomena."

"What makes you think that?" I asked.

If he hadn't been standing in the air at an angle to me I could've sworn he shuffled and looked down.

"If, well, what one hears about close encounters with these kind of machines is anything to go by."

Oh.

We all went out of the bay and patched to the surface cameras. The ship was outwardly unchanged, its aspect as improbable as ever. The sounds of disengagement clicked and banged through the walls and floor.

"Ship is clear to go."

"Firing secondary jets," said Camila.

A two-second burn took the ship clear, another stabilized its position a kilometer out from the asteroid.

"Engaging AG."

No blue nimbus was visible this time, nor any change in the ship.

"Okay," came Camila's cheerful voice. "That's it powered up in neutral. I'm going to ease it forward."

The ship moved. One moment it was there, the next it had stopped dead a kilometer away. Even those of us who'd seen the performance of the sled could hardly believe it. Roxanne Khan, who hadn't seen it, actually covered her eyes for a second. She saw me looking, and her briefly paler cheeks reddened.

"Rest in peace, Sir Isaac," she said under her breath. Then, in a clear voice:

"Cosmonaut Hernandez, take it away."

"Thank you, ma'am," said Camila. "Engaging forward motion."

The *Blasphemous Geometries* went away.

An instant replay of the view in the cameras, then of that on the

radar, showed only the briefest dwindling glimpses before it vanished from both.

Driver let out a long breath.

"Like a bat out of hell," he said.

He turned to the technicians.

"Can we raise her?"

"Sure."

He nodded at Kahn.

Very formally, she said: "Space station *The Darker the Night the
Brighter the Star* calling *Blasphemous Geometries*. Report, please."

No reply. Kahn repeated the call.

After another second, Camila's voice came back.

"*Blasphemous Geometries* to *Bright Star*. Craft operation is nominal, systems are nominal."

"Very good," said Roxanne. "Disengage forward motion, reverse
direction, and return to station."

"*Blasphemous* to *Bright Star,* uh, that's a negative."

"Is there a problem?" Roxanne asked.

This time the delay was about two seconds. It suddenly dawned
on me that the craft was already a light-second away: three hundred
thousand kilometers.

"No problem," said Camila. "I'm returning to base—Groom
Lake, Area 51."

Sometimes it's only when an assumption is destroyed that we realize what it was, or that we'd made it all. I had assumed that if
Camila were to go home she'd take me with her. I'd also assumed
that because I was in love with Jadey, I couldn't be in love with
Camila.

I alternated between rage at Camila and hope that she would
come back. That was a dream. Camila and Jadey were both—very
definitely and for the foreseeable future—in the real Dreamland. A
voicemail message from Jadey came in a few minutes after Camila
landed there.

"Uh, Matt, there's something I've got to tell you. The disk I
gave you wasn't the one I got from Josif. *That* disk had the information Driver leaked to one of our agents in the ESA apparat, about
the alien contact and the alien math and what it meant for crypto.
I zapped it across to Nevada from my office at work that morning.

I didn't know what was on it, natch, but I doubt it was even encrypted. No point, right? And the FSB must've read it, which started the whole ball rolling, bounced the E.U. into making the announcement. The data on the disk I gave you is on sites all over the Net, and has been for over a year. I downloaded it from one of them.

"We think the aliens spammed the space-drive info to widely dispersed sites without the knowledge of anyone on the station. It was in the form that the ESA systems on the station defaulted to for production specs. Nevada Orbital Dynamics has people who do web searches for flying-saucer stuff. This is because the company has turned up a few, uh, anomalies in the records. You know what I mean. Enough to make this sort of thing worth at least keeping half an eye on. Most of it's total crap, of course. They found the data in all that clutter and checked it out and it looked interesting, but they didn't have the necessary skills to deal with the ESA conventions and to actually run the systems analysis and production-planning because, as you know, these actually require hairy, kludged combinations of U.S. and E.U. tech.

"However, they knew a man who did—you, via me. And we always knew you could be counted on, politically. They hung back, though, until the thing could be authenticated. I'd already taken a download, lightly encrypted—I didn't know what it was. When I sent them Driver's message confirming the alien contact, they replied with a prearranged phrase which meant I should take the flying-saucer datadisk to you, and once you were convinced, to get you to America. The data wasn't important—*you* were important. If it hadn't been for Josif getting killed, which was sheer bad luck, and the crackdown, I'd have gone with you. As it was, my arrest at least served as a distraction.

"Because it was you we needed, and it was you the cops should have gone after. The data was out there all along."

I hung in the webbing for a while, on the side of a busy corridor, watching people pass like fish, their mouths working almost silently as they talked in the other, invisible web. I took out my hand reader, pulled down the completed production plans, and routed them through the station's transmitter to as many nodes as possible.

It wasn't really necessary, but it gave me some small satisfaction.

· · ·

I wasn't the only one who'd made false assumptions. The entire ship watched agog as recriminations flew around the science committee.

"None of us imagined that Hernandez would take the craft to Earth," said Roxanne. "Because we *assumed* that our security expert had good reason to trust Hernandez, or he'd never have allowed her to make the test!"

"Oh, I trusted Camila, all right," Driver said. "I absolutely took it for granted that she'd be off at the first opportunity. Like a bat out of hell."

"So why did you allow it?"

"Because that's what I wanted."

After the noise had died down, Lemieux said:

"Colin, my friend, please tell us, now there is nothing more to lose or gain—are you, after all, an American agent?"

"No," said Driver. "Hand on heart, mate, I'm not. I'm not now, nor have I ever been."

"So what *are* you?"

"I'm an Englishman," said Driver.

The CNN bulletins showing shaky amateur video from Groom Lake had barely faded when Major-General Oskar Jilek appeared on an E.U.-wide broadcast.

"A grave situation has arisen with regard to the rebel-held space station *Marshall Titov*. The scientific knowledge obtained by its historic achievements, which by rights should have been used for the benefit of all humanity, have been usurped by foreign agents and unilaterally applied to endanger the peace. The Emergency Committee of the European Union regrets to announce that its patience with the rebels is exhausted. Their escalating provocations and insolent demands have crossed a threshold. From this moment, the European Union is in a state of war with them. Their actions equally endanger the United States, and we urge upon that nation's government a course of action appropriate to the gravity of the situation.

"We have nothing to negotiate with the rebels. Any further communications to ESA, by anybody on the station other than Major Sukhanov, will be regarded as another hostile act. Major Sukhanov and his fellow hostages must be unconditionally released, and full authority over the station returned to Major Sukhanov within one hour. Otherwise, the Special Forces of the European Peoples' Aerospace Force will respond with all necessary force and without further warning."

Driver, too, didn't waste time. He ignored the scientists' committee. His face and voice filled the ship.

"Jilek is bluffing," he said. "We now know when the expedition left Earth orbit. An astronomer in Kazakhstan caught the picture, and some hacker in Sydney has just zapped it through to us. The burn was seven days ago. We have five days to build the engine and disengage the station from the asteroid. And then, people, *let's jump.*"

21

The Darker the Night the Brighter the Star

S HE NEVER CAME back?"

Elizabeth's voice sounds sad.

The hour is late, even for New Lisbon. The pithkie and the gigant at the bar are almost asleep, but they pride themselves on outlasting their customers. The pub is empty except for them, us, and few saurs, and who gives a fuck what they overhear?

I've told them my story, in a long wander that has taken us from the One Star Hotel through a succession of bars. We've eaten, at some point. I've kept the parts of the story I don't want humans to hear for our swift staggers through the streets, or the dives of the sister species.

"Of course she fucking never came back," I say. She flinches slightly, and I soften it. "She contacted me. We talked. She loved me, I think, but there was no way she could fly off in the gods-damned hell-spawned *Blasphemous Geometries*. The U.S. Air Force was all over it like flies on a shit."

"You still haven't told us," says Gregor, "what went wrong with the navigation. Did you miscalculate, or what?"

I stare at him. Sometimes I wonder, I really do. The myth of our navigation has served us well, but it must have served the locals too. It must fulfill some deeply-felt needs, to survive so long in the face of its brazen unlikelihood, to say nothing of its falsehood.

"We didn't navigate anywhere," I tell them. "The data I recovered might have been authentic, for all I know, but maybe only a kraken—or your artificial squid—could have made sense of it. Or it might have been complete garbage, intentionally or not. Whatever. I suspect the engine had a preset instruction to go here. All I know is that we set up what we thought was a jump across the

Solar System, and we found ourselves in polar orbit around Mingulay. We'd just figured out that it was definitely not Earth and definitely not the Solar System, when Tharovar's skiff turned up. A skiff—that wasn't the scary bit, we kind of expected that. The scary bit was when he dropped out of the airlock."

I fix on Salasso what I hope is a hard stare, but which is probably just a bleary look.

"You people have a lot of explaining to do."

The saur spreads his long hands. "I can't help you there. None of us knows anything of what any saurs in the Solar System may have done in historical times."

I wonder how much you would know if I stuck a probe up your arse.

I hope I didn't say that.

"I wonder," says Elizabeth, "if the computers on the ship still work."

"They probably do," I say. "Radiation-shielded, you know? All the equipment to reboot them. Hell, I could do it now. Except that Tharovar and his mates took us off the ship in a great hurry, and made a big fuss of us, and never, never let us back."

"That should not be a problem," says Salasso, "now that we know you can navigate. We never believed you had found Mingulay on your own, though we never contradicted you. We believed the gods had sent you here, and wanted you to stay here. Perhaps they did. They have some purpose in setting up this Second Sphere, but neither we nor the krakens know what it is. However, now that the krakens have given their judgement, there is no reason to stop you."

Gregor grabs the saur's arm.

"You mean we could try out the navigation on the *Bright Star*?"

"Yes."

He grins at Elizabeth, and even in my drunk and stoned state I can see that she, perhaps, does not entirely share his delight.

He turns to me.

"What's it like?"

"Come on out," I say.

We haul ourselves up and, arms around each other's shoulders, sway into the street. I lead them away from the streetlights, into a square where no lights burn. We look up at the Foamy Wake, at the blazing god, and we wait awhile, until we see the shuttling spark cross the sky from north to south, the *Bright Star*.

"You go there," I say.

You make your way through the ship's long corridors, with nothing in your hands but numbers. Your shipmates, your colleagues, your comrades clap your back and congratulate and encourage you, with an anxiety in their eyes that you hope you are not showing, yourself.

You approach the engine, diving down to its base, and you hope that what you are doing is entering the numbers in its alien mind. You confirm that everyone is ready.

You press what you hope is the right switch, and you—

jump, becoming light.